Thomas Simpson Sheardown

Half a Century's Labors in the Gospel

Including thirty-five Years of back-woods' mission work, and evangelizing

Thomas Simpson Sheardown

Half a Century's Labors in the Gospel
Including thirty-five Years of back-woods' mission work, and evangelizing

ISBN/EAN: 9783337072919

Printed in Europe, USA, Canada, Australia, Japan

Cover: Foto ©Raphael Reischuk / pixelio.de

More available books at **www.hansebooks.com**

Thos. S. Sheardown

(in 1865.)

HALF A CENTURY'S LABORS IN THE GOSPEL,

INCLUDING

THIRTY-FIVE YEARS

OF

BACK-WOODS' MISSION WORK, AND EVANGELIZING,

In New York and Pennsylvania.

An Auto-Biography,

BY THOMAS S. SHEARDOWN,

As related, in his 74th year, to a Stenographer.

WITH AN APPENDIX,

Containing additional Sketches, Notices of Mrs. Esther G. Sheardown, Histories, &c., &c., by other hands.

SECOND THOUSAND.

PUBLISHED BY
O. N. WORDEN AND E. B. CASE.
1866.

J. A. WAGENSELLER, Printer,
No. 2, North Sixth Street, Philadelphia, Pa.

In sending this work to the press, it can truly be said that its subject has contributed his share solely to gratify many old and new friends, and in deference to their views of its utility rather than his own. He is responsible only for that which appears as his.

The Sketch of his Life is printed as it fell from the venerated author's lips, except that verbal repetitions have been erased, a few omissions were afterwards supplied by him, and some narratives are so transposed as to make the whole as far as practicable appear in the proper order of time. The language—the forms of expression—have been retained, so as to make the whole an exact representation of ELDER SHEARDOWN—AS HE WAS, AND AS HE IS.

It is not issued as a literary recreation, but is designed to meet the wishes of very numerous deeply attached admirers of the man, and for all honest, hearty workers in the Lord's vineyard, who may open the volume. It is a deserved (though imperfect) memorial of ONE of those self-denying, pioneer ministers of the Gospel, whose abundant labors have been largely blessed in laying broad and deep the foundations of Christian Churches. His graphic portraitures of godly, active church members, on both sides of the Atlantic, may also, it is hoped, be of lasting benefit beyond the bounds of his acquaintance.

It may be asked, by some at a distance from the scenes of his labors, why a minister whose friends require this printed volume, even in his life-time, has not a more extended reputation? The query will be answered in the contemplation of the unremitting efforts revealed in the following pages. Yet it may be well here to say, that, as far as the writer has known or heard, Elder Sheardown has always been content with his field, and, unambitious of distinction abroad, wished to be "counted faithful" at home. He had passed the "half-way house of life," and had the charge of a large family, when he was set apart to the work of the ministry—and then began, literally in the woods, to organize conferences, and churches, which claimed him as their under-shepherd. To those bodies, individually and collectively, he gave his heart and hands, with a characteristic affection, solicitude, and devotion. Those scattered flocks he could not leave, except as he extended his lines of labor beyond them. From a log cabin in the primitive wilds of Catlin, his circuit advanced on every hand, and absorbed all his time and all his heart. Year by year his Gospel range widened, but—like a true husband and father—he always returned to his own house for encouragement, and then undertook wider excursions. Taking the south end (or head) of Seneca Lake for the centre of his field, the outlines of his "diocese," as Missionary or as Evangelist, extended to the borders of Lake Ontario on the north, to Binghamton on the east, to Jersey Shore (Pa.) church on the south, and to Whitesville, Allegany County, N. Y., on the west—the most distant point not being one hundred miles from his original church. In Chapter VIII., the reader will find an incidental notice of temptations—to quit the ministry, to vary his doctrines, and to seek a more popular and remunerative field—which were made and heroically subdued. These records will, it is hoped, be of material benefit, also, in showing that *every field of labor* affords sufficient material for *any preacher's best endeavors.* Thorough cultivation—continuous and unremitted—is as essential to success in the moral world as in the physical. And there is force in the suggestion of a late aged minister, " Whether, in view of the increasing ease with which is rent asunder the tender, holy, and confidential relation which should exist between pastors and people, God hath not a controversy with many of his churches?"

To the thousands who have heard the subject of this work from the stand or pulpit, no description of his person or manners is necessary. But, for the gratification and benefit of others—children of his former hearers, and entire strangers—it may be well to make a passing reference to his peculiarities, as gathered from persons who knew him best when he was in the meridian of all his powers.

Elder Sheardown is about five feet ten inches in height—compactly built, with no waste flesh—firm, flexible, strong of muscle—of a dignified, easy carriage, piercing eyes, and serious, commanding expression. He seems to have been always temperate—unless his multifarious efforts to preach the Word may have been excessive—industrious, frugal, constantly engaged in something practical, something useful.

As a speaker, he had naturally a very strong voice, and exhibited proof of his mixed ancestry, combining some of the smoothness of English oratory with the bold fervor of the Welsh. One minister, when asked to describe the nature of Sheardown's eloquence, said he could not analyze it; it appeared to him something like the sweep of a mighty whirlwind through a forest, prostrating in its course every tree, great or small, and giving living proof of irresistible POWER. A brother who heard him at Seneca Falls, in 1840, states that he was fairly magnetized by the peculiar traits of the speaker. He had never heard of Elder S., previously—but, from the outset, was rapt in admiration, not less with the solemn and momentous character of the truths presented, than with the torrent of burning words that rolled continuously from his lips, and the vehemence of his emotions. Every part of his body spoke with his tongue—the tears and perspiration seemed to mingle and flow from his face in streams—and there could not have been a dry thread upon his person.

The amazing energy of his administration of the Gospel message, rendered it impossible for his hearers to be wholly careless or asleep. The impressions of his preaching were indeed powerful, and often lasting beyond his knowledge. Eternity only can reveal the full fruit of his endeavors to win souls to the Redeemer.

His sermons were noted for their simplicity and evangelical character. The Bible was his standard of right and wrong. From it he found a lesson for saint and sinner, and each could understand the portion designed for himself. It is perhaps unfortunate that he *never wrote a sermon*—and to have *reported* one, when in the flush of his noon-day years, would have been as difficult as to have described thunder-peals while the rain was dashing upon one's roof. He *studied* his sermons, and had the *subject-matter* at command, but not the particular words, nor was the order always chosen before-hand. Some sketches of discourses, taken down by others, are expected for the Appendix to this work, but with no hope of clothing them with the life and glow of their delivery. They are *skeletons* —but only skeletons, and may suffice as outlines of his sermonizing. The rich, original, world-wide illustrations, and his apt quotations (in prose and verse) must be left to the memory of those who heard, or the imaginations of those who read.

Elder Sheardown was happy in choosing texts, and in selections for unexpected emergencies; and his well worn Concordance, his ancient " breeches Bible," and various Scripture helps, rarely confuted the impressions of his tenacious memory. In the pulpit, he was perfectly at home, and self-possessed—scanned his audience critically, reading them through as though they were transparent glass—and became " all things to all men that he might by all means save some." His public performances were rarely if ever prolonged so as to become tedious, for he knew when and where to *stop*—a knowledge of human nature quite desirable in this fast age.

He was eminently and emphatically a *man of prayer*, and in that exercise was most *importunate*—pleading with God as a trusting child asks a loving parent for that which can and will be granted. He prayed in faith—believing—and this work contains many instances of answers to fervent supplications. When singing, it was *with a will.* In public and private exercises, the same large-heartedness, and " wholesouled," straight-forward *devotedness*, characterized him. His daily walk and conversation convinced even unbelievers that his were the sincere out-breathings of one consecrated, soul and body, to the service of a Master he truly loved.

But the bow, always bent, loses its elasticity. He knew how to withdraw his mind in social relaxation, as well as how to concentrate it on the One Great Object. He can readily weep with those who weep, and rejoice with those who rejoice. One of the most genial of companions, he has always attracted, as with "hooks of steel," personal friends, male and female, of all ages and positions in life. Considering the stern nature of his work—preaching the self-denying doctrines of the Cross, so repulsive to the carnal mind, amid the antagonisms of evil and error he has encountered on every side—God has graciously shielded him from great abuse and bodily harm, and scattered much joy and gladness along his pathway.

Should any be disposed to think "that great, little word, I," is used quite often in this work, let it be remembered that it professes to be an *auto-biography*— that is, a record of one's life as related by one's self. From its very nature, that which, in another work, might appear egotism, is not in this. Elder Sheardown is the *subject*, and was requested to *prepare* it, and therefore we would and should expect a book chiefly *about* Elder Sheardown. He has "stuck to his text" as literally as most preachers do, and could hardly have been less personal and at the same time have answered the object in view and the earnest desire of long-tried, exacting friends. His generous and spontaneous allusions to worthy individuals with whom he has been associated, although not always essential to the main design, give vent to his intense feelings of love and gratitude, and show that he desires, incidentally, to place on record the labors of others as well as of himself.

When we engaged to issue this work, we stated that it would appear "as soon as *practicable*, the coming Autumn," and "contain, *probably*, 400 pages, and be sold at $1.50 per copy." That was at the close of the armed phase of the Rebellion, when it was believed there would be a fall in the rates for paper and for labor generally. Illness on the part of the Editing Publisher has delayed the printing, and the continued high prices of labor, paper, and everything connected with the publication, compel an increase in the price above what was intended.

While reading, it will be borne in mind, that, in the State of New York, the word " town" designates a sub-division of a county, and may include one or more *villages*. Some of the latter are "incorporated," while others are unincorporated. In Pennsylvania, similar sub-divisions of a county are called "townships," while the word *town* means an unincorporated, and "borough," or "burg" an incorporated, village. In this work, localities in those States are generally given in accordance with the legal designations of each—" town," in New York, being equivalent to "township," in Pennsylvania.

On every copy of this book, sold, a portion, satisfactory to Elder Sheardown, is secured to him or to his family.

O. N. W.

Lewisburg, Pa., August, 1865.

PREFATORY REMARKS.

For many years, there has been a strong desire, on the part of numerous friends of Elder THOMAS SIMPSON SHEARDOWN, that some records of his eventful life might be given to the public. Efforts made to secure the histories of Churches, and of Associations, in Southern New York and in Northern Pennsylvania, increased that desire, for it was found that *his* history and *theirs* were to a great extent identical; as he had labored long and faithfully while planting and nourishing feeble churches in those regions.

To the Chemung River Baptist Association, belongs the honor of projecting this work. The Minutes of their annual meetings, for 1863 and 1864, contain cordial endorsements of the effort, accompanied by the appointment of Brethren T. O. LINCOLN, P. OLNEY, T. MITCHELL, and D. GARTHWAIT, as a committee to aid in the preliminary measures. Brethren of the Bradford and other Associations co-operated with those of the Chemung River, and their united efforts have culminated in the present book.

It should be remembered, by the readers of the Auto-Biography, that although in earlier days its author wielded "the pen of a ready writer," yet, for many years, such has been the condition of his nervous system that he has been unable to write at all. It therefore became necessary that he should deliver his narrative in the presence of a stenographer, who was occupied *forty four days*, first in jotting down in short-hand, and then writing out in full, the subsequent pages. The details were mainly from memory, Elder Sheardown having unfortunately lost most of his private papers in 1854. Let any reader who would be critical as to dates, &c., bear that important fact in mind, and remember also that this severe and long-continued tax upon his recollections of the past seventy years, was made when the narrator was in the *seventy-fourth* year of his age. For that reason, all errors will be generously overlooked.

The humble writer of this introductory notice, believes that the request of his former pastor, that he should undertake so pleasant a part in the work, originated in the conviction, on the part of Elder Sheardown, that the writer knew him better—had heard him preach more sermons—and had (in attending protracted meetings, associations, councils, &c.,) traveled more miles with him—than any man now living. As a deacon in the first church of which Elder Sheardown was pastor, I was permitted to know him in all the intimacy which ever ought to exist between a pastor and the other officers of a church; and most cheerfully do I testify to his *prudence* and *wisdom* as a *counselor*, and to his *fidelity* as a *laborer* in the work of the ministry.

As an ordained minister, he commenced his career with a church gathered, by the Divine blessing upon his efforts, amid the privations of a new country, where he wrought with his own hands in clearing away the forest and providing for his rising family. Often did he preach three times on the Sabbath, requiring a walk

of twenty miles, returning home the same day. He
very seldom failed to meet his engagements, and was
usually on the spot half an hour before the time of
meeting. When asked if he never stopped on account
of the weather, he would say, " Not often. I make the
appointments, and not the weather. It is my business
to fill the appointments, and the Lord will take care of
me and the weather."

In estimating the value of the labors of our brother
in the ministry, it is well to take into consideration the
difficulties he overcame. A friend who has had the charge
of preparing this work for the hands of the printer, in
a letter to the writer of this chapter, makes a few suggestions, which I take the liberty of quoting in this
place :

"In reading portions of this narrative, we may be
inclined to censure our Baptist fathers for their inflexible determination to make all claimants of Christian
privileges produce evidences of their trust-worthiness.
None were more friendly, generous, and unsuspecting,
than were those hardy, orthodox pioneers, when satisfied of the merits of those desiring their confidence.
Sixty, forty, and perhaps thirty years ago, the land was
infested with unworthy strangers, claiming to be ministers of the Gospel. Associations annually warned their
people against such characters—some of them, immoral
men ; or of indolent habits, ' sponging' their living from
kind, charitable families ; and others, schismatics, and
errorists of various sorts, dividing churches, and de-
ceiving and misleading young and weakly members.
Some of the early ministers of the Chemung Association
were expelled from it, for grievous faults. In 1826, the
Association advertised, by name, *seven* imposters, pre-
tended Baptist ministers. In 1830, the same body
" request our brethren not to invite a stranger to minis-

ter in holy things, unless he exhibits credentials of recent date and unquestionable validity.' It is related
that when Eugenio Kincaid—then a young man—first
called on father Thomas Smiley, of White Deer Valley,
the latter could not invite the former to the full rites of
Christian hospitality, until he had catechised him to
ascertain if he were sound in the faith, and had the
proper credentials: (and on both points he was satisfied!)

"Of later years, religious periodicals, and more extended intercourse among members and ministers, have
combined to diminish the danger from imposters, and
to make Baptists more harmonious in sentiment and
practice. Our fathers were strict, necessarily so; and
although they may sometimes have been over-suspicious,
and were always liable to err in the execution of such
difficult and delicate tasks of discrimination, yet their
jealousy for the purity of the ministry, and the safety
of the flocks in their exposed condition, was defensible
on the grounds alleged. Coming among such people,
from England, after the war of 1812, without even the
form of a church letter, it is not singular that it took
some time for Elder Sheardown to win the hold he did
upon the entire confidence of the churches.

"Far less to be justified was the former tendency, in
England as well as in America, to discourage rather
than to encourage young converts in the improvement
of their gifts, 'sermon-wise.' The harvest field of the
world being ripe, and thousands perishing in their sins,
we are taught, 'Pray ye, therefore, the Lord of the
harvest, that he would send forth *laborers*.' If we pray
in the spirit of true prayer, we should look for evidences
of answers thereto. Elder Sheardown was baptized
when only *twenty-one* years of age, and seems to have
had at once mental, spiritual, and physical adaptations
for the ministry, as well as a burning desire to engage

in it. Yet he was thwarted and hindered, instead of being aided and encouraged, and had reached *thirty-eight* years before he was ordained. Those who have heard him preach, and who know the measure of grace and gifts given him, can never cease to lament that a dozen or fifteen of the best years of his life were comparatively wasted, before he entered fully upon the joyful and all-important work for which he was so peculiarly fitted, and in which he has been so much blessed."

The reader will very naturally be ready to inquire how it was possible for a man to succeed amid such discouragements and embarrassments as are hinted at in the foregoing extract, and revealed in the pages following. What was said of the lamented Dr. William Carey, may, (with a slight change of words,) be applied to Elder Sheardown :

" Yet, amidst all this, he 'abated not a jot of heart or hope.' Always serene, cheerful, and ready to benefit others, he pursued the plan which he had marked out, with the same unruffled calmness as though every one cheered and encouraged him. The secret of his success resided in the constraining love of Christ—in energy of will—in unconquerable resolution—and in indomitable perseverance."

From the beginning of the Slaveholders' Rebellion, Elder Sheardown exhibited a most ardent and outspoken patriotism. Thomas Mitchell, a neighboring pastor, well qualified to speak on this point, says :

" Troy, (Pa.) being a military depot from the commencement of the war, Elder Sheardown has given much attention to the soldiers who gathered there, particularly in the year 1861, and while a provost guard, (composed of invalid soldiers,) was kept in the place. He often preached to the volunteers, instructing them in the principles of religion, and inspiring them with patriotic ardor to go forth and battle for the right."

Many of the soldiers desired the venerable Elder should accompany them as chaplain, but his failing strength—having accomplished his three score years and ten—forbade him that pleasure. He, however, gave three of his sons to the service of his adopted country— John, one of Sheridan's noble "fighting men," and Samuel and Almon as army surgeons. John and Samuel have returned safely. But Almon—the Benjamin of the family—fell a victim to the climate, and to over-exertions among the sick and wounded. The father's heart was wrung with anguish as he laid his youngest child in his early grave, yet he was comforted with the assurance that he had given his life to a just and holy cause—a cause, thank God! now triumphant.

The institution of Sabbath Schools, the promotion of Temperance, of Ministerial and Popular Education, of Domestic and Foreign Missions, and kindred efforts for the elevation of mankind—as well as the more direct work for the salvation of souls—always met a welcome in Elder Sheardown's heart, and aid from his hands as he found opportunity. The present year, while the younger members of his congregation are engaged in Sabbath Schools, he retains their fathers and mothers for instruction as a Bible Class.

Although an inflexible Baptist, he has always secured and enjoyed the good will and frequent co-operation of members of other churches. Numerous revivals of religion in which he has participated, have swelled the ranks of Methodist, Presbyterian, and other denominations, as well as that of his choice and conviction as nearest the divine original in its doctrines and ordinances. The truly pious, of every name and condition, are his companions, and he loves to walk with them as far as they can agree.

Elder Sheardown descended from a long-lived family, and yet, considering the amount and the variety of both physical and mental labor he has performed, it seems a special mercy that he has been spared to a serene old age. In weakness and trembling, yet with much force and persuasiveness, he yet proclaims, usually twice upon the Sabbath, the "unsearchable riches of Christ," and thanks God for sustaining him under all his cares and responsibilities so long.

May his last, be indeed his best days !

And may these records of his protracted and toilsome pilgrimage, prove a source of consolation to his many friends, and inspire in every reader (and especially in the heralds of the everlasting Gospel) a desire to imitate his virtues, avoid his errors, and meet him in the better land !

A. C. MALLORY.

BENTON CENTRE, N. Y., June, 1865.

TO THE

CHEMUNG RIVER BAPTIST ASSOCIATION,

WHICH CALLED FOR, AND INSTITUTED MEASURES FOR ITS INCEPTION
AND COMPLETION;

TO THE CHURCHES

WHICH HE HAS BEEN INSTRUMENTAL, DURING HIS MINISTRY,
IN REARING;

TO THE MANY PERSONAL FRIENDS,

WHOSE CONFIDENCE HE HAS SO LONG, SO INTIMATELY, AND SO
UNINTERRUPTEDLY ENJOYED;

TO *ALL* WHO LOVE OUR LORD JESUS CHRIST,

This Auto-Biography is Dedicated

BY ITS

AUTHOR.

AUTO-BIOGRAPHY, &c.

CHAPTER I.—1791 to 1814.

My Birth, Parentage, Education, Mercantile Employments, Conversion, and Baptism—Peculiar and Profitable Usages of the English Baptist Churches—invited to the Village of Skidby, and, with much trepidation, opened my mouth for Jesus— Called to Account by my Church—Received Approbation to Improve my Gifts for Speaking.

BIRTH—PARENTAGE—CHRISTENING.

I was born, November 4th, 1791, in Little Coats parish, near Great Grimsby, in the county of Lincoln, England. My father, JOHN SHEARDOWN, was pure English; my mother, whose maiden name was ANN RABY, was mixed with Welsh. Religiously, they were strict adherents of the Established Church, until a few years before I was born, when they were hopefully converted, joined the Dissenters, and became members of an Independent church, (a branch of believers who most resemble the Congregationalists of any church in America.) At my birth, however, they had me "christened," and I had my "god-fathers" and "god-mothers," according to the Episcopalian formula. Consequently, the clergyman of that church considered me one of his lambs, and under his watch-care. I distinctly remember when he would take me upon his lap, and repeat to me the Catechism, in which I was taught, that, by my baptism, " I was made a member of Christ, the child of God, and an inheritor of the Kingdom of Heaven!" As light broke in upon the minds of my parents, I was taken from under the charge of my ecclesiastical instructor.

YOUTHFUL RELIGIOUS TRAINING.

My father always read the Bible, and prayed, in his family. From his prayers, I gathered in my early childhood the idea of a God, but I had no clear views of who or what He was. I thought Him to be some very superior Being, but where located I could not tell. Hearing my father ask God, in his prayers, for so many things that he needed, I was led to do the same. In my childish ignorance and simplicity, in little things that I wanted, of which I was denied by my parents, I would ask God to give them to me. I remember when I was so small that I played with a bow and arrow, and, as I often lost my arrow, I would hide myself in the grass, and ask God to tell me where it was; and, as I often found it soon after, that gave me encouragement always to go to Him for anything that I was greatly troubled about. My parents were very strict with their children, guarding them against all evil. The family always attended church on the Sabbath, and that day must never be desecrated by either children or servants. I recollect, one day, hearing one of my father's hired men using words to his team that I had never heard before. After he was gone, I stood upon the same stone that he had stood upon, and repeated his language at the top of my voice. My father heard me, called me to him, and asked me what I was saying, and where I heard those words? I told him, " from Richard." He took me kindly by the hand, led me into the house, and told me those words were very naughty, and God was angry with every individual who used them. He talked to me, and wept. The man was discharged, and that was the end of it—but, from that time onward, I dreaded profanity. Thus passed my early boyhood.

MY FATHER'S DEATH—THE PROPERTY.

My father died when I was about eleven years old, and, having died suddenly, he left no Will: consequently, under the English law of primogeniture, there was no provision for any of the children except the oldest son. When my mother died—which occurred after my removal to America—her Will was prosecuted in the Court of Chancery, and that used up the balance of my father's property. I do not know that any of the family reaped any benefit from it.

MERCANTILE APPRENTICESHIP.

My time was spent in school from my seventh to my twelfth year. For that day, I had obtained a tolerable knowledge of the English language, and made some little advance in Latin. In my fourteenth year, my mother bound me as an apprentice in a wholesale and retail dry-goods and grocery establishment. About two years after, my master failed in business, and I prevailed upon my mother, if possible, to get my indentures, which were kindly given up. She was then living in Great Grimsby, where my father died. She had watched my morals with intense anxiety. I loved her—and to this day there is no word, except "Jesus," in the English language, so dear to me, as "Mother." At this old age, I have no recollection of ever designedly doing anything that I thought would injure her feelings.

TRY MY HAND IN LONDON—AM ROBBED.

After my mother had got everything settled relative

to my indentures, I concluded to launch out upon the world for myself. She assisted me, and I started for London, knowing very little about a large city, although the place where I had been was quite a market-town, a borough, and a sea-port. Nothing of importance occurred on my journey to the great Metropolis. But I had been in the city only a short time, when I found my pocket was picked. I had a number of guineas—seventy-five, I think—which my mother had carefully sewed up in a little pocket, inside my vest. To my utter astonishment, my vest was cut, and the pocket and guineas were gone. I soon found friends, and got into employ. For years, I never mentioned my loss to any individual, but concluded, if that was the way the world was to use me, I must look out for it.

CULTIVATE MORALITY.

I reflected, "Now, I am alone, and will mark out a path that I must walk in if I am ever to be anybody." The first point was, I will be punctually honest : whoever shall be my employer, I will make his interests my own. I will never profane the Sabbath, but, under every possible circumstance, will attend church. I will never indulge in tippling, gambling, nor swearing—and will see to it that I am never found in lewd company. These resolutions, thank God! I was able to live up to. I was naturally light, vain, and fond of amusements. Perhaps my greatest sin was a passionate fondness for the theater. I was cured of that evil, by the following circumstance : A gentleman, on the stage, was performing his part in the "Castle Specter," and where he called upon God to strike him dead if he was not telling the truth, he fell lifeless upon the floor! From that time onward, my great anxiety for the theater was gone.

There was nothing in my daily life worthy of note as widely differing from that of other young men under like circumstances. I confined myself to the dry-goods business entirely, in a house that sold both by whole-sale and retail.

RELIGIOUS IMPRESSIONS.

Up to this time, I had always been the subject, more or less, of religious impressions, and at times was very much distressed in relation to my future state. I was unprepared to meet God, and often longed and wished that I were a Christian. While living in Brentford, seven miles west of London, I heard a very faithful minister, every Sabbath, and under every sermon felt worse. We had many clerks, both male and female, who would often speak about my being cast down, and would cautiously say they must rally me; when, in order to prevent them from thinking I was serious on the subject of religion, I would join with them in their merriment, and dissipate the feeling as soon as I could.

MY CHRISTIAN BROTHER-IN-LAW, NOT FAITHFUL.

My employer was also my brother-in-law. After going to church one Sabbath, on our return, as we were sitting in concert in the family circle, he said to me, "I am going down into the country, sir, and want to take the coach, at five o'clock in the morning, from Golden Cross, Charing Cross." I asked, "What coach will you take?" He replied, "I prefer to walk, sir, it being only about ten miles; but I wish you to go with me. We will start about two o'clock in the morning— it will be a pleasant morning walk." I was much de-lighted with the idea of walking in company with him, for he was a religious man, and prayed with us every morning and evening. I thought it would be a good opportunity for him to talk with me about the interests

3

of my soul. But, alas! although I taxed all my powers to draw him into conversation on the subject of religion, it was an utter failure. His only theme was the business which was necessary to be done while he was gone. I was the particular and confidential clerk, therefore had to submit to all the instructions he had to give concerning the things of this world. When I returned home, I felt sick, for I did neither eat nor drink while walking the twenty miles. That left me rather feeble, but it would not have been so much the case if it had not been for the distress of my mind. I went to my room, and laid down. I was soon called upon by one of the servants, who took to my sister the message that I was sick. She came, and tried to nurse me as best she could, but nothing that she could do would relieve the pain and anguish. Finally, one of the clerks came up to my room, and said I must get up, for there was a gentleman who had some business to attend to, and he wanted to have it done before the King passed through, on his return from Windsor to London, which would be in about an hour. Amidst the world of business, my convictions soon wore off in a great measure, and I resumed my former appearance.

REMOVAL FROM LONDON TO HULL.

Nothing especial occurred with me for quite a length of time. My employer was a member of a London linen drapers' company, who were opening new establishments in different cities and towns. One day he called me into his private room, where he told me he had bought an establishment in the city of Hull, and the stock would be ready to ship from London in a short time. He wanted I should take charge of the goods, get them all in order in the new store, and, when ready to do business, write to him, when he would come with a set of clerks to open the house.

VISIT MY MOTHER—MUCH ENJOYMENT.

The vessel in which I embarked, anchored at the mouth of the river Humber, opposite the port where my mother lived. I went ashore in the evening, and about nine o'clock found her, with her little grand-daughter, sitting around the table, with her daily companion—an open Bible. She embraced me with all the affection and love of a mother. When a boy at home, I used to read to her a great deal in that Book. While she was preparing me some supper, I took her Bible, and commenced reading at the place where it was opened, in the prophecies of Isaiah. I read several chapters. I never read the Scriptures with so much interest before. I thought my satisfaction in reading grew out of the idea, in my own mind, that it was because she was pleased to hear me read again. When ready to retire for the night, she showed me into my room. She said the house was new, the doors were swollen, and would not shut close, and therefore she left mine entirely open. When I was laid away in bed, she came into my room, and I requested her to put my curtains to one side, as I had to leave at four o'clock in the morning. Her lodging room joined mine. When she retired, she kneeled down by her bedside and prayed. I never had such feelings in my life, before. My mind was in a state that I cannot describe. Some time elapsed. I thought I must pray, but had no hope that God would hear me. I thought, if I could only remember some portions of my father's prayers, I might be heard; but I could not call up in my mind words that I could so connect as to make any sense. Then, I tried to pray in my own way. A thought struck me, that, to lie in bed and pray, did not become one in my state of mind. I got upon my knees, and prayed, and while praying, all my trouble appeared to be removed.

I fell into a sweet sleep, for a short time. Awaking, I arose, and bade farewell to that dear mother. I did not think, at that time, that it was any religious change, and I am not prepared to say, even now, that it was.

DARKNESS OF MIND.

My business called me to the docks, and about the ships, where I heard much profanity. It sounded more harshly in my ears than it had ever done before. But my cares and responsibilities soon wore away that blessed state of mind which I enjoyed when I left my mother's house. I punctually attended church, every Sabbath, hearing different ministers, but did not have much religious feeling. Afterwards—in immediate connection with a change of sentiments in a prominent minister—my mind became much interested in view of my condition.

MR. ARBON BECOMES A BAPTIST.

Rev. William Arbon, my favorite preacher in Dagger Lane, was a graduate of Lady Huntingdon's College, and followed the peculiarities of the clergymen in her connection. They wore the gown and bands, and used part of the liturgy, with other modes of worship, of the Episcopalians. At one time, having a number of children to sprinkle, he thought he would thoroughly investigate the subject. He was a Welshman, a ripe scholar, and had all the means for a close investigation. He proposed to base his sermon upon the First Epistle of Peter, 3d chapter, 21st verse: "The like figure whereunto, even baptism, doth also now save us, (not the putting away of the filth of the flesh, but the answer of a good conscience toward God,) by the resurrection of Jesus Christ." But he found that, upon that point, he had always been in error. When he went to his chapel

Sabbath morning, expecting to have the children presented for christening, he told his congregation that he should not attend to it, then. Returning home, after service, he took his gown and bands and threw them on the fire. His wife said, " William, you are crazy." He replied, " No, wife, I am clothed and in my right mind." In the afternoon, he preached on baptism, and told them it was his farewell sermon to them.

WAS BAPTIZED—A NEW CHURCH FORMED.

At that time, there were but two Baptist churches in the city, and they evidently saw that he was too good a man to be lost—consequently, they agreed to colonize a few members from their two churches, as a nucleus for a third. They at once rented a chapel in which there was no preaching, built a baptistery, and invited him to join them. A council was held, he told his Christian experience, was baptized, ordained, and called to be their pastor. He afterwards went down into the liquid tomb and immersed some who followed him from his original church, and also several converts who had not before made a profession of religion.

All this had passed, unknown to me, until I heard that he was preaching on Princess street. I immediately went and hired a sitting in his chapel, and my mind became very much stirred up in view of my condition.

BROUGHT INTO FULL HOPE.

A short time after this, I heard Mr. Arbon preach from Solomon's Songs, 6th chapter, 13th verse: " Return, return, O Shulamite ; return, return, that we may look upon thee. What will ye see in the Shulamite ? As it were the company of two armies." My eyes were opened. I did not only see men as trees walking, but I appeared to enter into the full-orbed light of the Gospel. Old things had passed away, all things had become new; and I felt, then, that it would have been no sacrifice for me to make, if a person had said to me, " Now, Sir, if you will give all you possess, you may go into that pulpit and speak half an hour." I would have given it, freely. I must confess that I did not know what I wanted to say—but I saw such a beauty in the plan of God's salvation, that I felt I must say something about it. I went home from chapel, expecting everybody knew just how I felt. I did not know, then, that this was religion. I thought, if it was, Christians certainly would know about it, and they would say something to me upon the subject. But, alas! not a word from any individual. My employer was a Baptist by profession, and afterward became a member of that church, but he never conversed with me upon the subject of personal, experimental religion. The idea appeared to be universal, in that day, when they saw a person who appeared to be under religious exercises, they must not say anything to him: God would do his own work.

THOUGHTS AS TO MY DUTY.

I was, otherwise, very happily situated. I had my own lodging room, where I could enjoy reading my Bible, praying alone, and meditating upon my situation—not knowing what this great change meant. The blessed Spirit, in a great measure, was pleased to give me a ground of hope, from the reading of the Word of God, that I was a Christian. In the multitude of the thoughts that were within me, this one struck my mind with great power: Now, if you are a child of God, He has claims upon you that He has not had before. I believed that I had duties to perform, and commands to obey; but I was ignorant of what they were. I thought they must be revealed, somewhere; and I was led to search, carefully and prayerfully, the New Testament. With my Testament open before me, and on my knees before God, I found it was my duty to be baptized; and Jesus revealed to me no other way, but immersion. I had never seen a person immersed. I had never heard what is called a Christian experience. I was continually passing through light and shade, no person saying anything to me relative to my condition. Sometimes I thought Christians knew all about the workings of my mind, but had no confidence in me as a Christian, and therefore withheld from me everything upon the subject.

INQUIRY MADE—BUT NO PROGRESS.

I was in the habit, after the business of the day was over, of taking a walk with my employer. One evening, while walking out pretty late, he remarked to me, "Sir, has not a great change come over your mind, in a short time?" This opened the door of my lips: it was, indeed, as oil to my head, and marrow to my bones. I told him many of the changes through which I had passed. We walked till a late hour, but I do not recollect, now, that he, as an individual, ever named to me the subject again, until I had become a member of the church.

A GOOD DEACON HELPS ME.

I did not know how to get my case before the brethren. There was a deacon of that church, whom I esteemed, very highly, as a great and good man. Being an upholsterer, he was doing with us a pretty large business. One day, while with him, I thought I would ask him some questions, but did not mean to betray myself. The first question was, what a person had to do, who wished to become a member of their Church?

He went on and told me, in the first place, the individual must make his request known to the pastor, or some of the deacons. In the next place, the pastor or some of the deacons would call upon the one thus requesting admission, and, when the individual had been conversed with, if they thought best they would lay it before the church. The church would then appoint a committee to wait upon the individual, and converse with him, and he with them, and they mutually pray with and for each other. If there were religious individuals in the family, they would be inquired of by the committee to know what kind of a life the applicant had been living, what was thought of his moral character, &c. The committee, and the candidate, would arrange the times of meeting according to their own convenience; and this was to be as often as circumstances would permit, for one month. Then the committee reported to the church their progress, and their observations in the case, if they had any, with several other matters of minor importance.

I had calculated, through this conversation, to keep myself entirely in the shade, but the good man read me all through. Immediately after the details were ended, he said: "Sir, you have been asking these questions on your own account?" and I had to own up the whole truth.

BEFORE THE CHURCH.

The month was passed through in this way, and I was notified to attend the next meeting of the church. On the appointed day I went, and met with several others, whose errand was the same as my own. We were put into a small room, or vestry, until the church had heard the reports of the committees relative to the evidence they had obtained of the genuineness of our conversion. We were then taken before the church, one at a time. When in the presence of the church, we were kindly invited to give a relation of our Christian experience. Here I stumbled. I told them I did not know what was meant by a Christian experience. A good old brother said, with an overflowing heart, "My dear young brother, it is very simple; just begin where God began with you, and talk out familiarly your thoughts, and actions, up to the present time." I related, as best I could, the way that God had led me. After I got through, the deacon went with me into another side-room, where I awaited the decision of the church. Then I was permitted to return to the room where the church were. During the examination, no two candidates were permitted to be in the presence of the church at the same time, (so that they might not hear or use each other's phrascology in giving in their testimony.) The candidates were received, and, the next day, were baptized. At this time, I was in my twenty-first year.

MY BAPTISM—PARTAKE OF THE LORD'S SUPPER.

On the morning of the day of my baptism—which was in the fall of 1812—the pastor preached a very strong and lucid sermon upon the subject. After baptism, the new members received the right hand of fellowship, from the pastor, with appropriate remarks to each individual. In the afternoon of the same day, the church celebrated the Lord's supper. It was a time of great interest, especially to the converts who were permitted for the first time to attend to that solemn institution.

CONFERRING WITH NO ONE AS TO DUTY.

Strange as it may appear, through all these important changes, I never so much as thought of advising with any individual, not even with my own mother, in relation to what I ought to do, and what I ought not to do. I was taught by the Spirit, and felt myself amenable to God, and to Him only, walking in the footsteps that appeared to me to be marked out in the example of our Lord Jesus Christ. The New Testament had been my only guide thus far, and I felt to trust God for the future.

TWO CHURCH PAUPERS, RICH IN FAITH.

Converts, in those days, were the same as now—babes in Christ, needing instruction from those in riper years. There were a very pious old brother and sister, who, although supported by the church, were rich in faith, and heirs to the kingdom of God. Their little attic room was always the converts' home. They would pray with us, and we with them, and here we were schooled, and nourished up in the things pertaining to the kingdom of God. Although many years have passed since then, and those pious friends long, very long ago, have entered into their rest, they live in my memory fresh and green as when I sat at their feet for instruction.

MEMBERS PUNCTUAL IN MEETINGS.

It was expected that the members of that church should attend all its meetings; if absent, they were supposed to be sick, or out of the city. Even if a member was missed from public worship on the Sabbath, it was seldom, if ever, that the deacons returned home without calling to ascertain the reason of the absence.

We were indeed a band of brothers, striving for the unity of the Spirit in the bonds of peace. Though my business responsibilities were great, yet, when in the city, I could always so arrange affairs as to be able to attend all the meetings of the church. For we were taught, in that day, to regard our religious duties as first, and business, secondary.

CHURCH ACTIVITY AND FAITHFULNESS.

Our pastor preached three sermons, always, on the

Sabbath; held prayer meeting on Monday evening, when he recapitulated his Sabbath morning's discourse; another prayer meeting, Wednesday evening; and such other meetings as were necessary, were appointed from time to time. If we were taken sick, the first thing was to drop a line to the pastor, or one of the deacons, informing them of our condition, and, if severely sick, a messenger was sent without delay. We always had a prayer meeting on Sabbath morning, at five o'clock in the summer, and at seven in the winter, to pray especially for the pastor, and that God would be pleased to bless His word through the day, in his public administrations. Members of the church, going from home, were expected to send a line to their pastor, notifying him of their intended absence, requesting him, and the church, to pray, in the public congregation on the Sabbath, for God's special protection and care in their behalf. On their return, the pastor would give thanks to God, publicly, on Sabbath morning, for protecting them on their journey. Such things, with us, in this fast age, are obsolete.

PRAYING, AND SEARCHING THE SCRIPTURES.

We had also, in those days, very interesting social meetings. A few converts and friends would meet at a brother's house to spend an hour or two in prayer and reading the Scriptures. The one who read, was expected to explain that which he had read. The reader, having been appointed the week previous, had therefore more or less time to prepare his mind for the work assigned him. Others present would criticise the remarks made by him, why such things were so; and in doing this, we always did it with the most brotherly kindness and good feeling. If there were any questions that we could not satisfactorily dispose of, they were generally referred to the pastor, who gave his views upon the subject. There was great familiarity between the pastor and his people. If at any time they heard him announce a doctrine or sentiment which they did not understand, it was customary to appeal to him for further enlightenment upon the subject. It was no uncommon thing for the pastor to be present at some of our little family meetings, and take part in the services; but never to take the place of the reader, or to give any explanations of a text unless called upon so to do. Those were very interesting seasons, and kept us from being alienated one from another.

SABBATH SOCIAL EXERCISES.

While a member of that blessed church, as I have said before, we had a prayer meeting at the vestry, every Sabbath morning. At that meeting, it was customary for some one to read a portion of Scripture, (more or less, as he chose,) and he was expected to give an explanation of what he had read. The reason for this was unknown at that time, to the junior portion of the church. The pastor, and older brethren, had adopted this plan in order to discover the gifts that were in the church. They generally arranged matters so that when it appeared to fall to the lot of an aged brother to read, he would very kindly invite one of the younger members to do it for him. Consequently, we never knew when we might be called upon; and this induced us to search the Scriptures diligently, always try to have a stock of information on hand, and to be ready on all occasions to meet such an emergency. This enabled the older brethren to notice the different gifts among the younger. When we erred in our exposition of any subject, the pastor, or deacon, or some one, would very tenderly endeavor to correct us. To these meetings, I am very much indebted, for what little amount of Bible knowledge I possess.

INVITED TO HOLD A MEETING IN SKIDBY.

While pursuing this course, one day, I met one of the aged brethren on the street. He said to me, "You are the very man I wanted to see." I asked him what he wanted of me? He told me that there was a little village, by the name of Skidby, some seven miles from the city, and that its people were living in great ignorance of the way of life. "Now, sir, I want you should go to that village, next Sabbath, and hold a meeting with them," remarking that there were but three or four in all the community, who might be said to be experimental Christians. I replied, "Sir, that I cannot do. In the first place, I do not know where the village is, and secondly, I have no acquaintances there." "That," he said, "will make no difference. I can give you the necessary directions." I told him, again and again, that I could not hold a meeting; that I had no gift, or calling, for anything of the kind. He, however, argued, "You can sing, you can pray, you can read the Bible, and you can talk some from what you read; and that will be meeting enough, for those poor, ignorant people." Still I persisted in my former statement that I could not go. He then importuned, "Now, you go this time, and I will tell you where to call. Enquire for Mr. William Wilberforce; he is a Dissenter, and he and his wife are very pious people. You need not fear, at all; the house in which he lives is licensed, by the Bishop of the diocese, for Dissenting ministers to hold meetings in. And now, sir, you must say you'll go." He pressed me so hard that I said, "Yes, I will go."

UNDERTAKE WHAT I DID NOT ANTICIPATE.

After hearing preaching the next Sabbath morning,

4

from my pastor, I went, afoot and alone, to the village, all the while pondering in my mind what course I should take. I had expected to meet only a few persons; but, to my utter astonishment, the house was not only full, but a number were on the green by the door and windows. The moment I went in, the gentleman named met me with all the familiarity of an old acquaintance. He showed me to a standing place, in one corner of the room, with a desk convenient for a speaker, and a beautiful white napkin spread over it, with a Bible, and Watts' old hymn book thereon. I had taken my own hymn book in my pocket, for I did not expect, in such a community, to find any Dissenters' hymn books. The very sight of that desk and Bible, impressed me as I had never been impressed before. Everything spoke, though in silence, yet louder to my heart than thunder tones, "This means that you are to preach." I took my seat behind the desk, thought a few moments, and came to this conclusion: "I will read, and sing a long hymn; I then will pray, as long as I can; then I will read a long chapter, (thinking I might be able to say something, from the whole of it, that would make a respectable talk;) then 1 will read another long hymn; and make a long, concluding prayer—and get out of this, the best way I can."

LED TO SAY SOMETHING—BREAK DOWN.

To my utter astonishment, when I had read the first hymn, they arose, and I saw there were three, four or more hymn books, and a group of youngerly folks who looked to me like singers. A man raised the tune, and gave the pitch, and they sang most heavenly; I was so enamored with the singing, that my troubles subsided, at least for a season. I prayed, and then read another long hymn, after which I read part, or the whole, (I do not now know which,) of the 3d chapter of Jeremiah's Lamentations. The first thing that I was really conscious of, was, that *I was in the highest state of perspiration, speaking from the 57th verse*, which reads as follows: "Thou drewest near in the day that I called upon Thee; Thou saidest, Fear not." I instantly broke down, and said no more. I then proceeded to read the third hymn, prayed, and dismissed the congregation.

ANOTHER APPOINTMENT—FEEL GRIEVED.

To my utter astonishment, Mr. Wilberforce jumped up and said, "This man will preach to us again, next Sabbath, at half-past two in the afternoon. The word *preach* almost petrified me. I said, as soon as I could speak, "No, sir, I shall not be here any more." But the old gentleman insisted upon it that I would be there, and told his neighbors and friends all to come out, for they would not be disappointed. I thought I was very much misused, so much so that I had some trouble to keep John Bull from showing his horns. The friends were very kind, and asked me to stay and have some refreshments, but I had so little fellowship with the old brother's conduct, that I would not stay with them even to eat, and went home feeling very badly—sometimes, crusty. When I went to church in the evening, no one said to me, "Where have you been?" and I was glad they did not.

RECONCILED.

On Monday morning, more calmly and dispassionately reviewing the scene through which I had passed, I was rather glad than otherwise that I did go. By Wednesday of the same week, I felt as though I was not sorry that I had to go again the next Sabbath—and, if the old brother had not said "preach" to the people, I thought it would have been a privilege for mo to go, but I could not bear the idea of *preaching*.

THE CHURCH CALLS ME TO ORDER.

On Thursday, the same Deacon with whom I had had the conversation about what was necessary for an individual to do in order to join the church, came into the store, on business, and said to me, "We have a special meeting of the church, to-morrow night, sir, and we would be glad to have you attend, at six o'clock. You will be there, will you? The meeting is important, and we shall especially need you." I told him, if Providence did not hedge up my way, I would certainly be there. I thought of the thing after he was gone. I had heard of no notice being given for a special meeting, and could not think what it meant.

HAVE TO TRY TO TALK AGAIN—BREAK DOWN.

At the appointed hour, I left my business, and went to chapel. I was walking through the aisle, to my own seat—the minister and deacons were sitting in what was called "the deacons' pew," at the foot of the pulpit—but, as I came opposite the slip, about to turn to my left, one of the deacons beckoned to me. I turned to see what he wanted. He said, "Come into this pew, and sit down beside the pastor." This was indeed strange to me—I did not know what it could mean. After sitting a few moments, the meeting was opened by singing and prayer, after which one remarked, "Shall we not proceed to business?" An aged brother looked up and said, "Our business is with you, Brother Sheardown." I arose and told them that I was not conscious of any wrong—I had not meant to violate any rules of the church, or any principle of Christian propriety. The first thing that came to my ears, was, "You have been preaching, sir, without our authority; and we do not suffer our brethren to run around, preaching, without our knowledge of it." I here referred them to the brother, then present, who induced me to go. They then said, "If you can preach to others, you can preach to us." I told them that I had not preached, and that I could not preach. They affirmed that I had preached, and that I must preach, to them, that night. When I saw that it was impossible to get clear, I said to the pastor—whom I loved next to my life—"Brother Arbon, if I must speak, will you pray?" His answer was, "If you are going to be a preacher, you must do your own praying." That, coming from the one who I claimed as my spiritual father, was the severest blow yet. I tried to pray, but know little or nothing of what it amounted to. They said, "Now, take your text." I named the 41st chapter, 10th verse of Isaiah, which reads as follows: "Fear thou not, for I am with thee; be not dismayed, for I am thy God. I will strengthen thee, yea, I will help thee; yea, I will uphold thee with the right hand of my righteousness." I felt pained, crushed, and distressed in heart. I commenced making remarks from the passage. After awhile, I felt some freedom of utterance. This part of the text struck me with peculiar force: "Fear thou not, for I am with thee; be not dismayed, for I am thy God." Then arose in my mind something like this: "Now, you are telling the people that you are not going to fear, and that God is going to help you:"—and I was broken down, and stopped then and there. I then told them, if they would only forgive me for going to Skidby on the Sabbath and saying what I did to the congregation, 1 would never do the like again; and I besought them with tears, to pardon me.

THEY REQUIRE ME TO GO TO SKIDBY AGAIN.

But nothing in answer to my petition. They said,

"You have another appointment there, and we do not allow our brethren to run at loose ends, and make appointments for preaching and not fulfill them." I told them I had made no appointment—then went on and recapitulated the conduct of the old gentleman who made the appointment, but that I did gainsay it, and gave him to understand that I should not be there. "Well, but did he not say, in your presence, that you would be there? that all might come? that they would not be disappointed? You should not have allowed the appointment to go out." I begged of them not to urge it upon me, but they said, "You must go."

CONTINUE SPEAKING AT SKIDBY AND BEFORE THE CHURCH.

The next Sabbath I went, according to *appointment*, with a determination of heart that it should be the last time. I got along a little better, that time, than the first—but, as soon as I had got through with the services, Mr. Wilberforce made another appointment for me, the next Sabbath. My spirit was somewhat subdued, and I made no resistance, for the church also had made an appointment for me to speak again the next Friday evening. This was in the latter part of the year 1813. I spoke to the church, once a week, for several months, and also continued going to the aforesaid little village.

FAILURE TO GET AT THE WORK.

During this time, there was a young brother who wished to preach. He appeared to have the "preach fever." Not so with me—mine was the *chill*, without the *fever*. This brother wished me to let him go with me to Skidby, and let him preach—which he did, to the best of his ability. He went again, and preached from Isaiah, 7th chapter, 25th verse, which reads as follows: "And on all hills that shall be digged with the mattock, there shall not come thither the fear of briers or thorns; but it shall be for the sending forth of oxen, and for the treading of lesser cattle." He was very much embarrassed, and talked pretty much all the time about digging with the mattock. It appeared to have made an impression on the minds of the children, for the next time he went they ran in the streets and cried out, "There comes the mattock man —there comes the mattock man!" I do not recollect that he attempted to preach much afterwards.

ENCOURAGED AT SKIDBY.

That village had been noted for its immorality; and it was very difficult for a Dissenting minister to go there, preach, and get away without personal insult. The clergyman of the Established church was also the Justice of the Peace in the place: consequently, it would have availed nothing to enter a complaint. But there was not so much as a dog to move his tongue against unworthy me.

SOME DISCOURAGEMENTS AT HOME.

Brethren of our church would occasionally go over with me, to hear me (as they said) "preach." One who sometimes went along, would use all the effort in his power to prevail on me to quit. He would often say, " You disgrace yourself and your family." Knowing, as he did, the situation in which I was placed, I thought it cruel in him. But it was the opinion of some good men, in that day, that if a young man could be induced to give up trying to preach, or by harsh means be driven from it, it was a proof that he was not called of God to the work!

DISTRESSED AS TO MY DUTY—THE LOAD REMOVED.

I had, all this time, a great anxiety to do good—to be the means of saving souls—but had not the least

evidence of being called to preach the Gospel. It wore
upon my physical nature, so much so that the first
inquiry of my friends was, "Are you sick, sir? You
look very poorly." My wife—for I was married, as I
will hereafter narrate—was afraid that I would die.
While thus afflicted, both mentally and bodily, I was
going to hear my pastor preach, one Sabbath morning,
weighed down with sorrow, because I thought I was
(like one of old) running, but had no tidings. I can
clearly see, in my mind's eye, now, the very spot, with
its surroundings in the street, where this passage of
Scripture came to my relief—Acts 9th chapter, 15th
verse: "But the Lord said unto him, Go thy way: for
he is a chosen vessel unto me, to bear my name before
the Gentiles and kings, and the children of Israel." I
felt, at once, volatile as air. My trouble was all gone.
I was as happy, it appeared to me, as it was possible
for any one to be. I cannot describe the state of my
mind at that time. I took my accustomed seat in the
chapel. I thought my pastor looked unusually lovely.
When he arose and read his text, he took the same
passage which had so richly relieved my own mind!
He appeared to enter into the very depths of my heart
—and, before he was through, I had no doubt left that
God designed I should preach his Gospel, as best I
could.

After that meeting was out, the brother who had endeavored to dissuade me from ever standing up before
the people again, said to me, "Are you going to
Skidby, to-day?" I answered, "Yes, sir." Said he, "I
want to go with you." We agreed upon a certain
corner of a street where we would meet. I was sorry
that he proposed to go, for I feared he would mar my
meditations, and disturb my sweet communion with
God. He heard me speak, and I asked him to pray.

After the service, he appeared to be in very good spirits; and when we had left the house to return home, he took hold of my arm, very familiarly, and said, "Brother Thomas, you *will* preach, in spite of all of us. You *have* preached, to-day. *And now, sir, I bid you God-speed.*" From that day onward, I had a comfortable evidence that God had been pleased to appoint me to the work of the ministry.

Marriage—Enlarged Itinerating Labors—Hard Times in England—Business Changes—Gillites and Fullerites—Visit to the Continent, with my Wife—Emigrate to America, and Settle in Seneca County, N. Y.—An Awkward Englishman, a Stranger among Friendly Yankees—Try to adapt Myself to the Ways of the Country—Arrival of my Family—Good News from Skidby.

OUR MARRIAGE.

As I have stated that I would say something in reference to my marriage, perhaps I may as well say it now as at any other time. When I made up my mind to change my situation in life, I thought everything, as far as domestic happiness was concerned, depended upon the choice that I should make of a companion. I knew there was One who could direct me aright: therefore, I concluded to ask wisdom of God. It was my special prayer, for weeks, that He would direct me. I told the Lord just what kind of a person I desired. In the first place, she must be pious: in the next place, she must have the same denominational views with myself. I told the Lord, He knew all about my temperament of mind, and I wanted whoever should be best adapted to my circumstances and feelings in this respect.

MY FIRST CHOICE.

After having prayed long and earnestly, I saw a certain individual coming into church. The thought flashed across my mind, "That, I should conclude, is the very woman to suit me for a wife." But, somehow or other, I had an impression that she was a married lady. I had often seen her, singing in the choir, but did not know her name. When church was dismissed, I said to one of the members, " Can you tell me who that lady is ?" The answer was, "Why! do you not know ?" I said, " No, I do not." He then replied, " She is the daughter of Brother Glassam, one of our members." I continued, " She is a married lady, is she not ?" The reply was, "No, she is a single lady."

In the evening, when church was out, I shook hands with her parents, (for I was acquainted with them,) and said, "I am going to walk home with you." I offered my arm to the young lady, (Esther, by name,) according to the custom of the country, tarried about an hour, had a little prayer-meeting, and said to Esther, on leaving, " If it would be convenient, I would like to call upon you, Wednesday· evening, at nine o'clock." She politely accepted the call. I visited her but a short time that evening, and left with the promise of another visit.

When I went the next time—which, by the by, was only the third—instead of meeting the young lady, the father met me, and wanted to know my intentions in calling upon his daughter. I told him they were all right, but if I could spend an hour with her, I could then tell him more about my intentions. The mother showed me into a room adjoining the sitting room, and presently the daughter walked in. We talked over, in one (to me) important hour, all that we had to say, relative to a union for life. She said she also had been praying for direction from God, in view of such a change, and had been deeply impressed, when she saw me, that that would be the man of her choice if he was not a married man. But I always walked with my sister—her husband being much from home—and many had taken us for husband and wife. I told her, that evening, in closing up our conversation, " Now, I shall not be in a situation to be married, under one year. Can you wait so long?" She answered, " Yes, O yes— anything that is best." I remarked, " Then, if God will, we will be married on such a day, one year hence, at eight o'clock in the morning. We can correspond at any time when we are absent from the city. But I never wrote a love-letter in my life, and probably never shall. I want all our correspondence to be of a spirit-ual nature. We will write in prose or poetry, which-ever suits the mind the best." The thing was settled, then and there. I then reported, to the old gentleman, our progress. We had a very pleasant year of cor-respondence, frequently walking and talking together as opportunity offered. I rented a house and had it furnished, ready to take her to, when she should leave her father and mother.

ECCLESIASTICAL IMPEDIMENTS.

In those days, though the Toleration Act had taken off many burdens from the Dissenters, yet they were not allowed to marry, or bury their dead, without the Episcopal service. We could only be married accord-ing to the formula of that church, and the ceremony could not be performed except between the hours of eight o'clock in the morning and twelve o'clock at noon. As we did not intend to have our marriage " published"—that is, read to the congregation, in the church, three Sabbaths in succession—we were obliged to marry " with license." Five guineas was the price for marrying in that way. The time had arrived. I went to the clergyman's house, about six o'clock in the evening previous to the day appointed, to obtain the license, which should be given twelve hours before celebrating the ceremony. The vicar was not at home, but his wife informed me that he would be at home, in all probability, before eight o'clock. I told her my errand, and the necessity of being married in the morning as soon as the clock had struck eight. She said, "Call again, sir, any time in the course of the evening." I called the second time—he was not in; the third time —all the same; the fourth time, at about ten o'clock in the evening—I knew, from what his wife said, that he was attending a party. I told her I would be in, about six o'clock in the morning, for my license, and must have it. She said, "Very well, sir—I will inform Mr. B." I knew that the responsibility rested on him, and not on me. The license granted at that hour would not be strictly valid, and, should it come to his Bishop's ears, the vicar must be the individual who must suffer.

A DRUNKEN MINISTER.

I went again in the morning, rang the bell, and soon a servant appeared who showed me into a small reception room, saying that Mr. B. would be in shortly. I thought, at once, the thing was understood. He very soon made his appearance, in his morning gown—apologized for having been out so late over night—said he was at a party, and, while around the convivial board, had taken too much punch: "In fact," he said, "I got pretty tipsy." I told him·that I knew that. Said he, "How did you know it, sir?" "I saw you, sir." "Where, sir?" "Standing at the corner of Princess street, resting your head against the wall." "Well," he said, "we will say no more about that." He went to a little closet in the room, where he had a case of old Madeira wine, brought out a bottle, two glasses, and a corkscrew, and said, " Won't you take a glass of wine, sir?" I excused myself, by saying, " I never take wine in the morning." He said he did not generally do it, but, when he had been out over night, in the morning he wanted a little to give tone and action to his system! While writing out my license, I should think he took over one-half or two-thirds of the bottle full. But I got the paper, and started for the woman, with her mother, father, and sister, and, just as the clock struck eight, we were in the church, ready to appear at the altar. There was a word in the marriage ceremony which was " worship." It came in the clause where it is said, " With this ring I thee wed, with my body I thee *worship*," &c. I was willing to love and cherish my wife, but was not willing to " worship" her. Therefore I substituted the word " serve," when saying over that part of the ceremony. He said, " worship." I tried it again, and gave the word " serve." He then turned his large Prayer Book the other side up, so that I could read for myself. I knew he was in my hands, for I could report him to the Bishop: therefore I read again, " serve." He said, "Very well, sir; *serve* it is, then; it will do just as well." So we passed on to the end.

I took my wife to her new home, with her parents and sister. Our breakfast was waiting for us. I dropped a note of invitation to our pastor and his wife to take tea with us and spend the evening. I then went to my business, and attended to it until about four in the afternoon. Returning to my home, we spent the evening in conversation, singing and prayer, when the friends retired, and we were left in possession of our own domicil. This was on the 23d of December, 1814. I shall have occasion again to refer to my wife, for she was my right hand, in affliction and sorrow, in joy and rejoicing.

ENLARGED LICENSE TO PREACH.

While trying to preach, my labors were for a time confined to the little village of Skidby, and to the church. (And here let me say, that when I spoke before the church, there were none present but those who were members of that body.) Things went on prosperously with us, and, in 1815, I received permission from the church—or what is termed, in America, a "license"—to exercise my gift wherever God in his providence might open a door.

SUFFERING AND CRIME IN ENGLAND.

Those were times that tried both State and Church. The American and French wars were about closing. Breadstuffs were extremely high. Flour was two dollars and twenty-five cents per stone, (fourteen pounds.) Bankruptcy and failures, of every kind, had been the order of the day, for some time. The poor tax of our firm in Hull, one year, was about eleven hundred dollars—a rate of taxation which Americans never yet endured. The operators in mills, factories, &c., were sore pressed to obtain the small pittance sufficient to keep them from starvation; and many died of actual hunger. It was a common-place thing to see, in the daily papers, accounts of men being found dead: " Verdict given, Died for want of food." I saw, on one occasion, as estimated, one hundred and forty thousand operators, gathered at Manchester, parading the streets, emaciated and care-worn. Their banner was a bread loaf, dipped in blood, with an inscription of red letters upon black ground, " BREAD OR BLOOD." The soldiers were let in upon them, after they had assembled in St. Peter's Square, Market Street Lane, to be addressed by a Mr. Hunt, who presented himself as one of the great reformers of the day. But the whole scene was summed up in the utter dispersion of the motley crowd, by the swords and sabres of the military. Highway robberies, shop-lifting, house-breaking, and murder, were every-day occurrences. None but those who lived in that day, and witnessed the scenes, can form any adequate idea of the wretched state of the nation.

NEW CHURCH ENTERPRISE.

But I wish not to recall the picture of those dark days in England. Therefore I will return to that which concerns me most, and review circumstances more congenial to my nature. About this time, our church had to give up their chapel—for what reason, I do not now remember, but my impression is that it was decided, in a suit which had been for many years in the Court of Chancery, against those from whom we had rented. We then removed to a house, called Salt House Lane Chapel. Soon after that, it was thought best, by some of the church, that a few should take letters and build up a new interest in a low, wicked part of the city. We obtained a building, and fitted it up, for a place of worship. I was one in the enterprise. Our pulpit was supplied by such ministers as we could obtain. Part of the time it fell to my lot to·do the public speaking. I also continued my labors in the little village previously alluded to.

HOPES FRUSTRATED.

A new thought came into my mind—that, if God would prosper me, as he had done, I might in a short time be able to preach the Gospel to the poor, anywhere and everywhere, as opportunity might offer, and sustain myself. But God's ways were not my ways, nor His thoughts my thoughts. For, though I had sailed, more or less, in different crafts, I had got my foot upon a ship that I had never sailed in before—that was a *partner-ship.* I became a junior partner in the firm, but very soon found the vessel was leaking, and the probability was that she would founder, sooner or later. In her, I lost a great portion of the earnings that I had been laying up for years. I concluded to leave Hull, and commence anew.

REMOVE TO PONTEFRACT.

In the spring of 1818, I located in the old borough of Pontefract, in the same county, doing some business on my own account, and some on commission, and making about a comfortable living. But my hope of becoming a minister of the Gospel, preaching to the poor, and sustaining myself, gave up the ghost. Yet I continued to preach, in villages near the city. There was no Baptist church in' Pontefract, and the nearest was in Leeds, some eighteen miles away. But I felt that the poor villages needed the Word of life. I also preached for ministers in the place, and ministers in the country. No matter, to me, what their denominational name might be, if they were only orthodox churches.

TOO MUCH METAPHYSICAL PREACHING.

Here permit me to relate a little circumstance which occurred while I was in that place. Some three miles distant, there was a village of several hundred poor and ignorant people, the men being generally barge-men and coal-heavers. But there was an Independent chapel in the place, with a pious church, and a minister whose soul was in the work. He was a man of good education, and well understood how to use that education in the field of his labors. He called upon me, one day, to see if I could preach for him for three weeks; he had obtained a supply for other three weeks, and was to be absent six weeks. The other brother he had obtained, was from the Bradford Theological Institution. I supplied the church the first, and the young brother the next three weeks. After the pastor returned, he came up to town, to express his thanks for my labors. I was engaged in business when he came in, and asked him to walk up stairs into the sitting-room, where Mrs. Sheardown would visit with him until I was at liberty. Soon, I heard Bro. Lees laugh, most heartily—only as such good-hearted, whole-souled men know how to laugh. When I went up-stairs, I inquired the cause of the wave of merriment which had subsided. Bro. Lees said he had been relating to Mrs. Sheardown a circumstance that occurred during the labors of his young collegiate, as given him by the brother himself. He thought he had preached a very big sermon. In that sermon, he had said a great deal about "metaphysics," and metaphysical reasoning. He was quite anxious to know what the people thought of his sermon : therefore, he concluded to mingle with the congregation, as they retired, hoping that he might hear their opinions. He was close in the rear of two good old mothers, who, with locked arms, were nudging along the sidewalk. One said, " O, what a blessed *sarment* we had ! I never *heered* such a one." The other said, " What part did you like the best ?" I *liket* it all, but that part I *liket* best where he told us the *Gos-pill* was both *meat and physic*." The circumstance was so humiliating to the young man, that he told the pastor that, in future, he would try and use such language as the people whom he was addressing could understand. (If this should meet the eye of any aspiring young man, whose bumps of self-esteem are very large, may it be a word fitly spoken!)

ITINERATE AMONG THE POOR.

While residing in Pontefract, I had all the week-day evening preaching I could do, compatible with my busi-

ness. My great object was to present to the people,
Jesus Christ, the only Saviour of sinners, and that He
was able and willing to save to the uttermost all who
came unto God by Him. The operatives in that manufacturing district—in fact, in all the land—continued to
be sorely pressed for food; and it was to me a luxury
to spread before them the bread of eternal life.

DOCTRINAL DISSENSIONS.

At that time, there was great excitement in the Baptist churches, growing out of *Gill-ism* and *Fuller-ism*.
Although the beloved Fuller had recently (1815) gone
to his rest, he had tapped a new vein of theology, that
was just beginning to pour out its light upon the world.
Dr. Gill had long been the standard of divinity, and it
was very hard for some to give up his favorite dog-
matical theories, and many, both ministers and laymen,
were deeply imbued with the spirit of hyper-Calvinism.
But Fuller had hidden the leaven in the measure of
meal, and it was working powerfully upon the minds of
many, so that, when a minister was the subject of conversation, the first question generally was, "Is he a
Gill-ite or a Fuller-ite?" and the churches were much
divided in their views. I recollect that Mr. Arbon once
said in a sermon, "If faith is not a duty, then unbelief
is no sin." Two or three of the old members immediately took their hats and deliberately walked out of
the church, saying they would never sit peaceably and
hear such Arminian stuff as that.

VISIT TO FRANCE.

While residing in Pontefract, in the early part of
1820, business called me to the continent of Europe.
While in France, I learned more about the "mother of
harlots and abominations of the earth," than I had ever
known before. It would not have been safe for me,

had it ever been known that I had a Protestant Bible in my possession. In traveling by the *Diligence*, it was almost a daily occurrence to have to take off my hat to the images of their saints, posted at the corners of the roads; and, on one great festival day, I had to bow my knees in the street until the *Grand Costodia*—the bust of St. Peter, and other relics, which were carried upon the shoulders of twelve priests—had passed by!

A LONE CHRISTIAN WOMAN.

While in that land, I met but one Christian. That was a lady, whose acquaintance I made accidentally, while walking one morning on the beach of the Bay of Biscay. In passing her, I gave the customary salutation, in French. She answered very politely, and, turning around immediately, she added, "*Anglaise, Monsieur?*" She detected my English accent in pronouncing the French. I entered into a conversation with her, in which she gave me a short history of her life. She was born in London. Her father, an English officer, was killed in battle. She and her mother were then in France, where the daughter married a French officer, and, subsequently, renounced her Protestantism, and became a Catholic. Afterwards, she became convinced of the great sin, (as she expressed it,) of renouncing the religion of her fathers. Her exercises resulted in her hopeful conversion to God. Seventeen long years she had cherished that hope in secret, all the time conforming to the externals of Romanism. She said that I was the first person to whom she dared to divulge the fact; for, if her husband should know it, he would take the first opportunity to plunge his dagger into her breast. I spoke to her such words of consolation, and encouragement, as I could, under the circumstances. I saw her no more, but hope she may be found among the redeemed of the Lord, in that day when God shall make up His jewels.

MRS. SHEARDOWN'S ADVENTURES.

While in France, my wife came over, to make a short visit to the country that was then so bitterly hated by the land that gave her birth. Her introduction was very unfavorable. I had written her that I would meet her at Calais, on the given day and hour that the packet from England was expected to arrive. The vessel came, in an hour or more before the expected time; consequently, I was not down to the port when it arrived. She could not speak a word of French, and as soon as the ship was hauled up to the dock, the *gens-d'armes* (armed police) came on board, demanded her baggage, and sent it away to the Custom House. She herself was taken by a class of men who looked, to her, the meanest set of ruffians she ever saw, and posted away, to a prison looking house, where they put her in the custody of some old French women, to be searched. She scolded, in her language, and resisted all she could, but they continued unpinning, &c., until they had searched her person thoroughly. They found nothing contraband concealed about her, and she was released. I was waiting at the depot to receive her. She was so frightened, that she looked unnatural. I should have given her the particulars that would be required of her on her arrival, in my letter, had I not expected to have been present when the vessel came in. A few weeks taught her, that she was not in the land of her nativity.

VISIT HOLLAND—THOUGHTS ABOUT AMERICA.

My business was nearly done up, and we should soon have returned home, but I had to go to Dunkirk, in Flanders, and took my wife with me, that she might see more of the world.

For several years, I had been very anxious to visit America. I had read many exciting works respecting the land of liberty. A particular friend of mine, a deacon of the church where I had my standing in the City of Hull, was induced to go to America by the flattering accounts, in English publications, of a Dr. Robert H. Rose and others. I had got the impression that America was the garden of the world, and that the regions around Mont-Rose, in the "Beech Woods," were the · very flower-beds of that garden. My friend, the deacon, wrote me flattering accounts of the country, but did not like the Beech Woods, and finally moved to Philadelphia. I had great confidence in him, for he was to me a brother beloved. But after I was married, and settled in life, I gave up the hope of ever seeing the new world. I could not endure the thought of tearing my wife away from all her friends, and taking her to a distant land, where, perhaps, she might never see them again. By doing this, I thought I should have a poor, broken-hearted wife.

SHE PROPOSES EMIGRATION.

But while we were at Dunkirk, conversing on our pillows, without any reference to America or any other foreign land, she broke off from the subject then under consideration, and said, "How long I have been wishing that you would take it into your head to go to America!" I was perfectly startled. I said to her, "My dear! can you leave father, and mother, and friends, to go to a land where you may never see them again?" She answered, "If you think it best, I can." I said to her, "I can never take you to a country that I have never seen. Would you be willing to stay with our friends until I go over and explore the land, and then, if it looks best for me to stay there, can you undertake the voyage

across the Atlantic alone, with your two little children?"
She said, " Yes! The same God who protects me here,
can protect me on the waters." I told her I would
bring my business to a close as speedily as possible, and
start for the land of promise.

PREPARE TO SEE THE NEW WORLD.

I finished my business, and went up to London to
take ship. I found I had to wait there some two weeks
for the vessel to sail.

HINDRANCES.

I found, also, that difficulties of a new cast would be
liable to meet me. No individuals could leave England, at that time, who were mechanics, or who had
served an apprenticeship to any kind of business.
None but those who were farmers, or laborers, could
get away, unless smuggled. However, I concluded to
pay my passage, and enter on board as a passenger for
New York. The vessel went down the river, some
thirty miles below London, to Graves End, the final
place of her clearance. Here I found that all the passengers must come ashore and repair to the alien
office. There the questions were of such a nature as
I had not anticipated. While others were interrogated,
I found that they must have a voucher, or recommen-
dation, from some prominent individual, testifying that
their object in going to America was to possess land
and follow the avocation of agriculturists. Many of
the passengers had vouchers from the overseers of the
poor in the places where they had lived. Those were
very readily passed. When it came to me, I frankly
told the officer, that I did not know that I was required
to have such a voucher, and had none; but I would
give him the address of an individual of high standing,
in a certain rural district, who would answer all his

inquiries on the subject of the land business. He did not appear to see through it: because, before he could get the information from that individual, I would be tossing on the Atlantic! After we were all through, however, he ordered every individual to rise and stand before him, while he read to us the Alien Act—thereby alienating us for ever from his Britannic majesty, his Britannic majesty's government, and all his Britannic majesty's dominion—from any hope of protection by that government, from henceforth and forever! All safe on·board, we weighed anchor and gave three hearty cheers for the land of promise!

OUT UPON THE OCEAN—STORMS, &C.

After we had cleared the river, and got fairly into the sea-way, we were busily engaged overhauling our sea-stock, &c. By-and-by, a request was sent to the Captain, from some of the cabin passengers, to have the decks cleared, and give them the privilege of having a dance. But, to an experienced eye, it was very evident there would soon be other business for the voyagers. In about fifteen minutes, a squall struck the vessel, with a greater degree of violence than any had expected, carrying away her fore-topsail, and using the ship rather roughly. All was bustle, as it ever is on such occasions. The dancing party had enough to do to wait upon their sea-sick stomachs, and we never heard another word about dancing through all the voyage.

We parted with our pilot at the Downs, and laid our bows for the goodly land. The charge for a steerage passage was forty pounds sterling, and we had also to provide our own sea-stock (provisions, &c.,) for eight weeks, the voyage usually requiring six weeks on an average. Cabin passage was probably twice as expen-

6

sive, at that time. Ours was an American vessel, named *The Criterion*. She was an old vessel, but sailed fast, and nothing specially alarming occurred.

REACH NEW YORK HARBOR.

For several days, we were making a very good run, after which we experienced heavy weather, with some terrific gales, which kept the passengers, not accustomed to the water, snugly hatched down below. I always had the privilege of the decks. Having been on the water considerably, and never troubled with sea-sickness, I could always lend a hand, to help the men in any time of need. We left with our ship's company one man short, and two were injured so that they were not able to do duty: consequently, a raw hand was better than none. We made sight of land after four weeks' running, and put ship-about for the night, thinking, probably, the next day to be in Sandy Hook. But a very heavy gale of wind, blowing off the land, sent us out to sea; and it was ten days before we made the sight of land again. The ship being old, and badly strained by stress of weather, began to make water pretty fast. The pumps had to be worked, day and night, and the male passengers had to take their turns at pumping. When we sighted land again, it was about ten o'clock at night, I had retired to the fore-top, where I could be alone and enjoy my thoughts. I saw from the fore-top that we were running the land down. I cried to the officer on deck that we were running·right ashore. The word speedily rang out from the officer on deck, "Topsail-sheets and halyards haul—ready about." As the ship came about, her keel grounded on the bottom. We fired several shots for a pilot, and got an answer about daylight in the morning. ·The pilot came on board, and ran us safely into the

Hook: and as soon as the wind veered, (which I think was not until the next day,) he brought us safely up to Quarantine. Here, our ship and passengers being examined, and all found right, we proceeded up to New York.

GO UP THE HUDSON.

I spent but a short time in the city, and took a sloop for Newburg, not knowing where I should go, or scarcely what I wanted. But, after all my cogitations of heart, I made up my mind that I could proceed to Mont Rose, and see what I thought of the country after a personal examination.

MEN FROM THE LAKE COUNTRY.

Landing in Newburg, late at night, I went up to a tavern or hotel to stay. There I fell in company with some good, honest sort of men, who said they were from the "Lake country." They informed me that the "Beach Woods country" was a poor, barren, miserable region, and that it was not fit for "chipmucks" to live in. I must confess I knew no more about what a "chipmuck" was, than a wild Arab knows about English grammar. But those, whom I had thus met, appeared to be very kind, and very communicative. As they were in Newburg with teams, they offered to give me a passage with them to their homes, "between the Lakes." I thankfully accepted their offer, and cast my lot with them. I was deeply interested in everything I heard and saw, and in due time we arrived at the place of our destination—Covert, Seneca county, New York—in October, 1820.

BECAME A CITIZEN OF YORK STATE.

Every one appeared to be friendly, open-hearted, and gave freely of what they possessed, (which, by the by, was abundant,) for eating and drinking. The father of one of the men whom I had traveled with, was an intelligent man, formerly from Long Island, and pretty well posted in relation to the country. I made up my mind that I should stay in that place until the arrival of my wife. I wrote her several letters, but received none in answer. I was perplexed and troubled, but when I came to inquire of individuals, what they thought could be the reason that I received no answers, they looked upon England as being so far out of the world, that, if I got an answer in a year, I would do very well The mails, from the Lake country to New York or Boston, were very uncertain in that day. The last letter I wrote to her, (which, happily, she received, and the only one she had received,) gave her a particular account of my whereabouts, and all the directions how to proceed until she got to Newburg.

CHEAP LIVING—MY GREAT AWKWARDNESS.

Having concluded that I should make that my stopping place, I asked the gentleman with whom I was staying if he had anything that I could do, as I wanted to earn enough to pay my board. He told me board was nothing. I believe, at that time, wheat was selling at three shillings (37½ cents) per bushel, and everything of an eatable nature about the same proportion. He said, if I had a mind to work some, I might go and thresh some wheat he had in the barn, and take care of the horses and cattle, which I was very glad to do. I wanted to learn the ways of the country. I worked just as I pleased, but I had never threshed wheat with a flail, or taken care of cattle. He had to show me how it was to be done; and he promised to give me all the wheat, pork, &c., that I should want for my family.

One day he remarked to me, "Now, we must go to-day and get up some wood." The team was harnessed, and everything ready; he then gave me a chopping axe, and took one himself, when we started. But I had never seen a chopping axe before, nor had I ever seen any individual cut down trees, American fashion. I had seen the English choppers prepare to cut down a tree. They would get some able man to climb the tree, take up a strong cable rope, and make it fast to the top of the tree; then put all the strain they could on the rope, and fasten it to another tree, if there was one, and if there was not, to a stake firmly driven into the ground. Then they would sit down on the ground, with an axe resembling what I should now call a long-bitted post axe. They would cut all around the tree, close to the ground, but when it was almost cut off, would be very careful to keep from under the side where the rope was made fast to draw it over. I told him how ignorant I was about the chopping business. He said he would show me how it was done. I stood, and looked with astonishment to see how he made the chips fly. After the tree was felled, he said to me, " Now you cut off that limb, and let me see how you will perform." I thought I must strike very hard, and I expected to see the chips fly, but, instead of that, the axe flew out of my hands, two or three rods. I went and picked it up out of the snow, and he laughingly said, "I dare not stay within a half mile of you." But he ventured to give me another trial. He told me I must hold to the helve with one hand tightly, and let the other slide up the helve. But my hand would not slide, therefore I had to let go with that hand entirely, so that, when the blow came, I had but one hand hold of the helve. He enjoyed my ignorance, and was very patient with me, appearing to think, if he could learn me to chop (as he said) it would be a great feather in his cap! Every opportunity, I would get an axe and go off alone; and kept on trying, until such time as I found I was getting a little *sleight*. This encouraged me, and I felt determined to be a chopper.

So in relation to all the business of the backwoods. I worked very steadily at one thing or another, until spring. I then bought three acres of land from the father of the man with whom I was boarding. It being cleared up, I could do nothing with it until the spring was fairly in.

One day, the old gentleman said to me, "I want you should come with me into the sugar bush." We went, and he showed me what was to be done, describing all the process of tapping trees and manufacturing sugar. He said to me, "Now I want you to tap all the maple trees in this piece of woods, and, when you get tired, come down home." I did not go home, though I was very tired. I thought I would set all the spiles we had taken up. He did not know what might have happened me; I might have cut myself, or something: so—at a late hour—he came where I was, and said, "Do the trees run good?" I told him, some run, and some would not run at all. He walked around with me through the bush, and I certainly had tapped three basswoods to one maple! My friend concluded he might as well do the tapping himself.

I had gained, through the winter, some knowledge of American husbandry, but more in theory than in practice. The old gentleman told me, one day, that I must plough a part of my lot, which had never been broken up, and put corn on it. It would have to be ploughed, he said, twice; the second time, it would have to be cross-ploughed. I know something about ploughing, from observation in my travels through the country, but the labor part I had never performed. He lent me a plough and chains, and a neighbor furnished me a pair of oxen. But they were rather fractious—probably growing out of my awkward way of handling them. Sometimes the plough was in, but more frequently it was out of the ground ; some of the time I was holding to the handles ; at other times I was thrown on the ground. There were some pines on the lot: I would get the plough hitched to a small root, and then whip up the oxen, and the first thing I would know, the root would break, the ends spring back and take me on my shins; so that, before the day's ploughing was through, my shins were pretty well scarred, and bloody. But I thought, legs or no legs, I must have this part of the lot ploughed : so I persevered to the end.

MY FAMILY ARRIVE.

Now I will return to my wife's coming into the country. In the letter of directions that I had sent her, I requested that she should write me as soon as she arrived at New York, then come up by boat to Newburg, which she did; but I received no letter from her, consequently she become tired of waiting. Supposing there might have been a failure in her letter, and finding some English people coming into the Beech Woods, (which would be on her way to the Lakes,) they engaged a team in partnership, and started on. One of them wanted to go to Great Bend, on the Susquehanna River, which was on her direct road. On arriving there, she wrote to me again, and waited some two weeks, but no answer came. She then hired a team to bring her and her two children from there to the place where I was stopping.

One day (in the month of May, 1821,) I was standing in the door-yard, talking with the gentleman I was boarding with. We saw a team coming over a little rise in the road, some thirty or forty rods distant. He jokingly said, "Yonder comes your wife." I answered, "So she does," not realizing scarcely what I said. I waited and looked with intensity; and very soon, indeed, I saw that it was she. The driver had said to her, as they were passing over the little rise of ground, "There are two men yonder now, if one should be your husband!" She replied, "If he would only move, I should know him." Just at that time I moved down towards the road, when she exclaimed, "That is he, indeed!" It was a joyous and happy meeting, after having been parted more than ten months. She had had a boisterous passage, for something over six weeks. But, with all the toil and labor of the voyage, and traveling from New York city to Seneca county, she had never been discouraged; her spirits remained buoyant to the last.

That afternoon, a good old lady—who was, Yankee fashion, asking all kinds of questions—inquired of my wife if it did not almost break her heart to leave father, mother, brothers and sisters, perhaps never to see them again? She said, "No. When parting with my friends, while they were all in tears, I had no tears to shed. My mother said to me, 'Esther, why don't you weep?' I replied, 'I cannot weep—*I am going to see my husband!*'"

LAST INTELLIGENCE FROM SKIDBY.

For the purpose of bringing into view, at once, all connected with my Old World life, I will here narrate a fact somewhat out of the order of occurrence as regards time.

During a long period, in America, I had much

trouble, not knowing what had been the effect of my labors in the little village where I first preached the Gospel. As I will hereafter notice, it rose up before my mind, by day and by night, that I did wrong in leaving there. I had no hope of ever ascertaining whether any good results had followed. But, after my ordination, I met one day, on the highway, a gentleman, who said, "Elder, there is a letter in the Post Office for you." (We had but a weekly mail.) I replied, "Much obliged, sir—I am going down to the office." Said he, "The 'Squire told me to tell you it is a shipping letter—he thought you would be very anxious to see it." I passed on to the office, and called for my letter from over the seas. At once, I saw that it was not from any of my regular correspondents, for I did not know the handwriting of the superscription. I opened it, and was then convinced that it was from some one who had never written to me before. I cast my eye to the bottom of the page, and saw the signature—"J. Jefferson." It did not strike my mind at the time, who that was. The next page seemed to be written by an old fashioned writer—the characters looked very much like the round hand-writing of my father. I saw, at the bottom, the name, "Wm. Wilberforce." The next page was in the hand-writing of a female, and subscribed, "Jefferson." I then understood who the writers were. The old gentleman (Mr. Wilberforce) was the man at whose house I first opened my mouth for Jesus. The lady (Jefferson) was the daughter of Mr. Wilberforce, and J. Jefferson, was her husband. Those kind friends had inquired, and sought out my far distant residence, on purpose to inform me as to what God had wrought in their midst. By those letters, I learned that Mr. and Mrs. Jefferson were both hopefully converted under my labors. The father named several texts of Scripture, from which I had preached, and under which a number of other individuals had been brought to the knowledge of the truth. Among these was a young man, a plowman for a neighboring farmer, who appeared to have talents, which, if cultivated, promised usefulness in Zion. He studied two years in Dr. Steadman's Institution, at Bradford. There had been built, in Skidby, a neat brick chapel, which was occupied by a church of about one hundred members, and that young man was their pastor.

This information took away all the burthen from my mind—believing that God had done by me all that He intended I should do in that place. And I have never had any anxiety about them since.

CHAPTER III.—1820 to 1826.

As it regarded my ignorance of the ways and customs of a country so new and peculiar to me, I have hitherto been somewhat particular on several points, but will say no more at present, and now enter upon the darkest page of my history.

RELIGIOUS OPPORTUNITIES.

When we had become settled, after paying for my three acres of land, I had just seventy-five dollars to begin the world with. That was no discouragement to me. But my religious life was a great concern of mind. I attended church, the first Sabbath after I arrived at my stopping place. I thought it was the most singular congregation, and place of worship, that I had ever seen. But what astonished me most, was the preaching. I have no doubt of the goodness and piety of the minister, for God had done a great work by him. A short time before, he had moved Westward, and was then on a visit, to see his old friends, and attend to some unfinished business. I made some remarks relative to his preaching, when a gentleman replied to me, "Any person who finds fault with Elder T.'s preaching, cannot live in this community." But I thought I would continue to attend meetings, and form acquaintances with the church members. I had not yet reflected upon my peculiar situation, for I had left England without a church letter. While absent from the city where I had my standing, the few brethren and sisters, before referred to, who designed to form the fourth church, found that they were not able to sustain themselves; upon which, they dissolved, and joined other churches in the city. My father-in-law wrote, soon after, to let me know what had taken place. But I was not concerned, because I knew that I could obtain a standing in any regular Baptist church, in England, when God in his providence should cast my lot wherever there was such a church: all I would have to do, there, would be to prove my baptism, and give a relation of my Christian experience. I always said, when conversing with any of the members of the church, that I was a Baptist in my own country, and told them the circumstances under which I left; but no word of encouragement was given me, nor any invitation extended for me to become one with them.

IN A BACKSLIDDEN STATE.

At that time, a strong temptation beset my mind, that I would say little or nothing more about it—at all events, I would never lisp the first word that I had ever preached—and get along as best I could. I found my religious enjoyment to be waning, though I continued to pray in my family, and pray in my closet— but not so frequently as I had been in the habit of doing. Very soon, I became backslidden in heart, and too much so in life. Still, I continued to meet with the church every Sabbath, and occasionally attended their covenant meetings, but all was cold and dark. They would ask me to speak, which I think I never refused to do; but something all this time was whispering within, that I . had better *live more.* like a Christian, and *say less* about it. Those were most painful days to me, and I thought any place better adapted to me than the church of Jesus Christ. I would rally at times, and feel very anxious for a standing in the church, but whenever I made any move towards it, I was always answered, " You can never get into the church, sir, in this country, without you bring a letter." I had always been honest in telling them my real condition; that I could-give them evidence, in letters which I had by me, that I was a member, in good standing, of a regular Baptist church in England; also, that I could give them the name of a brother, a deacon in the church, who saw me baptized, and knew my Christian walk and character, and who might easily be communicated with, for he was then living in the city of Philadelphia. All that, they would answer, will not supply the place of a letter. I told them the reason I had none was because the church had disbanded in my absence, and I was left alone in the world—but that, if I was in my own country, I should have no trouble in obtaining a standing in any church of our order. They never asked me how I would, and I never thought it best to tell them, for I did not think it was my duty to dictate to them, or to introduce new laws among them.

DISCOURAGEMENTS.

There were brethren in the church who I esteemed very much, but only one with whom I was perfectly confidential. When I received letters from England, they always were of a religious character, and I let him have the privilege of reading them, as they delighted him much. I now had a new trial, or temptation, pro-

7

sented to my mind: it was, that I had sinned against God in not remaining in the little village where I first preached, and that God had forsaken me because it looked as though I had forsaken them—and I could not return to my native land. In the first place, I had not the means to cross the Atlantic again. And in the second place, I had been alienated from the British government—from all support, recognition, or protection thereof—according to law. Therefore (I came to the conclusion) God had left me to myself, to take my own way, and to walk after the sight of my own eyes. The bitterness of such thoughts can be realized only by those who have experienced them. It appeared to be a settled point, in my mind, that I never should divulge the fact that I had once tried to preach.

ALMOST DETECTED.

About that time, I received a very interesting letter from my father-in-law, in England. In it, among many other things to which he referred, was the effect of the last sermon he heard me preach before I left my native land. Upon meeting with Deacon Porter, (the brother previously alluded to,) I said to him that I had another letter from England. He asked me if I had it with me; I told him I had. He said he would like very much to see it, if it was consistent. I said, " Certainly you can, my brother." I handed him the letter, having forgotten all about the preaching part until he had had it in his possession, long enough to read it almost through. I would have given anything I had if I could only have obtained it from him. But, strange as it may appear, not a word was said by him relative to the preaching. And, some years after, while conversing with him upon the subject, he told me that he thought it was some other individual whose preaching my father-in-law referred to, instead of my own. I had feared, for some time, lest he would leak it out to some of his friends ; but, not hearing of it from any one, I concluded he had forgotten it, or must have overlooked it.

I employed myself, part of the time, in teaching school, and the balance of my time in laboring at anything that I could do. The state of my mind became more and more depressed, and I was alarmed at my situation. The church was supplied by different ministers, the greater part if not all of whom I trust now are in the better world. They at last obtained a pastor—a man in years, and I thought a very good man—high in doctrine, and strict in discipline. He was more like a preacher, to my view, than any I had become acquainted with in this country. I thought, now, perhaps, this man can do me good. So I kindly invited him to come and spend a day with me. He gave me the promise, which he fulfilled.

ANOTHER DISAPPOINTMENT.

This, I think, was the Friday before covenant meeting. I frankly opened all my heart, and read to him my English correspondence, except the letter that spoke about the preaching. He had questioned me, and we had talked familiarly together. I had kept nothing back, in order that he might know my case just as it really was. Something, I do not now recollect just what, prevented me from going to the meeting. A good Dutch mother in Israel, with whom we were intimate as a family and neighbor, called at my house on Saturday evening, on her way home from the covenant meeting. I was busy cutting wood by the door. I went into the house to carry some wood, and found the old lady, weeping bitterly, and talking with my wife. I asked her what was the matter? She said, "I'm kilt, I'm kilt." I replied, "Sister L., what has killed you?" She said, "Our minister." "Why, what has your minister done?" She said, "He told us to-day, in meeting, that he had been to see that foreigner who calls himself an Englishman; he had had a long interview with him; he is a very smart fellow," said Elder W., "and is capable of doing good, or a great deal of harm; and I would caution you against having anything to do with him." I thought, then, the last blow had been struck; that it was more than I could bear. Still, I continued to go to church on the Sabbath; but it was very seldom that I went to any other meeting.

RELIEF COMES, AT LAST.

That good man died, soon after, and another pastor was chosen, in the person of Aaron Abbott. He very soon heard of me, and proved to be one of the most genial spirits I had ever met with on this side of the Atlantic. I found that he appreciated what I told him; we wept, and prayed together; and many of the dark clouds that were about my mind, were in a measure dissipated. He said to me, " Would it not be a privilege to you to belong to the church?" I said, "Yes; if I can not have a home in the church, I can not have any home on earth," for I told him I was entirely alone in this new world, (as far as kindred or connection were concerned,) except my family. Having made him acquainted with my situation, he said, "Now, my brother, is there any way that you know of, whereby you can become a member of the church?" I told him that I knew of a way, but I did not like to name it; it looked so much, to me, like pleading my own cause. He replied, "Name it to me; what we say is confidential." I told him the only way, as I viewed things, was that I should give proof of my baptism being legitimate, and that, if the church gained evidence that I was a Christian, they could receive me into their fellowship. He answered, "That is it. Now, will you and your wife attend the church covenant meeting?" I told him we would. "Then I will try to open the way to them."

WE JOIN THE CHURCH.

We attended. The circumstances were laid before the church, by the pastor. My heart was broken. I confessed my wanderings and alienation with bitter tears, I trust, of repentance. As soon as the brethren and sisters saw the thing in the light as presented by the pastor, they were astonished that they did not see it so before, and we were received into the church. That was a good day. Nevertheless, there were many thing that corroded my very heart; but nothing equal to the continual anxiety growing out of the idea that I had excluded for ever all the pleasantness that I had enjoyed while preaching to the people in the little village where I first commenced.

TAKE THE LEAD IN MEETINGS.

The pastor was a great lover of the old fashioned conference and prayer meetings. He often appointed them at different school houses, invited me to attend them, and, if there was no leader in the meetings, to take the lead myself. I was delighted with the invitation, and was willing to go anywhere, because it gave me opportunity to talk upon the subject of religion. I was once in one of those little meetings, at the Kingtown school-house. God was refreshing my soul while speaking, when a good old mother, (Robinson by name,) exclaimed, "Why, this foreigner can preach! You have preached," she said, "haven't you?" I said I had always been in the habit of speaking on religion, more or less, ever since I was converted.

EXERCISES DURING SICKNESS.

In 1825, I was taken severely sick, with what was called the "old lake fever." While confined to my bed, I had a great deal of reflection in reviewing my life. One day, my wife came to my bedside, and said to me, "Can you remain alone a little while?" I replied, "Yes, but where are you going?" She remarked, "I want to go down to the brook and do some washing." It was but a few rods from the house, and I told her by all means to go; that she might not be troubled about me. While she was absent, I passed through a scene that I shall never forget. I was looking at my watch, which was suspended where I could see it. It was just fifteen minutes to eleven in the morning. After this, whether asleep or awake I know not, but the first thing that appeared to me was every part of the known world in which I had ever been, either by sea or land. It appeared as distinctly as though it were drawn out upon a map in living characters before me. Immediately after this, I saw every sin I had committed, as distinctly and as clearly as I ever saw figures. The last and greatest sin of all appeared to be my neglect of preaching the Gospel of Christ to perishing sinners. The next appearance was, that I was in impervious darkness. I then saw all the iniquity of my life, in mass together, piled up like one mighty thunder cloud; and, rising up in the centre, was the sin of my keeping back from proclaiming the riches of Christ to my fellow men. At this moment, I appeared to be upon an inclined plane, about four feet wide. On my right hand, was a gulf more dark than the darkness that I was in; and on my left, rising up like an immense mountain, was this black cloud of sins. The plane on which I was walking, inclined more and more towards the gulf; for it was a sidewise inclination. I thought

that I still tried to keep walking forward, but the path
became considerably crowded with travelers like myself. I could hear them dropping into the gulf, before
me and behind me. Sometimes I thought I should lose
my foothold, and fall into what I thought to be the
bottomless pit. When it seemed as if I could not keep
my feet much longer, I saw a little light, not larger
apparently than a pin's head. I thought something
whispered, " Never mind your feet, but keep your eye
upon the light." The light appeared to expand slowly.
I do not recollect that I ever turned my eye from it.
Suddenly, the plane became so inclined that my feet
were just about to slip, when, instantly, the light shone
with the greatest refulgence that can possibly be
imagined; and at that instant, the darkened cloud fell
just behind me, right into the gulf, with a tremendous
crash. I appeared to be in universal space; and as my
eyes reached into the far distant glories that were before
me, I said, "Lord, I shall live, and I will preach the
Gospel of Jesus Christ!" At this instant, my eye was
upon my watch; it wanted twenty minutes to twelve.
I was bathed in tears, and the subject of such abounding
consolation as I had never experienced before. My
wife came into my room a few moments after. I had
turned my face the other way. She gently put down
the covering, saw the situation in which I was, and
exclaimed, "Are you worse?" her tears flowing in
great profusion at the same time. I said, " No, I am
better—I am better. Leave me alone. My choicest
friends are only a burden to me." Such was the
abounding consolation of soul and mind, the savor of
which remained with me more or less through all my
sickness.

ECSTATIC ENJOYMENTS.

My fever was of a very dangerous nature. It ran

some thirty-one days before it arrived at its crisis. My senses were good, and my mind clear, all the time, with some very small exceptions. I was reduced so low that I could not raise my hand, and finally could not speak. While I was in this low condition, many of the brethren and neighbors were in to see me; and several of them I could hear talking to my wife, saying that I could live but a short time. It grieved me very much to see her weep under the influence of their con] versation, for I felt confident that I should live, yet had not strength to speak and express my hope. I had had that assurance through all my sickness. One night there was standing by my bed-side, with others, my confidential friend, Dea. Porter. This was about eleven o'clock. I spoke out, the spectators said, in my usual tone of voice, saying, "Dea. Porter, pray." The deacon at once said, "What do you want I should pray for, Bro. Sheardown?" I proceeded to tell him. All present were bathed in tears. The deacon said, "Stop! I am a child compared to you." Some said they thought I talked half an hour, others twenty minutes: but the most composed thought it might have been about fifteen minutes. When I had done speaking, my strength was almost entirely gone, and I was perfectly exhausted. I always loved to hear the deacon pray; but, on that occasion, it appeared to me that it was the most insipid prayer I ever heard. I could hear the people say to my wife, "It is a revival before death; he will die about twelve o'clock." But, the next day, my physician pronounced me better: the fever was broken, and he saw no reason, with good care, why I might not recover. My faith was in God, yet I believed in all the means that could be used. I felt afraid, at times, that my watchers might make a mistake in giving the medicine, and that might end my life. From that time, I began very slowly to amend; and, through the blessing of God, was finally restored to perfect health.

DESIRE TO REMOVE MY HOME.

This severe sickness did not appear to have undermined my constitution, for in a few months I was as hale and rugged as I ever had been, from anything that I could perceive. But my mind passed through a great change, and I was desirous of leaving the place. I inquired of every person whom I met, or was acquainted with, if they knew of a good place where I could obtain wild land at a cheap rate. I was finally told that in a place called Windfall Settlement, beyond Ithica, there was land, that could be obtained on easy terms. I thought I would not move prematurely; I would wait until I could see some person who had been there, in whom I could confide as giving me a correct account of the settlement.

I had a great desire to locate in what was called a new country, providing I could find one that suited me. When I had been about eighteen months in America, I thought I would like to go and see some unsettled lands, but it was not worth while for me to go alone. Consequently, some time elapsed before I made a start. Unexpectedly, one of my neighbors said to me, "Some of us are going out to look out wild land: don't you wish to go along?" I said to him, "Where are you going?" The answer was, "Somewhere west and south of the head of Seneca Lake." I concluded to cast in my lot with them.

There were five of us. We shouldered our knapsacks, stored with provisions sufficient to supply us when we got beyond settlers. They all had rifles, and told me I must have one too. I told them I might as well take a broomstick as a rifle, for I was as ignorant of handling a rifle as a cow was of handling a musket. So we went forth, and came to where Havanna now stands. There were a few houses there; one called a tavern, stood near the bank of the inlet. There we made one meal, to save our provisions. We then proceeded on our journey, and very soon found ourselves in a dense forest. Wandering along, toward night, we happened to come to a log house or shanty. The occupant was a Mr. Wakeman. He was very kind, and told us we must stay all night with him. He was poor as poverty, but entertained us with narratives of his own history and experience. He had fought in the last war, was taken prisoner by the British, and had been sent to one of the British Isles, where he remained three years a prisoner, which had very much broken down his constitution. In conversing with him, I found him a man of ardent piety; a Free-Will Baptist by profession. He had squatted in the woods, commenced a little clearing, and appeared very sanguine that he should get along in the world, and finally pay for his farm, (which he did, in time, and more too.)

PROSPECTING FOR NEW SETTLEMENTS.

In the morning, Mr. Wakeman gave us directions which way to go to find the best lands. We ranged the woods several days, and walked a good many miles. One lot of land he pointed out as being very superior; if we followed down a certain stream, we should come to an Indian camp, called Cole's Camp. This, to be sure, was a beautiful little spot; but I thought I would not live there for all the land I had seen. On our return home, night overtook us in a very dense forest, on what is now called Post Creek.

We were in a balsam swamp. The night became very dark, and drizzling with rain. We exhausted all our means in trying to get a fire, but failed, and decided we must locate so that each man might "tree" if the wolves should come upon us. Soon after coming to this conclusion, we heard a cow-bell, when we plucked up courage, and started where we thought the bell was. We stopped to listen, and found it was coming towards us. It proved to be a boy with a yoke of cattle, and a small grist of corn meal in a bag hanging over the yoke. He had been to mill, at Printed Post, some fourteen miles from where his father lived. The oxen kept the path, and we followed on with the boy, making a very good rear guard for the little grist. These faithful cattle led us to the house of a Mr. Haskins, where we tarried for the night. This must have been something above what is now called Beaver Dams, in the town of Catlin. We found one or two other settlers in the morning. From thence we posted our way home between the Lakes. When I got home, my neighbors inquired how I liked the new country; I told them I would not live there if they would give me all the land I had seen.

MR. WAKEMAN, AGAIN.

After this disgression, I will return to my preparation to go out to see the Windfall Settlement, before referred to. Spring time having arrived, people told me that it was the time to go if I wished to commence in a new country. My wife and I had talked the thing up, and the day was set for me to start. But the workings of Divine Providence I knew nothing of, until they manifested themselves to me. My wife and I were both from home. I do not recollect whether we had gone to meeting, or where, but I think not both to the same place, for I was the first who got home. My oldest child told me that there had been a man there from Catlin, with whom I had once stayed all night. He left his name as Bradley Wakeman, saying that I must not (for he had heard that I was going to move from Covert) go anywhere until I had been at his house again. His mind was deeply impressed that that was the place for me, and that God would make me useful to the people. The idea struck me with power, that God must be in this. How the man should have heard that I was intending to move, I do not know. . I told my wife that I should not go to the Windfall Settlement, but should start in the morning for Catlin, and, if I felt no better suited than I did before, I would then go to the Windfall Settlement, as I had intended. After I had started for the old gentleman's, I felt as though every step I took was like going home. Arriving there, I went out with him into the woods, and looked about. A certain lot of land, called No. 5, that he had showed me when I was first there, he informed me, was taken up, but that there was plenty more quite as good. The land had been in market but a short time, and settlers were beginning to drop in. I saw nothing in the country of that forbidding character that appeared to me the first time I was there. I finally went and viewed the lot on which the Indian camp, or Cole's camp, was. It looked to me like a paradise, and I had no disposition to look any further. I immediately retraced my steps, went to the land agent, (who lived in Caroline, Tompkins county,) and articled for eighty acres, being one half of said lot.

CHAPTER IV.—1826 TO 1830.

This was in the Spring of 1826. Mr. C. had taken
up the lot adjoining, and was about to move on it. I
made my boarding place with that young, married
family—a family which has always had a very warm
place in my heart. He was the son of one of the
deacons of the church to which I belonged, in Covert.

OUR WILD-WOOD HOME.

I went to work, with a will, on my new lot—where
not a stick had been cut—built me a log house, cleared
four acres smooth and clean, and sowed it to wheat
that fall. I moved my wife and children into my new
house, and we felt happier than we had ever done
before since we crossed the Atlantic, although we
lived that winter without either door or windows in
our house. We had our cow, and she was permitted to
range the large field without enclosure.

8

ATTEND AND ADDRESS MEETINGS.

I think it was the second Sabbath after 1 went into the woods, in the spring, that I saw a man who asked me if I did not want to go to meeting? I replied, "Yes, but where is there a meeting?" He said, "On the side of the mountain, this side of the inlet." That, I think, was about one mile and a half from the present village of Havanna. The old gentleman who was to preach, was Eld. Sted. He said some good things, and some very strange things. After the sermon, according to almost the universal custom of the day, a prayer was called for, and opportunity given for exhortation. The minister asked me my name? I told him, and then inquired, "Do you preach here again, next Sabbath, my brother?" He said, "No, sir." I said to him, "Will you say to the people that I will preach here, if God will, next Sabbath, at two o'clock in the afternoon?" He gave the notice that "Brother *Shwovenshear*" would preach there next Sabbath at two o'clock. He got my name all wrong, but I did not stop to have him correct it. I found he had got a *Shear* into it, so I concluded it would answer every purpose.

I felt in that little log school house, with a few people around me, that I was in the very height of earthly felicity. From that time onward, I preached wherever a few individuals could be gathered together.

HUNT UP SCATTERED BAPTISTS.

Shortly, I began to say to myself, "Is it not time that I began to look around and see how many Baptist brethren and sisters I can find?" The town was twelve miles by six in size. All I could see or hear of, were seven, with my wife and myself. I felt encouraged, and thought that presently I would get them together and form them into a conference. Settlers began to come in pretty fast, and we finally formed a conference. "Organized by appointing Eld. J. Reynolds, Moderator, and Bro. T. S. Sheardown, Clerk. . When the following brethren and sisters presented themselves: Brn. A. Vandeventer, J. Wixon, W. Dewith, P. Tanner, D. Weed, T. S. Sheardown; Sisters A. Pierce, C. Vandeventer, S. Lafever." Mrs. Sheardown was unable to attend that day, but joined afterward.

By this time, a great change had come over me. I was as familiar with the country as though my parents had been frontier settlers. Every few days, people were coming in, wishing to be taken into the woods, with the view of purchasing land. No matter what we were doing, when any person called on such an errand, it was always a rule with settlers to drop everything else and spend a day, and if necessary even more, in tracing lines and showing them what was for sale. I felt as much at home in such business as I ever did in the streets of a city in the old world. We were very anxious to have people settle among us, and never grudged the time that we devoted to such purposes.

PECULIARITIES OF PIONEER LIFE.

The first of the settlers were generally young married people, from between the Lakes. I had become practically acquainted with the labor of a backwoods-man, so that all the people were willing to change works with me. I could do a satisfactory day's work at chopping, and stood "A No. 1" as a logger. Of course, we had our privations, but we bore them with manly courage; and this taught us how to appreciate and enjoy the few blessings by which we were surrounded, with thankfulness of heart.

When we were in our incipient state as a settlement, we had a great distance to go to mill. One man proposed to build a grist mill, if the settlers would turn out and help, which they very willingly did, without pay or reward. This made it very convenient for us, providing we had anything to take to mill, (which was not always the case.) I was solicited to teach three months' school, one winter, in the place known to this day as Crawford's Settlement. It was about two miles from where we lived, to the school house, the path (or sled road) the greater part of the way winding through the woods. The going was pretty bad, having had some snow and rain, and there were several slough holes in the path, which made it considerable of a labor, but nothing discouraging: all was bright and hopeful beyond these small difficulties.

A DAY'S WORK AT MILL, SCHOOL, &C.

One morning, Mrs. Sheardown said to me, " I have baked up the last meal we have got." I had two bushels of corn that I obtained from between the Lakes. I shouldered the two bushels of corn, and took it to the mill, (which was three-quarters of a mile or more, beyond the school house;) then came back, taught the day's school, and at night went and got my grist and backed it home, so that we could have some meal for supper: for this was all the bread-stuff we had in the house. This was hard work, but still we remained hopeful for the future.

It was very common for me to commence chopping in the morning while the stars were yet to be seen in the sky, and, only spending a short time for dinner, at five o'clock in the afternoon quit, wash up, take some refreshment, go from three to five miles, preach a sermon, then have a prayer meeting, and return home

the same night, to be ready for labor the day following. I would generally cut down a large tree over
night, and take it for my breakfast spell to cut it up in
the morning, and often would kneel down by the side
of the tree, in the gray of the morning, before I began
work, and have a good time communing with my God.
Then I would sing my favorite hymn:

> "In the desert let me labor,
>   On the mountain let me tell,
> How he died, the blessed Saviour,
>   To redeem a world from hell."

My "stent" would often be done before my wife
gave the signal for breakfast. I was always in the
habit, let what come that might, of attending family
worship before breakfast; because I found my children,
and any persons who might be in the family, would be
on hand at meal times: consequently, I never was
troubled with any scattering of the family after breakfast.

RARE ENJOYMENTS.

Perhaps there never was a more friendly, congenial
class of people, than those who became settlers on that
new tract. Although most of them were unconverted
people, yet they were a kind, frank, sympathetic class
of men and women. Aristocracy was unknown. We
were very much alike as it regarded our means of
living. We often had "back-woods sociables," but
they were very different from the "sociables" of the
present day, for then we had no tattling, bickering, or
backbiting. We appeared to know nothing but pure
friendship and sociability, and seldom had an evening
gathering but that religion was a topic of conversation.
Even wicked men wanted to know something about
the Bible, and they knew that I was willing to give

them my opinion, and the reason of that opinion founded upon the word of God. We were blessed with a community (both males and females) who loved to sing, and we would sing the songs of Zion with such power and pathos that a person might have thought we were training ourselves to sing in that better world. Then we attended prayer; and, if very dark, we lighted our torches and wended our way through the sturdy forests to our respective homes, the fathers carrying the babes, and the mother's tongue continually going, " Do see that that young one don't get cold—feel of its feet." Those were mothers indeed, very tender of their offspring. And a blessed thing that they were, as things have turned out, for they were doing a great business, which has only been developed since the commencement of this wicked, Heaven-daring Rebellion. I have no doubt but many of those infant boys, that were thus carried in the arms of their fathers, *have made their mark during this awful war, for I know of some of them who have.*

ENLARGE MY FIELD OF LABOR.

My mind continued to be more and more deeply impressed relative to the moral condition of the people. The sphere of my labors was all the time enlarging; for, wherever there were a few settlers dropping in, in the remoter parts of this new region, I used to follow up. All were glad to have religious meetings in their houses; and if there were but a few that could come to meeting, that few would always be there. The town of Jersey, lying westward of ours, was the greater part of it a wilderness; and there were but very few ministers in all that region of country. I can call up in my mind, now, only one, and he was the old Mr. Sted, a Free-Will Baptist preacher, to whom I have referred. There were, in his connection, some few brethren who would talk to the people, and try to do what good they could.

I was acting as school commissioner. In the extreme northern part of the town, there was what was called a "half share school district;" that is, the school house was located in the town adjoining, and the district made up of parts of the two towns. This made a great deal of trouble. Judah would envy Ephraim, and Ephraim would vex Judah, and the commissioners from the two towns were often called to settle some difficulty. On one occasion, it was so late before we got through with our business, that I had to stay all night, with Esq. Tracy, at whose house we met. After the other commissioners had gone home, I commenced talking with the 'Squire about the interest of his soul. I found him an intelligent man, free to converse upon the subject, and we talked until a late hour in the night. I felt, that night, as though, indeed, I was about my ·Master's business. He said to me, "Sir, don't you preach sometimes? I think I have heard of your preaching in Crawford Settlement." I told him I tried to. In the morning, before I left, (which was very early,) he entreated me, with a great deal of tenderness, to come and preach at his house. I told him I would be very glad to, and that, if I should be called there again on business, I would arrange to preach at his house in the evening; and I very soon had the privilege of doing so.

I began to feel, then, that my field of labor was extending well to the north. Invitations began to come from the Beaver Dams, and from some parts of the adjoining towns west of us; so that I found myself under the necessity of going out several evenings every week. I had planted the banner of the Gospel at head quarters in Crawford Settlement, and that I always reserved for my Sabbath morning appointments.

While thus engaged in preaching, one of the deacons from between the Lakes, (a member of the church where I had my standing,) came out to visit one of his children. He stayed over the Sabbath, attended meeting with us, and we had a good time. I felt strong in the Lord, and in the power of his might, and was very much comforted by the presence of Deacon Cole. The church in Covert had heard that I was preaching, and at one of their covenant meetings it was proposed that I should be called to order because I had said nothing to them upon the subject. When they had made their remarks (some of them) about calling me to order, Deacon Cole arose and said, "My brethren, let Bro. Sheardown alone; God is with him, and he will ultimately do a great work in that new country." My old confidential friend, Dea. Porter, remarked, "I agree with Dea. Coles. I have long thought that Bro. Sheardown was just where God would have him; and, for my part, I believe all will come out right in the end."

The Lord had sent in among us, here and there, a few Baptists. We appeared to gain a little strength, though there was nothing very elating, only that every individual who could, would always attend meeting, whether it was preaching or prayer meeting. We never wanted for a congregation, winds blow high or low. And thus all moved on, laboring at their daily avocations, and toiling in their moral calling as professed brothers and sisters in the Lord Jesus Christ.

CONSTITUTION OF THE CATLIN CHURCH.

We concluded, when we numbered nineteen members, to organize ourselves into a church, to be known as the First Baptist Church in the town of Catlin. The preliminary steps were taken, with much prayer, and great searching of heart. I wrote the Articles of Faith and Covenant, part of them by the light of my burning log-heaps at night. Having obtained letters from our respective churches, we perfected our voluntary organization, May 31st, 1828. Next, invited a council, to see if they would fellowship us as a Baptist church in regular standing. At the appointed time, (June 25th, 1828,) the council came together, in the barn of Bro. A. Vandeventer. It was a time of trial for me. I had been, to the Conference, as pastor and clerk; in fact, all its business had gone through my hands. I wrote the letters of invitation, and signed them by the authority of the church. The council was principally gathered from between the Lakes. I think all the ministers, except one, were from that region. When the council was organized, and ready for business, one minister arose with a letter in his hand, saying he should never have stirred one inch to come there, if it had not been that he concluded that it was sheer ignorance of the individual who wrote the letter. I began to feel very intense upon the subject of ignorance. I was aware that I knew but little, but I was not aware that there was anything betraying ignorance, neither was there anything incorrect, in the letters that were sent. He was asked, by one of the brethren of the council, where the difficulty lay? He replied, " Your letters can not be like mine, or you would have seen it at once." He then pointed to the letter, as he held it in his hand, and said, " See here !" (beginning to read :) " The First Baptist Church in the town of Catlin, to the Baptist church of [such a place,] sendeth Christian salutation. Beloved brethren, we invite you to send your pastor and chosen brethren to sit with us in council, to see if you can fellowship us as a regular Baptist church." " Now," he said, "I never before saw such a letter as that, in my life. If they are a church, what necessity was there of sending for us? I always thought that letters were sent to call a council to *organize* a church." I had been appointed by the body (the church) to be mouth for them. I told him, as I understood it, it was our business to "organize" the church, then to call a council to see if they could *fellowship* us as such; but no council could make us into a church, if we were unwilling, on our part, to enter into that relation. There was a great deal of *pro* and *con* in the council, among the lay brethren; the ministers said but little. Finally Eld. Abbott, of Covert, arose, and said to the objecting brother, "If you have come here with the intention of helping to *make* a church, you might just as well have staid at home." This led to further altercation; but finally the council decided that the letters were correct. Then they called for our Articles of Faith and Covenant. There was one Article which embraced remotely the doctrine of the pre-existence of Jesus Christ. The brother who was in so much trouble about the letters, was now in more trouble about the doctrine, stating that whoever composed that Article was an Arian. The inquiry was made of some of the brethren, where they got the Articles of Faith. They told them that Bro. Sheardown wrote them. At once, the objector pronounced the doctrine to be heterodox. I told the council, that, inasmuch as I was responsible for the doctrine inculcated, not to get into litigation over me, but set me one side; and if the council thought best to expunge the article, or to alter its phraseology, all right; but to fellowship the little church, for that was my life. The council almost unanimously agreed that they could not fellowship the church unless I was an integral part of it. It was proposed by some of the council, that the objecting member should write an Article in place of the one that was the subject of dispute. It was written, and presented to me to see if it would meet my approbation as well as the one that was inserted in the church's Articles of Faith. I told them that the doctrine involved in the new Article was Unitarianism. This led to further debate. Eld. Abbott said he would write an Article that Bro. Sheardown and the council would all coincide in. It read as follows: "We believe that Jesus Christ ever was, is, and will be the medium of communication from God to His people." I told them that I was perfectly satisfied with that, and thought it far better than the one I had written myself. Then the council moved on, and fellowshiped us as a church. This was indeed one of the hard days of my life; yet, after all, a day that afforded the greatest satisfaction, perhaps, of any.

LICENSED TO PREACH.

At their covenant meeting in July, 1828, the church gave me a formal license to preach.

FATHER CATON'S VISIT, AND RIDE.

We had in our little church a brother and sister from Romulus, Seneca county, where they had been under the pastoral charge of Rev. John Caton. Bro. Caton was a very large man, in body, mind, and will, and imbued with all the spirit of the Revolution. He was once on the staff of Gen. George Washington; and a man who had been so near the father of a nation, may well be considered of some importance. This brother and sister had been down to visit their friends, and they had told father Caton some of the peculiarities of the Englishman who was preaching to them in the woods. The old gentleman said to the brother, "Is your minister sound?" He replied, "I think he is." A short time

after, the brother was going down again to see his
mother, and said I must go with him, and preach to
Eld. Caton's people. I concluded to go; and the first
thing after we had arrived in the place, the brother
went to Eld. Caton, and told him that his minister was
out with him, and, if he thought best, he should like
very much to have him preach that evening. The
Elder said: "My brother Abraham, is he sound? There
are so many of these young upstarts who are rotten
Arminians." The appointment was talked up, and the
Elder concluded, as he was rather infirm, that he would
have the services at his own house. He said, "I do
not think it best to make much fuss about it; and if it
was to be in the school-house, there would be a great
many people turn out, if they heard of it, who, perhaps,
would not come to my house; and I should like to hear
the man for myself." I had made up my mind, if I
preached, I should preach on faith and repentance; but
I must do something to convince the old father that
I was "sound." Consequently, after I had named my
text, I employed, as an exordium, a long quotation from
Paul to the Romans and Ephesians, relative to the purposes of God, embracing the doctrine of election, and
justification by the imputed righteousness of Jesus
Christ. This lubricated the old gentleman's throat so
effectually, that he swallowed down everything I said
relative to man's accountability, and the sinner's obligation to repent of his sins, and believe on the only
begotten Son of God, so that he might be the happy
recipient of the hope of eternal life, which God, who
cannot lie, promised in Jesus Christ before the world
began. As soon as the remarks were ended, the Elder
rose up in his majesty, and endorsed the doctrine,
eulogized the young speaker, and told how thankful he
was that he was not trammeled with Arminian stuff.

When we parted, he promised, if Bro. Abraham would come after him some time, he would make us a visit, and preach for a week, on condition that he could be carried from place to place, so that he might preach every day as long as he should stay with us. Of course, all this was agreed to.

In the fulness of time, (December, 1828,) Bro. Abraham arrived with his former pastor. We were much rejoiced at the coming of the patriarch. All were ready to make him as comfortable as their circumstances would admit; and he appeared to be well pleased with the attention paid him. He being very corpulent, as well as aged, we always minded to give him a good locality in the ox-sled, by which we moved him from place to place. After having attended a meeting in the afternoon, (when he preached plump two hours, if not a trifle over,) we were to travel two miles to the meeting in the evening. Bro. Abraham figured largely among the friends, doing all he could to make everything go off right, so that Eld. Caton would give a good account of us when he got home. We loaded up our precious freight—Domine, brethren, sisters, and children—(for we must always have the children along, and this was a very prolific place)—and commenced our passage to Bro. Abraham's, to be ready for the evening service. Our path lay all the way through the woods, just wide enough for a sled to pass, winding about amongst the trees. After we had reached the summit of a rise of ground, we then had a descent, some parts of which was very steep. The oxen found the draft was over, and, as the sled began to crowd a little, they had an inclination to run away. Abraham, the pilot, hallooed at the top of his voice, "Hwo! hoi! gee!" but the oxen minded not. Increasing their speed at every step, by some means they caught the sled against a' sapling, which swept off the temporary box, and all the passengers, into the snow, except the minister. I started with all speed on the track, (for then I could run like Cushi,) expecting every moment to find our guest lying in the snow, if nothing more or worse. After having run three-quarters of a mile or more, I saw, on the plain below, the breath of the oxen rising up like the smoke of a furnace. They had stopped of their own accord, and lo and behold ! there sat the good old man with his feet stretched out before him upon the only bottom board left on the sled, with his hands clinched, almost with a dying grip, on each side of the board. He looked up with a perfect stare of amazement, and before I could ask him if he was hurt, he exclaimed, "I didn't know but I was going into eternity, but I thought I would hold on to my board." And he had held on, for the perspiration was standing in drops upon his face. After we had loaded up again, and got the old gentleman to the house, he appeared to wake up to the circumstances through which he had passed, and exclaimed: " I have had a great many rides in my life, but I never before had such a ride as I have had this afternoon." However, he concluded, after all, that he had come out the best of any of us, for he had ridden while we had to walk, and run after him through the snow. But this was about the summing up of his labors with us. He has long ago entered into his rest.

SENECA ASSOCIATION—COVERT AND OTHER CHURCHES.

Recalling those incidents, leads me to notice, here, the situation of the Baptist churches in that garden of the State. I may often- refer to circumstances that happened among them, inasmuch as it was the region of my first settlement in America. There are many things that are riveted upon my mind, some of which

I hope never to forget, in this world or the world to come.

I think the church in Romulus was the first Baptist church between the Cayuga and Seneca Lakes, and was organized in 1795. By whom gathered, I have not the means of knowing: but I do not think that that church ever sent out many branches.

The Covert church appears to have been more fruitful. This church was organized in 1803. She covered a vast territory. In 1853, I was invited to attend her jubilee meeting, (the 50th year of her standing.) The pastor, Rev. C. Wardner, was requested to present a history of the church. I was requested to talk upon the subject of the Seneca Association, of which she was a member. I had known more or less of the movings of the Association from the day of its birth. I think I was present at its first annual meeting; but, being a stranger in a strange land—alone, while in the midst of hundreds, knowing no one, and but few knowing me —my spirits became depressed, and I returned home before the session closed. If my memory serves me, it was held in Farmerville, in 1822. I believe there was but one Baptist church building (or meeting house) between the Lakes, when I settled there. There might have been another, but I do not know of any except the one at Covert; and that was a rare model of architecture for the time. The people went into the gallery from out of doors, going in at the gable end of the building. The first time I saw it, I could but admire the patch work. It was not, I believe, plastered all over: only here and there a patch put on, and everything else about it appeared to be in keeping with what is already named. The centre of the church was at Thomas' Settlement called so after their first pastor, Minor Thomas. They had a covenant meeting, not only there, but they had another at the house of Thomas Horton, at the head of Seneca Lake, about twenty miles in a south-west direction. They had another, I believe, in Virgil, Cortland county, (in about a south-east direction,) which must have been some thirty miles from the common centre. I think they had another in Ovid, on the north, between Covert and Romulus. This certainly goes to show that that part of the country must then have been sparsely settled. It also implies that the pastor must have been a very laborious man.

In the best sense of the word, Covert was a "mother church." She had begun to marry off her children just before I came into the country. In 1817, the church in Enfield was formed. The same year, the church in Mecklenburg also was formed. In 1819, the church in Trumansburg was formed. In 1820, the church in Newfield was formed. In 1821, the church in Lodi was formed. In 1828, the church in Ovid was formed. In 1838, the church in Danby was formed. There are others, the time of whose organization I do not recollect, neither have I any means of knowing.

In looking over the ground, now, I am ready to say, "What hath God wrought!" If we commence at the head of the Cayuga, we find a good Baptist meeting house in Ithaca, and starting from that point we will pass through to the outlet of the Cayuga and Seneca Lakes. We find respectable meeting houses in the following places: Newfield, Mecklenburg, Bennettsburg, Trumansburg, Covert, Peach Orchard, Farmerville, Lodi, Ovid, Ovid Village, Romulus, Fayette, and Seneca Falls. There was one in Waterloo, but I believe, for want of good financiering, it was finally sold, and whether they have ever built another I do not know. Also one in Geneva. Truly, the Lake country is the land of Baptists.

The greater part of this territory is covered by the Seneca Association; and although it is years since I have traversed that delightful portion of the country, yet the blessed scenes through which I have passed, in the school houses and barns, before many of those church buildings were erected, have left a deep impression on my mind. I have preached in nearly all the meeting houses above named. Several of their dedications I attended, and have held protracted meetings with them, the remembrance of which is as cooling waters to the thirsty soul. When the churches of the Seneca Association took me by the hand, as pastor of the Catlin church, and gave me that hearty welcome, which spoke loudly to my inmost soul, with their hand I had their hearts also. And at this late day, notwithstanding so many of the older brethren and sisters have passed away, I love the churches still, and am ready to say, now, if I forget you, let my right hand forget her cunning. I shall have occasion frequently to look over that field so dear to me.

MY ORDINATION TO THE GOSPEL MINISTRY.

Returning to the church at home, I find that on December, 1828, (the same year I was licensed,) the church invited a council to confer as to my ordination. The council met and I was ordained. The proceedings of this council are appended to this narrative.

LABORS IN THE TOWN OF READING.

Having occasion again to go to Esquire Tracy's, on school business, an appointment was made for me to preach, the following Sabbath, at Miller's school house, within the town of Reading. I found an old gentleman there, a Presbyterian minister, who, though to me a stranger, proved to be a very fine man. He said, by right of appointment, it was for him to preach: but, inasmuch as the people had come together expecting to hear me, I must preach. That led me to leave another appointment. I continued to go to that school house, about once a month. My foreign accent, and my old country appearance, if nothing else, induced the people to come together. This was an older settlement than the one in which I lived, south of it, and the people very generally came out to hear. A Baptist woman in the congregation, made herself known; she lived four or five miles down the Lake; she said her husband was unconverted, and she had long been praying for him.

THE BAG WITH HOLES.

In the congregation were two good men, originally from the East, where I believe they both held the office of deacon, or ruling elder. The great difficulty, here, was, that they wanted somebody to rule over, for there were but very few professors of religion in the place. On one occasion, I preached from the text, "And he that earneth wages, earneth wages to put into a bag with holes." As soon as I had concluded, one of these men arose and said, "If you have preached the truth, sir, I ain't a Christian—I ain't a Christian!" The answer was, "I do not know whether you are or are not a Christian, but I know I have preached the truth." Nothing more took place at that time. The Baptist sister was in attendance with her husband, and he, being a wild, jocose sort of a man, kept joking her, all the way home, about her religion being in a bag with holes. He said that old uncle D. found that all his religion had run out, and did not think he was a Christian.

When the time rolled around for another appointment, the man said to his wife, "Let us go again and hear that fellow who preached about the bag with boles." They came, and she introduced him to me after the services. I said a few words to him about his soul, and the necessity of immediately seeking the salvation of God. I saw the muscles of his face twitch, and his chin quiver; he turned his back, and abruptly walked away. I felt that God had fastened his own truth in his heart, as a nail in a sure place.

"THE SOUND THEREOF."

The next time I spoke there, I saw a female, apparently about in middle life, very much exercised. Some times she would weep bitterly, and at other times would smile almost to laughter. As soon as I had said amen, she arose and exclaimed, "And thou shalt hear the sound thereof—and thou shalt hear the sound thereof!" Everybody was aroused by her apparent energy of expression, and (as they said) disturbing the meeting. It was with difficulty that I could get her so composed as to find out what she meant. She said, for many days she had felt herself such a sinner that there was no way for her but that she must go down to hell. She proceeded to give a relation of her trials, and the course she had taken. She went to Eddytown, a small village about a mile from where she lived, to lay her case before a minister. He told her to stop her crying—there was no necessity for her to be so—it was just as easy to get religion, as it would be for her to turn her hand over: all (he told her) that she needed, was barely to resolve to lead a better life. She resolved, and re-resolved, but felt worse and worse. When she got to her father's (for she was a maiden lady) her brother-in-law was there, and was telling about a strange kind of a man, preaching at the Miller school-house, near Irelandville, who had been telling the people a long story about a bag with holes. She said to her brother-in-law, "I

must go and hear him—when does he preach there?"
He replied, "To-morrow—and if you want to go, I will
take my team and carry you, for I want to go, too."
She remarked, that, all night long, she walked the room
in the greatest agony of soul. The words she uttered
in the congregation, came to her mind—"and thou
shalt hear the sound thereof." She never thought
whether they were in the Bible or not. As the time
approached for her brother-in-law to call for her, she
was so fearful that he would not come in season, that
she started afoot and alone, all the time having this
impression—"And thou shalt hear the sound thereof."
I think she said there was no one at the school-house
when she got there. It pleased the Spirit of God to
take of the things which are Christ's, and show them
unto her. She went home rejoicing in the Lord, and
told every one she saw what great things Jesus had
done for her. She scattered the blessed fire for nearly
ten miles along the Lake road.

The next thing was, that invitations began to come ·
in to preach in certain places on that road. The husband of the sister previously referred to, was under
pungent conviction, and entreated me to make an
appointment at his house, with which I had to comply.
These were the first stores gathered from nature's
quarry to be put into a new organization, for it was
the starting period of the beloved church in Reading.

Although I had a great many different places to
preach at, and no way of going, then, except on foot, I
always preached three sermons on the Sabbath, mind-
ing the places were not so far apart but that I could
reach them at the appointed time.

VISITS TO AND FROM THE BIG FLATS CHURCH.

Previous to this, we received a visit from two

brethren of the Big Flats church, south of us. They had heard that there was somebody preaching in Moreland, and came ten miles to see what we were doing. They appeared to enjoy themselves, and when they left, said they would give a good account of the land. They promised to come again, on the day of our covenant meeting, the time and place of which we gave them minute directions, so that they might find the house of the brethren where it was to be held without trouble. On the day named, we were all assembled, except those who were sick or away from home; for if any sisters were unable to travel, some brother would go with his ox-team, bring them to the meeting, and carry them back again. Just after singing and prayer, behold! in came our visitors—Dea. John Brown and Cornelius Low. Bro. Low was quite an eccentric man, and always had much to say allegorically. In the course of his highly figurative conversation, he said there was one portion of the Bible which he could never understand: the passage was about Jacob's flocks—the "ring-streaked, speckled, and brown." In looking at our sisters, he said it was all clear to him. I do not know as it regarded the "ring-streaked," but I do know that many of the female members were "speckled and brown," for they were to us, what God intended—help-meets—and were ready to acknowledge it. They spent a great deal of time out of doors, picking up and burning brush, often helping their husbands to brand up their log heaps until midnight: and, to tell the truth (which we always wish to do) they were pretty dark complexioned, varying in proportion to their exposure to smoke, fire, sun, and wind. I have no doubt the good old brother often repeated his exposition of Jacob's flocks. But we derived some very important information from our visitors. We heard of the state of religion in the valley, and got from them a description of their pastor, Rev. Philander D. Gillette—what a good work he was doing*—how everybody was following after to hear him preach—also that he was very desirous to come and see us, but, like myself, he had a very large field, and pretty hard to till. He sent word that he wished to see me, and form an acquaintance.

PHILANDER D. GILLETTE.

Subsequently, I determined to make *his* acquaintance. Not knowing exactly where to find him, I inquired, and was informed he had gone up the river, probably to Bro. Bennett's. I steered my course in that direction, and met a man riding along the road in an old-fashioned wagon, driving a good horse, which Bro. Gillette always did. When he got almost to me, he exclaimed, " Halloo ! is your name Sheardown ?" I told him it was. " I knew it was," he said—" our brethren had described you so minutely, that I knew you must be the man : for there is not, I think, another drab coat like yours in the country." I preached for him, that evening, in a school house, and arranged with him for an exchange. From that time onward, our hearts were knit together like the hearts of David and Jonathan.

THE OLD SISTER'S CHASTISEMENT.

But that *exchange* was a bad one for me. I preached to the people as well as I could. The very moment I closed, a good old mother in Israel was on her feet. With a shrill voice—(I had often been startled, in the woods, by the sound of the owl, but never did I hear, I thought, such a human voice : and perhaps, after all, it

---

*In 1827, Big Flats church had 103 accessions by baptism, and 28 in 1828.

was not so much the voice, as the words she pronounced, or rather screeched)—she exclaimed: "O,
Lord! I wonder if this is Elder Sheardown, I have
heard so much about? He has only said one word
that I was glad to hear, and that was 'Amen.' O,
my Lord!" she continued, " if Mr. Goff could rise from
the dead, and hear such preaching where he had
preached so often, what would he say ?"

I was not only, as the sailors say, taken all aback, but
I was in a sinking condition. There was about half an
hour's recess, and then I was to preach again. The
friends were very kind. One said, "Go home with me,
and take some refreshments." Another said, "I live
pretty near by—go with me." I told them I did not
want to eat, and should not until I had preached again.
I saw a pile of straw behind a barn, and crept into it,
as well as I could, until my watch told me it was time
for me to go to my meeting. How to go, I did not know.
I thought I could never stand another such a volley.
But I buckled up my harness, and bared my arm to
wield the sword of the Spirit again, continually praying
that the Lord would deliver me from the fear of the old
sister. I preached from Paul's words, (Rom. 8th chap.
1st verse,) "There is therefore now no condemnation
to them which are in Christ Jesus, who walk not after
the flesh, but after the Spirit." I said a good deal
about walking after the flesh. As soon as I said Amen,
the good old lady was upon her feet again. I thought
I was surely elected for another shot. But, instead of
that, she exclaimed, "O, Lord! forgive me—forgive
me! Such a whipping, I never took before. O, the
man has paid me more than double interest!" She
wept, and confessed—and I must say, I was very glad to
hear her. It appeared as though she could not give up
her walking after the flesh. She began to entreat every

one to forgive her. I felt somewhat better—but I acknowledge that, from that time to this, I have feared an old woman more than all the Doctors of Divinity before whom I have ever preached.

This opened the way for frequent exchanges with Bro. Gillette. And if, on any occasion, I found him preaching in any part of my large parish, it was all right: or, if he found me over the line in his diocese, it was all the same. We labored much together, aiding each other at every turn—neither of us jealous that the other would take the crown, but continually praying and preaching that the crown might flourish on Jesus' head.

ITINERATING ON MEAD'S CREEK.

After this digression, we will return to the more immediate field of my own labor. I had established a preaching place on Mead's Creek; on Nash's Hill; at the lower part of that creek I preached occasionally; also in a region known as Knowlton's Settlement. These points were in Steuben county, ten to eighteen miles from my home. I had other appointments—one where Millport now stands, in Chemung (then Tioga) county, and another in the town of Reading, before referred to. My traveling was all on my own feet. One severely stormy day—when it rained sleet and snow—I called at the house of a good old Vermont brother, of Revolutionary memory, to take dinner. In walking through the mud and snow, I had caught one shoe under a root, and torn a large hole in the upper leather. After dinner, a son of the old gentleman (a man approaching middle life,) said, "Elder, is it not lawful to do good on the Sabbath day?" I answered that the Saviour had taught us that doctrine; "then," he said, "take off your shoe, sir, and hold up your foot." He took a rule from his pocket, and measured my foot for a pair of shoes.

"Now," said he, "I am going to make you a pair of Gospel shoes." I remarked to him that I had a pair of Gospel shoes that I had worn a great many years, and they were as good as they were the first time I put them on. But he waggishly replied, "They are not adapted to those feet, or otherwise you would not have had that large hole in your shoe, but I will make you a pair that shall fit your feet, and that will not tear by catching them under a root when they are wet." He made them, and such a pair of shoes; I never had seen, nor worn before; I never wore them out; for after I had worn them long, I finally gave them away to a poor man who I thought was worse off than I was.

COMMENCE HORSE-BACK LABORS.

Soon after this, a door for more enlarged operations opened by a man offering to sell me a horse. Of course, it was a cheap one, but proved to be very good. I only gave forty dollars for the horse; I borrowed a saddle and bridle; and then felt, perhaps, as lofty and well pleased as some of our Generals do when they are fully equipped on their war steeds.

Labor was increasing on my hands all the time, and there was nothing for me but to arrange so as to give my whole time to the vineyard of my Master. I could endure, physically, in those days, a great deal. I could walk twenty miles in a day, and preach three times. Often, my evening appointment would leave me some eight miles from home, and a great part of the time through the wilderness; but there was nothing discouraging in that.

One Saturday, I was in a very great strait. My appointments were standing for the next day, and I could not meet them short of traveling thirty miles about, and if I did that I must stay out from home over night,

10

which I felt was not duty in the situation of my family.
I said to my wife, "Now, I ought not to go to my appointments to-morrow." She replied, "Yes, you must;
you can get back to-morrow night, late, can you not?"
I replied, "Yes, but it will be very late." Yet she
encouraged my heart to go, and had my pledge that I
would get back as soon as I could. I redeemed my
pledge, and arrived home between ten and eleven
o'clock, Sabbath evening. I felt tired, but not tired
out. I arrived home at a providential time, but had no
rest that night!

WINTER TRAVELING.

I will not dwell, at present, longer upon my pedestrian
excursions, but return to my horse-back labors. I occupied the saddle during spring, summer, and fall; but in
the winter I traveled in a cutter of my own making,
which I could at any time build in about two hours.
All I wanted was an axe and an inch auger. I traveled,
generally, in a covered cutter, the cover nicely woven
with hemlock boughs. Taking my auger with me, and
a good jack knife, if I happened to break-down, I could
repair damages anywhere in a very short time, and
pass on again, never discouraged at the toils and the
dangers of the way.

DOMESTIC ARRANGEMENTS.

Perhaps there may arise in the minds of some reader
the inquiry whether I was "worse than an infidel" in
that I did not "provide for my own household?" and
what became of the wife and large family, all this time?
I will tell you my plan for providing for them. Brethren
and sisters were able to do but very little towards their
support, and I managed the matter as follows: I hired
the best back-woods young man I could find, and gave
him the best wages! My object in doing this was, in

the first place, to have a man capable of taking care of my family. In the next place, through the winter, he was chopping. I bought a good yoke of cattle, on a year's credit, but minded to buy in the spring of the year; then he was prepared for a summer's work; he could break up some ground for potatoes and other roots, get in some oats, and a little corn. When the time came to burn the fallow that he had cut in the winter, he was prepared to aid those who had no teams : consequently, by changing work with himself and team, it brought in a great deal of labor in return; and, as we always logged our fallows by changing work, he generally got his seeding done in good season, from seven to ten acres of wheat. I had all the wheat, and the gifts of my brethren and sisters. So I was enabled to pay my hired man, and have provisions raised to meet all the real necessities of my family. When I was at home, I always doffed the clerical dress, (which, by-the-by, was very simple,) and put on the tow frock and trowsers, and went at it myself, with all my energy, to aid the young man in anything he had to do, either at home or in paying work where it was due from us to any of our neighbors.

I recollect, one season, hiring one of the most thorough-going men in all our region, but fearfully profane. My brethren said to me, " Why, Elder, what do you mean in hiring T. E. ? He is the worst fellow for profanity there is in all the region, and will spoil all your children." I told them, I thought not! I never had any person around me who did swear, and I did not think he would use profane language with me or with my family. The reply was, " I should be very sorry to trust him." I remarked that I did my own hiring and made my own bargains.

When I engaged the man, I said to him, " Now,

Mr. E , you are just the man I want, as it regards your knowledge of business and your willingness to do. But there are some things that, if they must be done, I must do them; and there are other things which you must do. Now, sir, you are in the habit of using a great deal of profane language. I never have any swearing around me, or on my place, and I will not hire any man who is addicted to swearing." He looked amazed, stood a moment or two, then said, "It is a bad practice; I can quit it." "I know that, sir; now, will you do it?" He said, " Yes," I replied, " Very well, sir; I knew you could quit it; therefore, it will save me trouble, for I was going to say to you, that if you must swear, leave it undone until I come home; then tell we what you wanted to swear over, and, if I thought swearing must be done, 1 could, may be, do it better than you. But I am rejoiced that you conclude voluntarily to quit the bad practice. Now, sir, there is another thing: I don't want any individual to work for me who gets angry and unreasonably whips his team, or pounds his cattle with a handspike," &c. He said, " That I can get along with, very well. I know I have been addicted to doing so, but it is a bad way to treat a team." I then remarked to him, " Now, sir, there are other things. One is that the family must have all their wants supplied. If you are told by Mrs. Sheardown that milling must be done, or anything else of like importance, do just as I should, drop everything, and attend to it. There are little things about the house that I might speak to you about, but you have the acknowledgment of all that I am acquainted with, that you have always been, from a boy up, very good to your mother. This will lead you to notice the lesser things. And yet another point, sir, and that is, we try to bring up our family religiously. When I am at home, I read the

Scriptures and pray with my family; when I am absent, Mrs. Sheardown does the same; and I want you, sir, always to be in the house at the time of family prayer. Now, if you are ready to make a bargain with me under these considerations, from the information I have received, and from my personal knowledge of you, I am prepared to hire you for one year. What will you ask for your year's service, taking your pay at the end of the year, except what little you may need for your current expenses?" He replied, "I do not know, Elder; I wish you would say what you will give." I told him that "I had never been found fault with for oppressing the hireling in his wages. I have never given more than one hundred and ten dollars, and do the washing, boarding and lodging: but I think you will suit me, and you are capable of earning more than a common man; I shall entrust all in your hands; as to your labor, I do not want you to make a slave of yourself, and I will give you one hundred and thirty dollars for the year." He appeared to be abundantly satisfied, and so was I. Mrs. Sheardown said he was as kind a man as she would ever wish to have come into her family; everything was done, and done in the time of doing it. Some time before the year closed, he gave good evidence that he was happily converted to God. This was the plan I adopted to support my family, with the assistance of a few dear brethren doing what they could, so that I might give myself more untiringly to the work of the Lord.

By this time, the older part of my children began to be very useful, both in-door and out: they were brought up to work, as soon as they were able to do small things; and as soon as the boys were able to use an axe, they were employed in underbushing; those that were lesser, doing the out-door chores. The girls were equally busy in the house, learning to spin wool and flax, milk cows, &c. In the winter, those that were old enough, went to the district school; and as fast as they grew up, I sent them away to school, or gave them the best advantages we had in our own vicinity. So that, by a kind Providence, I was able to give them a good English education; and my secluded location secured them from the contaminating and corrupting influences so prevalent in more populous places. I always endeavored to impress upon their minds to necessity of preparing to rely upon themselves. We had twelve children, four of whom died in infancy. Of the eight who survived, five were sons, and three daughters. Through a merciful God, I am now able to rejoice that seven of the eight have a hope beyond the grave.

I had made a beginning at Reading, and on the upper part of Mead's Creek, where I thought (under God) I should be able to raise two churches. It was not so clear in my mind that, in any other of my preaching places—whatever might appear in the future—I should succeed in building independent interests.

DIVISION OF CHRISTIAN AND CHURCH EFFORTS.

Perhaps I had as well, here, state something relative to my management in those places, remote from the church in Catlin, which was my grand rallying point. Therefore, I would say that, when any individual was converted, if it was possible, he came to the church, told his experience, and was baptized at our regular baptizing place for the church in Catlin. After a few had been brought in, I called them a Conference in their own neighborhood, when, for the accommodation of families and those that had no means of conveyance, the church voted them the privilege of receiving members, in conjunction with a committee sent from the church to act with them; then these were all considered as baptized into the fellowship of the original church. Next, the church voted to grant them a monthly meeting, which we generally termed a covenant meeting, at which meeting as many of the brethren from the home church would attend as possible. The next move was, the church voted that the pastor should break bread to them, as a part or branch of the mother church. Under this process, they grew up, and our views as Baptists became better known in the neighborhood.

My places of preaching were in barns, saw-mills, school-houses, private houses, and in the open air, for we very often had such large gatherings that there was no building in the neighborhood capable of holding them.

TOWNSEND SETTLEMENT CHURCH.

About this time, we gave letters to some brethren and sisters to organize a new interest in the same town in which the mother church had been gathered. This church was known by the name of the Townsend Settlement Church.

There were on Nash's hill, in Hornby, (a town lying west of Catlin,) a few brethren and sisters who had once been organized as a church under the missionary labors of Eld. T. B. Beebee; but they had no organization or visibility when I found them: they joined the Catlin church—consequently, those who were baptized were baptized into the Catlin church. All this time, I was gathering more or less at the rallying point on Mead's creek. In time, it was thought best for the brethren and sisters on the hill to join the few on the creek. This gave them strength enough to be recognized as a church.

I had now on my hands three churches, besides two or three covenant meetings.

The Conference in Reading continued to grow, and the Lord was working by his Spirit in all these places.

TRULY LIVING CHURCH MEMBERS.

The question may perhaps arise, how could one man do the necessary labor for the growth and best interest of those scattered over so large a field? In the first place, just as soon as persons were converted, we set them at work, and they worked with a will. They were live men and women. They would have two, three, or more prayer or conference meetings in the week. All would sing who could, and all would pray and talk; and it was no uncommon thing, when the pastor passed his regular round, once in two weeks, or once in four weeks, that he would find, under the labors of those brethren and sisters, two or three hopefully converted to God. They worked, expecting that God would bless their labors. When they prayed, they believed that God would hear them; and one peculiarity of the times was that we had no long prayers, no long talks. They knew when to stop, as well as when to begin. Their meetings were lively, full of the Spirit, and they attracted the attention of the unconverted; so that, whenever they held their little meetings, the house or school-house, whichever it might be, was generally well filled. So we continued to labor on.

It was thought best to make an effort, through the brethren in Reading, to prepare for an organization there. There had been once a small church in Reading, but it became scattered, and lost its visibility. There were a few old-school, anti-mission, anti-temperance, anti-everything good persons, who were trying to cling together, but who had no fellowship whatever for what they termed "New-Lights." In January, 1834, a church was fellowshiped, by a council of brethren from between the Lakes.

MASONIC EXCITEMENT—UNJUST ACCUSATIONS.

With many mercies, the churches also had their times of trial, unknown at this day, except by the older members.

I refer, now, to the days of William Morgan, when the Anti-Masonic and Masonic advocates were so belligerent. While considering the matter, I reflected, that, wherever evil existed, the only reformatory power is to be found in the Gospel of God's salvation; when that is experienced, it works reform that will be permanent. I well knew that my bark was but small, and it would be safest to keep well in-shore, lest peradventure I should be swamped amid the fearful storms that were beating upon Zion. My desire was, as far as possible, to preach Jesus Christ and Him crucified. For some time, I met with very little opposition or trouble from either party, and thought all was going well. My aim was to run in the middle channel, and steer as clear as possible of arguments and conversations on either side. I desired to save our churches from ruin, for I thought there were good brethren on both sides of the question.

I had a preaching place in the suburbs of a little church, within the bounds of my labors. A barn was prepared on purpose for worship through the summer season, with seats for the congregation, and a stand, elevated some two feet above the main level, for the speaker. One Sabbath afternoon, as I was going to this station, I left my horse about a mile behind, to feed while I was preaching, and took it afoot. Up a little rise of ground, in sight of the place of my appointment, I saw quite a crowd in the barn-yard. A brother was walking ahead of me a short distance; when I came up with him, I said, "Why, what are all the people doing, out of doors, to-day?" He remarked, "You will find out, sir, that the people are not all out of doors. I presume the barn is full," and he said, I think, "you will find out what it means before you get through. If you ain't mobbed, to-day, it will be a wonder to me." I inquired, "What is the matter?" "Matter enough," he said. "The Anti-Masons have found out that you are a Mason, and they are determined not to hear you preach. The Masons are here from all around to protect you, and have you preach. It is a well known fact," he added, "that you used to attend Masonic lodges in England." "Well, what next?" "They say it can be proved that you have attended Masonic lodges in this country, and the public will put you where you ought to be." "Well, is that all?" He answered, "No. They want to know what fellowship you have for Masons who are Christians?" "Anything more, sir?" "No. It will be best for you to find the other out by experience." I remarked to him, "Very well, sir. I presume there will be no trouble about this thing."

As I passed in through the people, I saw there was a good deal of whispering and blinking of the eye at me. I pressed forward, and, in the majesty of my religion, took my stand, and laid out of my pocket, as usual, my hymn-book and Bible. There appeared to be some commotion, but not much. I remarked to them, "Now, I want to say a few words before I open religious services. Although my congregation, to-day, is much larger than usual, yet I feel a peculiar satisfaction, in looking it over, that I know almost every individual present. I have preached to you, in different places; and I have always had this satisfaction, that, when I looked upon you, you always appeared as though you believed what I was telling you was the truth. I have just learned, as I was walking up the hill, that there are certain statements made relative to me—first, that I am a Mason. Now, then, I tell you, candidly and honestly, that I am not, nor never was, though I have wondered perhaps a thousand times why I was not, for my business life always threw me more or less amongst the Masonic fraternity. I know nothing about them in their organic or individual relations to each other. I understand it is also said to be susceptible of proof, that I have attended Masonic lodges since I have been in this country. This is a grand mistake, or a palpable falsehood. As it regards there being any *proof* of my ever attending Masonic lodges in the old world, I do not believe that any such proof can be brought. I have yet to find the individual, on this side of the Atlantic, who knew me in my own country. I am not going to deny that I ever was in Masonic lodges in that country. It was very common with the fraternity to have their lodges open, on a part of St. John's day, for all those who wished, to go in and see their tables set, and the badges, medals, regalias, pictures, &c., which adorned the walls of their dining rooms. When passing those places, I have turned in with others, (for hundreds often went as curiosity seekers.) So that part of the story is true, from my own confession, not from testimony. I have been in Masonic lodges, in my own country; but never in the time of their sessions. There is another thing you desire to know, and that is whether I have any fellowship for Masons who are Christians. My answer to that, is this: I understand it to be God's work to change the heart of man, and turn him from nature to grace; and now, if God makes Christians of Masons, it would be vain for me to undertake to undo God's work, and pull down that which I am laboring so hard to build up. As it regards church fellowship for Masons, if a man has more fellowship for the Masonic fraternity than he has for the church of God, I have no fellowship for him as a Christian; consequently, my church fellowship would rest on the same base. Now I feel that I have conscientiously declared to you the whole truth; and I read in your countenances, that this is an honest declaration of fact; we must believe the man. Therefore, I will now preach to you, as best I am able, without meddling with a vexed question that I know but very little about. My great object in coming among you, from time to time, is, that I may do you good for eternity. The Lord bless you. Now we will sing" such a hymn. My congregation was never more attentive, and I do not recollect that from that time onward I ever was called on publicly to say pro or con upon that subject.

CONFESSION MADE.

I was aware that Satan had been at work somewhere, but where, to me was unknown. About a year and a half, perhaps, afterwards, I was preaching in a school-house, when a brother and sister, whom I was intimately acquainted with, were present. She appeared to be very much affected, and said to me, after the evening service, "I want you to go home with us, to-night." The reply was, "It is too far. This has been my third sermon to-day. I have ridden some twenty miles, and my horse is tired and hungry. It is very dark and cold. You must excuse me." She replied, "I can not." At this moment, her husband came up, repeating the same invitation, with great earnestness. From the visible excitement in which they both appeared, I concluded to go. Notwithstanding it was late when we arrived, we must have some supper. The woman appeared to be in tears all the time. She finally took her seat between myself and her husband, and exclaimed, "I can bear it no longer." Of course, I wondered what was coming. She remarked, "Do you not recollect preaching in such a barn, at such a time, when there was a great excitement about you relative to Masonry?" I answered, "O yes, I remember it well, though I have thought of it but very few times since it transpired."—"Did you ever learn, sir, who got up that report?"—"No, madam, nor I never cared; and I do not want any resurrection of it." She exclaimed again, "I can not bear it any longer! I was the individual who raised that report, out of the rough. O, how it has pressed my conscience! Do forgive me! do forgive me!" I remarked, "That was very wicked. I hope and trust God has forgiven you. If so, I had much rather be taking my supper, than listening to any confession you may have to make to me." The dear woman had laid off the burden of her conscience, and I judged by her actions her relief was very great. After supper, we all kneeled down and prayed together, and it appeared to me, by her earnest prayer and broken heart, that God had been pleased to pardon her sin. I never loved them any less as Christians. To me, her conduct was conclusive evidence that God had put away her sin.

STEUBEN ASSOCIATION.

I shall always remember the first Association (except the Seneca) that I visited. It was good old Steuben. When I attended its sessions for the first time, it convened in the old Baptist meeting-house in the town of Wayne, in Steuben county. I was almost a perfect stranger to every one present. There were two or

11

three, in company with me, who belonged to that Association. I was wearing the old, veritable, drab coat, and was invited to preach. Some said I was an Englishman, some said I was French, some did not know who I was, or what I was. I think it was the introductory sermon that I preached. Why it was so, I do not know—whether they had omitted to appoint one, or whether the individual had failed to come. One of the friends with me pointed out a certain individual and said, " That is Eld. Sanford." When I had entered the pulpit, the good old man looked up and said, " Now, you see what a great congregation of people you have to preach to. You young men are in the habit of mumbling, so that half of the people can not hear you. Speak out, young man! don't be afraid." In those days, my lungs were very strong, and if showing zeal for the Lord of hosts could be manifested through sound, I was capable of convincing people that 1 possessed a good deal of zeal. When I was through, the Elder complimented me for having "spoken up."

One reason why I loved always to meet with this Association, perhaps, is the fact that I always had to work. Their gatherings were so large, that few if any meeting-houses in their bounds would comfortably hold the people. Therefore, while the Association was doing its business, my place was in a wagon, or under the shade of a tree, and sometimes in a little grove, if there was one near by. If there were two meeting-houses in the same place, we were sometimes permitted to occupy one of them, so that those might hear preaching who were unable to get into the house appointed for the sitting of the body. I acknowledge that I delighted in open air preaching, for it was so much in keeping with my labor at home.

ALFRED BENNETT.

On one occasion, the Association met in the town of Prattsburg. They had what is termed a log meeting-house, far too small to hold the hundreds of people who had come together, and we repaired to the woods. I was invited to preach the first day. Eld. Alfred Bennett, (so widely known, and so much beloved by the churches, not only as a pastor, but also as a missionary agent,) being present, I invited him to pray before sermon. The sky had been lowering, and there were indications of rain. The thunder muttered upon the distant hills. The good man, when in prayer, appeared to be talking with God face to face. He said, "Now, Lord, thou knowest all about us; in what a helpless state we are. We have no shelter to flee to. We are here to worship Thee. And now, do not let it rain upon us and scatter us; for what should we do?" The thunder appeared to come nearer by—the blue-winged lightnings scathed the brow of heaven—everybody was looking for a severe drenching—but, to the utter astonishment, perhaps, of all present, there was not enough rain fell to cause a man to put his coat on, (for scores were in their shirt-sleeves,) while the rain continued to pour down all around us, sometimes within a quarter or a half a mile of the place where we were gathered. It was proverbial for many years, in that region of country, that Eld. Bennett kept back the rain by prayer.

OLD ELDER LAMB'S FAMILY.

At night, a number of us went to tarry with that man of God, Eld. Lamb. He had raised a good many lambs, and the greater part of them had become shepherds. While conversing with mother Lamb in relation to her family of boys, she said she hoped they were all converted, except Thomas. If my memory serves me, he was the youngest. She wept while talking about the dear young son—said he was a thoughtless boy, very shy of ministers, and had a peculiar aversion to having any one speak to him on personal religion. "I have," said the good mother, "but one hope of him, and that is, when I brought him forth, I know I dedicated him to God." I mingled my tears with hers, for her expressions broke up the deep fountains in both head and heart. Upon inquiring how I could see the young man, that I might have some conversation, his mother informed me that she had found him in the barn-yard. I walked up the lane, and took a seat on the top bar of the fence, so that, if he came out, he must either climb the fence or crawl through underneath. As he came within speaking distance, I inquired, "How do you do, sir?" He made a similar inquiry, firmly and kindly. I remarked, "You have got a pair of beautiful cattle, there." He replied, "Yes, very good, sir." I saw other stock that I could speak well of—for his father was a good farmer, as well as a good preacher—asked the age of a certain orchard, how long his father had lived there, and other things, until his embarrassment appeared to be gone. I spoke of his brother Reuben— what a blessed thing it was that he had been converted in the days of his youth, and had concluded to be a minister of the Gospel! I found him perfectly spellbound—talked to him about his own soul: he wept bitterly—his heart appeared to be stirred. When I returned to the house, he followed part of the way, and I continued my onward pace, pondering what the result of the conversation might be. When it was time to go to the evening meeting, the mother said she could not find Thomas. I said to her, "Do not be troubled about him. You will find him in some solitary place, in-door or out. Be of good courage. Pray on. God will give you your son."

When the meeting in the evening closed, most of the people had passed out at the door, and—as in those days we were not blessed with beautiful chandeliers and fine lamps—the home-made tallow candles afforded us all the light we had. In the dimness, some one thought he saw a large dog in one corner, but, on going to drive him out, found it was a young man. I overheard some conversation as I was exchanging words with a friend at the door, and, looking to see what was the matter, saw Thomas Lamb, so deeply troubled that he could not speak; his body almost prostrate, through the anguish of his heart. I put one arm around him, and started for home, pointing, as best I could, to the Lord Jesus Christ as able and willing to save to the very uttermost. The night was very dark, and we moved slowly, for he was full as much as I could sustain. We had come to the foot of quite a pitch or rise in the road, and I was almost ready to conclude that my strength would give out before I could get him up the pitch. All at once he lighted up, appeared to have recovered strength, and exclaimed, "How light it is! What a beautiful night!" He said his fears were all removed, he felt the burthen of his heart gone, and went home to greet that beloved mother who had consecrated him to God from his birth.

On my return, Eld. Sutherland was quite anxious that I should take his road home. The good old gentleman said I must preach in Penn Yan, Yates county. He had the use of the Court House. I do not know whether it was Court week or not, but there appeared to be a number of professional men there. I tried to preach from this text: "And be sure your sins shall find you out." I had a very healthful season for the soul, and plenty of labor.

In 1838, Steuben Association reported 522 accessions

by baptisms, (of which 149 were in the Penn Yan
Church,) and a total membership of 1891.

CHAPTER V.—1829 TO 1836.

*Missionary Excursions into Pennsylvania, Varied with Abundant
Labors in New York State—Back-Woods Narratives, viz: Extensive Revival on Tioga River and Crooked Creek—Edsall
Mitchell, Middlebury, Head-Quarters—Words with Eld. A.,
an Antinomian—My Deacon's Sole Missionary Tour—Camp-
bellite General's Attack and Repulse—Baptism of Mr. Tuttle,
Inn-Keeper, Aged Eighty-Five Years—Conversion of Mr. B.,
of Knoxville—Three Poor Families near or on Pine Creek—
Two Females come Through the Thunder-Storm to Hear
Preaching—Securing a Preaching Place in Tioga, (Willardsburg,)—Relation of Eld. Broakman's Early Days—Renewal
of Baptist Interest in Sullivan: Reynolds: Rockwell—Origin
of Bradford Association: Eld. Dimock—Morgan Family—
Conversion of Von Puttkammer.*

Inasmuch as the Saviour gave commission to His
disciples to "go into all the world, and preach the Gospel to every creature," I thought I must occupy as
much of it as lay in my power.

FIRST VISIT IN PENNSYLVANIA.

In 1829, I was called into Pennsylvania, to sit with
a council to recognize a little church at Middlebury,
Tioga county. That, I think, was the first time I
had passed the line of New York State.

Soon after, I was called to sit in council at Mitchelltown, (near what is now Tioga Village, then known by
the name of Willardsburg.) Elders P. D. Gillette and
Wise were the other ministers, who, with myself and
chosen brethren, were to examine, and, if thought best,
ordain, two candidates for the ministry. One of them

boasted that he was a great linguist, and my fear was that he knew too much to be very useful. The other knew less, and could murder the English language equal to any other man, yet he was pious and earnest. In view of all the circumstances, and the destitution of the country, we thought best to ordain them. The first individual, so long as I knew him, never amounted to much, but the other has always been doing some good.

Those two visits gave me something of a view of the vast destitution of that part of Pennsylvania; but I could not see how I could render them any assistance, for I had already more on my hands than it appeared possible for me to get along with.

Bro. Edsall Mitchell, of Crooked Creek, (Middlebury church and township,) wrote me a very urgent letter representing the destitution in Tioga county. My heart was pained within me. I did not know what to do. But God, in the plenitude of his mercy and grace, was raising ministers, while we were organizing churches. Among those I had baptized in New York State, were a dear young man, named Wadsworth, and his wife. He was an Eastern man, who had enjoyed the advantages of a good New England school, and graduated, I believe, at the Musical Academy in Boston. He was indeed one of the sweet singers in Israel —a man of rare talents, and commanding appearance— and my hearty desire and prayer to God was, that he might become a faithful minister of the New Testament. While I was praying, God was working by His Spirit upon his mind. It was always my aim to culti- vate a habit of familiarity with all my brethren, and especially where I thought I saw traits befitting a preacher of the Gospel. In conversing with him, one day, he told me, with tears and trembling, the exer- cises of his mind relative to being enabled to do something more than he had hitherto been able to do for the conversion of souls. I gave him such advice, and such encouragement, as I thought duty under the circumstances.

A second pressing letter was received from Brother Mitchell, urging me to go to his house, and he would show me something of the desolation of the land. I said to Bro. Wadsworth—who was in comfortable circumstances—"Now, take your horse, and go with me into Pennsylvania." His inquiry was, "Where are you going?" I told him I did not know, but showed him the last letter I had received from Middlebury. I also said, "I want tó preach at Mitchelltown, on the river— then we will steer westward."

EXTENSIVE REVIVAL ON TIOGA RIVER AND CROOKED CREEK.

We stopped and held the meeting on the Tioga river, at evening, and from thence proceeded to Bro. Mitchell's, up Crooked creek. The good man met us at the door, but was so overjoyed and choked with tears that he could scarcely speak. I thought, surely, God must be in this. We had left another appointment, at Mitchelltown, for our return—and two brethren had besought me to preach at Willardsburg also. I gave them the day and the hour, so that they could give notice and obtain a place for preaching in. On the evening we reached Crooked creek, I tried to preach in the schoolhouse. They wished another appointment on my return, at the house of Dea. Keeney, in the evening—and an affirmative answer was given to that request, also.

The next morning we proceeded, guided somewhat, in this to us unexplored field, by the information we received from the former-named brethren. We were told where we could find one or two Baptist brethren, on Pine creek. There was not much difficulty in obtaining places in which to preach, or people to hear, for it was a new thing to have a minister among them. By the aid of those few brethren, we had as many appointments as I could fill, aided by Bro. Wadsworth's praying, and talking after sermons. We were able only to approximate the region of real destitution, pressed on every side by the cry, "Come again! come again!"

Returning, we commenced filling our appointments. At Dea. Keeney's, it was a dark, lowery evening, but the house was filled to its utmost capacity. God appeared in our midst by the power of the Holy Spirit. In vain we strove to dismiss the meeting, for the people seemed unwilling to go away. After a season of prayer and exhortation, one rose up manifesting a hope in the Saviour; another followed, and another, I think four or five in all. We thought we were ready to depart on the morrow, early in the morning; but God's ways were not our ways. Those individuals, after having been fellowshiped by the few Christians who were present, wished to be baptized. I know not what to do. The conversions seemed to be sudden, and yet the converts gave signs of a death unto sin and a quickening by the Spirit of God. I felt anxious to get away early in the morning. When my mind was made up to baptize them, I asked Dea. Keeney if he had any pitch-pine? if so, I would baptize them that night, for Crooked creek ran but a short distance in front of his house. But the good old man had no torch-wood. It was then after midnight. I gave the people notice that I would preach at day-break, and baptize as near sun-rise as possible. We dismissed the meeting, and I retired to bed to review the scenes of the evening, and prepare for the morning.

Next day, the people were in very early. I heard

them, but, suffering from an intense headache, I remarked to the brother who was with me, "Get up, Samuel—go and pray with them. I thought I heard the sound of distress. I will be out of my room, shortly." Very soon I heard praying with great anxiety; I could not remain on my pillow, but dressed, and went out into the congregation. There were two men on their knees, and Bro. Wadsworth was praying for them. I thought I knew one of them, and, from the account that had been given me of his character and opposition to religion, the probability was that he was profanely infidel, and what is commonly called "a pretty hard case." The other one I did not know at the time; he was from the river, and had heard me preach at the ordination of the two brethren previously referred to, when I formed a little acquaintance with him and his wife. After my brother was through, I kneeled down behind the two men, laid a hand on the shoulder of each, and commenced praying. I was pressed to plead with God that they might not be beguiled and lose their souls by the inebriating cup. The first described man was but little moved. The other one—to me, that moment, unknown—expressed himself, afterward, that he knew that that prayer was all meant for him. He appeared to be the subject of deep conviction. After prayer, I preached a short sermon, and then prepared for the water. The heavens had cleared away their darkening clouds, and the king of day came forth from the chambers of the east in all his glory, just as I was going down into the creek with the first candidate. I baptized the believers, and they went on their way rejoicing. (And here let me say, I have no knowledge of any of those converts ever falling back. It was my privilege to see one of those brethren, a few months ago. His whitened locks bespoke the great change which thirty years or more had made in his physical system, yet he was hoping that by-and-by he would lay hold upon eternal life.)

We made some calls, and gathered fresh information from Bro. Mitchell, then wended our way down to Willardsburg, (now Tioga,) to attend the appointment given out through the two brethren, already referred to.   When we reached the little 'burg, I saw those two friends, standing in the street.   We rode up to them, and passed the compliments of the day; but I saw, by the countenance of one especially, that he was much cast down.   One of them, at last, remarked, "Eld. Sheardown, you can't preach here.   We have tried every way, to get a place for you to preach in, but we have failed."   The other, an aged man, added, "I told you it would be so.   The folks in Willardsburg won't come to hear preaching—and they never ought to have another sermon preached to them."   This was a good man, but very stern in his way of expressing himself. The younger—a man with a family—began to weep. I said to him, "God help you, my brother! don't weep.   Where is the use of crying?   I will preach in this 'burg.   Wadsworth, my brother! rein up your horse here beside mine.   If there is nowhere else for me to preach, I will preach sitting on my horse.   Then, if the Anakims are likely to overpower us, it will be soon enough for us to flee, and we shall be already mounted."   This was opposite the tavern.   While I was turning the circumstances in my mind, a gentleman came up to those brethren, and began conversation. I heard him say, "The man may preach in my bar-room, if he pleases."   I remarked, "Thank you, sir.   I am much better treated than my Master—he was not permitted a place in the inn."   We turned our horses under the shed, and went into the house.   The landlord appeared to be kind and pleasant. But the notice was not spread, so the people did not know what was going on. I remarked, "If we have any persons to meeting, we must ring our own bell. Now, Bro. Wadsworth, sing one of the songs of Zion—something that we can both join in. We sang a piece or two, but none came in to hear. I walked out upon the platform in front of the house—a kind of piazza—without my hat, and commenced singing at the top of my voice, walking to and fro. By-and-by, a little crowd came around, and once in a while I would hear it said, "He is a crazy fellow— he is a crazy fellow!" When I thought perhaps all were gathered that would be drawn to the point, I said to them, "Come in—come in! I am going to preach to you." With this, they all entered; the landlord made it just as comfortable as he could; and I preached from the text, "Jesus Christ, the same yesterday, to-day, and forever." It was a time when sinners felt, and felt intensely—one was under powerful conviction.

Meeting being over, we proceeded two miles or more down the river, where the evening appointment had been left. There we found a different kind of a tavern from the one we had just left. It was a "Baptist tavern," kept by the ancestors of all the Mitchell family in that neighborhood. The old gentleman (Richard Mitchell, Sen ,) was without the church at that time, but mother Mitchell clung fast to the wreck. The *first* "Tioga, Pa.," Church joined the Chemung Association in 1814. It was probably composed of members throughout the country, and held its meetings at different points. In 1822, the name of "Sullivan" appears in the Minutes in the place where "Tioga, Pa.," had stood, with delegates from the vicinity of Sullivan— and the same year, a *second* "Tioga, Pa.," was received into the Association, with delegates from the vicinity of

12

Tioga. Elisha Booth, an ordained, and David Short, a licensed minister, and Bro. John Main. Elisha Tucker, D. D., was engaged in teaching school in Tioga, and there preached his first sermons, in 1816. But this new organization became scattered. There might have been more than one brother still living in membership, and, perhaps, six or eight sisters.

After refreshment, we had a season of prayer, and then went to the old school-house, which looked to me like a palace built for God. In the course of my sermon, I remarked that the waters of Crooked creek empty, above us, into the Tioga river—gave a short sketch of what we had seen, felt and enjoyed, up that creek, the night before, and on the morning of that day—and then observed, that, as the waters of the creek, in which I baptized that morning, flow into the river, so I believed the waters of God's salvation would flow to that people. A dear sister—the daughter of the good woman ta whose house we stopped—lived in the house adjoining the school-house. After meeting, she said to me, "Eld. Sheardown, it looks to me, sir, almost like blasphemy, to talk about God blessing such a wicked people as we are here." We were to tarry all night with her family. After singing and praying, I thought her husband appeared somewhat moved, but not powerfully. We retired at a late hour.

About one o'clock in the morning, some person awoke me out of a sound sleep, and I heard the expression— " dying !" I rose up quickly, and inquired, " Who is dying ?" He said, " Poor Thomas and his wife." I inquired, " Where are they ?" He replied, " In my kitchen—and, for God's sake, Elder! make haste." Partly dressing myself, I went to see what was the matter, and found the two kneeling down together, weeping bitterly, in great anguish, over a sense of their lost condition. I prayed with them, tried to instruct, and to take from them every dependence but Jesus Christ. The man proved to be one of those for whom we had prayed in the morning at the meeting on Crooked creek. Before daylight, both husband and wife professed to have obtained the pardon of sin. The next thing was, they wished to be baptized. I was again deeply tried to know what was duty in the case. The first idea, almost, that struck my mind, was, baptize a rum-jug, and it is a rum-jug still. I retired to a joint in the fence, and there prayed that God would give me wisdom, and enlighten my path, so that I might do what would be well pleasing in His sight. While in this struggle, I thought I had an evidence that it was duty to baptize them. (Eld. Samuel Grenell proved to be in the neighborhood, and, being a connection of the man and wife, he, I believe, baptized them.)

We were to start for York State as early as we could get breakfast. The dear brother, who had been weeping in Willardsburg because he could not get a place for me to preach in, came to bid us good-bye. But I remarked to him, " We are not going yet, Bro. Adams. Here are two candidates to be baptized." He inquired " Who are they?" I answered, "Thomas and his wife." He appeared to be perfectly awe-struck. " Why," said he, " it was only the other day that I saw him drunk." I replied, " I cannot help that. I believe God has converted him ; and, if converted publicans and harlots may enter into the kingdom of heaven—why not this man? Now, my brother, I want you to put a boy upon one horse, and send him up the river; and another on your other horse, and send him down the river. Call at every house, and tell everybody they see that there will be a covenant meeting this morning at nine o'clock, and that Thomas and his wife are to be baptized." The messengers went forth, and the people rallied to see this great sight. At the appointed hour, the school-house was a perfect jam. Weeping and anguish appeared to take hold upon some of the old members who had been excluded for intemperance. (Let me here say, that we acknowledged the few sisters, and Bro. A., as a church, for the women had always maintained their regular covenant meetings.) I talked to those who were desirous to return, as best I could, impressing upon their minds the magnitude of their sins. I told them I felt as though confession only was not enough to satisfy the community in the midst of which they had fallen. I inquired for a temperance pledge. One was brought. I read it over again and again, and said to the brother that was to be baptized (if fellowshiped by the remnant of the church,) "Will you sign this pledge?" He said he would. I then asked the same question to such as had fallen into bad habits and lost their standing in the church. They answered, "Yes."

When we had got through that part of the service, I remarked, "Now, before you sign the pledge, and before I can advise this little body to receive or restore you, I wish to pray; and while I pray, I want you to stand, and hold up your right hands as a token, that, by the grace of God, you will not violate this pledge." They were immediately upon their feet, and there was weeping aloud on every hand. After prayer, the pledge was signed, the converts related their experience, and the backsliders were restored upon their confessions. The former were received by the church, and baptized. After some of the best advice and instruction that I was able to give them, the benediction was pronounced, and we started on our journey about one o'clock in the afternoon.

The next Sabbath, I was preaching in Reading, New

York, within a school-house known as Devins' school-house, at one of my regular appointments. Before I closed my sermon, I saw in the crowd, Bro. A., from Tioga. The tears were coursing down his cheeks. As soon as I had said "amen," I added, " Bro. A. tell your story : I know you are after me." He remarked that "the people in Tioga are in a dreadful state of mind ; weeping appears to be all that many of them can do ; and I want you to go home with me." I said, " Very well, sir, I am ready." He said, " When?" I told him, as soon as I had dismissed my meeting. I was sixteen miles from home, and had another appointment on my way.

Arrived at home that night, and the next morning started for Pennsylvania. Arriving at father Mitchell's, on the river, I learned that a minister of another denomination had heard of the moving in the neighborhood, and on Sabbath made an appointment for Monday evening. Some of the people felt rather indignant, because he had been told that a messenger had gone out to York State, and they expected me back with him ; and although it was not certain, yet they had every reason to believe that I would be on the ground, Monday night. I told the friends to have no feeling on that subject; we would all go to meeting, and try to do good. We heard a sermon that appeared to be antago- nistic to Baptist sentiments and Baptist views, and many things were alleged, that, as a denomination, we have never believed or practiced. I knew the preacher personally, and he knew me, but he paid no regard to me. That, however, made no difference in may feel- ings in relation to the well-being of the souls that were gathered around us. He preached a very long sermon, after which he remarked, that " there may be some one, here, perhaps who would be glad to speak, but we have not the time to spare. I have some other things to say to this congregation, and especially to any that may have been recently converted. I design having an organization here." (That was not his word, yet it implies what he wished to perform.) He told them, if they would do so and so, he could come there and preach to them as often at least as once in three or four weeks. The meeting held to a late hour, and he did all the talking. His last remark amounted to this: "Now, to-night, must determine whether I shall come here any more or not: if there are any who will comply with my wishes, I want you to manifest it by rising up." But none arose. He then came to a very righteous conclusion, by saying, "I perceive I am not wanted here."

I stayed with them several days, and had sometimes two meetings in the day, and sometimes only in the evening. The blessed Saviour was pleased to claim the purchase of his blood in the conversion of many souls. I was under the necessity of returning to New York, but left an appointment when I would be there again. I do not recollect whether I baptized any that time or not, and the records of the church in these days are lost, (so I am told by the clerk,) up to the year 1845, so that I am deprived of obtaining the exact dates when and how many were added unto the church. This, however, was the beginning of what is called to this day "the great revival on the Tioga river."

The work continued to go on in my large charge in York State. Yet I saw very clearly that I must devote more time to the field in Pennsylvania than I had yet done. I find, by referring to the records of one of the little bodies where I was preaching, in New York, that they passed a resolution, that "we willingly relinquish our pastor for one-half of his time, to go and labor in the destitute regions of Pennsylvania," (and it is worthy of notice that that little body had claims upon me for only two sermons a month.) This was a great relief to my mind, and there were one or two young brethren who could occupy the ground during my absence.

For a length of time, every visit I made into Pennsylvania, I baptized more or less—rising of forty, I think, in Tioga. But I kept Middlebury as my radiating point, and continued to make further inroads into those regions where they had no privileges of a Gospel nature.

The father of my Bro. Edsall Mitchell was one of the first settlers in Tioga county; and the whole family (like others of that day) loved to hunt. Being thus extensively-acquainted in the woods, he (the son) could conduct me to every settlement, however small. I rode with him a great many hundred miles, and the remembrance of those excursions is very sweet to this day. I owe a great deal to him, for he conducted me sometimes through woods twelve or fourteen miles without a house. A few months ago, I had the privilege of spending some time with him, recapitulating the dealings of God with us. He is now tottering on the brink of the grave, but rejoicing in the hope of the mercy of God.

AN ANTINOMIAN TROUBLER OF ISRAEL.

I recollect, one time, I had an appointment at the house of a Bro. Steel, on Pine creek. When I rode up, I saw a little, knurly kind of a man, holding a very fine horse by the bits. The first impression of my mind was that the man had stolen the horse, for I had not seen such a one in all those parts. My congregation was together, with few exceptions, and I was just about to open my meeting, when the man came up to me, reached out his hand, and said, " I suppose I shake hands with Eld. Sheardown," I replied, " I suppose

you do, sir." He said, "I am the far-famed Eld. A."
The reply was, " Some men are famed for their good
deeds, and some for their bad ones. Pray tell me, sir,
on which of these grounds your fame has extended ?"
He paused, and acted as though the shot had taken
effect; the reply was, " I suppose, for my bad deeds."
He was answered by my saying, " I suppose, then, sir,
the greater part of what I have heard about you, is
true. Now, when I am at home, I keep good company;
therefore, mean to when I am abroad." He said, " I
have been waiting in this place twenty-four hours on
purpose to hear you preach." I remarked, "Very well,
sir; my business is to preach to sinners." This ended
the conversation, and I passed on to my services. I
had another meeting in the evening, a short distance
from there; he was again present; but, from that day
onward, I did not see that he ever spent much time in
waiting to hear preaching from me.

FRIENDLY METHODIST FAMILY.

One of my principal places of speaking, on that part
of the creek, was at a tavern kept by one of the kindest,
best-hearted men I have ever met with. His wife was
a Methodist, and a choice spirit, amiable and kind.
Since that time, that dear man has been converted, and
is (for anything I know) a living member of the Methodist church. He has served as Sheriff of Tioga county
for one or more terms. I never meet him but I receive
smiles and tears.

THE PEOPLE LOVED TO HEAR PREACHING.

In those days, I would generally ring my own bell
and make my own appointments, never thinking to
ask whether they were desirous to have preaching, but
taking it for granted that it was always welcome. I do
not recollect, now, that I ever came near being "bluffed

off," but once, in all my travels—and that was in the case of Mr. Tuttle, which I will come to presently.

CONVERTS, REMOTE FROM CHURCHES.

Whenever I had evidence that souls were born of God, I baptized the converts, if there was not a Baptist church within fifty miles. Under such circumstances, I gave them a certificate, stating that they were baptized by me, and recommended them to any church of our order.

THE DEACON'S MISSIONARY TOUR.

On one occasion, after my return home, while attending covenant meeting in one of the little churches that I had gathered, I was reciting some of the privations and difficulties I met with in these new and sparsely settled regions. While I am pleading with them to spare me a little more time to devote to the poor, hungry souls, that were so willing to receive the bread of life, I remarked that no one knew what a minister is exposed to, who travels through the little back places in Pennsylvania. One of the deacons—a right hand man to carry on meetings in my absence—tapped me on the shoulder, and whispered, "Stop, Elder—they won't believe you." I remarked, "If the friends are incredulous, I wish some would take a tour or two with me, and I think they will not consider the little things that I have named, are exaggerations." He replied, "I should like to go with you." The answer was, "Do, my brother: go, and see, and feel for yourself." He said, "When are you going again?" "In two weeks, if God will." This deacon was a Dutchman, and always kept an excellent horse. He concluded, at the appointed time, to explore the field, or part of it.

As Providence would have it, it was to be one of my hardest tours, and—being about the middle of March—

in about the worst time of all the year. Before I had returned from my last trip, two young men in Tioga county—unconverted men, yet who often traveled many miles to hear me—had said to me, "Now, Elder, we want you to go down to Blackwell's and Lloyd's. We are going down there, and, if you will let us take appointments for you, when you come again, we will be at home and go with you." One remarked, "It is a bad ride down there, and we should not like to have you go alone." I gave them the appointments, which were faithfully circulated. This appeared to me to be very timely in order to give my new fellow-laborer a large experience in a little time.

The pastor and his deacon started on the trip. The latter looked proudly at his beautiful dappled steed, which had always been fostered in a warm stable with the best of care. He soon began to complain that his horse was losing flesh, but I endeavored to comfort him by saying, "We are not yet fairly in the field." "Entertainment for both man and beast" every day becoming more scarce, instead of a good, comfortable stable, the horses would have to be hitched for the night under some old log shed. We were riding about twenty miles, and I generally preached three sermons, each day.

When we had come down off the mountain, wending our way to a certain creek, (the name of which I have now forgotten,) I preached at the house of a man named Braughton. It was agreed at what hour we should start, under the leadership of the two young men. The creek down which we traveled entered into Pine creek but a short distance above Mr. Blackwell's, where my first appointment was. In passing down this little creek, we had to ford thirteen times in going about nine miles. The fordings were very difficult, for the creek was frozen on both sides, but open in the middle. The deacon

was always the last to put his horse in, and I really
was amused, for I thought sometimes it was difficult to
tell which was the highest—his head or his shoulders.
He had evidently got what is generally termed his
" back up."

But the great struggle had not yet come. When we
reached Big Pine creek, our guides declared it impossible to cross at the fording place, it being frozen on
either side, and open in the middle, and the boys said,
from the depth of water, we could not get out on the
other side if we got in. My own experience and observation confirmed the truth of the statement. What
must be done? In looking at the situation in which
we were placed, I said to the deacon, "If God will, I
shall fill my appointments." "How will you get
there?" "I shall get there, some way. We can go
down to the eddy, and cross afoot on the ice." But
the second appointment was in the evening. Now,
what must be done with the horses? "Hitch them safe
to some saplings, leave them, and let us take it afoot."
The boys fell in with the idea. The deacon thought it
unsafe to leave horses under such circumstances, without any feed or shelter, as the wolves might come and
destroy them.

But we were not to leave our animals thus. One of
the boys said, "Now, Elder, between here and the Big
Eddy, the creek will be open, but it is very swift, and
the bottom very rocky, and bad to ford." We rode
down to the place spoken of, and found it as described.
We concluded to take the ford and try it. It was
agreed that I should go first, seeing that my horse was
thoroughly trained to such adventures: for fording rivers and creeks, under almost all circumstances, was a
part almost of his every day business. I made the
passage, though it was very rough and difficult, for my

horse, by the strong current of the water, and in winding around the large stones or rocks, had gone down stream a great many rods. When I made the opposite shore, I called to the boys to put in higher up, as it appeared to be less dangerous. After we were all safely landed, one of the pilots found we were on an island—and the danger was not yet passed. The other branch of the stream we must cross, in order to get on the side on which the man lived in whose house our appointment was made. One said he would go down a little way and try the ice. In crossing, his horse broke through with its hind-quarters, and we feared for a second that horse and rider both would be lost. It was open water at the head of the branch, and to my mind it was much better to risk the open water than the treacherous ice. The place where we thought to cross, was not so very wide, but it might be deep: the water being muddy, we could not see the bottom: but the appointment must be filled. I therefore concluded, if the deacon must stay behind, 1 must in. I got on my knees on the saddle, crossing my feet (as I had often done) just behind the saddle, and put my horse in: he just made the passage, without swimming; the opposite bank was very bold, and, as soon as my horse's nose touched the bank, I jumped from my saddle, with the bridle in my hand, and, "chirping" to my horse, (as I was wont to do when I wanted him to make his best effort,) he came out all right. The other young man tried it next—then the good deacon—and we were all safe on the bank of deliverance.

We had a blessed time at the meeting, without a thought of the dangers and trials through which we had passed. By the time we were ready to return, the stream had fallen some, but still it was March traveling. We succeeded in filling all our appointments, and returned safe at home, after a tour of two weeks or more. The deacon's horse looked as though he had seen very hard times, and truly he had, for he was not accustomed to "go on a mission." When the Deacon was questioned by the friends relative to the journey—whether he found it as bad as was represented by the Elder—I cannot say what would be his reply, but I dare say that the one-half of it he has never told.

HOME RECREATIONS.

Having arrived at home again, the old field must be gone over. The little bodies, unconnected with the church, must be seen, covenant meetings attended, prayer meetings, preaching, and baptizing—for it was a rare thing, in those days, to pass a month without baptizing some. It was a common occurrence, when I reached my house, to hear, as the first item of news, that such a one is converted, and such a one. Frequently, from three to ten were reported, who had been brought into the kingdom in my absence. Sometimes, on arriving home, I would find my wife with four or five young people, over whom she had been weeping and praying, having prevailed upon them, after the meeting was out, to come with her, that she might have an opportunity to labor with them. So my own dwelling was the spiritual birth-place of many souls brought to the truth as it is in Jesus. The deacons and other gifted brethren would give me an account of the interest of the meetings at the different points. The home work being done—which would require about two weeks of incessant ministerial labor—then I would take the saddle again for the back-woods.

BATTLE WITH A CAMPBELLITE.

Those were the days when Campbellism was making bad work, not only in the feeble churches, but was
13

seriously affecting the minds of unconverted people. I
remember having met a gentleman—for his title was
"General"—not far from Wellsboro', whose wife's
mother was a Baptist. I frequently stopped to refresh
with the family, and preached occasionally. The
General still lived with his wife's family, and would
always endeavor to get into an argument with me,
when there, about baptismal regeneration. But he
was very much like Gen. Taylor's troops in Mexico
—he did not know when he was whipped! Having an
appointment at his father-in-law's house, I concluded to
talk truth to him: then he would not feel at liberty to
answer while I was yet speaking. I had studied my
sermon in my saddle, from the Saviour's words to
Nicodemus: "Marvel not that I said unto thee, Ye
must be born again." (John iii: 7.) The day was
very rainy, and I was pretty well saturated, having
had a long ride, the last part of it (about eight miles)
through the woods. I cannot say that I had not a dry
thread about me, but I was thoroughly wet, from head
to foot. When I reached the house, I found the young
folks, but the father and mother had gone to York
State. The storm was such that I could expect but
very few—perhaps a dozen people—at meeting. Had
it been fine weather, I should have expected enough,
from a distance, to have made quite a congregration.
I made up my mind that I should have to take another hand-to-hand combat with the General. But,
to my astonishment, the people came through the
storm, and filled the room. It is seldom that I have
felt more grateful to the God of all my mercies, than I
did on that occasion. I preached my sermon, as best I
could in my uncomfortable condition of body. As soon
as I had said amen, the General arose, and controvert-
ed the doctrine which I had advanced   I said little or

nothing, but let him talk in peace until he was through, when I remarked, "Now, sir, I have very little reply to make. I have a few questions to ask, and that is all. Since I saw you last, I have learned that you have been baptized, by torch-light." He replied, "Yes, at twelve o'clock at night."—"Now, for a question or two. Do you really believe, that when you were immersed, your sins were all washed away?" The answer was, "I do, sir."—"After that act, sir, do you now consider yourself in a state of perfection?"—"As far as my sins are concerned, I do, sir."—"Did that act of baptism place you in an immutable state, so that there is no danger that you will ever sin again—or, in other words, that you are incapable of sinning?" The reply was, "I suppose not, sir."—"Then you are liable to sin, are you?"—"Yes."—"Do you believe a sinner can enter the kingdom of heaven?"—"No, sir."—"Now, then, what must you do, in order to be saved from the sins that you may commit after your baptism?"—"I suppose, sir, I should have to be immersed again."—"Well, sir, after this second immersion, if you should fall away and sin against God—your conscience be smitten that you had done wrong—and, while thus reflecting, by a flash of lightning, or the falling of a tree, or some other casualty, you should be instantly killed: what would become of you?"—"I don't know, sir—I had not thought of that." I had but one more question to ask, and that was to my congregation. I said to them, "Now, all of you present, whether saint or sinner, who believe that I have preached the truth, and that the last speaker is in error, signify it by rising on your feet." I think there was but *one* (except myself) who did not rise, and the reader may guess who that was.

THE AGED INN-KEEPER, CONVERTED.

An unconverted man said to me, one day, "I wish,

Elder, you would preach at Knoxville," (on the Cowanesque river.) I told him I thought I would get an appointment there, but could not see my way clear to give them a sermon until I should pass through again. I did not always know how many appointments I had to fill, until I arrived at Bro. Mitchell's on Crooked creek. That was my head-quarters and I had given him encouragement, that, if he saw any person from some remote little settlement, where no minister ever went, I would go there and preach, provided he made the appointment with the understanding that he should pilot the way. But I thought probable that, the next time I was through, I could preach at Knoxville, and therefore made an appointment, for a certain day, at half-past two o'clock in the afternoon. Notice was given out in the school.

When the day arrived, a Baptist sister, who was passing through the village, heard of the meeting. She tarried to hear me, and, after sermon, came and shook hands as cordially as if she had always known me. She remarked, "My name is Weeks. I am a Baptist. Where do you preach to-night, sir?" I replied that I had no appointment that night, but had one for the forenoon of the next day, in Mixtown, or what was often called New Hector. She at once said, " You must preach for us, to-night." I inquired, " How far do you live from here?" She said, about six miles. I remarked, " Why, that would be useless—your neighbors could not get the word, and I, perhaps, should have no persons to preach to." She replied, "Yes, you will have persons to preach to. To be sure, we are very scattered, but I am on horseback, and I will publish it to every house as I go up the river, and I know who to tell to go and notify their neighbors; and when I get home, I will start the boys out, to let all my neighbors know that there is to be preaching to-night. Now, I want you to understand that the preaching is not to be at my house. When we have any person who comes there to preach, they always preach at Mr. Tuttle's. You cannot miss his house, sir—it is right on your road, up the river—a very large house, with red gable ends, and the front white. It is a public house, and has a large sign up—'Entertainment.' You will most likely meet with the old gentleman: you may know him as soon as you see him, for he is palsied on one side. His wife is a very excellent women—but he himself is very crabbed and cross—and, if he should abuse you some, you must not pay attention to that. I shall call and tell him of the appointment, so that you may not be quite a stranger to him; but do not feel bad, sir, if he scolds considerably."

COOL RECEPTION.

Having received this information, and the good woman having gone homeward with permission to ring the bell for me, I got my horse, rode along as directed, came to the house, dismounted, and went into the bar-room. There was the old gentleman, evidently armed and equipped to meet me. I said to him, " My name is Sheardown. Mrs. Weeks said she would make an appointment for me to preach, here, to-night, sir."— " No sir," said he, " you ain't agoing to preach here. I wont encourage you lazy vagabonds, running around getting your living out of the poor folks, professing to be preachers."

. I replied, "I shall preach here. Have you a hostler, sir ?"—" No !" he said, " not for such lazy fellows as you." I said to him, " Well, sir, if you have no hostler, tell me where I shall put my horse." He replied, " I

tell you, you shan't stay."—" I tell you, I shall ; and if
you will not tell me where to put my horse, I will put
him in the best place I can find."—" Then," he said,
" take him across the road, and put him into yonder
long barn." I took him to the tier of stables, found
some good hay overhead, and let him go to eating.
Going back to the house, I said 'to the old gentleman,
" Now, sir, I am a good hand at waiting upon myself.
Please tell me where I can find some oats. I want six
quarts for my horse."—" We haven't got any," he said.
The reply was, " I know you have got plenty." He re-
torted, " But you shall not have them." I replied, " I
will have them. Your sign says to the traveling public,
'Entertainment for man and beast,' and if you do not let
me have the oats, I will pull your sign down." He exclaimed, with a word that I am not at liberty to use,
"Take my keys, unlock such a bin on the stoop, and
take what you want." I got my six quarts of oats, at
the same time telling him that I always intended to
pay my way.

After returning from the barn, and conversing with
Mr. Tuttle a short time, he appeared to be a little softer.
I asked, " Have you no women around the house ? I
want something to eat." He replied, " Very well—go
into such a room, and you will find the old woman—
tell her what you want." I found the lady. She appeared like a mother indeed. The moment she knew
who I was, she anticipated my wants, and brought on
mince pie and other good things to meet the necessities of the hungry body. I ate hastily, for the time of
my appointment was near at hand. I preached that
evening to quite a congregation, and felt the presence
of the Lord very precious. The people appeared to be
over-awed.

I had another appointment soon, at the same place,

when everything appeared to go off smoothly. The old gentleman was good-natured, and ready and willing to let me and my horse have all that was necessary for our comfort, without fee or reward.

FRUIT IN OLD AGE.

Some time afterwards, in making a tour over the mountains with my pilot, we found it very bad traveling, it being about the middle of March. There was much snow and ice in our paths. I said to Brother Mitchell, " We must make the best of it. I want to go down in the valley before school closes for the day in Knoxville, as I have no appointment for the night, and will preach there—it will be easier getting a congregation." And I added, " Now, we must not stop at father Tuttle's"—for we were to pass his door, and if we stopped we should be detained so long that I could not be able to get my appointment circulated. However, both of us complained of our feet being very cold, and concluded we had better stop ten or fifteen minutes, see how the old gentleman was, and warm our feet. We had but just dismounted, when a son of the landlord came up to us, with an overcoat, and a whip in his hand, apparently fixed to leave home. I addressed him as " Brother Tuttle"—for he was a Methodist class-leader, and I think an excellent man—and inquired, " Where now—where are you going, sir?" The tears came to his eyes as he replied—" To York State; I was going to see if I could find you." Seeing that he was so much affected, I thought perhaps the old gentleman was dead. He said something about his father, which his choking with heart-feeling prevented our understanding. But he immediately took our horses, led them to the barn, and said, " Go in." We entered the house, and found the old lady, and a little grand-daughter, I think, with her. She raised her hands, and in her way began to praise God, and weep; and the girl, sympathizing with her, wept too. Bro. Mitchell said, "What is the matter, mother Tuttle? what are you all crying about to-day?" She tried to tell, but I was not yet able to understand what was the cause of the apparent sorrow. The son returned from the barn, saying, "O, there is a God in this—there is a God in this!" We had not yet taken off our over-garments, because my motto was, onward to Knoxville! He said, "Sit down, brethren, and I will try and tell you all about it. My father," he continued, "is con-verted. He has had a very severe attack of sickness, and is still quite unwell. He had desired me to go to York State, find Eld. Sheardown, and, if possible, have him come home with me, for he felt as though he must be baptized before he died. Now, you must stay and preach with us to-night, and we will see how things will turn out." I still plead that I ought to go on, but he overpowered me with his argument. I thought, Who am I that I should resist God? So I concluded to stay and preach, and he sent off the runners to give general notice of the meeting in the evening at his father's. I said I should like to see father Tuttle. His wife and son, Bro. Mitchell, and myself, went into his room. He was in bed, but looked up and exclaimed, "It's him! it's him!" He got hold of my hand, and wept like a child. He said something like this to his son: "There, now, I feel better; I want to get up; I want to talk with Eld. Sheardown." We left the room, and they got the old gentleman into his large arm-chair. I conversed with him to see what evidence I could get that God had wrought a work of grace in his heart. He gave large evidence that he was dead to sin and alive to God. I asked him if he thought he would be able, after sermon, to. talk to us, and tell us how the Lord had dealt with him, especially since the first time I had preached at his house. His reply was, "Yes, I want to tell all about it."

MR. TUTTLE'S EXPERIENCE.

There was a very general turning out in the evening, and after sermon I remarked, "Mr. Tuttle thinks he has experienced religion, and is going to tell us something about his feelings—how he has felt, and how he now feels." The old gentleman had some two or three times of commencing, for something would strike his mind, relative to his change, that he had not named before. He said he must tell everything; he did not want to keep anything back. A death-like stillness prevailed through the congregation.

After he had got through, I said, "If it is God's will, I shall baptize father Tuttle, early in the morning." I spoke after this fashion: "Now, in the first place, I want to say to every individual present, who professes religion, whose hope is based upon repentance toward God, and faith in the Lord Jesus Christ, if you can receive the experience of this aged man, believing that he is converted—born again—rise on your feet." What few Christians were present, to an individual, arose. I then said to his pious son, (who was a man in the meridian of life,) "Can you personally feel to fellowship your father as a Christian?" He almost wept aloud, and said, "Yes." I then said to all present, "I do not care who you are, what you are, or how wicked you may have been; if you think that Mr. Tuttle is a Christian man, rise up on your feet." They all arose.

I was preparing to dismiss the meeting, (for it appeared that I had nothing more to say, except to give out the morning services,) when the old man broke out and said, "Don't go away yet; don't go away yet; I have not done confessing to my neighbors." And such a flood of confessions the old gentleman poured out, as is seldom heard. I then gave my appointment for the morning: at daylight, preaching, and after the sermon, we were to repair to the river, which ran but twenty or thirty rods in the rear of the old gentleman's house, for baptism.

THE BAPTISM.

In the morning, at the time of appointment, the house was crowded. When all was ready to repair to the Jordan, the first thing to be considered was, how we should get the old gentleman down. It was proposed to carry him in his arm chair. We had plenty of power, for there were a number of strong, athletic men, who were anxious and willing to do what they could. They fixed a piece of board or scantling underneath the chair, the bearers on either side, and some walking behind, steadying the sedan, until we arrived on the bank of the stream.

After he was set down, he said, "Carry me under that buttonwood tree." They took him up, and carried him just where he wanted to be. "There," he said. "Here is the spot. When I knew not what to do with myself, I crawled down here; here I prayed, here I felt happy, and right there," pointing into the river, "I prayed that Elder Sheardown might baptize me." He was a very corpulent, heavy man. I do not know his age, but it was said by some that he was eighty-four; others said he was eighty-six, but I did not ask any of the family his age.

After singing and prayer, I said to the congregation, "You all see the difficulty that I am in. It is impossible for me to get this palsied man in and out of the river, alone. Now, who will go into the river with me, and, when I am ready, assist in this solemn business?" "I will," was responded all around me. But his son spoke out, "I will go in with the Elder and my father." I inquired something about the depth of the water, for the river was roily, and I did not know how the bar lay. Every individual appeared to be interested: one said, "It is so deep there, Elder;" and another said, "It is so deep there," and pointed it out. I told them what depth of water I wanted, and the place was designated by throwing a stone where they thought I should have the depth of water I desired. I went into the river, explored it, found the place I needed, and came out.

Next, we got the old gentleman out of his chair, and I told his son how we must handle him, how we must get him in and out of the water, &c. I told him when I said, "I baptize thee," (for that was always my last word, bringing the word and action together)—then he must let loose of his father; but, the moment he saw his face coming to the top of the water, he should take hold of him with me, raise him up on his feet, and hold him perfectly steady. But the good brother, instead of obeying me, obeyed the impulse of his own warm heart; for, when he ought to have had hold of his father, he was clapping his hands, crying, "Glory to God! my soul is happy." But I was able to raise the old gentleman on his feet, and steady him a second or two, until the dear son got hold of him. We locked him in our arms; he stepped with one foot, and dragged the other after him; we got him safe back into his chair, and in carrying him to the house he said to the men, "Set me down, set me down; I can walk—I know I can walk." They said, "No, you can't walk." I said, "Give him that cane; he can

walk; set him down." I suppose it was the action of
the cold water on his palsied system, that might last
him to the house, and it did; but many published it as
a great miracle. This was the last I saw of father
Tuttle. He died some time after this, (I do not know
just how long;) his son told me that he died in hope of
eternal life.

ALL GOING WELL IN YORK STATE.

My face was now turned towards home, filling my
appointments, in Southern New York, bordering on my
mission field in Pennsylvania. Arriving at home, 1 as
usual began to gather up the fragments, so that nothing
might be lost. The brethren had enjoyed good seasons
throughout that field of labor. I seldom spent two
weeks at home but I had more or less to baptize, some
things to set in order at the different stations, my working brethren and sisters to encourage, and lay out new
labor for them while I should be absent on my next
missionary tour; and I had brethren and sisters who
would work with a will, some who never-faltered.
Having straightened up the ship at home, and got her
fairly on her course; I was ready again to depart for
another wilderness campaign.

CONVERSION OF MR. B.

Riding through a neighborhood in Tioga county, six
or eight miles from Knoxville, I was hailed by a man
at whose house I had stopped once or twice by invitation. If there can be anything good in an unconverted
man, who believed in annihilation, he possessed that
quality, for he was very sociable and benevolent. He
invited me to dine with him, and fed my horse, that I
might be better prepared to go on my way. He asked
me if I was going to Knoxville? I replied, " No, sir."
—"Now," said he, "1 wish you would let me make an

appointment for you there, because there is one individual in that village, who is a very wealthy man, but one of the queerest, wickedest men you ever saw. I thought that if I should go down there and have a talk with him, and tell him that I am going to make an appointment for Eld. Sheardown, a particular friend o mine, he will come to meeting. He never goes" (I believe he said) " to any meeting; but, if he can get a minister into trouble in any way, it affords him a great deal of satisfaction. One day," he said, "Rev. Mr. C. called at his store, and said, 'Mr. B., I want to see your wife.'—'Very well,' he replied, 'she's a pretty woman, and I will go to the house with you.' He took the minister around, seated him in a cozy little room, and asked him if he had read the news? Mr. C. replied he had not, 'but,' said Mr. B., '*I* have got the paper in my pocket: here, sir, you take and read it until Mrs. B. comes in.' He went out at another door, for there were two doors to the room; one he went in at from the street, and the other led into the interior of the house. Mr. C. commenced reading, and waited more than an hour; becoming tired, he thought he would go and look up the lady; but, behold! the inner door was fast; he thought that some trick must have been played upon him, at which he took umbrage, walked out at the door he came in at, and went off, without seeing the lady. The secret was, Mr. B, when he went out, locked the door, put the key in his pocket, and never told his wife that a gentleman was waiting to have an interview with her.—Now I thought, sir," said the Esquire, " I can induce Mr. B. to come and hear you preach. I will go down with you, and use my best endeavors to prevail upon him to come out and hear you." I told him to take his own course: he might make an appointment for a given day in the distance, at half-
14

past two o'clock in the afternoon, and I would make it in my way to take dinner with him, and we would go down in company.

I made my connection at an early dinner hour. The Esquire was very fast to inform me that the appointment had been well circulated, and that Mr. B. had promised to come and hear me preach. He said his women folks were going down with him, and he wanted one of the young men should ride my horse and I ride in the double wagon with him and his family. Any way suited me, therefore I piled in with the family. He left us at the place of the appointment, and I did not see him again for some time. He came just as the congregation had about got together and said, "Mr. B. wont be here; he is in one of his tantrums: I never saw him in a worse." I said to him, "He will be here, sir, I believe, and I wish I knew him personally, but I do not know that I have ever seen him. Now, sir, when he comes in, (for I believe he will,) I wish you would just draw your fore-finger across your brow, so that I may know him." He smiled and said, "Very well." Mr. B. came in during prayer. When I commenced reading my hymn, I saw Esq. C. give the sign; he turned his eyes partly over his shoulder; behind him sat a tall, gaunt-looking gentleman, his hair standing every way like the quills of a porcupine. My anxiety to know the man, was, that I might see whether I could gain his attention or not.

After meeting, his wife very kindly invited me home with her. I consented to go; she took me through the bar-room, and there was Mr. B. She introduced me; he started back a pace or two, and said, "Why, this is the man who preached to us." I said. "Yes sir."— "Well, wife," said he, "you take care of him; you are the woman for ministers." She was a Baptist sister, of exalted piety. One of Mr. B.'s peculiarities was that he always, in choosing a wife, (for this was his third,) looked out for a pious woman.

The evening passed along; I saw nothing of Mr. B.; he was not in to tea; but I should think about seven o'clock, he came into the sitting-room, running his fingers through his hair, and paced the room backward and forward several times without saying a word. He then went out, and after a while came in again, smoking a pipe. I remarked to him, "Mr. B., it looks quite sociable to see you smoking." He replied, "Would you like to smoke with me?"—"I would, sir, if you please." He said to one of the children, "Go and get some clean pipes, and some of that best tobacco." He sat down, and I thought that he had taken, (in some measure,) the bait.

I remarked to him, "Your saw-mills on Pine Creek are about in running order again." (This was after what is termed the great May flood, when mills as well as other property had been very much damaged.) He said to me, "What do you know about my mills on Pine Creek?" I told him I was very well acquainted there; that I stopped and preached to the hands, some-times, when I was passing by, when it was not likely to interfere with their labor; and went on to inquire after some other mills that he had on different streams. "Why, how the ——" (I liked to have said *devil*, but I won't say it,) "do you, as a minister, know so much about saw-mills?" I told him I always calculated to notice everything that I passed, and gather some information as I went along, and that some of my best preaching places were among such establishments. I found he was becoming quite tame. He said, "I am not known by the name of B. I pass, both in the country and in the city, by the title of the Lounger of the West."

He then endeavored to entertain me with a lengthy anecdote relative to a scene through which he passed in the city of New York. "At such a time," he said "I was down to the city, buying goods. I bought some of my goods at the firm of a father and son: the father was very aged, but the son was a real business man, in the vigor of life; they were the most religious people, sir, you ever saw. I bought a great many goods of them; we always had a very good understanding. The son said to me, after I had made my purchases, 'Now, sir, I should be very happy to have you take tea at my house this afternoon, at such an hour.' I replied, 'I cannot do that, sir; I am here, you see, as the Lounger of the West, with my cow-hide boots on, and everything else in proportion, and I am not fit to go into company, especially if there are to be ladies present.' He told me that it would be a little family *te ta tee;* in the course of the evening there might perhaps be a friend or two dropping in, but no one whom I need be troubled about. I finally promised him I would go. Then, the first thing was to get shaved, the old boots blacked, coat brushed, and rig everything in the best style under the circumstances. To my utter astonishment, after tea, we were shown into another apartment, (a very beautiful, elegant room;) soon after, gentlemen and ladies began to drop in, and the first thing I knew I was in the midst of a cotillion party. Of course, I must figure with the rest, and a pretty figure I was. Now," he said, "after all was over, I was waited on to my room for the night. It had then got to be twelve or one o'clock. I had not been long in my room before I heard this pious gentleman praying. I thought to myself, good Lord, these people could not pray when I was up! How very pious they must be."

After he was through with his relation, I said to him, "Mr. B., I have learned two things, sir, from your anecdote. The first is, you do not think much of people who keep you up till twelve or one o'clock at night at a cotillion party; the next is, sir, that you have no confidence in those who pray after you have gone to bed. Now, sir, I am in the habit of praying every night, when I go to bed, certainly, either before or after I retire."—"Why, would you like to pray now?"—"Just as you please, sir; but I shall certainly pray to-night, and I should like you to have a good opinion of my Christianity."—"Daughter," said he, to a lovely child, "fetch in some more candles. Now, maybe the man would like to read."—"I should, sir, if it is your pleasure."—"Bring your mother's big Bible." While this was doing, I looked at my watch, and said, "It is very near twelve o'clock." I read a portion of Scripture, kneeled down, and prayed, after which I said I would retire. He took a candle and waited on me to my room. He said, "There, sir, this is the best bed and room I have got in my house. I hope you will enjoy it. Pleasant dreams to you, sir; good night."

On my pillow, I reviewed the scene, from the time Esq. C. had solicited an appointment from me, with the understanding that he was to go and get this gentleman out to meeting. I believed that God was in this movement, but how, I could not tell. I was always in the habit of rising early in the morning, and I found that they did the same. We had an early breakfast. After breakfast, I commenced conversation again in reference to large tracts of wild land that he owned, after which I said to him, "I should like, sir, to look over your establishment here. I have about an hour that I can spare. I was brought up, in early life, to business, and it always does me good to see a prosper ous man.

He replied, "I shall be very happy to show you what little we have here." He went on speaking of some conveniences about his house, the tavern where he lived, then took me to the store, from there (I think) to the tannery, and from there led me along to an old building in the mouth of a little ravine: at once he stopped suddenly, and said, "I won't take you any further this way; this is rather a bad concern; that building," he said, "is my still-house; it came very near being carried away by the freshet, and I wish it had." He said, "It is poor business; I think I shall never work it again. Now," said he, "I must show you the grist mill." He took me into the grist mill, through every nook and corner, until I was almost covered with cobwebs and flour dust. Every once in a while, he would give the meal a brush off me with his hand, but (as his hand was always very mealy) he left me in a worse plight than I was before. Yet he was always very careful to say, "I am sorry, sir, that you are getting so much of this white upon your clothes." I told him it made no difference to me, as I was used to the rough and tumble of life, and if it was not white it was just as likely to be black, from helping some poor man who might be trying to get a black brand on to his log-heap—for I never rode by a man, and saw him in trouble in getting a log up on his heap, but that I jumped from my horse and assisted him what I could. "Why," said he, "you are a queer fellow. I never met with just such a one before."

After I had gone through, I said, "Now, sir, I will have my horse, and pay my bill. Have you got a boy around that will saddle and bridle my horse?"—"Yes, I will do that." We went to the stable, and found my horse in as fine trim as though he had come out of the hands of a perfect groom. He saddled and bridled my horse, and brought him out. I asked him how large my bill was? He said, "Nothing at all, nothing at all."

After I had got into my saddle, he said to me, "Ah, now you must dismount, and go back with me into the house." I went back with him; he took me into the bar-room, unlocked the bar, went to his decanters, first taking out one stopple and then another, smelling of the contents, finally took a bottle and glass, and set them down, stood a moment, put them back, and came and took a seat by me, and commenced conversation again. I thought then, and I think now, his great object in this manœuvre was to get me to drink something, but he was afraid to ask me.

I then walked out to my horse at the post, and got into my saddle. He said to me, "Now, sir, whenever you come this way, make my house your home. The best I have shall be at your service." I said to him, "Mr. B., I am very much obliged to you. And now, sir, I expect you are honest in what you say, and I accept your invitation. But there are some things about this, that perhaps I should do well to name. It is reported, far and near, that Mr. B. is the most profane man there is in this country, and is in the habit of getting into what the people call 'tantrums.' Now, sir, if I should call upon you, and you should be in your business, I shall not come and interfere with you, for the sake of seeing you, for men never wish to be interrupted when they are crowded with business matters; and I don't want, sir, that you should ever come where I am when you are in those tantrums. I profess not only to be a Christian, and a Christian minister, but a gentleman, and when I call at your house, sir, if you can step aside from your business, I shall expect to have your company, and that we shall try to be sociable and do each other good. My great object is to benefit the children of men. Now, sir, I have said this to you in the honesty of my heart, and I hope we shall often meet to enjoy seasons of conversation together."—"Go on, sir, go on; you are the queerest fellow I ever saw in my life."

The next time I staid all night there, he and his wife were away from home. I was well cared for, and in the morning asked the young man for my bill. " O," said he, "father told us, if ever Eld. Sheardown came here, and he was not at home, to let him have the best the house afforded, and never charge anything." I thanked him, talked with him a moment or two, and went on my way.

The next time I was there, he was at home, and I had a very pleasant time. He said to me, with tears in his eyes, " Now, sir, if you will come and live in this village, I will find you a good house to live in, and see that you lack for nothing, and I will build you a church in the corner of my orchard there—that beautiful place —that shall cost three thousand dollars. I will enter into bonds that shall be perfectly satisfactory to you, to do all that I have said." I told him my calling was of such a nature that I could not settle anywhere. Things were assuming such features, in York State, that it was necessary for me to curtail my labors in Pennsylvania.

The next I heard of Mr. B , a man rode up to my own door, soon after daylight, with a jaded horse, which looked as though he might have been going all night. I invited the man in, and called one of the boys to take his horse. He said he had come, on express from Mr. B.'s, for me to return with him with all speed; that Mr. B. was very sick, and the probability was that he could not live. I questioned the man in relation to how he was taken, what was the matter, what the physician said about him, how long he had been sick, with a great many other inquiries. From the man's account, I gathered the idea in my own mind that his sickness would not be unto the death of the body, for everything indicated that he was under the greatest distress of mind for his sins. I told the man that I could not go; that I had other engagements that I must fulfill, and that I could not save Mr. B.'s life. "But you return home, as soon as you can, and say from me to Mr. B., that no earthly power can do him good; there is but the one Physician, and that is Jesus Christ. Tell Mr. B. to commit himself, soul and body, for time and eternity, into the hands of the Saviour, and he will be well enough."

For some years, I heard nothing from Mr. B. One day in 1854, my senior Deacon, who had heard me speak in reference to the gentleman, and knew something of my anxiety to know his condition, said to me, " Your old friend, Mr. B., is living in Elmira. Would you not like to go down and see him?" I said, "Yes, indeed, I would." He replied, "To-morrow morning I will take you down there. I am acquainted with him. He is a very different man, now, from what he was when you first knew him." We made the call, and found him at home. He was a good deal haggard with the toils and cares of a long and arduous business life, but I had scarcely entered the room before he recognized me, and embraced me with the greatest rapture. After we had talked a few moments, he said, " I want to pray. Let us all kneel down and pray together." The scene was what I can not describe; the feelings of my heart no human tongue can tell. This was the last interview I had with Mr. B. How different from the first! I hope and trust he now is in heaven.

THREE POOR FAMILIES.

I had been traveling some in Potter county, Pennsylvania. When I came to a school-house, if there was school, I would arrange with the scholars, at noon, to run around and give notice to a few of the nearest neighbors, who, with the children, would make up quite a congregation, and I would try and preach to them Jesus and the resurrection. Then I would inquire the course in which there was another school-house, and, if it was in my reach before school was dismissed, would get out an evening appointment, then find somebody with whom I could stay all night. Thus pushing around from place to place, I finally crossed the line into Tioga county, and preached in a settlement where I had spoken a few times before. There I met with two or three Baptists. After the meeting was out, a man came up, shook hands with me, and called me by name. I had to look pretty close, for all the light we had through the service was from a few slivers of fat pine, inserted in the jams of the old fashioned log-house fire-place. He asked me if I would not go home and stay all night with him. I told him I preferred not going any further, if I could stay where I was; but he insisted that I should go with him. I asked him the distance. He said not over a mile. His wife was in company with him, and I concluded that if she could walk that distance through the pitch darkness, I certainly could ride. They were both irreligious. I talked with them, prayed with them, and endeavored to point them again to the Lamb of God that taketh away the sins of the world. I had preached to them in York State. They appeared to be among the very poor, but what they had was free as water. My horse faired a great deal worse than myself, but he said nothing, had no fault to find, for he had learned, no doubt, that the mission field was often very scarce of provender.

In conversation with the man, early in the morning, after having eaten a very light breakfast indeed, we talked about the way to Phœnix Run. He wanted to know how far from Pine Creek. 1 told him, as near as I could guess. " Well, now," he said, " Elder, you are a pretty good back-woodsman, and if you can keep the course through the woods as I will give it to you, you will strike the Run at the foot of Round mountain." I thought that there were so many mountains, and round ones too, that it was not a very definite direction. He said it was only eight miles through the woods, but there was no path, not even marked trees, by which I could be guided. He pointed out the direction, where the wind was, and said, if I kept the wind so and so, I would no doubt come out right. I concluded to try it, inasmuch as it was going to shorten, very greatly, my travel. Having got perhaps two miles into the deep wilderness, my horse made signs that there was some-thing around that he did not like very well, for he was always afraid of wild animals. While talking to him I heard the brush crack. My horse jumped, and I looked around, but saw nothing. Very soon, I heard it crack again, and thought perhaps it might be a panther drawing his heavy carcass along; but, in a little open-ing to the right, I saw a man, and he saw me, and as we approached each other I hailed him by his given name, " Oliver! what are you doing here, my brother?" He was a young man whom I had baptized, with a number of others, some time before, on Pine Creek. I asked him where he was steering to? He said, " To the creek."—" Where do you calculate to strike Phœ-nix Run?" He replied, "At Round mountain." I asked, " Why do you call it Round mountain?"—" O," he said, "the people have names for almost all these mountains." I asked him if he had ever been through this piece of woods before? He said, "Yes, once." I remarked, "I think you are bearing too much to the right, otherwise the wind has changed." He said he thought he was pretty near right, but would not be sure; and as we kept talking and moving on, he added, if we are right, we shall come to a house, pretty soon. I said I had never heard of a house anywhere in that part.

While we were talking, "There," said he, "I see the break, now, in the woods." We soon came to what back-woodsmen call a "slash fence:" there might have been, perhaps, an acre, the timber of which had been cut down, and left on the ground just as it fell. As we could not get through this slash fence, we consulted which was the best way to get around it, and had just started to work our way, when I saw some children. They must have been playing at hide-and-seek, for those that saw us began to shout and scream, and very soon I saw three or four more little ones crawl out of a very large hollow bass-wood tree that had been cut down but was lying up on other timber. I saw at once that they were not all children of one mother.

While we were talking and amusing ourselves with the children, we arrived pretty near to the house. There did not appear to be a vestige of anything growing, but what had sprung up wild from the bosom of nature. I said to the brother with me, "Hold on, I want to stop at this house." I went up to a rude door that was partly open, and knocked, but no answer. I always had one question to ask first, when I called at an isolated dwelling, and that was, "Where is your spring?" I opened the door, and asked the question. There were two women in the house; one answered, "The spring's down by that hemlock tree; the gourd shell is there, sir." I then told them my name, and that I was a Baptist minister; I asked them if they knew the course I should have to take to strike Phœnix Run, near the Round mountain. They told me that I was on a pretty direct course. All this time, I was surveying their habitation. I asked them how long they had lived there? They replied, "Over nine years." I asked them where they were from? They said they were from York State. I asked them from what part of York State, but got no answer. I asked them what county? No answer. What town? All silent. I then concluded that, very probably, they were like several others whom I had met with, in isolated places, who had left York State for a cause. I asked them if they had a Bible? They said, "No." A Testament? "No, sir." Why, what books have you? "Not any." Have you not an Almanac? "No, we have not any books." I talked to them some in relation to the interests of their souls. They were intelligent, looked tidy in their persons, their garments well patched. I put it down that those females had seen better days. They had but one room. The floor appeared to be made of split chestnut; chamber floor, they had none; chairs, and tables, were not there. I saw a small quantity of crockery, more or less broken. They had no chimney; the logs had long been burned out where the fire was wont to be built, and a very large slab-stone, standing edgewise, served for a fire-back. There were some small pieces of venison hanging in a little smoke. Blocks, like shingle-blocks, appeared to be their seats. Their bedsteads (one on either side of the room) were very rude, but convenient: they had bored into the logs with a two-inch auger, and inserted cross-pieces, which were put into a

15

hole of the same size, in what might be termed the bed-posts. One difference I observed, between the bed-posts of civilization and those that were on the borders, was, that while we have but two posts on a side, theirs appeared to have three, with the head part some inches higher than the foot. On the cross-pieces appeared to be laid slabs or boards, (I could not say which.) I inquired for their husbands. They said they were out hunting. I would have given them my Bible, but it was the only one I had with me, and it would have been very difficult for me to have made my way home without a Bible.

My companion left me soon after we arrived on the Run, and I continued my course. Judging my horse by myself, I knew he must be very hungry. I was passing a little log cabin, something like seven miles from the settlement below, where I calculated to take my dinner. I was somewhat acquainted with the people living in the cabin; they were pious, good people, but very poor. I saw, amongst the boys laying around the house, some very nice fresh grass, which I did not see on the mountain, for it was now about the middle of May. I thought I would ask the privilege of turning my horse loose there a short time. I inquired of two children if their father and mother were in. One said no, the other said yes. While I was speaking, the good woman came to the door, very glad to see me. I told her that I wanted to let my horse pick a little of that grass, and I would stop ten or fifteen minutes. She asked me what time of day it was; I told her, about eleven o'clock. She said, " Now, Elder, you must stop and take dinner with us." I told her she must excuse me, for I must go on, very soon ; (and I knew that, if I stopped to eat, I should " eat the children's bread.") But she was so importunate, that the thought struck me, if I do not stay, she will think that it is on account of their poverty : so I concluded to tarry. She said to two little boys, "Run down to the creek, and catch some trout." They were gone but a short time, and returned with a good string of trout. I saw her dress them, nicely, and put them into an old-fashioned frying-pan, minus butter, lard, or anything of the kind. She baked them in her pan, and put them on her table. She said, " Now, Elder, I cannot give you what I have not got; this is all we have, eatable." I sat down with her, asked a blessing, and we partook of the fish. It was, indeed, a " fish dinner." She remarked, " We should not have been so badly off, had it not been that my husband went down the river, and he is detained at tide-water. We expected him back some three weeks ago, and are looking for him every day. You must not be discouraged, and not call again, because we have so little." My heart was deeply moved, and my eyes could not refrain from weeping. We kneeled down and prayed, and if ever I felt humbled in view of the many excuses that had been made around my own table, when we were abundantly supplied with the necessaries of life, it was on this occasion. I left that house, I thought, a better man than I was when I entered it. Proceeding on my way, I reached my appointment in the evening, seven or eight miles below.

ANXIOUS HEARERS, THROUGH A THUNDER STORM.

On another occasion, not many miles from that place, I had an engagement where there were a saw-mill or two, and three log-houses. Preaching was to be in the afternoon. I had about eighteen miles to ride, at ten o'clock, A. M. My first offset was through a piece of woods, perhaps eight miles. I had not been in the woods long, before I heard it thunder. It was evident that it would be a shower of some magnitude, and, from the way it appeared to be coming up, I knew I could not escape. I rode through the whole of it, and the shower was traveling the same direction that I was. Arrived at my appointment in due time. My congregation, of course, was but small, but I had all that were around the establishment. They remarked, "The shower has been very heavy, sir." I said, "Yes." They said, "You must be very wet, indeed." "I am, but I am used to it." When we were together, I sang and prayed, preparatory to my sermon. After prayer, I saw that, during that part of my service, my congregation was increased by two females, apparently as much drenched with rain as I was. After service, I went into the adjoining room, (it was a double log house,) because there was a little fire there. When I entered, I found those two females standing by the fire. I said to one, "You had to come through the rain?" "Yes," she replied. "Ain't you sorry that you came to meeting?" She replied, "No sir, for I have not heard a sermon, until now, since I left York State."—"How long ago is that?"—"Three years, sir." The other one, added, "Nor I, either; the last sermon I heard, was preached in York State."—"How long ago, madam?"—"Over five years." My heart began to grow tender. I was sorry I had not given them more of the bread of life. After conversing with them a short time in relation to the interests of their souls, they remarked, almost simultaneously, "We heard of this meeting by accident: a man was passing through, and, among other things, he told about a meeting being here, and we concluded to come." I inquired, "Where did you come from—from what part?"—"From a little, new settlement, above, sir." I said, I did not know there was a settlement, anywhere above. One remarked, "It is about seven miles—seven miles, sir." "You came down on foot, did you?"—"O yes," was the reply, "and through the thunder storm." One said, "It was very severe, sir. When we got out to the clearing here, there were thirteen dry trees, burning, on the side of the mountain; they had been struck by lightning." I said to them, "You will not return, I suppose, until morning?" One looked me in the face, and, the tears brimming upon her eyelids, said, "We must go back, to-night, sir; *we have left our babies at home.*" That broke my heart, (and why should it not, as long as a parent's heart was beating within my own bosom?) I said to them, "Why, it is now five o'clock; you cannot reach your home before dark, can you?"—"Yes, sir, we shall get home, if all is well."—"I care nothing about it," said the other, "if we can only get through Wolf's Hole before night sets in." I parted with them, never to see them again. But such thirst for the waters of life, as was manifested by those friends, ought to put to shame thousands of professing Christians, who live within sight and sound of God's sanctuary, who, if it is not just so pleasant, and just so convenient, appear to opiate their consciences, and make up their minds that they are not called upon to go out to serve God under such unfavorable circumstances!

GETTING A PREACHING PLACE IN WILLARDSBURG.

My face was very soon turned homeward, taking Middlebury and Tioga churches on my way. This was a time of great interest with the latter body. My mind was much exercised as it regarded a common centre for that dear church, now largely increased by a group of precious converts. Its original location was Mitchell's Settlement, two or three miles below the village. Naturally, where a church is first established, there is an attachment to the locality, which some who live in the immediate vicinity feel reluctant to give up. It is like moving the ancient land-marks. My judgment was, that, for the church to grow, it must eventually have its rallying point in Tioga village, and for that I had thought, prayed, and labored. But whenever it was remotely hinted at, that Tioga would one day become the common centre, you could very clearly see that it disconcerted the older members. An empty house in the village I caused to be obtained for preaching, thinking that finally the members' minds might be turned so that it would appear to them duty, there to erect the banner of the cross. I do not say too much, (and the older Christians will sustain me in the assertion,) that the village was the hardest place to obtain a congregation, anywhere in that part of the country. Not that I mean to say they were sinners above all; but they had formed habits of Sabbath desecration; there was no charm in the Gospel to them; and Jesus was as a root out of dry ground.

It was very difficult, at my first outset, to obtain a place to speak in. But one gentleman, whom I have always highly esteemed for his kindness, said to me, if I would preach in his wood-shop, he would have the upper part of it cleared out, and he thought it would make a very comfortable place for meetings. I said to Mr. C., the owner of the shop, "It is a great favor, sir, for which I am very grateful, to God and to you." My first effort in my new meeting house was very scantily attended. The next thing that absorbed my mind, was, how shall I get a congregation? I hit upon this plan. Perhaps some of my brethren may think that there was too much of the human hand in it, but thus it was: I was preaching up the river from Tioga, down the river, and up Crooked creek, and my arrangement was for a simultaneous rally from those places, where I had good congregations, thinking perhaps I might provoke the people in the village to good works. I said to my friends in those localities, "Next Sabbath, at one o'clock, God willing, I shall preach in Mr. C.'s wood-shop, in Tioga. And now, can not a number of you, young friends, get up your teams, with as many as you can, and come into that place as near one o'clock as possible?" When the time arrived, I was on the look-out. I saw the dust rising a short distance down the river, and up the river, and up Crooked creek. They were driving like Jehu, showing their zeal for the Lord of hosts by their fast driving. They rounded to at the place appointed. Many of the people wondered what was the matter. The result was, I had a very large congregation, and from that day to this, whenever I have preached in that village, (which has been frequently,) I could never say that I wanted for hearers.

This church, since the days referred to, has passed through a variety of changes. They had the elements of a strong church—members, wealth, and position; but the greater part were located near the old hive. After some time, they agreed, I believe mutually, to build a house of worship in the village. It is well located, and adapted to the size of the village. And had they only remained united among themselves, they might have been the most prosperous church in any of these northern counties. But, alas! it has not been so. Difficulties of one kind or another would arise, and many became alienated in feeling. I thought, sometimes, they would become moral cannibals, against whom Paul warned the Corinthians: "For, if ye bite and devour one another, take heed that ye are not consumed one of another." But I bless God, that, amidst all their changes, there have always been a faithful few who would hold on to the promises. They have had a great many pastors, some prudent, and some I fear imprudent. Still, by the grace of God, they continue to this day, and I think in a better state than they have been for many years. My anxiety for this church and community has been very great. And how could it be otherwise? Here was the first door that opened to me in this State, and here God was pleased to give me a large portion of the richest sheaves I ever gathered for Him.

BRO. BROAKMAN BROUGHT IN.

In that first revival, while God was bringing in many of the more influential part of the community, there was one—a tall, lank-looking lad—who professed to be converted, but who was rough, and unprepossessing in appearance as could be imagined. When we were hearing experiences, he told his, but there was an unwillingness, on the part of some of the church, to receive him. Eld. Gillette had come from Elmira to aid me. I described to him the circumstances, and said, " Now, my brother, what shall I do? I believe the boy is converted, but I doubt whether the church will receive him. He wants to be baptized, and I am desirous to baptize him." He replied, it would not be exactly orthodox. But I would baptize him. I talked with some of the leading brethren, and told them what I should do. They remarked, it would be far better if all could be agreed. It appeared to me that they scarcely could help being agreed—that there could be nothing in the way to a just cause. He was received, and baptized. The poor young brother afterwards went to work in a lumber bush, and had one leg broken, but was kindly cared for by a dear family in that region. I have walked in sight of that young man these many years. Religion appeared to do everything for him, soul and body. He began to work at the carpenter's trade, and became a master mechanic —also a good English scholar (although a German)— taught school—was tried about his duty to preach— was licensed by the church in Tioga—manifested considerable adaptation to the work of the ministry—and was finally ordained, in Catlin, Chemung county, January 15th, 1851. I think, under the circumstances, he has become a good minister of Jesus Christ. He surmounted many difficulties, and remains to this day a brother (to me) much beloved. That was no other individual than the present Eld. S. M. Broakman.

THE REVIVAL IN SULLIVAN TOWNSHIP.

Another circumstance, not far from this time, occurred, to me of some interest. Having gathered together one evening at the old school-house on the bank of the river in Mitchelltown, I saw in my congregation a brother and sister I had known between the Lakes. The man was a Methodist, and his wife was a Baptist, of talent, and piety. In our conference meeting, after sermon, she arose and spoke through her tears with great earnestness, beseeching the people to spare the minister to go up into their neighborhood and preach for them. The brother, after she had got through, made some appalling references to the destitution and moral condition of the place. It appeared that there was a Baptist church, so called, but the pastor was a whiskey drinker, and believed that every day was alike; consequently, his children were often employed on the Sabbath, laboring, while the father was preaching. She concluded that they could not go home unless they had an appointment to take. I finally said to her, "My sister, have your kettle boiled, your tea-table set, and, precisely at sundown, I will, through Divine Providence, be at your house [on such a day.] Have my appointment for early candle-light." I had in company with me a young man who was studying for the ministry, and who kept an account of my appointments, when and where. He remarked to me, "You can't do it, Elder; we shall be in Potter county, the night before." The reply was, "I know that, my brother. But, if the Lord permits me, I shall fill my appointment as committed to those friends."

When the morning of the day came, I knew that it was not far from fifty-four miles to the place of my destination in the evening. We took a very early start; there was some snow on the ground, and we were on runners. We made pretty good time, until we got into the township of Middlebury, where the snow left us, and the hubs were pretty sharp, but we made out to arrive at Bro. E. Mitchell's. I told him I wanted dinner, or something to eat, and my horse fed, as soon as he was in a condition to eat. I added, "Now, Bro. Mitchell, can you lend me a saddle and bridle? I must be at Bro. Reynold's, at sun-down, this afternoon." I said that I would leave, in exchange for the saddle and bridle, my cutter, harness, and Bro. Smith. I got on my faithful old pacer, and (as we generally say) "put him through." Just as the sun was dropping below the foot of the horizon, I arrived at the place of meeting, and found everything, that could be desired, ready for myself and horse. It is seldom the missionary meets with a better home than was found there. I preached that evening to a very large congregation, in Bro. Reynold's house, and made appointments, after sermon, for the next day.

My impression is that I preached four sermons that day, (I know I preached three,) on the subject of faith and repentance. My sermon in the evening was at the same house where I preached the night before. It was a time of great breaking down. There were some present from the former named (would-be Baptist) church. They felt very intensely. One brother arose and said that he had been excluded for paying (I think it was) two-and-sixpence to the Tract Society; another said he had been excluded for joining a Temperance pledge or society; and so on. It was very evident that God was doing his own work by his own appointed agency in that place.

I left another appointment, but, before leaving in the morning, I said to Bro. Reynolds, "Now, my dear brother, God is going to begin a good work among you, and I feel an assurance, that, if I live to come back, I shall find some precious souls converted. Amongst them, I shall expect to find your dear little daughter. And now, my brother, if she is converted, it would be pleasant for her to go with you; but I expect, if soundly converted, she will want to be a Baptist. Do not stand in her way, but let her take her own course, and God will bless you both." His heart appeared to be broken, his head a fountain of water, and his eyes filled with tears, as he replied, "I have never asked God where my children should go, or into what church; but I have asked Him, a great many times, that He would convert them." We parted, I trust, well filled with the Spirit.

When I returned to fill my appointment, I heard, before I was well out of my saddle, from the lips of sister Reynolds, (for she came into the door yard to meet me,) "Our daughter is converted, we hope," and such a one, and such a one. After the evening service, we

heard the relation of their Christian experience, received the statements of some of the brethren who had
been excluded, (to whom I have before referred,) and
formed a kind of church nucleus, (I think we called it
a conference.) In the morning I was to baptize. It
was very cold, the streams hard frozen, and water near
by was rather scarce. I got up early, and said to Bro.
Reynolds, "Now, where can we baptize those candidates? The ice will have to be cut, and necessary pre-
parations made." He said, "It is all done, sir. I have
been and done it myself." That truly bespoke the
character of the man.

From that little gathering, I believe, the foundation
of the Gray's Valley Baptist church, (in East Sullivan,)
Tioga county, was laid. There was a Bro. Myron
Rockwell, who had trials about preaching. He identi-
fied himself, I believe, with this little body, and a son
of the brother at whose house I preached, I believe had
been baptized between the Lakes. Eld. Rockwell has
preached for them a great deal, and the young Bro.
Reynolds for years has been a consistent Deacon of
the church. The church on what is called the State
Road, might be termed an offshoot from that in Gray's
Valley.

It was still impressed on my mind that my labors in
Pennsylvania must very soon, in a great measure, come
to an end, and I hoped the young man whom I have
before referred to (then traveling with me,) would answer to fill my place in that mission field. He had no
cares, but just himself and horse, (which, by-the-by,
was a very good one,) and in this respect all appeared
to be favorable. He was ordained in one of my
churches in York State, in the town of Reading. He
entered upon his work, and I thought was pretty well
broken in for a young man. But, some way, he failed

for want of adaptation to the field: when the rough and tumble was left to him alone, he did not appear to be equal to the emergency. I would not imply by this that he might not be adapted to other fields of labor.

FORMATION OF BRADFORD ASSOCIATION.

During those years, Campbellism, with its baptismal regeneration, was flooding Northern Pennsylvania, and the billows were making a desperate effort to run over into Southern New York. In 1830, I think, it made its appearance as far north as Trumansburg, be-tween the Lakes. There was an old organization, called the Chemung Baptist Association, which became a perfect wreck by Campbellism and Antinomianism. The churches in Bradford county, and part of Tioga, Pennsylvania, appeared to suffer most, and indeed all of them have not yet got entirely over those days of adversity and alienation. Bro. Gillette exerted his in-fluence to save the remnant of the churches along the border, by finding a home in the Seneca Association, in York State. I remember Rev. D. M. Root, from Troy, in Bradford county, and brethren from Middle-bury and Tioga in Tioga county, from Wellsburg on the Chemung, and from other places, sought an asylum in the same Association. When the storms of error had in some measure passed over, the churches in Bradford county (with some from Tioga) rallied and formed the Bradford Association, about 1835. I be-lieve I was present at its first annual meeting, which was held in Columbia township, Bradford county, in a school-house on what was called "Baptist Hill," not far from the present house of the Columbia and Wells church. The venerable Davis Dimock, of Montrose, Susquehanna county, was present, and was chosen Moderator of the Association. Bro. E. Mitchell, of

16

Middlebury, had a connection living there, whom he
desired to see, and invited me to accompany him.
The Moderator was anxious that a sermon should be
preached on Foreign Missions, and that a collection
should be taken for the same. But it appeared there
was no one ready or willing to preach on that subject.
Bro. Mitchell arose and said he had with him a ministering brother, who, he thought, would preach, if invited. Eld. Dimock shook his head, and remarked that
error was prevailing so much, he wished one of their
own brethren would preach the sermon. He being
in the chair—though not a member of the Association—
and a man of extensive influence and known reputation, his words had great weight. However, no individual was found ready to preach on the occasion.
Bro. Mitchell again urged that the stranger with him
should be invited. I thought, " Why should not Eld.
Dimock, the chairman, preach it himself?" and proposed the thing. But that was waived, and I was
asked some questions relative to my views of missions.
I said little in answer, but remarked that I hoped, if I
should preach anything heterodox on the subject, the
Moderator would be kind enough to stop me, and I
would willingly desist and thank him for his honesty.
I received the invitation, and preached from Psalms,
72d chapter, 8th verse: " He shall have dominion also
from sea to sea, and from the river unto the ends of
the earth." The collection, I think, amounted to a
little over six dollars. It being their first effort, they
felt much gratified at what they had done. The
Moderator kindly and affectionately gave me his hand,
saying, " This is the doctrine, my brother, which we
want preached throughout all this region of country."
I thought the Association parted under very encouraging circumstances, and hoped and prayed that their

benevolence might grow with their growth, and strengthen with their strength. I have lived to see the day when that desire and prayer are in a great measure answered.

LINDLEY AND LAWRENCE—MR. AND MRS. MORGAN.

Another reminiscence of by-gone years puts my mind in connection with one I had known across the Atlantic. When referring to my difficulty on coming to this country without a church letter, I stated that there was a brother, residing in Philadelphia, who was formerly in church fellowship with me in the old country. I was almost as familiar, with his children, as with my own. In 1830, or thereabouts, I was much surprised by a gentleman and lady riding up to my door. Whom should she be but the daughter of my dear Bro. Bernard? She had married a gentleman called Col. A. C. Morgan. She had heard of me, and came to meet us again face to face. He had bought a large tract of wild land, and gone into the lumbering business at Lindley, near the State line. They gave me a very pressing invitation to visit them with my wife, and preach. In the course of time, a door opened, and for the first time, on that part of the waters of the Tioga river, I endeavored to speak for God. Col. Morgan was a gentleman of superior business talent, but was an unconverted man. When passing up and down, making my tours into Pennsylvania, it was often convenient for me to call and try to pay my way in preaching. My heart was much moved in relation to the place. I received a line from Mrs. Morgan, stating, in language the most encouraging, her hope that her dear husband was converted to God. I was going up the river very soon, when we had a pleasant interview. I left an appointment to preach on my return, when God was pleased in the multitude of His mercies to pour out His Spirit, and a number were hopefully converted. Things looked, to human observation, to be very fair for the growth of a comfortable little church.

REV. AND COL. PUTTKAMMER.

There was living with Col. Morgan, a German—a talented young man, of superior education—but his mind very dark as it regarded the plan of salvation. He had supposed he was all right, and safe for eternity, because the priest had made him a Christian when he was a little baby. However, it soon became evident that he was in trouble about his soul. I shall never forget the time when I took him by the arm, as we wended our way to the bank of that beautiful stream. Sitting on a fallen buttonwood tree, I endeavored to open unto him the way of eternal life through faith in the Lord Jesus Christ. He professed faith in Him. After some time, he left the employ of Bro. Morgan, and fell into the hands of another pious family. He soon became anxiously desirous to do something for the salvation of others, and would try to distribute tracts or anything in his power. But God appeared to have a duty for him, and to preach the Gospel became like a fire in all his bones. He became a member of the Lindley and Lawrenceville Baptist church. I had lost track of him for some years, when I heard that he was preaching to a German congregation in the city of Rochester. It was reported that he was the son of a German prince, and was exiled from his home and his country in consequence of having placed his affections upon a young lady in whose veins did not run royal blood. I did not have this from himself, for I never pried into his secret affairs, and he always appeared to be very reserved when conversing about his home and the events of his younger days. The next I heard from him was that he was the pastor of the German Baptist church in the city of Albany. But I have been informed that the same brother (Alexander Von Puttkammer) has since honorably served as Colonel of the 11th New York Battery in the Union contest against the Rebels.

CHAPTER VI.—1830 to 1860.

---

*Formation of Caton Church—Three Days' Meetings: Views as to
their Errors and Benefits—Labors as an Evangelist, Chiefly in
New York State—A Variety of Revival Incidents and Peculiarities—Chemung River Association—Protracted Efforts in
Caton—Trumansburg—Steuben County: Hunting Foxes up at
Babcock's: Backslider Reclaimed—Howard Flats: the Universalist Preacher, Struck Dumb: a Pentecostal Deacon, Con-
founded: Gunpowder Plot—Seneca Falls: Old Ship Zion—
Big Flats: Roads Blockaded with Gates, and the Guilt Con-
fessed: the Young Horse-Racer and Gambler—Yates County:
the Wicked Valley: Happy Change: Disturber Silenced—
Crooked Lake—The Agricultural Sermon: the Card Player—
Political Alienations: an Offended Member Prays Against his
own Church: Another Confesses his Annoying Partizan Songs
—A Church Opposes its Pastor as to a Protracted Meeting, but
Relents, and is Blessed—Rochester Meetings—How a Sign-Post
was Torn Down—Personal Appeals, or Individual Efforts—
Singing in Open Meetings.*

Having retired from my field in Pennsylvania in a
great measure, I was next on the look-out for some
other destitute place on the Southern tier of counties
in York State.

CHURCH IN NO. 1, (NOW, CATON.)

I was conversing with a brother, in the town of
Hornby, who tried to preach a little himself. He informed me that, in a remote settlement in what was
then called " Number One," now known as the town
of Caton, in the south-east corner of Steuben county,
there were a few brethren and sisters who had moved
in some years before. Remembering the day of the

covenant meeting of the church from whence they came, they met together, the same day, for conversation on the dealings of God with them. There were but few Christians in the settlement, the major part of the people being unconverted. He entreated me to go and see them, for it was a very rare thing for a minister to pass through that place. If I would promise to go, he would go with me. I could not state the time, but he said, when you get ready to come this way, call on me, and we will go over and see how they do. The first opportunity I had, I called on him, and said, "Can you go to 'Number One?'"—"Yes," he said, "do you want to go to-day?" I replied, "Yes, if we can get there in time to circulate an appointment for the evening." He said, he thought we could. We were both well mounted, but the day wore away so fast that I was afraid we should not be able to get many out. He said, "We can expect only a handfull of people." I remarked to him, "If we do anything, we must make a fuss about it."

As we entered the settlement, he said, "We will stop here." The day was very cold, and we both needed a stopping place. We inquired for the man and woman, or the heads of the family? They were not at home. There were some stout, lusty-looking young men, and one or two of the daughters who were well able to set the table. I began to talk about the state of religion, when one of the young men turned around to me and said, "We never have any preaching here, scarcely, and I don't care much whether we ever have any more such preaching as we have had, or not." I asked him if he was a professor of religion? He said he was. I told him I was glad of it, for I was a Baptist minister, and wanted to preach. He replied, "I don't think we shall care about hearing you. We have been taken in, here, too much, by strangers." I remarked to him that there must not be much time lost in getting out the appointment.

"I shall preach, sir, and I shall not notify the people myself." He said, "I should like to see your credentials." I told him my credentials he had no business with. "You are acquainted with the brother who is with me, and by him you have been sending invitations for me to come over and preach. I am come, and there is no time to be lost, parleying about credentials. And now, sir, I want you to start, and start speedily; and I want you should run, not walk, but run from house to house, just as fast as you can, and tell them that Eld. Sheardown is going to preach, to-night, at the Miller school-house. Now, don't you delay, sir."—"But I have not time," he said. "It makes no difference to me, sir, whether you have time or not. You have got to do as I tell you; and now, make all speed, and just give the notice; do not stop a moment at any house to talk, but do up the work effectually." I finally got him started. And he went like a rolling ball before the wind. He called at a certain house, and said there would be preaching that evening at the school-house. The lady said, "Stop! I want to know by whom."—"I don't know," said he, "he is the queerest fellow I ever saw. He almost swore that he would preach."—"Is he alone?" was the inquiry. "No, Bro. W. is with him."—"Well, then, it is Eld. Sheardown."—"I don't know, it is Shear-something; but I must not stop, or he'll be after me, as no fellow before ever was after me." He did the work faithfully, excited every individual he saw, and himself was a perfect eccentric. Perhaps no person who got the word, failed to be at the meeting that evening. My text was, "And thou hast well done that thou art come."

RELIGIOUS MEETINGS FOR DAYS.

That night was the entering wedge, that opened the way for my going again. I was solicited to go and preach three or four days, or as long as I could. They said the people would drop everything, and attend meeting, any time when I could make it convenient to come. I sent them word at what time I would be there. The appointment was made, and the few Christians were ready to go to work. We had a blessed season. Several choice spirits were converted to God. It was remarked, by many, that there were not more than two or three men in the settlement who were not converted, or under pungent conviction, and those few were scoffers. One, especially, would tantelize the pious by saying, " O yes, you have a great deal of feeling, now, for us sinners; but, as soon as Sheardown is out of the place, there will be no more praying for sinners."

A TEST OF FAITHFULNESS.

Something like a year or more after this, one of my good deacons was with me as we passed through that settlement, and I preached over night, ready to depart early in the morning. We started not far from sunrise. There was a little snow on the ground, the morning cold and chilly. Our course lay through a long strip of woods, on a road very seldom traveled. I saw some men coming towards us, and said to Deacon Overhiser, my companion, "There, I believe, come some of our Number One brethren;" and surely they were. We stopped and talked a few moments. I got out of my saddle and hitched my horse to a little sapling. The brother inquired, " What are you going at, Elder ?"—" I am going to have a prayer meeting here in the woods." I was very desirous to know whether those young brethren kept their mouths open for God, and it appears to me to be a very good time, for my own soul needed a morning baptism. There was a very inviting spot, a fallen tree, lying close by us. "Now," I said, "we will all kneel, here together, for a precious season in praying. I will lead the circle, and then the rest of you follow on. We will all pray."

After I had prayed, and the brother who was with me, I thought I heard the stepping of a horse pretty close by me. The thought flashed over my mind that one of our horses must have got loose. I looked up, and to my utter astonishment there were a man and horse standing still. The man had dismounted, and held his hat in his hand. I have seldom heard more fervent prayer put up for the unconverted sinners in the settlement, than had been lifted that morning, and by those brethren. When I rose from my knees, I at once recognized the man. I took hold of his hand, and said to him, "Now, sir, 1 hope you are convinced that praying for sinners, by Christians in Number One, did not cease when Sheardown left." He was pale as ashes, and trembled like a leaf in the autumn breeze. I have never learned whether he was converted after this, or not; we parted, and each went his own way.

There were some peculiarities about the meetings held in that settlement. We worked all day for God. Our prayer meetings commenced at five o'clock in the morning, no matter how dark or stormy. Some would bring their day's provisions with them; others would scatter to the nearest neighbors, and, (with the exception of two or three short recesses,) we would continue until nine o'clock at night. No wonder, in my mind, that God should bless such a people. They were soon organized into a church, and erected a comfortable meeting house. Like all other churches, they have waxed and waned, but, by the grace of God, they continue to this day.

THE STUBBORN HUSBAND BROUGHT IN.

There is one circumstance connected with that revival, worthy of notice. I stopped at the house of a Bro. Woolcot, near by the place of worship. A number had stayed there through the night. He had plenty of provisions, and, as it regarded the lodging, it made but little difference, for the soft side of a pine board was good enough for any of us. Among the guests, one night, was a female who hoped in the mercies of God, but whose husband was a very wicked man. She lived three or four miles from the place of meeting, and wanted he should let her have a horse to ride, but he refused, and was pretty abusive with his tongue. She had a baby some six or eight months old. She told him she should go to meeting, if she had to walk and carry her baby, which she did. I arose, as usual, in the morning, about five o'clock, to go to the prayer-meeting, and in passing the barn of my host (which stood close by the way-side,) thought I heard a singular noise. It was raining hard, and had been all night. I listened a moment to hear from whence the sound came, and found it was some person praying in the stable; it was a female's voice, and evidently in a great struggle of soul; the subject was her husband, and that God might so control him as to bring him to the meeting. My heart was stirred; I believed that God would hear her prayer; but at the time I did not know who she was. It came out in the meeting that it was the dear sister whose husband would not provide a way for her to attend. From report, he was a profane, wicked man. We had not been in meeting half an hour, before he came in—a large, heavy Dutch-

man, thoroughly drenched with rain. Before he had
got to the middle of the school-house, perhaps he meant
to kneel down, but he came down in our midst like an
ox from the felling axe. He told us he had started,
over-night, to come to meeting, and had been in the
woods, and in the fields, and all over, almost, except
where he ought to have been. His own remark was,
that he had been "lost all night;" and how he found
the place of meeting, he could not tell. The first thing
that he appeared fully to realize, was, that he was a
penitent, confessing sinner. He professed, in the course
of that little meeting, to have a hope in the Gospel of
Jesus Christ, which I trust he had.

PROTRACTED MEETINGS

Had now become very common in the churches. In
1830, I received the first invitation to attend a three
days' meeting with the church in Trumansburg. We
held services the appointed time, but were under the
necessity of stopping, because our time (which was
limited to three days) had expired. It was customary,
when such meetings were held, to invite ministers and
brethren, from neighboring churches, to come in and
help; consequently it made, in show, a great work, and
many indeed were the happy recipients of Divine grace
in those three days gatherings. But, no matter how
deep the work of grace appeared to be, we must dismiss at the close of our appointed time. There was a
strange infatuation among many of the brethren relative to doing God's work, and some even thought it
was presumptuous to have such meetings. I have often
closed labors, when my inmost heart was grieved. We
could see God *so willing* to work by his people, and
ready to save; then why should the work cease? But
extra labor for the salvation of sinners was then in its
17

infancy, and God must have praise that the eyes of the church were opening to the great duty of being workers together with him, let the time of special labor be longer or shorter.

I had well learned that the Gospel was the only power of God unto salvation, and, believing this, I saw the necessity of a more continuous bringing in contact the sinner and the Gospel. And holding, as I do, that all the power is of the eternal Spirit, in order to be the recipients of that power the church must learn to let go everything else, and labor in holy consecration and dedication to God, with an unshaken faith in His promises. Divine efficiency and human agency thus united together, will produce the desired end. I have lived to learn this fact, that, while without God we can do nothing, nevertheless, it is essential for us to do our duty, as it is for the farmer to till his ground and sow his seed, to be enabled to gather a harvest.

I also learned that it was not the best way for the church to gather in a great deal of aid·from abroad, because it appeared to divert the minds of the public, as well as the church, from the great, important *responsibility that rested upon each one.* They were continually finding fault with this sermon, or the other sermon; one liked this preacher, and the other liked that; and it was indeed as in the days of the Apostles, some for Paul, some for Apollos, and some for Cephas. It created in the·churches, as well as in the congregations, a kind of "itching ear." Some good ministers would be put very low, while others, who appeared to have greater gifts for talking, were valued just in proportion to the volume of their voice, and the multiplicity of their large words, though the greater part of what they said would perhaps have little or nothing more to do with the salvation of the souls of men, than the chattering of the crane has to do with the music of heaven. Hence, by degrees, it was found that the better way was for the pastor of the church, and one brother from abroad, to do the greater part of the preaching; it produced a better effect, and left a more abiding influence, than was attainable from all the foreign aid that could be brought in. It was necessary, at times, for some churches, that were in a very low state, to invite some good, Holy Ghost, praying brethren, and sisters, from the churches in the vicinity, to labor with them. But, as it regarded the preaching, after the novelty of the speaker had passed away, (which generally would in the course of a few sermons,) then the church and congregation would settle down calmly and dispassionately to listen to the truth that should be advanced.

This work appeared to be just suited to my views of the Gospel, with its adaptation to the necessities of lost sinners; and my whole soul went out after it. Consequently, a new field of labor, in this department, began to spread out before me. From this time onward, I was engaged more or less in such evangelizing labors. The little churches, which, under God, I had been enabled to raise, were now supplied by permanent pastors, (an account of which I shall give, more minutely, hereafter.)

It is a palpable fact that these special meetings did not always produce the desired good. And a variety of causes, in all probability, led to the failure. I think, for one, that the fault has been either in the churches, or in the evangelists: for, whatever passes through human hands, will in a greater of lesser degree be defective. While God works by agency, that agency must of necessity be of God's appointing. Wicked and designing men, perhaps, have sometimes palmed themselves off upon the churches; and on the other hand, churches have sometimes sought for men who were capable of getting up the greatest excitement. I believe that no individual was ever converted to God without being excited; yet there is such a thing as *genuine* excitement, and also *superficial* excitement. Some seem to think, if they can only have "the whirlwind and the fire," it is all that is necessary; but this whirlwind and fire do not appear always to be the means that God blesses to the salvation of sinners. Genuine excitement, I suppose, is occasioned by the truth of God operating upon the hearts of the children of men. Hence, the Gospel becomes the power of God unto salvation to them that believe. The effort to bring men to God, very often, fails, because there is more trust and confidence put in THE MEANS, than FAITH IN THE GOD OF THE MEANS; and the result will be, in every case, that more or less superficial professors, or unconverted people, will be brought into churches.

INJUDICIOUS MODES.

I remember, on one occasion, stopping in a village for the night, where there was a protracted effort going on. I was invited to preach, but declined, on the ground that I did not know the state of the meeting, neither did I know the class of Gospel truths that had been presented to the people. I tarried and heard the sermon, and think I was a prayerful observer of the *modus operandi* as it passed before me. I felt, under the sermon, as though I was standing close behind Moses when God spake from his burning pulpit on Sinai's trembling mount. The effort appeared to be carried onward without one ray of hope to illumine the dark, obscure winding to the very mouth of the fearful pit of long despair. No Jesus appeared, no invitation given, no up-lifted cross, no running blood to quench the fearful flame, or waters of life to cool the thirsty tongue! I anxiously looked for the result, for I felt under a hardening process. I could not see, in saint or sinner, any marks of deep contrition, nor any livening up of the consciences of God's professed children. When the sermon was closed, the anxious were called forward—all very well in inself, providing they had been really anxious for the salvation of their souls. Some few cold, stereotyped prayers, were offered, and the anxious were requested to rise, after which the leading spirit of the meeting said to those inquirers, "Now we are going to sing a verse, and all you who are willing to give your hearts to God, when we come to the clause,

'Here, Lord, I give myself away,'

bow your heads." Several of the anxious complied, and as soon as this was done the individual said, "Remain on your feet until I count you." His eye ran over them, and he then announced to the congregation, "So many more converted—so many more have given their hearts to God—so many more delivered from the power of Satan." I had but one ejaculatory prayer to offer, and that was, "From such awful deception, good Lord, deliver us."

There has probably been too much desire, in the hearts of many professed evangelists, to aim at numbers, so that, at the summing up of a few weeks' labor, it might look like a great work. And such individuals were sure to say, before they left the field, privately to some friends, "Now, just pass this through the papers, if you please, so that the churches may see, for their encouragement, what a great work of grace has been done amongst you," when in fact it was too evident, in a very short time after the close, that there had been but very little if any work of grace at all.

SCRIPTURAL EFFORTS, LARGELY BLESSED OF GOD.

Notwithstanding there has been a good deal of chaff among the wheat, nevertheless I believe, in my inmost heart, extra efforts, when rightly put forth, have resulted and must result in the salvation of immortal souls. Yet, in order for this, the truth as it is in Jesus must be proclaimed, attended by the demonstration of the Holy Ghost and power, and that will bring about this greatly desired end. Sometimes a church will send for an evangelist, in order that they may have what they call a good time. They will pray, sing, and talk, with a great deal of emphasis, but they do not appear to possess that peculiar state of mind which is necessary for them to be workers with God. It is often necessary, I think, in the first place, to *take away from the church all human dependence*, just as much as it is to endeavor to *take away the sinner's dependence,*- or that in which he trusts. I have never known it fail, in all my observation, that, whenever a church of Jesus Christ, under the proclamation of God's precious truth, was brought down at the feet of sovereign mercy, and was led to cry out, as did Rachel of old, "Give me children or I die"—I have always noticed, that, under those dying pangs and labors of soul, sinners have been converted to God, and Zion has been increased by an addition of living members.

NECESSITY OF UNION—HUNTING FOXES—UP TO BABCOCK'S.

I have before my mind's eye, a circumstance which may be worthy of narration, to show the importance of church harmony in working for the salvation of sinners. I was called, by a church in Steuben county, to hold a protracted meeting with them, and entered into an engagement to be there on a certain day, some weeks in the future. When the appointed time had come, I was traveling along to the place where I had been directed to stop, and had to pass the meeting house. Seeing horses, wagons, and everything to indicate that there was a gathering inside, I concluded to stop and see what was going on. I found it a prayer and conference meeting, appointed in order to have everything in a state of readiness to proceed with the work. After the little excitement of recognition was over, I requested them to proceed with their meeting. They sang beautifully, prayed loudly, talked freely, and appeared to be filled with joy and rejoicing. One of the deacons remarked to me, "Now, Elder, we are all ready to go to work. I do not think you ever met with such a church in your life. We are all right."— "You have told the truth, my brother," was the answer, "for it has never been my lot to meet with or see the church yet that was *all right*, just as God would have them." The reply was, "Well, sir, you will find that you have nothing to do but to go to preaching, and souls will be converted right away." Instead of this encouraging and quickening my faith, it had quite the opposite effect. But I gave out the appointments for the next day.

We commenced with a prayer meeting at nine o'clock in the morning, preaching three times a day, &c. I tried to preach as best I could, but my words appeared to be like the chattering of the crane or swallow. The unconverted came in, and filled the house to its utmost capacity; there was evidently a great deal of conviction amongst them; but not the first sign of any coming into the kingdom of Christ. I was conscious where the difficulty lay, and came to the conclusion that it was necessary to press home upon the church the truth of God in order to break that pleasing monotony of religious service that they appeared to be possessed of. I still found that they traveled the same round, like the blind horse grinding at the mill.

THE EVILS DEVELOPED.

After making a new consecration to God, and pleading for special aid, I concluded to preach a sermon to them of such a character as (I hoped) would tell in bringing them into the path of moral labor. After it was through, I remarked, " Now, brethren, I want you to go to Dea. Babcock's upper room, to-night, every one of you, and we will go to hunting foxes. I think we shall find some, either small or big." Some of the leading brethren appeared to be very much put out in consequence of so much being said about Christians before the unconverted, and manifested a great unwillingness to go to the place designated; they appeared to be parleying upon the subject. I remarked to them, " You can do as you please, brethren ; go to Babcock's, or let this be my farewell sermon with you. Suit yourselves." My dear Bro. A. C. Mallory was then spending some time with me, with the expectation of coming into the ministry.

After we had got seated in the upper room, the brethren declared themselves aggrieved, and wished that I had never come; they thought there was more harm done, already, than all the good could counterbalance that might be done, if the meetings should continue. Bro. Mallory arose, with his large heart and big tears, and said to them, " Do not be so hard, my brethren. Eld. Sheardown is a man of a great deal of experience and observation. I know him of old. He either sees or feels something that has led him to take the course he has." After his remarks, one of the brethren arose and said, "Now, do not make strange of this thing, brethren; you know, as well as I do, that there is difficulty among us. You know that I have not come to the communion in a very long time, and you also know that I very seldom meet with you on any occasion; and you know the reason why. I am not sure," he continued, "that this is the proper place to talk this business over, but I have carried it as long as I can." I remarked to him, "Bro. S., this is the very place and time. This work must be done before God can consistently bless." "Shall I tell it, then," said he, "just as it is?" I replied, "Yes, tell it, just as it is; untie the bag, and let all the cats out here in our midst; then we will try and take care of them."

This offended brother was a business man, and it was one of those hard seasons or crises in monetary affairs, of which he felt the pressure. The difficulty with the church, as then stated, was, that the various pastors they had had, for some years previous to this, were requested, if they thought proper, to do their trading with Bro. S., who was encouraged, that, if he would wait upon the pastor, they (the brethren) would take in their wool and corn and cancel the debt at the expiration of the year. This they had failed to do, year after year, until the brother became jaded in his feelings, and pressed in a pecuniary way, so that he was sore from head to foot. He was replied to by some of the brethren, that "we can not do it now; it is no time to talk up such things in a protracted meeting, and we have not come out prepared to meet anything of the kind." I remarked that it could as well be done then as ever, and asked the brother if he could give the amount due him. He said he could, and stated the sum total. I recommended that it should be raised on the spot, and wished them to take their own course to do it. They tried by subscription. One dear brother, broken down in his feelings, and subdued in his spirit, said, " Brethren, I do not feel able to do a great deal, but I am very anxious to get this whole thing out of the way. I will give fifty dollars, notwithstanding the long continued sickness of my wife, which, you all know, has been a great bill of expense to me." But, having failed in the subscription, "equality" was then talked up; and, by equality or assessment and subscription both, I believe, the amount was raised.

The next point was, when shall it be paid? I remarked, " It can as well be paid to-night, as any other time." The plea was they were unprepared, and it would require a little time to get the funds together to cancel the debt. I answered, " I know that, and perhaps one word from Bro. S. will decide the point at once." The question was put, " Are you willing, my brother, to take the obligation of these brethren, thirty days after date?" He said, " Yes."—" Now, then, for pen, ink, and paper; let those due-bills be drawn, and signed, here, to-night, and put in the hands of our grieved brother." All was done up. The church appeared to be humbled, and the brother satisfied. I then remarked something like this: " Now, my dear brethren, if there are any more foxes that spoil the vines, do let us have sight of them, to-night, that we may not be at the trouble of digging them out of their holes."

One other domestic difficulty was also settled by the church thus assembled. They felt they were chastised, appeared to bear it meekly, and said they believed there was nothing else of moment among them.

FRUITS OF RECONCILIATION.

I remarked, " Now, brethren, if your ways please

God, He will give us an evidence of it on the coming day, if we live. But what shall we expect as an evidence that all is right? There are a great many sinners in this place, under the most pungent convictions. Now, to-morrow morning, after sermon—for I do not wish to make any extra effort to bring about the end I have in view, but we will take this as an evidence that our ways please God—I will say to the great congregation, "Is there any individual here, who last night went from this house loaded down under a sense of a guilty conscience, as a sinner against God, and feeling as though he or she must perish unless God should have mercy upon him or her? Now, if there is one such present, who feels this morning that God has put away his or her sins, and who enjoys a comfortable hope in His pardoning mercy—rise on your feet."

When the invitation was given, five individuals, I believe, arose in different parts of the congregation. The Saviour had set the captive exiles free, and had put a new song into their mouths.

That was the beginning of one of the choicest seasons that perhaps I had ever experienced in protracted effort. The pastor of the church was a young man, not yet out of his studies at Hamilton; consequently, it fell to me to baptize the candidates. I think, as the avails of the labor of that dear church, in connection with the young man, and my unworthy self, I was permitted to baptize ninety-nine. A Presbyterian brother told me that he had devoted a great deal of time to riding through the community, and was perfectly acquainted for several miles around; he thought, from his calls, and personal conversation, in the meetings and out of them, that there could not have been less than near four hundred souls hopefully converted to God. They came from eight to ten miles distant, with their double teams, bringing in from ten to sixteen in each wagon, bivouacing for the day, going home at night only to return early the next morning. And I believe, to this day, it is a common proverb in that region, if there is any difficulty, in a family, church, or neighborhood, that they "ought to go to Babcock's."

A BACKSLIDER BROUGHT IN.

An item in relation to an excluded member of that church, and I shall leave it. He had adopted fatalism as the foundation stone of his creed—"that if a man was to be saved, he would be saved; and if he was decreed to be lost, he would be lost." He stated to the congregation, that, when he heard of the meetings, he made up his mind to attend every one in his power, and see how the machinery worked. "The first move," he said, "did not stir me, for I saw that those who were professing to be converted, were all young people, perhaps in their teens. The Elder said," (he remarked) "'Brethren, you see that God hears your prayer; that He is willing to bless: now let your faith rest upon the promises of God, and you shall see greater things than these.'" He continued,-"I watched with a great deal of interest for greater things. By and by, another class of people appeared to be coming in, but they were a class who I did not think were over-smart. Then the Elder jumped up again and said, ' Now, brethren, hold on upon the promises of God; keep very low at the Saviour's feet; talk but very little; pray a great deal, in your families, in your closets; nay, let your every breath be the breath of prayer: and you shall see greater things than you have seen.' I said to myself," he continued, "now you think you have done wonders. But I should like to see you take such men as Esquire P., our Supervisor, and that class of people. Then I

will begin to think there is something in it.   If I can
see them come forward and act in this thing, I shall
believe it is of God, because I believe they are honest
men, and they wont be drawn in by the shallow opinions that have induced those others to come.   To my
utter astonishment,," said the old man, "the first thing
I knew, behold there were Esquire P. and his wife,
weeping, upon the anxious seat.   I said to myself, I
am now taken in my own traps, but I will wait and see
how they come out.   Very soon, they were converted.
I can not gainsay their conversion.   I used to think
that I knew the power of religion upon the heart."   At
this point, the gentleman became bathed in tears, and
again he continued: "The next individuals I noticed,
were Mr. Beach, and some others whom I had singled
out as men who knew too much to be induced to make
a profession of religion without experiencing its power.
The controversy between myself and God's work had
to be given up.   I hope, my brethren, I shall never
live to get into that awful state of darkness and opposition to the works of the Lord again, for God is certainly in this place and I know it not.

UNIVERSALIST MISCHIEF-MAKER CONFOUNDED.

While Eld. D. M. Root was pastor of the church at
Howard Flats, he was very anxious to have some
ministerial aid, and I endeavored to assist him.   It
was another very sterile place in the great field, and
appeared to be almost impervious to the Gospel of our
Lord Jesus Christ.   We opened the meeting, not knowing when or how we should close, for God has never
permitted us to look into the future, or judge from the
outward circumstances.   I expected that the powers of
darkness would come up in solid phalanx against the
little host of God's elect.   We very soon had a house

filled to its utmost capacity, and the people listened to the truth with as much decorum as could be expected. The time passed along—brethren and sisters prayed, and, as usual, not very much affected by the scenes that were passing before them.

One individual always remarked in his prayer, "O, Lord! give us a pentecostal season—let us see things as they were on the day of pentecost!" I said to him, one day, "Do you believe, my brother, that God will answer your prayer?" He hoped so, he said, or he would not pray. I continued, "Now, Deacon, if the Lord should be pleased to give us but a small portion of the Spirit that was poured out on that occasion, I am afraid you might find yourself unprepared to receive it." The dear man felt rather touched by the remark, though I endeavored to make it as free as I could, that he might not think that we were doubting his piety or honesty: for I was well aware, if God should shake the heavens and the earth, there should be a terrible outcry when the adversaries of Zion should lay weltering in their moral blood.

I remarked, one day, to the congregation, "We have preached to you the twenty-seventh sermon, all bearing upon your duty to God, and the fulness of salvation to those who repent and believe; but you are yet unmoved. Now, on such an evening, (which I think was Thursday of the same week,) *I shall tell you the worst of it.*" On our way to the church, at the time indicated, some individuals fell in with us in the street, and one politely said, "Are you going to church, brethren?" One of our brethren replied, "Yes sir." I looked up into their faces (for I had paid but little attention to them previous to the remark,) and saw one of them was a Universalist minister. I said, "How do you do, sir?" He said,

" Very well. How is Eld. Sheardown ?"—" Very well,
sir."—" What meeting have you at this hour, sir ?"—
" Prayer-meeting, sir, previous to the evening services."—" What time do your evening services commence ?" He was told the preaching would commence
about half-past six. He remarked that he was glad to
have an opportunity to go to church. We went on
together. I opened the meeting ; he sang beautifully,
but did not appear to have any praying to do.

The prayer and conference meeting having closed, I
opened the more public services. My text on that
occasion, (for I was to redeem the pledge that had
been given—to tell them the worst of it,) was from a
part of one of the Saviour's parables : " The rich man
also died, and was buried ; and in hell he lifted up his
eyes, being in torment." As soon as I read my text,
the Universalist drew from his pocket or bosom quite
a large piece of paper, and commenced taking notes.
He wrote, probably as fast as he could, through the
whole sermon. I was samewhat acquainted with the
way in which the Devil very often undertook to dissipate the truth of God, by getting up an argument, if
possible, on the subject of salvation. When I closed
my sermon, I was led to deviate some from my common
course, and felt as though a season of prayer would be
the best thing for us under the circumstances.

An invitation was then given for some brethren to
kneel at the breast-work at the foot of the pulpit, and
pray for the anxious or inquiring sinners. Probably
eight or nine bowed down, and one brother led on in
fervent supplication for the unconverted. The brother
next to him was Thomas Clark, who was looking forward to the ministry, (and, some time after, was
ordained.) With other language, he uttered in his
prayer something like this : " O, Lord God ! here is a

wicked man, an infidel, I believe, who has been taking a schedule of the minister's sermon. If he shall rise to-night to endeavor to explain away the truth of God, when he shall look upon that schedule let him be struck with blindness." About this time, the Universalist came out of his seat, which was very near the praying group, with his paper in his hand. "O Lord," Bro. Clark continued, "if this man shall undertake to speak in order to cast dark shades over the truth of God, let him be struck dumb. O Lord, if he shall go into the Academy, next Sunday, to his appointments, and undertake to deceive immortal souls and lead them down to destruction, let him go swift down into the pit! But now, dear Lord, if there is a drop of mercy in the bowels of heaven for such a wicked sinner, may he repent of his sins, to-night, and God have mercy upon him!" I think I never felt more of the power of the Spirit of God under prayer, than I did while this dear brother was pleading with the Almighty. His prayer was lengthy, but full of the Holy Ghost and faith. Fearfulness and trembling appeared to take hold upon the congregation. When he said "Amen," they all arose from their knees, as though the mutual conclusion was that there was no more praying to be done at that time. The Universalist retired, after prayer, to his seat, paper in hand.

The next remark was, "Now, if there is a convert, or any dear brother or sister, who feels as though he or she had a word of exhortation, speak on." He came out of his seat, put himself in a speaking attitude at the foot of the pulpit—we were all looking, eyes and ears open, to see and hear what was coming—but not a word was said: he returned to his seat. One or two brethren spoke a few words. He came out the second time, and all eyes were upon him, waiting for what he had to say; but he said nothing, and returned. After another short season of conversation, he went through the same manœuver; and as he turned to go away for the third time, I brought my hands together and exclaimed, "*God be praised! my brother's prayer has been heard in heaven, and answered. The infidel is struck dumb!*" He took his hat, then left the meeting.

That was the last time I ever saw him. I have heard, since, that he was converted under the labors of Bro. Marsena Stone. If so, indeed he is a brand plucked from the burning. I do not know that I have any reason to doubt it. Still I have thought a great deal of a remark made by an aged brother who lived in the same place where he had lived. When I was relating the circumstance to him, he said, " I think, if he is converted, he had better come back on the ground where he has done so much evil. To me, it would have been far better than to go to the West."

THE NEW GUNPOWDER PLOT.

After this, things went on in peace for a few days. Our meeting-house was badly contrived. It was warmed by a large stove, which would admit wood perhaps three feet long, and stood directly in front of the pulpit. Consequently, when the house was full, it was necessary to let the fire go down until after sermon. The sexton (who was also a good deacon) managed the fire as best he could. I saw, one evening, he had not put in the wood—I thought, at all events, I saw the brick that closed the draft of the stove was not removed as usual. I spoke to the deacon, from the pulpit, in a low voice, saying, " Remove the draft; they are cold in the back part of the house." He came to me and said, " I dare not remove the brick, sir. I have been informed that there is somebody here who calculated to throw gunpowder into the stove." I said, "O no, such a man would be a bigger fool than Nabal." He removed the brick, and all went on right.

Next Sabbath morning, I went to church very early. Every person who has known me through life, knows that I am always among the first at the house of God. There was no one there but the sexton. He had on a very heavy fire. I said to him, "Deacon, you are warming things up this morning." He replied, "Yes, I came very early, on purpose, for I am aware that the people who come in from a distance will be very cold." We had been out of wood, and I had said, several days previous, to the congregation, "We want wood, the sexton says, and we will omit services this afternoon, and try and get some wood. We will make a wood-bee. I will go also." A brother remarked, "I don't know how we can get to the wood. It will take most all the afternoon to open the way through the drifts." I said, "There are a number of dry hemlock trees, standing not far off on a knoll, there in the field. I wish I knew who owned them, I would see if he would not let us have them to supply the church." A man arose and said, "Some of them are mine, sir. You are welcome to all you want. You may cut them down, and take the bark off. There is a green maple you may have, and the bark and the green maple will make very hot fires." I thanked him for his kindness, and told him we would accept his proposition. We had been burning this fuel some days previous to the Sabbath morning that I was praising the deacon for having such a good fire. He said, "Now I will go and fetch my wood, ready to put in the stove after sermon. When he came in with the second armfull of wood, which was laid down near the stove, I was musing, and looking at him piling it up. There was one stick that caught my eye. I said to him, "Deacon, where did you get that stick of wood?" He replied, "In the wood shed." I said to him, "That is not our wood." "I see it is not, sir," he said. "How came it there?" "I don't know," he replied. "Now, sir, there is something wrong. My impression is that there is a charge of gunpowder in that stick." His answer was, "O, no, I think not. It is a stick that has been used for something, and has had a pin driven through it." I said, "Hand it here; let me look at it." It was the quarter of a very good sized white beach, that looked as though it might have been cut and seasoned a year. The pin had been cut off with an axe, in doing which they had lightly glazed the stick, which showed that it was a very recent work. I said, "Lay that stick in the pulpit; I shall preach about it, to-day." He laid it in the pulpit, under the injunction that he should tell no man.

I had for the text, that morning, Zech., 4th chapter, and 7th verse: "Who art thou, O great mountain? Before Zerubbabel, thou shalt become a plain; and he shall bring forth the headstone thereof, with shoutings, crying Grace, grace unto it." While preaching on the subject of opposition and persecution that had been raised against the church of God, I remarked, "Perhaps our congregation will say, why talk about persecution? That belonged to the dark ages of the world. We live under a government that protects all religions alike." But I remarked, "I have an engine of death at my feet"—then stooped down, took up the stick of wood, (which I was not able to lift with one hand,) and said, "Now, this stick of wood was brought from our wood-house, this morning, and would have been put in the stove, after sermon, providing it had not been so very different from the wood that we are burning.

This stick, I have no doubt, contains a charge of gun-powder." The congregation appeared to be panic struck. I saw a few individuals turn very pale. I asked, "What is the matter with some persons in our congregation, that they look so pale and nervous? Is the poor, wretched, dastardly coward, who has committed this wicked and diabolical act, among those pale faces? What would have been the consequences? Look here—if you are in the congregation, you miserable wretch of wretches—see this dense crowd! look at these mothers and children, crowded around this stove, the mother with her infant in her bosom, others with their little ones by the hand! Why do you want to kill those mothers and children? to tear this house to pieces, and destroy God only knows how many lives in this congregation? If I am the one you are after, you know my path. I cross this little field every night almost, in the dark, when I go home to the pastor's house. Why not have taken your rifle and have picked me off on my way there? The Devil would have called that manly action; but all hell would be ashamed of such cowardly, wicked work, as this. Now, I want a committee appointed, to examine this stick of wood, and report, this afternoon, how much gunpowder they find in it. I do not want one Christian on that committee. All you citizens who are men of character, are fit persons for such an investigation." Four or five gentlemen volunteered to examine it, and the report (in the afternoon,) was, that there were in the stick of wood at least two large musket charges of powder, which might have destroyed, for what I know, half of the congregation.

I was informed, some time after, by Dea. F., that a certain individual "came up missing" that afternoon, and had not been heard from since. The Devil's agent had outdone his master. The Lord poured out his Spirit most gloriously, and I trust eternity will reveal many precious souls as sheaves gathered at that meeting for the garner of the Almighty.

THE PENTECOSTAL BROTHER, ASTOUNDED.

One word more about the pentecostal brother, and I dismiss the present narration. When the long gathering cloud was about to break upon us, probably there might have been over fifty, in different parts of the congregation, at the same time, crying out for mercy, or entreating to be prayed for. Stout men were on their knees before God. But, in the height of the excitement, our astonished church member exclaimed, "If this be religion, I do not want it." I replied to him, "Do not undertake to steady the Ark of God. Remember Uzza!" And, in a moral sense, I think he shared Uzza's fate, for I do not recollect his praying again in the process of the meeting.

THE "OLD SHIP ZION."

I had been holding a meeting with the church in Phelps, Ontario county, under the pastoral care of Rev. I. Bennett. When I closed there, I was solicited by Rev. Z. Freeman, then pastor of the church, to assist him, at Seneca Falls. It was in the spring of the year, (in March.) We opened our meeting with some prospect of good. Every person acquainted with Brother Freeman knows something of his untiring labor in his calling. He said to me, one morning, " I wish you felt like taking a walk with me." The reply was, " I suppose a walk would do me good, but my mind is very heavily taxed." He replied, " Let us take half an hour's walk, and it will clear your head some." After we had walked a short distance, he said, " I wish to call here—and that is the great object I had in view

when I invited you out—to see if we could not make
an impression upon Capt. S." I inquired his business.
He said he had quite an extensive boat-yard. I asked
him if he thought he was from the banks of the Cayuga?
He said he believed he was, and that his father before
him worked more or less at the same business. I told
him, if so, I had formed an acquaintance with his
father, the first year I was in the United States: he
lived on what was called Crowbar Point. "No doubt
the same man, my brother. His wife, I think, is a
very excellent woman, and he is a fine man, but unconverted, and my great business is to see if I can induce
him to come out to meeting." We made our call, conversed with his wife, and had an interview with him,
but he said it was not possible for him to attend, as it
was almost time to open the canal, and he had a vast
amount of business to perform before that time. He
had quite a number of hands working in his yard.
Among them were several ship carpenters from New
York.

We had about given up the hope of making any inroads upon them, because they could not be induced to
attend the meetings. Near by was a Methodist brother, one of the excellent of God's earth, who frequently
called upon me. While out to dine one day, he was
present. The conversation in the first place turned
upon his former occupation: he had once been a Captain of a North River craft, but at that time (if my
memory is correct) was an agent for some house in
New York, buying flour, and perhaps other property.
After this conversation, he began again to lament over
the condition of that yard full of men. He thought it
was very bad that they could not be induced to come
to meeting. I told him, if he would do what I would
require of him, I thought that they could generally be

moved upon to attend. He said he would do anything that lay within his power. I told him he could certainly do what I required. He replied, "1 suppose, sir, you would not make any unreasonable request." I said, "No, by no means." The difficulty in my mind was, not so much in drawing the people out, as it was whether we had faith enough to hold them after they had once come. He said, "Well, sir, name it, and I will do my best." I said, "My brother, I want you to see Capt. S., if you can, before you make the effort: ask him the privilege of saying a few words to his work hands, just at the time when the bell rings for dinner. I want you to be on the bow of some boat that is on the stocks, and sing out to the men, just as you used to when you were acting in the capacity of captain on board your vessel—say to them, that there is a man preaching on the other side of the river, or outlet of the Seneca, at the Baptist church, and if you will oblige him with your presence, on Thursday evening, he will preach about 'Old Ship Zion;' he will take you from her keelson to her maintop-gallant-royal. He is very desirous of having some hearers who might detect him in his errors, and give him some information. Now, boys, will you come, Thursday night?"

He did his work, and they came, almost to a man. The text was 107th Psalm, last clause of 3d verse: "So he bringeth them into their desired haven." After going through with the sermon, while a short time was spent in conversation and prayer, I was circulating among the congregation, looking for those men. I took one by the hand and said, "I am indeed glad to see you, sir." While I was holding his hand, I saw marked upon his arm, (for his sleeves were partly rolled up,) an anchor and cable, and remarked to him, "Where was that put on, sir?" He said, "On the other side of the

Equator." I told him I was very happy to meet a man who had crossed the line, because he might be able to point out to me some deficiencies, no doubt, in my discourse. He replied, " Captain, you have seen a ship more than once." Having passed a few remarks with him, I left him, to look after others. Speaking with him the second time, I observed, " Sir, I suppose you are aware that I have left out one of the most important things about the vessel." " I think not, sir," was the reply, " I don't recollect anything. I think you have done all that Mr. Kennedy said you would do." I said nothing pointedly to them in relation to the salvation of their souls, for I deemed it inexpedient just then.

When I returned to my pulpit to dismiss the meeting, I remarked, " I have made a very grand mistake, in leaving out one of the most important things connected with the ship; and to-morrow night, if God will, I will tell you what it is. I wish to have your presence again." I took for my text, next evening, " Which hope we have as an anchor of the soul, both sure and steadfast, and which entereth into that within the veil." Their feelings had become enlisted, and they generally attended with us. But, after all, my heart felt sad—I did not know that any of them had been benefited for the eternal world.

Some years passed. I was about leaving home to attend a meeting, six or seven miles down the river from Owego. A person having died four or five miles from my home on the road which I was to travel that afternoon, a messenger came after me to preach the funeral sermon. I promised, on my way I would stop and attend the services. I was intimately acquainted with the greater part of the people who lived in that settlement, and, when I drew up to the school-house, saw a horse, sulky, and harness, which were different from anything I had seen in that neighborhood before. While I was hitching my horse, and thinking whose establishment that could be, a gentleman came up to me, took me by the hand, and manifested a great deal of pleasure at meeting me again on earth. I said to him, "Sir, there is something in your countenance that is familiar, but I do not know you." His eyes filled with tears as he said, "Do you not remember, sir, when you were in Seneca Falls, that the carpenters of the boat-yard were invited to attend your meeting?" I said, "Yes, sir, very well. I passed through scenes there that are fastly riveted upon my memory."—"You recollect, then, sir, no doubt, preaching about 'Old Ship Zion.'" I said, "Yes, sir, very well indeed do I remember the two nights I preached on that subject." His tears flowed as he added, "I was induced, by those two sermons, to set my foot on board that Ship, and I bless God that I am permitted to see you. I feel, now, as though I am bound for the desired haven. I was passing by here, and saw the people gathering. I asked them the cause, and they said Eld. Sheardown was expected to preach a funeral sermon." He continued, "It struck my mind that it might be a great deal of comfort to you, if you could know the fact, that one poor soul, at least, was blessed by that effort. I want very much to stay," he said, "but I cannot. I am out here picking up timber for boat-building; my hands have already gone on into the woods, and I must immediately follow them." I hope, when "Old Ship Zion" rounds-to at the pin-head in Glory, I may meet him there!

UNLAWFUL DISTURBANCES, OVERRULED.

Perhaps it may be thought by some that it is hardly compatible with the design of a sketch of my life, to
19

be incorporating so many protracted meeting incidents. But they are an essential part of my ministerial career, and to me at least are full of interest. One who has spent much time in evangelizing, might fill a volume with sketches which he considers profitable reading and worthy of a permanent record. I will venture to narrate a few more.

In January, 1839, I was invited by Rev. A. Jackson, then pastor of the church, to labor at Big Flats—a field well known to me as the old stumping ground of my dear Bro. Gillette. Before he had got through describing the state of the community, and the situation in which the church was with some exceptions, I feared it would be pretty hard work, inasmuch as at the time I was well worn with previous labors. 'But I agreed to meet them at their appointed time, and do what I could.

A few days after the meeting had opened, early one morning, one or two of the brethren came to me and said, "Now, Elder, we must close these meetings." The inquiry was, "What is the matter?" "Why, last night, sir, after the meeting was out, as the teams were going home loaded with our families and friends, we found that those large farm gates, with their big sweeps, fences, rails, &c., were laid zig-zag across the roads; and it is a thousand chances to one, that half of them were not killed."—"Well, brother, who was killed? who lamed? whose horses' legs are broken?"—"Why, through a merciful Providence, there was nobody injured, but they run a very great risk—too much to run again." I remarked, "If this is all the faith in God that you possess, I should not wonder much if the Lord should see fit to suffer some of you to be killed, for being so frightened and cowardly, while you acknowledge that He was on the side of His people. I won't give my consent to close the meetings. I have never known a great work of grace, but what the Devil got very mad. If God helps me, I will try and preach here until my bones bleach on the moral battle field, or we shall see things in a different shape."

Elder Jackson was a good man to stand up in the face of the enemy, and my heart felt encouraged that God would work by His people as soon as He consistently could. We soon had evidence that God was *convicting* men of their sins. Every day the work appeared to deepen and widen, and soon we began to rejoice that He was also *forgiving* sins. One peculiarity of the meeting was, that orthodox Christians living in that community, of different sentiments, took right hold of the work, apparently forgetting, for some weeks, the peculiarities of their respective denominations.

One evening, a female was converted, and felt very anxious for the salvation of her husband, but he appeared not to be able to pass the strait gate, though evidently under deep conviction. He remained so for some time. I questioned the woman, (believing she was converted, and would tell the truth,) if she knew what was the difficulty with her husband. She said she did not. I inquired what had been their habits of life. She said that he often spent his Sabbaths in fishing, hunting, &c.; yet, from all that I could learn from her, there appeared to be nothing in the way of his coming into the kingdom of Christ, providing he was honest in the feeling he manifested. I saw him the next day in the congregation, apparently very deeply exercised; I pressed through the crowded house to the slip where he sat, talked with him, gave him such advice as was with me at the time, prayed especially for him, and he prayed vocally for himself. Still there appeared to be no God at hand. During the next services, he arose and exclaimed, "Shall I tell it? Shall I tell it?" He again exclaimed, "I must tell it, or go to hell." I remarked, "Tell it, be what it may." He exclaimed, at the top of his voice, "I am the man who helped to put the rails and gates in the roads!" I observed to him, "You say you helped: now tell who aided and abetted in the work? Who assisted you?" He paused and looked around. I said, "Tell us who helped you, or you will, after all, I am afraid, go to hell." He commenced naming certain individuals in the congregation, who must have felt as much ashamed as though they had been caught in their neighbor's sheep-fold.

There was another very singular circumstance connected with that meeting, which shows the power of God in his mysterious way of dealing, oftentimes, with very wicked men.

THE HORSE RACER AND GAMBLER, ARRESTED.

One day, after the afternoon services, I was going to a house close by my stopping place, (which was with one of the blessed good Deacons of that church.) The day was cold, stormy, and snowing. A youngerly kind of a man, a perfect stranger to me, said, after we had passed out of the house, "I am glad, sir, that you are taking in hand that dancing school at the village: it exerts a very deleterious influence on your meeting. I hope the committee will be successful, and may prevail with the landlord to postpone the dancing, at least until after your meeting." I had hold of his arm, and as we were passing along I remarked to him, "Sir, do you profess religion?" He said, "No, sir, I do not. I am very far from that."—"I wonder, sir," was my reply, "that you feel so much interested for the welfare of other individuals, and you yourself have no part or lot in the great matter of salvation." He said, "Now, sir, I will go back to the church," (where many were tarrying for the evening services.) I asked him to go and take some refreshment with me, and told him he would be welcome. I was very desirous to know more about his case, but he finally returned to the church, saying, "I hope to see you again this evening."

I found him, when I returned, on his knees, with a number of brethren around him, praying alternately for his salvation. I went into the seat, kneeled by his side, and prayed, after which he remarked, "I want to speak a few words to you, sir. I should like to tell you who I am, and what I have been." He remarked, when in conversation with me, "I was born in Connecticut; my father and mother were Methodists, I believe very good people. We used to have prayers in the family when I was a lad at home. I had a great passion for riding horses, and when my father and mother left me at home alone, I would get father's horses out, take them into a back field, lead one, and ride the other, and thus try their speed at every opportunity. I became quite an adept at riding." I think he said when he was in his twelfth year, his father and mother went from home, (whether to be gone for the night or not, I am not able to say,) and there was horse-racing, something like a mile from where they lived. His father, he said, charged him, over and over, "Now, you must not run away and go to those horse races." He promised he would not, but, as soon as he thought they were sufficiently out of the way, he started for the ground. This was the last day. There was an animal called the "Little Virginian": her owner was very anxious she should run, but he could not find a rider light enough. The lad listened to the conversation, stepped up and said, "I will ride her, sir." The man inquired, "Are you in the habit of riding horses?" He said, "Yes, sir, and I can make that little mare do her best." He was engaged to ride; he rode, and won the race. The owner of the mare kindly said, "Now, my boy, I want you, and I will make a man of you, if you will come with me. You shall be my rider. Now, will you go?" The boy said "Yes." "Well," said the man, "we must go right away." And so he concluded to go, and kept traveling down South as far as New Orleans.

"My employer," he said, "always took me with him; I lived as he lived, and he treated me no doubt as he would his own child. He gambled a great deal: it was about his main business, when he was not engaged in racing. I learned to gamble; he taught me all the arts and tricks he was acquainted with. I finally thought I was a master hand, and, seeing him often take great piles of money, I concluded to begin for myself. I commenced," he said, "on my own hook, and from that day almost to the present, it has been my business, more or less. Sometimes I was very rich, and sometimes very poor, without the means of getting a meal of victuals."

I asked him, "Did you ever attend church while you were engaged in this nefarious business?"—"Yes, sir; gamblers almost always attend church; it is a very good cover for a gambler; if you are seen frequently at church, people will not be so suspicious of you."—"Well, sir, when did you quit gambling?"—"I came into this region of country, several months ago, perfectly broken down. My means were all gone, and when I tried to gather up, everything turned against me. I was at Wellsburg, and used to hear Eld. Brown preach. He often spoke to me, when I would give him an opportunity, and talked on the subject of religion. That was very favorable for me, because Wellsburg is a small place, and a man is very easily found out in those little villages. I thought to myself, I had stayed there long enough : I could not effect anything, and came to Big Flats, where I thought I must do something. I concluded to go to work in the broom manufactory."

"All was going on with me, sir, as usual. But I dreamed, last night, that I was in Wellsburg. I heard a person say, ' Eld. Brown is dead; they have sent for Eld. Jackson to preach his funeral sermon.' I concluded to go to the funeral. The corpse was brought into the meeting house, in the coffin. I heard Eld. Jackson preach. After the sermon was over, Eld. Brown rose up in the coffin, pointed to me, and said, ' Sir, I have warned you to flee the wrath that is to come, and now God has permitted me so far to rise from the dead as to give you the last warning. If you do not repent, now, you never will repent.' While I was pondering it in my mind whether I should repent, now, or wait a little longer, something (I can not describe it) came, caught me up in his talons, and carried me off with all rapidity : just as I came in sight of the most awful place I ever saw, I wope up. I felt sick. I was boarding at a Baptist woman's—a member of this church. When I came down stairs in the morning, she remarked to me, ' Why! you look like a dead man : what is the matter? are you sick?' I paused, I did not know what to say. I said, ' No, not really sick : I had a very strange dream ; it appears to have unmanned me.'—' What have you dreamed?' I commenced relating it. Just as I had got through with the narrative, a lady came in—I believe she is a member of this church, too—and said to the woman with whom I was boarding, ' Have you heard the news?' ' No, what news?' ' O, dear Eld. Brown is dead, and they have sent for Eld. Jackson to come and preach at his funeral.' " He continued, "I was crushed down. I sat down, and felt as though I had not power to stand up. I concluded, at once, if I was able I would try and come to this meeting—that, after all, the warning of Eld. Brown might have that impression upon my mind, that should make me a good man—that I might serve God."

After our conversation, it was imperative that I should take hold of the meeting, preparatory to the sermon. In the course of that evening, while some brother was praying, the young gambler was hopefully converted. Then, his great anxiety appeared to be, "Are my father and mother alive? Have I broken their hearts? May I never see them again? I have never written to them, and have never heard from them since I left. But I shall see them, if they are alive, as quick as I can get there." I remarked, "I will have a further conversation with you, sir." I inquired for him the next day, but was informed that he had started for Connecticut—he could not rest until he knew the fate of his parents. I thought, in view of this occurrence, "God preserve our children, our young men, from the dark and wicked pathways of the horse racer and the gambler!"

GOSPEL TRIUMPH IN A DARK PLACE.

It was always gratifying to have a call to preach the Gospel in places where sin and wickedness abounded, because, (I have thought) some ministers appear to studiously avoid them. And indeed we often find, in some of those lesser places, the deepest sinks of sin and pollution, anywhere on this side of the kingdom of darkness.

I had an invitation to go to a certain place in the

State of New York. The person who invited me, said, "Now, sir, I want to tell you the truth. It is the wickedest place, probably, in seven counties. I don't know whether you will be able to preach or not. Things have been in a very bad shape there for some time. But something must be done, or the wicked will tread the little church beneath their feet. I made some inquiries to know what the great difficulties were. He said there was a class of men who feared neither the laws of God or man. They had almost driven every minister, who had tried to preach there, from his pulpit. I was somewhat acquainted with the brother who had been trying to preach to them, and believed him to be a very good, but by no means a great man. His knowledge, perhaps, of human nature, was not large, and he had been badly used.

I came to the conclusion that I should try what could be done. I rather feared to open the scene entirely alone, for I was informed that they had given notice that an Englishman would preach at their meeting-house, the next Sabbath morning, and also that there was a combination, embracing both males and females, who sometimes had gone so far as to use a large syringe and throw from it dirty water into the minister's face, while preaching. They had been prosecuted again and again, and fined from twenty-five to seventy-five dollars; but they would club together, pay their fines, and very soon get up another insurrection. I concluded to stop in a neighboring town, where I was intimately acquainted with the Baptist church and their pastor, the Rev. J. H. Stebbins, (a choice young brother—a man after my own heart,) and try to get, from some of the leading brethren, consent for him to be present with me at the opening of the meeting. They cheerfully consented, and he as willingly accepted my invitation.

We arrived at the place, on Sabbath morning, about ten o'clock. The church was not enclosed by any fence; the lower pannels of the outer doors were broken in; and the vagrant sheep appeared to have enjoyed the shade of God's house and made it their place of retreat from the flies. There were a few old sheds, but they were so near falling down that we dared not hitch our horses under them, but tied them to a fence, and went to reconnoiter the inside of the house. There was no sign of a path, through the grass-plot that was spread out in front of the sanctuary, and no marks of life, inside or out, except that of sheep and cattle. I said to my brother, "This is a hard looking place."

Time arrived for meeting, but no person came. I was examining the inside work, and saw a hole in the front of the pulpit. I put my eye to it, and could see a small glimmer of light from the outside. I said, "Bro. Stebbins, look here: this has been done by a rifle ball." After examining it, he concluded that it was indeed a rifle shot; it had passed through the front of the pulpit, between the studs and through the siding.

While we were pondering those things in our minds, and what would be the result of labor in that place, an old gentleman came in. We inquired of him, "Is there meeting here to-day? We thought you were to have an Englishman to preach here."—"Well," said he, "we had some ground to expect it, but I presume he has heard of us, and will not come. If he is wise, he'll never show his face in this place." I asked him what hole that was in the front of the pulpit? "O," he said, "it was made by a wicked man who swore he would shoot God Almighty's house down." We asked him if it was in the time of service? He said, "No. What few of us were here, had just got out of doors."

About this time, one or two others came in, and, a little before noon, we might have had a dozen hearers. I said, "Now, friends, I am the Englishman for whom the notice was given to preach here, at half-past ten this morning. For some cause or other, there are but very few present. However, we will sing and pray, and then I will try and preach a short sermon to you, after which I will tell you what I want you should do. After preaching, I said, "Now, I want you should run around among your neighbors, see every person you can, and tell them that the stranger is here, and will preach this afternoon, at two o'clock, and he wishes everybody who gets the word to come out and hear him." They stirred the turbid pool, and several came out in the afternoon. We made another appointment for the evening, when the congregation was much larger.

I went right on, and made my appointments for Monday, paying no attention whatever to what we had heard. The house which was assigned for me as a boarding place, was a very good place. The man was very eccentric, and could drop down from the sublime to the ridiculous the quickest of any one I ever saw. One specimen of his peculiarity will suffice. We were attending family prayer, and before rising from our knees he turned around upon his knees and exclaimed, "Elder! was not that a fine roast pig we had for dinner, yesterday?" Notwithstanding all this, some of the family were pious, and it is seldom that an evangelist, in such a place, meets with a better home.

We asked the old man in relation to the trouble that they had, and why they could not hold meetings in peace? He remarked, "I can not tell you anything about it, because I can not tell it bad enough; but if

you do not find it out, to your sorrow, I shall wonder."
I know no other way than to pray and keep the
powder dry.

On Monday, everything went off very well. Tuesday, not anything occurred very bad. I preached
three sermons each day. I think it was on Wednesday
afternoon that I saw them passing around slips of
paper in the gallery. Things looked to me as though
the hosts were marshalling for an attack. I stopped
preaching suddenly, and said, "There, now! there is
always something troubling me when I am trying to
do good. There flashed across my mind what I had
heard on my way to this place. You do not know me,
here. I never was through this hollow but once in my
life, and then I was on my way to Rochester, and made
no stop. But in the towns, South and East of you, I
am considerably acquainted; and it is always customary, when I am in any of those places, and they
know I am on the travel, to ask, 'Where are you going
Elder?' I answer, to such a place. When on my way
to this place, I was asked, 'What are you going to do
there?'—'Going to hold a protracted meeting.'—'Why,
you cannot do anything there: they will skin you.'—
'Very well,' I would reply, 'God permitted me to have
a skin, and if he permits the Devil and his emissaries
to tear off my skin, I wont find fault.' Others have
asked the question, 'Where are you going?' and when
I have told them, they would say, 'Why, it is impossible to do any good, there: I think it is the wickedest
place on God's foot-stool.' I observed that I did not
know anything about how wicked the people were; I
had heard that they were a wicked people; and where
shall we go and not find wicked ones? The final answer was, 'Well, try it, and if you come out with a
whole shirt or a whole hide, I shall wonder.' This is

the character you have abroad, in the neighboring towns. These are the interrogations and sayings I have met with, on my way hither. Now, I want to be able to say, hereafter, that I cannot vouch for it that one word of all this is true. So far, you have treated me as kindly as I could have expected to be treated. And I want to say to you, if you are the people as represented to me, I shall find it out. But there is one thing more. I profess to be a Christian minister, and I hope a gentleman in manners; and now I wish you to watch me with all interest, and if you hear me say anything, or see me do anything, that you think beneath my character, as a minister or a gentleman, just come right to me: I will gladly receive you. Point out my fault, and convince me of my wrong, and I will get down on my knees to any of you, if it is a child five years old whom I have injured, and confess all my faults, for I have no business to act wickedly. Now, keep your eyes steadily on me, and your ears open, to see and hear all that is said and done." I saw that they were calmed, so I proceeded with my sermon, and closed the day without the least sign of a break out.

The meeting continued well for a day or two, when I saw the same evil spirit manifesting itself. I stopped suddenly again, and said, "Now, what do you suppose I am thinking about? The miserable things that I told you before, are now troubling me again, though in a somewhat different way from the first time. I am now thinking what those people will say to me on my return, (for I shall pass through some of the same neighborhoods that I did in coming out.) You have treated me very kindly, I feel very happy amongst you; every one looks pleasantly at me; I am well cared for; and I expect, when I go back, I shall tell a story that will startle the people a great deal more

20

than the stories, I heard on my way out, startled me. I think I shall have it to say, that I have seldom fallen among a people who have treated me more kindly, or heard me preach more patiently, than you have in this valley; and I expect, that if people shall again tell me this bad thing and the other bad thing of you, I shall be able to reply that I left here at such a time, and must say the people are not deserving of the character you are giving them. I believe I shall give a very different report of this place, than, perhaps, has ever been given before. Now you watch me, so that I do not do wrong, and tell me of it if I do. I will watch you, and if you do anything wrong you cannot help but acknowledge that I have a right to demand the same from you that you demand from me. We are going on in peace, as we have so far. I am going to do you good, if I can. And I pray that I may not be left to do you any harm. We have met as friends, we will try and part friends, and I know I shall give a good report of you when I leave this place. Now I will finish my sermon, and I hope these things will never trouble me again while I am with you."

That evening, or the next, when the meeting was dismissed, I heard a man call out in the darkness, "Where is the Elder?" with a prefix, that I will not name, to the word "shame." I concluded, of course, that the one inquired after was myself, and said, "I am here, who wants me?" A man came up to me and said, "It is a shame, with so many folks here, for you to have to walk to Mr. ——'s such a dark night as this. We have got a carriage here, sir: wont you ride? We don't go your way, but that is nothing; we can soon take you home, and turn about and come back." Perhaps there might have been four or five in the carriage, (for it was what some folks call a wagon.) As soon as we were fairly in the road, the driver cracked his whip, the horses sprang with a will, and I said, "That is right, sir; I always feel safe with a good team and a good teamster—let them slide." They turned me up to the door of my boarding house, and lifted me out of the wagon. I thanked them kindly for the great trouble in coming so far out of their way to take me home. They replied, "O, it is a pleasure, Elder, to do it—it is a pleasure, sir—it is a pleasure, sir."

God very soon began to magnify the riches of His grace in the conviction and conversion of both men and women—not a dog moved his tongue—the congregation was still and solemn as the grave. The few brethren and sisters felt as though God was on their side; they were strong in the Lord and in the power of his might; they found that their bands were loosed, that their feet were upon the necks of their enemies, and Christ was claiming the purchase of his blood. We labored on successfully. It was evident that that community was not what is often called a "Gospel-hardened people." They had not heard enough of the Gospel, perhaps, to harden them, in the common acceptation of that term.

I well recollect, while preaching one afternoon, a solemn awe appeared to rest upon every one present, when a young man arose and exclaimed aloud, "I shall be damned! I shall be damned! O, I am lost! O, I am lost!" The congregation were pretty much all in tears. I stopped preaching. He cried out, again, " I must pray, I must pray, or be damned!" He kneeled down of his own accord, and prayed in his own way, audibly, so that perhaps every individual in the house could hear him. He arose from his knees, took his seat, and appeared to be calm and placid. I moved on

with my sermon, and had spoken perhaps five or seven
minutes, when he again arose, and exclaimed, "I am
afraid I ain't saved! O, I ain't saved! I must pray
again. O, do let me pray !" I told him to pray on his
own way, asking God simply for that for which he felt
so much need—to be saved. The sermon, of course,
came to an end, in about the middle of it. But that
made no difference. I never saw the time when I
wanted to preach, when sinners wanted to pray for the
salvation of their soūls. Their previous pastor or
preacher—although, as before remarked, a very good
man—had scarcely dared to show himself in the house
of prayer, but he was now greeted cordially on every
hand, and everybody appeared to love Eld. D.

I do not now know how many were baptized, but
quite a number. I recollect one incident that occurred
at the water's side. There was a poor, miserable,
wicked backslider, who had made more or less trouble
for individuals through the greater part of the meeting.
He was talking boisterously against Dea. K. and Dea.
G. He finally addressed himself to me in a very
unbecoming manner, when a stout, athletic man, came
up and (I am sorry to say) made use of a word that I
can not use, adding, "I will shake you out of your
boots, if you do not leave this place, immediately.
What ! abuse this man, who has treated us like a gentleman ever since he has been here? Now, if you do
not hold your tongue, and get away from here, I will
knock you until you will not be able to get away." I
saw no knocking, but I did not see or hear anything
more from that individual. We closed in great peace,
God giving us a gracious blessing, and I returned home
rejoicing.

A MARVEL AT CROOKED LAKE.

Twenty-three or four years ago, I was called by Rev.

A. C. Mallory, then in his first charge, to hold a meeting of days with him and his people. I could not deny him any aid that was in my power to render, for I had promised him and God that anything at any time (other things being equal) that I could do for that church, should be cheerfully done. I knew everything would go smooth as regarded him and myself, for we were not only like David and Jonathan, but like Paul and Timothy. God was pleased to hear the prayer of his people—and, by the agency of the ever-blessed Spirit, many souls were hopefully converted. One circumstance connected with this meeting, has always appeared interesting to me. A number of converts, and a large congregation, repaired to the head waters of Crooked Lake, where Bro. Mallory was to administer the first ordinance of the Gospel to those who had previously been born again. As we were passing down the hill to the place of baptism, I saw that the lake was frozen some distance out from the shore. Many, no doubt, observed this as well as myself. The crowd came upon the beach, and, while passing through the preliminary service, the anchor ice appeared to break loose from the shore, and commenced receding into the lake, so that, by the time my brother was ready to administer that sacred ordinance, the ice was sufficiently out of the way, apparently standing at bay by God's command, like the liquid walls of the Red Sea. After baptizing quite a large number (I do not recollect how many,) we retired from the water's side, where prayer was wont to be made. The ice gently began to return, and ere we had arrived at the same elevation at which we were when we first saw it on our way down, the ice had entered its former position. We never thought that God wrought a miracle for us, but to this day I have never been able to give a scientific answer to the many inquiries that have come to me, as to the cause. I leave that for those to solve who have a more philosophical pate than mine.

THE AGRICULTURAL SERMON AND CONVERT.

I was invited to hold another meeting, with a choice church, where I was some acquainted, and a pastor I placed among the best in my knowledge. When I arrived at the pastor's house, his wife remarked, " Mr. R. is not at home, sir, just now. Will you be kind enough to put your horse in the stable?" I replied, " Yes, ma'am, I am always able to take care of my own horse, when able to ride." I did as requested, and was kindly received. Shortly after, a girl of fourteen years came in with a pailfull of hot apple-sauce, a present from a neighbor to the pastor's family. While the woman of the house was taking care of the sauce, I was talking with the girl about the interests of her soul. I inquired her name, which she meekly gave. I remarked I did not know a family of that name in the region. She said, " I am living near here, sir, but my home is quite a distance from this place. I live with Mr. ——." I said I could not call him up in my memory at that time. She inquired, " Which road did you come here, sir?" I told her. She remarked, "You passed the house. Did you not see, a short distance from here, a very fine brick house? It looks like a mansion." I replied, I did. " Well, that is where I am stopping." I asked if they were professors of religion, there? She replied, " No, sir."—" Are there no persons in your house who are Christians?"—" I think not, sir. O, stop—I think I am wrong. Grandma lives with us. I have often heard her praying, all alone, in the garret. So I should think she was religious."

About this time, Mrs. R. came in with the pail nicely washed, and remarked, "This young friend is a member of my Sabbath-school class. I think a great deal of her. I hope she will be converted in these meetings." I said that we had conversed some on that subject, and I felt sorry to learn from her that the family with whom she lived were not religious. I then asked the girl, "Will you take a message from me to Mr. —— and Mrs. ——? Tell them you met, at the pastor's house, the minister who is going to aid in the protracted meeting. Say to them that he thinks it is very wrong for any person—and especially for those to whom God has been so very kind in giving them the good things of this world—not to love and thank Him for it. And that Eld. Sheardown sends his kind regards to them, and invites them to come and hear him preach. Now, will you do that errand, just as I have told it to you, as near as you can?"—"Yes, sir."

The pastor's wife smiled as she inquired, "Elder, what do you know about Mr. ——?" I replied, "Nothing at all—but I know if he is not converted, he ought to be." The response was, "If you knew as much as we do, perhaps you would not manifest as much anxiety."—"Then I am very glad I do not," was my reply. "Is he an Infidel?"—"I don't know."— "Does he attend church?"—"Very seldom. But my husband will tell you all about it, probably, when he comes home." Bro. R. shortly arrived, when his wife reported the circumstances of the conversation with the little girl, and the message I sent—and both, I thought, treated the subject very lightly. My spirit was grieved, but I made no reply.

As the days passed away, my frequent inquiry was, "Was Mr. —— in church?"—"No, indeed not: what makes you so concerned about him?" My reply would

be, " He must come—I believe he will be converted."
The pastor remained incredulous.

Notice was given that on such a day I would preach
an Agricultural Sermon, and hoped that the scientific
farmers especially would come and hear. The gentleman referred to (to me unknown) was said to be a
model farmer. On hearing the request, (as I was
afterward informed,) he said, " I will go and hear that
man preach about farming—for, if he knows anything
about it, he is about the first minister I have ever seen
that is worth a snap at farming. He may learn me
something, but I doubt it." Just before I commenced
the sermon, the pastor said to me, " Do you see a
gentleman sitting by such a window, with florid face,
a scarlet silk handkerchief on his neck?" I looked up
and said, " Yes, who is it?"—"That," he replied, "is
Mr. ——." My heart filled—I could not restrain my
tears—for I had not ceased to pray for him from the
time I sent the message. My text on that occasion
was, " They who sow in tears, shall reap in joy." During the sermon, he rose up several times, and appeared
very uneasy, as though he was tired of sitting, or some
other trouble. When I closed the services, I went
down to the last step of the pulpit stairs, (which was
close by the door,) shook hands with some friends as
they were going out, and when he came along, kindly
offered him my hand, called him by name, and said,
" A very pleasant day, sir." He passed on, and I said
no more.

He continued to come, and was very soon deeply
affected. I concluded to approach him, and have some
conversation about the interests of his soul. He remarked that he supposed that there was no hope for
him. I inquired the reason. He said, " Sir, I arose
two or three times to speak while you was preaching

the agricultural sermon. I felt so convinced of my state, that I thought I must do it. I have thought, ever since, that that was the time, and I let it go by. I thought it would be considered rude, and out of place, to speak during the sermon, and I think now, sir, that there is no hope for me." I invited him forward to an anxious seat. He came without hesitation. He told us how much he needed religion ; what his fears were ; as for hope, he had none. I gave him the best advice and instruction I could, but he remained in that gloomy, dark, troubled condition. He would talk, confess his sins, pray for himself, become perfectly prostrate while trying to pray, but all did no good. I had been led into the secret of the trouble. One evening, after all effort appeared to be ineffectual—when he had prayed and wept, and became almost as weak as a child—I said, " God help you, sir, to go home and confess to your wife and children." This was spoken audibly, so that all might hear. He took his hat, and left the meeting.

I heard no more of him until about five o'clock the next morning. I was awake, and thought I heard an unusual noise somewhere near the house. The first thing I distinguished, was a rap at the door. The pastor got out of bed, and answered at the door. The next thing, I heard my brother say, " he is in his room ;" and very quickly followed a rap at my door. I was about half dressed, and opened the door, when who should appear but Mr. —— and the pastor ! He threw his arms around me, and brought me on my knees on the carpet, (and he came with me.) The pastor and I prayed for him, but he had got such a death-like grip upon me, that I could not rise. Finally, the pastor left us alone, when I talked and prayed with him until about seven o'clock in the morning, when his

ebullition of feeling appeared to subside. Yet I could
see no signs of a regenerated heart.

Before he left, he remarked, " I do not know what to
do, sir. I have special business to-day, in a village
twenty miles from here. I must go—I ought to go—
but how can I go? I can not look at any person without shedding tears." I advised him, by all means, to
redeem his pledge. On his knees, he told me, perhaps,
all his troubles. I said, " Go, sir, take your wife with
you in your buggy, and do your business."

He was expected back that night, and when we met
in the church for prayer meeting in the early evening,
his case was brought up for special prayer. [He remarked, in relating his experience to the church, that,
the night previous to his coming to my room in the
morning, after he had done his duty, he laid down, but
whether dressed or undressed he did not know : he had
no recollection of taking off his clothes ; he dreamed,
he said—for he called it a dream, yet he did not know
whether he was asleep or awake—that the last day
had come ; the judgment was set ; it appeared to be
moving towards him like some mighty cloud, and he
expected in a few moments it would break upon him,
and that would be his eternal doom. Just before it had
arrived over his dwelling, he saw Elder Sheardown
holding up his right hand and praying God to stay the
judgment until he should be converted. He thought
he looked out of the window on the south side of the
house, and saw the same terrific appearance coming
from the south ; and at the same moment he saw the
same hand uplifted, and the same prayer offered, that
the judgment might be stayed until he had repented.
The next that he appeared to realize, he found himself
in my room, in company with the pastor.]

He took his wife with him, as advised to do, to

transact his business. On the borders of the village to which he had gone, there is a beautiful farm, of which he had often said, (as reported to me,) that, if he had that farm, he would ask no odds of either God or man. He was driving along the road, just before sundown— one of those beautiful autumn sunsets, with a clear sky, serene, frosty air, the seared leaves and the last rays of the setting sun throwing beauties all around that habitation—and as he cast his eye upon it, he thought he never saw such a change as had taken place. There was nothing in it, or about it, to him desirable. While these thoughts were passing his mind, this passage of divine truth came with great power and sweetness to his heart: "In my Father's house there are many mansions; if it were not so, I would have told you. I go to prepare a place for you, that where I am there may ye be also."

His soul was happy, and a sweet sense of pardon rested upon his mind. These circumstances, I think, took place at the same time that earnest prayer was going up for his salvation at the church. I saw him, with several others, follow Jesus in the first ordinance of the Gospel, in Cayuga lake. The last I heard of him (for I do not know whether he is living or dead) was that he was striving to make his calling and election sure.

THE CARD-PLAYER DETECTED.

Another incident, in the same meeting, may be worthy of notice. One day I preached a very pointed sermon on card-playing and other kinds of gambling. After the meeting, a member of the church, who I believed to be among the best of men, remarked, " You have preached a good sermon, sir, but it will be lost on this community; we have not got the people here who are addicted to the habits that you have been talking about." I replied, "I am very glad of it. I hope it may be lost for want of adaptation to the community, or any part of them." Things passed on but a very short time, when a lovely young man, the son of the brother just referred to, appeared to be under wonderful conviction. When interrogated in relation to when he first felt the magnitude of his sins, his answer was, while listening to the sermon on card-playing. He said, "I have often stayed at home, when father and mother went to meeting on the Sabbath, and some young friends would come in, when we would play at cards until about the time for them to return from church; then we would adjourn, to meet again, if the weather was pleasant, in the afternoon," in a certain piece of woods, which he designated; and of all his sins it appeared to him the sin of playing cards on the Sabbath was the greatest transgression. The dear young man was hopefully converted to God, and for all I have ever heard of him have every reason to hope the work of grace upon his heart was a genuine one.

EVILS OF PARTIZAN SPIRIT.

Permit me to relate, here, a few facts by way of warning or caution against the difficulties which may arise out of undue political excitements. It will be fresh in the minds of many of the older members of the churches, that there were fearful alienations in the election of 1840. I recollect of holding a meeting, with a certain church in the Lake country in which I was considerably acquainted. The pastor was a very good man, and I had some hope of seeing much of the salvation of God, if there was not something beneath the surface that we could not see or reach. Commencing labors, as usual, a large congregation was gathered together. Truth appeared to tell upon the hearts of impenitent sinners. It was a common-place conversation, that men in their prime, and some almost in the evening of life, appeared to be powerfully moved, even to tears. Yet we did not appear to be in possession of that converting power which comes from above in answer to the prayers of God's people. I felt in my own heart that it was very up-hill business, and often conversed with the pastor, why things should remain in their present state—so much powerful conviction, and still no evidence of regenerating grace. His answer was about the same, always—that he could not tell—but it was evident that there was something wrong. Brethren appeared to be honest in their confessions; they would pray, exhort, and sing, but the real motive power appeared to be absent. The word had gone out that such and such men were under conviction, and brethren and sisters came in from neighboring churches. They took hold, and labored, apparently in the Spirit. We began to find here and there a hopeful convert, apparently very weak, but still giving signs of spiritual life. They appeared to be willing to do their part of the labor, but they had not that vivacity which is generally found in new-born souls. We struggled on until it was said by some that there were perhaps forty hopefully converted to God.

I had heard a certain individual pray, several times, in the meeting, that the Lord would be pleased to bless the effort put forth for the salvation of souls. I heard him pray, the last evening of the meeting. In that prayer, he expressed great satisfaction that it was just as he had prayed daily that it might be—that little or nothing had been effected! I felt intensely under such a prayer—how it could be, that there could be such a contrast between the former, and the last, closing

21

prayer of the meeting—and endeavored to ascertain the reason. I was told, that the house of worship had been opened, as the most convenient place for one political meeting, and that the opposite party (to which that brother belonged) made application for it, but were not permitted the use of it. I watched with some interest the ultimatum of the meeting, relative to the converts. We were told some went to such a denomination, while others went to other Baptist churches; and the summing up, according to the statement of my informant, was, that *not one* was added, as the result of that meeting, to the church where the labor was performed, although, I think, some did not live more than a rifle shot from the meeting house! This was a very melancholy report, and I hope my ears may never be saluted with the like distressing details.

LACK OF CONCERT IN EFFORTS.

In the winter following the political struggle just referred to, after the excitement had in a measure passed over, I had given a pledge to a dear brother minister, laboring in a little church with some strength and moral power, that, if God spared my life one year from the time, I would be on hand and try, by the grace of God, to assist him in a protracted meeting. The understanding between the pastor and myself was, that if any obstruction should be thrown in the way, so that it should not be considered best to make the effort, he would write me in season. I received no letter, consequently concluded the way was open, and shaped my course accordingly. I wished to redeem my pledge to the day, and in so doing had to drive sixty miles in my buggy through one of the coldest days following a January thaw. I arrived just about dusk, and saw a

number of people standing around the pastor's door.
I believe there was but one member of that church
whom I had ever seen, and I had never before been in
the town. I drove up to the gate, sat in my buggy,
and thought, "Now, this is the house—I cannot be
mistaken," for I had inquired but a short distance back,
and it answered the description that had been given.
The thought struck my mind, "Is it possible that Eld.
Dudley is dead?" Still, I sat in my buggy, taking it
for granted that some of those men, standing in the
door-yard, were members of the church. I remarked
to them, "My name is Sheardown." They looked at
me, but paid little attention. One individual looked
around, and proved to be the brother who was in company with the pastor when I gave the pledge in Vienna,
the year previous. As soon as he recognized me, he
came up, and gave me a warm shake of the hand. I
said to him, "Now, sir, I am here, and, if I am wanted,
will get out of my buggy, for I am very cold. If not,
I will drive on a little further, and put up for the night,
for I am wanted in Lyons." By this time, the pastor
was out, and cordially received me. But I saw there
was trouble with him. He wept, and smiled at times
through his tears, and finally said, "It is my donation,
to-night. Now go right in, sir, make yourself at home;
I will take care of your horse." I requested him to
direct me to a part of the house where I might meet
his wife, or some of the family, and obtain a spot to
wash and make my toilet before entering the crowded
part of the house. I succeeded. As soon as it was
known by many that I was present, they said, "Now,
can not we have a sermon to-night?" My reply was,
"Not from me; but if you will come together to-morrow night, at the church, you may, God willing, hear
me preach."

The bustle of the evening over, the pastor and his little family and myself alone, I inquired about the prospect of a meeting, and what appeared to be the state of the church, the feeling of interest in relation to attending meeting, and all the little inquiries that necessarily come up between pastor and evangelist on their first meeting. He replied, "O, we shall have meeting." But there appeared to my own mind to be something very indefinite in answer to many questions that were put. I could not fathom the mystery. He had provided a very pleasant, cozy place, as a domicile for me—everything desirable—library, stove, bed, everything in fact, of this kind, that was calculated to make the inmate comfortable. He told me, the next day, he had an appointment for me in the evening. I went to church—a small congregation. I inquired of him, "What is the order of arrangements for your meeting?" He answered, "You may give notice that you will preach again to-morrow night," which I did, still wondering that he had no plan to name relative to his future movements.

I attended the meeting agreeable to appointment— was again requested to have meeting the next night— and this, I believe, brought us to about the close of the week. Then it was necessary that something definite should be decided upon relative to our future labors. He said, "Well, now, I will tell you what I want you to do. I want you should give notice, Sabbath morning, of just as many meetings as you feel able and willing to attend through the week." I replied, "I should like very much, my brother, for you to make some statements, yourself, concerning your meetings, and give the notice yourself." But he evaded and said, "You must do it," and everything was very dark. I could not pierce the gloom—his conduct appeared to me to be inexplicable. So I made appointments to suit my views and feelings, in view of the work to be performed.

I had now got upon the track, but the great thing was, the motive power did not appear to be there. Some of the brethren and sisters of the church attended, but I believe not by any means all the pastor expected. Some were always willing to pray, and willing to talk. I tried my best to rally the forces, and marshal them in the conflict, for we expected a hard struggle, and indeed it was for many days. There was no lack of attention to the Word, and the feelings of the impenitent appeared far above those of the church.

There was one little circumstance that I have never been able clearly to account for, in relation to myself. On the pastor's writing desk, with some open letters and papers, was a letter superscribed with my name. I had seen it, every day; had taken it in my hand, looked at the direction, and laid it down again—never thought that it belonged to me, and it was not my business to be quizzing any of his papers.

My spirit became crushed very much. I endeavored to cry mightily to God to know why He was thus contending with us. I knew it was for His glory to save sinners, yet it looked to me as though the effort must fail. In the multitude of these thoughts, after having said everything that I thought I could say, to admonish, to stimulate, and to stir up, yet, to bring into action the sacramental host, in that place, appeared to require a power that I was afraid God had not given me. I made up my mind to preach from the text, " Sanctify yourselves against to-morrow; the Lord will do wonders among you ;" and I preached from that text as well as I could. The morrow came. I was preaching in the afternoon, when there flashed across my mind what I had preached the evening previous. Everything appeared to remain the same, and the thought struck me, that now the people will say, "To-morrow has come, but you have lied in the name of the Lord—things remain as they were." I came very near breaking down entirely, but a flood of tears came to my relief, and I was enabled to double the cape and very soon feel the effects of the trade-winds. I had scarcely said amen, when a leading member of the church, who had been standing through the services in the broad aisle, (for the church was a perfect jam)— his countenance often had paled, and his chin quivered —this brother then, with one mighty effort, threw his arms around his pastor's neck, and they came down upon their knees in the midst of the great congregation. The member cried out, "O, Bro. Dudley, forgive me, forgive me! Whenever you brought up the subject of a protracted meeting before the church, I always opposed it. You remember, at the last meeting when you named it, I took my hat and walked out of the covenant meeting. I would not hear you, and about all the church followed me." This lifted the latch, opened the door, gave me an admission into the secret audience chamber, and shed a light upon those difficulties that had so much hindered our progress.

Returning to my room after service, the first thing I did was to take up the letter referred to before, and on opening it I found that it was a letter that had been written to me, at a very late date, by the pastor, (in which he appeared to have little hope that it would reach me, previous to the appointed or promised time that I was to be with him and his people.) But the letter had never been sent. The secret came out, that when that leading brother had induced the church to follow him from the meeting-house, there were but two left—the pastor, and one very good man—who finally came to the conclusion, that the pastor should go home and write a letter, if so be that it might reach the evangelist, and turn his steps another way. The brother was to remain at the church, take the letter, and drop it in the office on his way home. When the pastor returned to the church with the letter, the brother who had remained in waiting said to Eld. D., "We must not send this letter. I have been praying, ever since you left; and when I prayed we might succeed in preventing Eld. Sheardown from coming here, all was dark and gloomy in my mind; but when I felt reconciled to let the thing stand as it is, and let the man come, all appears to be bright as day. Therefore, I say, let the providence of God rule in this thing. After he comes and preaches a few sermons, he will get the people out, and we shall see what the mind of the Lord is. If he must leave, I will pay his traveling expenses, and we will get out of the thing the best way we can." This, of course, previous to the confession, was all in the dark as it regarded myself.

POLITICAL STUMBLING-BLOCKS.

One other instance that occurred in this meeting. I have said it was the winter following the great political conflict of 1840. We were moving on; the power of the Highest appeared to rest upon the people; and converts were daily multiplying. There was a brother of rather superior talent, one of the sweet singers in Israel," who had got pretty deep into my heart. He labored well. There was a certain other gentleman, unconverted—a man rather above mediocrity in his appearance and all his demeanor. His wife, and a little niece, I believe, were hopefully converted to God.

He appeared to be the subject of very deep conviction, and remained in that state some days. We could not see what obstacles were between him and the Saviour. I observed, that while the brother just referred to was talking, this gentleman's tears dried up. He looked, to me, as though he had speedily got into a hardening process. I concluded to watch the thing closely, as the convicted man very soon gave all the evidence that he was the subject of great anxiety of soul. For two or three meetings, when the above-mentioned brother spoke or prayed, it produced the same effect upon the trembling sinner. I concluded there must be something wrong, and in consequence took the brother by the arm and said to him, "Do you think you have made all the confession you ought to make? or is there something left behind?" He remarked, "I do not mean to be dishonest. I think I have done in that respect all my duty." Of course, I could not say that he had not, and had no business whatever to judge his heart. But the circumstances that had appeared before me were fraught with something that indicated wrong.

While preaching in the afternoon of the same day, I made some stirring remarks in relation to brethren throwing stumbling-blocks in the way of sinners, growing out of the political excitement of the times. It was a perfect digression, the remarks not growing out of my subject at all, but they passed for what they were worth. Immediately after sermon, the brother arose, called the gentleman by name, and, with a heart apparently dashed like a potter's vessel, said, "O forgive me, forgive me—I have done very wrong; I know it, now. I did not see it, before. Your politics were the opposite of mine. You know I would often drive around, on your carriage road, with my buggy blazoned with "Tippecanoe." I would sing a song, crack my whip, and was gone. I knew it would make you mad. I did it wilfully. I am very sorry. If you can, I want you should forgive me; and if there is anything else, that I do not see, that I have done, that is in the way of your soul's salvation, do tell me. I would not stand between you and the salvation of your soul, for the world." While this confession was going on, the gentleman's face became placid, his countenance as Lebanon! He hopefully passed the strait gate, and found joy and peace in believing.

But I feel something like Solomon, when he declared of making many books there is no end. So it is in relating interesting anecdotes growing out of extra efforts. A very few more *must* suffice.

MEETINGS IN ROCHESTER.

In the winter of 1844, I was engaged with the church in Palmyra—that beautiful village, and interesting field of labor. A short time before closing our effort, I recognized in my congregation a dear brother in company, apparently, with a gentleman I did not know. When the meeting was out for the afternoon, I was met by Bro. J. M. French, with whom I had been in intimacy long before he was converted. His house was often my resting place, where everything that his large heart could suggest, and his liberal hand supply, was always at my service. He had formerly lived on the Big Flats in the Chemung valley, but had been converted in the city of Rochester. He introduced to me, Dea. Barton. They very soon made their errand known. They had come after me to hold a meeting with the Second Baptist church, Rochester. They were commissioned to take me or my pledge, as soon as the meeting closed in that place. I felt very much exhausted, as that was the fourth meeting that I had labored through without rest, except the little respite I had in traveling from one place to another. I would gladly have plead off, on the ground of my worn-down physical system, but they smilingly said, judging from the sermon they had heard, they would be willing to risk the physical weakness! We had a little conference together, when they gave me an account of their condition as a people, stated what difficulties it appeared to them we should have to surmount and then said much in relation to the favorable circumstances that presented themselves.

When I arrived in the city, I went to the church in the evening. They had been worshiping in the basement, where we found a number of brethren and sisters, praying. Things appeared to look favorable. I had an introduction to a few deacons and brethren. Dea. Smith—that eminent man of God, who some few years ago was removed from our fellowship as a church to the fellowship of saints and angels in the upper sanctuary—remarked, " Had we not better go up into the audience room for preaching, to-night?" I replied, " No, my brother, let us labor here until God says, Come up higher." An evening or two after, before it was time to open the services, Dea. Smith said, " Now, what shall we do? The basement is full, and the sexton informs me that there is a crowd outside that cannot get in." I remarked, " This is the voice of God saying to us, Go up a little higher." So we repaired to the audience room above. We had a very blessed time. Week after week, salvation's streams were full banks. My dear brother, the pastor, baptized, I think, as the avails of the meeting, over seventy. I shall never forget the love of Christ that so richly abounded in the hearts of the brethren and sisters, and the hallowed influence that appeared to rest upon everything around us.

The morning of our final separation, at the house of Deacon Barton—where a number of precious brethren and sisters had met together to join in prayer, and take the parting hand—was the most like heaven of anything I have ever met with on earth. I think I speak the feeling of every one present on that occasion. Bro. Hotchkiss, the pastor, presented me with three volumes of D'Aubigne's Reformation in Germany and Switzerland. Permit me to inscribe here this token of esteem and respect to me, as a memento of my love and esteem to him, that it may live when I am dead, and the volumes with their inscription may have passed into other hands:

ROCHESTER, March 14th, 1844.

DEAR BROTHER SHEARDOWN,—Will you do me the favor to accept the accompanying volumes, as a slight tribute of respect and esteem. They may serve occasionally to revive the recollections of those sweet and hallowed scenes through which we have passed together, while ministering at the altar of God. Confident I am that they will live in my memory as *illuminated* and *sunny* spots on the checkered canvas of my life. And I live in the animating hope that we may be permitted to *recount* these seasons together on the fair fields of final rest. Wherever you may be called in providence, you will have my warmest Christian regards. Our brief acquaintance has won for yourself the truest and strongest affection of which my nature is capable.

Fraternally Yours,   V. R. HOTCHKISS.

Bro. Hotchkiss afterwards was chosen a Professor in the University at Rochester, and is now serving, a second time, as pastor of a church in Buffalo.

Since the time referred to, I have enjoyed a great many good seasons with the Baptists in Rochester. Although some have gone to their rest who labored so faithfully together, yet there remain many dear brethren and sisters, who have a warm place in my heart, but whom I never expect to see again until we meet on the other side of the river. I have become like Jacob of old, well stricken in years, and leaning on the top of my staff. But it is a pleasing thought that there is no old age in heaven. The great and all-absorbing question is, What can we do that shall most glorify God while we remain on the earth? I have very lately returned from almost the vestibule of the upper sanctuary, and this may be my final adieu to my friends in that city.

HOW A SIGN-POST WAS TORN DOWN.

One Sabbath afternoon, while holding a protracted meeting in a village in Steuben county, we had to give up the school house where we held services, on account of its having been pre-engaged by a minister of another denomination. A Presbyterian friend called at my stopping place to know if I would speak in a tavern, providing it could be obtained. I replied, "Yes, to be sure—I had rather preach than lie still, and I do not know that there is any place on God's footstool where the Gospel may not be preached." He said, "At what time shall we make the appointment?" I said, "At two o'clock." He remarked, "You need not fear but you will have a congregation."

At the appointed time, I found the corner room of the tavern crowded. My stand was near the door, between the bar-room and dining room, the bar directly at my right hand. Before announcing a text, I said, "I can not preach, unless I first ask a question. It has been asked perhaps thousands of times on the very board on which I stand. The question is, ' *What shall we drink?* '" The landlord, who was sitting a short distance from me, dropped his head. I continued, "You will find my text in Exodus, 15th chapter, last clause of 24th verse: ' What shall we drink?' " I saw no immediate effect from my sermon.

A year or two afterward, while traveling some distance from that place, I met a man on horse-back, to whom I bowed. He said, " Good morning, Elder." I remarked, "I know your countenance, but your name I can not call."—" Do you not," said he, "remember pulling down my sign-post?" I replied, "No, sir, I do not remember having done such a thing."—" Do you not remember preaching in my bar-room, and asking the question, What shall we drink?" The reply was, "O yes, I do not mean to forget that; but I did not know that I had pulled down your sign."—" You did, sir,—for I never had any rest in my soul until I got out of the business. I sold my property, at a loss of six hundred dollars, in order to get clear of the concern.

PERSONAL APPEALS, OR INDIVIDUAL LABOR.

During protracted and other meetings, it is very common to hear prayers for the salvation of a whole neighborhood, or village, or city. But I have never known such prayers answered. And I think the better way is to single out individuals—go to them, alone, and talk about the interests of their souls. Yet it becomes us to be sure that our way is clear, lest we receive the rebuke, "Physician, heal thyself." Never undertake the work, unless your own heart is imbued with the spirit of Jesus.

Personal labor must be done by the private members of the church. The pastor, or evangelist, can not do all. Every individual must do his or her own duty. It is a fearful thing to deal with the souls of immortal beings. If we err, the error may be a fatal one.

22

I have on my mind a circumstance that took place during a protracted meeting in a rural district in —— county. While passing through the congregation, conversing with different persons on the great subject of the salvation of the soul, I met a lady, a school-teacher by calling, apparently twenty-five years of age, of manifest intelligence. I said a word or two to her about the Saviour, and passed on. One of the brethren said, "Elder, what did you make out of that young lady?"—"Not much," I replied.—"Nor never will," a deacon remarked. "Did you not know, Elder, that she has sinned away her day of grace, and can never be saved?" I replied, "No, sir, I do not. And by what authority have you come to that conclusion?" —"It is very generally believed, by professors in this place, that it is so. Moreover, while she was attending a meeting of another denomination in the village, the ministers told her to her face that she had sinned against the Holy Ghost, and there was no mercy for her."

This representation made me feel intensely, and I determined to make every effort in my power to do her good. The first opportunity I had to converse with her, I learned that she had been raised under the influence of infidelity, but was not herself an infidel. I tried to point her to the Saviour. She replied, "It is of no use, now. I am already lost—Christians tell me so." I asked, "Do you ever pray?"—"No."—"Did you ever pray?"—"Yes, some time ago—but I can not pray, now."

On subsequent interviews, her mind appeared to have grown more dark, and her countenance was more sad. At length, I asked, "Would you like to be saved?"—"Yes, but it is impossible." Said I, "Permit me to ask you if you have a room by yourself, where you board?" She replied, she had. "Now," I continued, "I shall not ask you to pray, because you have told me you can not. But I expect to retire to my room, about ten o'clock this evening—and I request you to retire to yours, about the same hour—put out your light—kneel by your bedside—do not pray, but remember, every moment, that Eld. Sheardown is praying for you. Remain on your knees half an hour—I shall close my prayer about half-past ten."

The next evening, I met her in the church, and asked her if she had complied with my request. She said she had. "Will you do the same duty to-night?" Her answer was, "I will."—"How long do you wish I should pray?"—"Until midnight," was her reply. I remarked, "Do not pray for yourself until you seem forced to do it."

The day following, she informed me she had redeemed her pledge, and I inquired what were her thoughts while alone upon her knees? She replied, "I never felt so in my life." Before parting at evening, I inquired, "Do you wish me to pray again for you to-night?" She replied, "Yes, sir."—"How long shall I pray?"—"All night, sir." Her tears began to flow. The Lord was pleased to encourage my faith by giving a little sight. I said, "Will you PRAY FOR YOURSELF, to-night?" The reply was, "Yes." Near two o'clock, the next morning, the blessed Spirit came down like Peter's sheet, and our prayers were taken up to heaven. I felt assured the good work was done. During the day, she attended the meeting, evidently rejoicing in the salvation of God.

This is an extreme case. I do not give it as a sample of the moral labor to be performed by brethren and sisters. Yet there are many cases quite as difficult, in every field. I have known men so steeped in sin that

I feared lest God in His wrath should suddenly take them away in all their guilt. For such individuals, I have often spoken privately to some faithful Christian,. giving them (if they did·not already know) the particulars of their case—and, if circumstances demanded it, have appointed a continuous secret prayer meeting, day and night, wherein the time was so divided that vocal or ejaculatory prayer should not cease to ascend until it pleased God to manifest His justice or His grace. This method prevailed in the case of Mr. ——. He had been an infidel of high order—yet, even after his infidelity had given up the ghost, and he was invited to take the anxious seat, he declared, again and again, "Put hell on my right hand, and an anxious seat on my left, and I will jump into hell in preference to going to an anxious seat." But he did enter an anxious seat —was converted to God—and has long been a shining light in Zion.

SINGING IN OPEN MEETINGS.

It has always seemed to me that singing is a sublime part of public worship. But *adaptation* in singing, is just as essential as in preaching. In protracted meetings, I generally dispensed with the formalities of choirs. Guided in a great measure by circumstances, I could not mark out a path in which I should always walk. On Sabbaths, I often desired the choirs, as such, to be in their places—and, sometimes, felt it duty to secure their assistance, if possible, during every meeting.

By way of illustration, I will describe a scene that is irrevocably impressed on my memory. While attending a session of the Canister River Association, in a beautiful village in Allegany county, New York, the little church seemed desirous I should tarry, and hold a meeting with them. They had a large, well-trained choir, and I remarked to a brother, "You have a lovely group of singers."—"Yes—but they are unconverted." My heart was moved for them. Before the Association was dismissed, notice was given that the church would, that evening, commence a series of meetings, to continue so long as it appeared to be duty. I said, "It seems that 1 am to 'remain here, to proclaim unto you the way of life and salvation. Now, I have one request to make of some dear friends, and I hope they will not deny me. I desire that part, if not all of the choir, will be with us, every meeting. I have been perfectly delighted with the execution of the pieces performed during the Association. You are so good judges, that I will give you the privilege of making your own selections, whenever you wish." I believe they made every effort to be present. There were three young men who appeared to be able to lead the choir. The singers became very much interested, and one young lady professed conversion. One afternoon, I preached on the Judgment. When the sermon closed, one of the leaders announced the "Judgment Anthem." He sounded— but, in taking the pitch, he struck as far from it as *Old Windham* is from *Coronation*. He tried again, but failed, and took his seat. Another leader made an attempt, but he also failed utterly. Then, the order in the gallery was, *heads down*—except the young female convert, who remained firm on her feet, her countenance as placid as the waters of the Siloam! Looking at them through my tears, I was forced to exclaim, "No wonder you could not sing, with the dread realities of the Judgment, like drops of boiling lightning, scalding your guilty consciences! Now, dear friends, you need the balm of life. We invite you all to come down, and take those seats, which we will vacate for you.   Then kneel, and pray for yourselves—and Christians will pray for you." During this time. the converted lady was passing through the gallery, conversing. I continued, "Now, all of you, come down." She added, "Follow me!" and the gallery was evacuated—the congregation singing,

"Come, ye sinners, poor and needy."

Nearly all that group of young persons, as I hope, received the pardoning grace of God.

During protracted meetings, and in our conversation, anxious and prayer meetings, my general course was to omit reading hymns. The first thing was to ascertain if there was among the members, any quick, off-hand singers, and engage them to be ready, at any desired moment, to sing—and seldom to sing more than one or two verses at a time. One great difficulty is to select both words and tunes to meet the state of feeling in the congregation. While laboring to arouse the church from a state of supineness, we would select hymns corresponding in sentiment with the following:

"My drowsy powers, why sleep ye so?"
"Oh for a closer walk with God!" &c.

If exhorting sinners, hymns of this class are preferable:

"Hearts of stone, relent! relent!" ·
"Come, ye sinners, poor and needy."
"Sinners, can you hate the Saviour?"
"To-day the Saviour calls," &c.

If listening to converts telling what God has done for them, we would sing—

"O how happy are they."

If we were hearing converts relate their experience, in view of baptism and church fellowship, we would give out such as the following:

"In all my Lord's appointed ways."
"Come, happy souls, adore the Lamb."
"Christians, if your hearts be warm."
"O, Lord! and will thy pardoning love."
"From whence doth this union arise?" &c.

In the converts' or young Christians' meetings, we should choose a class of Zion's songs like

> "Am I a soldier of the cross?"
> "Come, let us ascend."
> "When I can read my title clear."
> "Our hearts by love together knit." &c.

Singing is not only a delightful part of divine worship, but also an exercise that God often blesses to the conviction and conversion of sinners. On one occasion, as I well remember, while singing that good old revival hymn,

> "Amen! amen! my soul replies,"

as the meeting was dismissed, a gentleman of high standing in the community was most powerfully convicted. Before he had passed ten rods from the meeting-house, he said to a brother on the road, "Do pray for me!" The brother replied, "Let us kneel down." They knelt together, on the snow, in the midst of the dispersing congregation, and, while prayer was offered up in his behalf, he passed the strait gate, as I trust.

It is very desirable that evangelists, and all who conduct prayer and conference meetings, should have their memory well stored with appropriate hymns and tunes. If they wish to give out a hymn of five or six verses, it should be sung at intervals.

I repeat that *adaptation* is as important in singing as in preaching. The solemnity of a meeting is sometimes dissipated by some one ranting something as entirely out of place as it would be to sing the words,

> "All hail the power of Jesus' name,"

in the tune *Mear*. We should "*sing with the spirit and the understanding also.*"

CHAPTER VII.—1844 to 1852.

REMOVAL FROM CATLIN TO READING.

In 1844, I resigned my pastorate at Catlin—which, indeed, had only been nominal for some years—and, in answer to a call from the church in Reading, removed my standing and took charge of the last-named church. It was a painful task for me, with my wife, and some of my believing children, to have our names taken from the records of the Catlin church, where there were so many associations and Christian ties, which had bound us together for so long a time. Yet duty appeared to call, and I knew nothing but to obey. The Reading church had been in some respects unhappy in their choice of pastors—were somewhat divided among themselves—and it appeared I was the only man in whom they could be agreed. They promised me that I should have my liberty to attend protracted meetings, by getting them a supply, or, if that could not be done, they would cheerfully endeavor to sustain meetings themselves.

FLANK MOVEMENT CONTEMPLATED.

There was another inducement. Jefferson—now

more generally called Watkins—at the head of Seneca Lake, had gone up, under my own observation, from three or four houses, to a flourishing little village, which had all the appearance of becoming quite a mart for business. There was no Baptist church in it, nor any Baptists that I knew of. In locating for Reading, I pitched my tent a little nearer to the head of the Lake than to Reading Center, the location of the Baptist church. I had it in my heart to try and do something for the rising village. I hoped, at least in a few years, to be able to cut loose from the church in Reading, and endeavor to plant the standard on some unbroken ground. Jefferson was near by me, and appeared to claim my attention more than any other. Things went on, with the pastor and people in Reading, perhaps as comfortably and with as much good feeling as could be expected. It was not a hard task for me, in those years, to preach three sermons a day, and travel several miles, for I had a good horse and buggy, and, by making due calculations, through a kind Providence I could always meet my appointments in season.

RECONNOITRE AT JEFFERSON.

I was called, two or three times, to the head of the Lake, to preach at funerals. The people gathered almost in mass. I inquired if there were not some Baptist people in that village? I was told that there was a Mrs. C., whose parents I had formed an acquaintance with on Five Mile Creek, in Steuben county, when she was a girl at home. I thought if I could gain her influence, I might get into some place to preach. True, I had been told that it was no use for a third denomination to come into that village, as the other two were in perfect harmony, and could do all the preaching it was necessary for them to have! However, I looked at the thing, and found indeed that the head of the Seneca was a part of God's world, and, if so, I had a right to go into it and preach the Gospel of our Lord Jesus Christ. I made inquiries for a school-house in which I might preach, but found there was no admittance. After having made a thorough effort, I failed in obtaining any place where I could set my foot and unfurl the banner of the Gospel.

INVITED TO LECTURE ON ROMANISM.

Things passed on a short time. I was very uneasy. I thought I could not live, within two miles and a half of such a place, and have no right of inheritance there. A circumstance occurred, one day, which proved to be the opening wedge. I was riding in my buggy, with my daughter, Mrs. Dillistin, when we met the pastor of the P. church. He held up his finger, as though he wished me to stop, so I stopped. In company with him was a brother, (a Mr. D.) who I highly esteemed from the acquaintance I had with him, and thought him a good man. One stood on one side of my buggy and the other on the other, with each of them a foot upon the forewheel of the carriage, (as we were on descending ground.) The clergyman said to me, "Eld. Sheardown, you are the very man I wanted to see." I inquired after his wants. He said, "The Roman Catholic bishop has been in our village, and has moved minds that I thought could not be moved. And now, sir, I wish you to come down and review the Bishop. I will tell you all I know in relation to the course taken by him." I replied, "Sir! I am not unacquainted with the course the Bishop took. I understand all about that. But, sir, I am not the man to review the Bishop. That is your ground. I have no inheritance in your place—not so much as to set my

foot upon. You had better do that work yourself."—
"No, sir," he said, "your age, and your experience in
Papal countries, make you the very man. And now,
sir, I cordially invite you to come down. You shall
preach in my church," (for they had a place that was
called by that name.) "I will make the appointment
for you, stand by you, and aid you all that is in my
power." I still told him that I could not see it my
duty, under the circumstances, to undertake such a
work. He urged me to give him an appointment for
the next Sabbath. I told him I would think of it, and,
if it appeared to be my duty, I would drop him a line
permitting him to make an appointment.

On my way home, I overtook an old Revolutionary
soldier, eminently pious—I thought him the most
godly man in my acquaintance—an "elder" according
to the forms of the church, the pastor of which had
just asked me to review the Bishop. I drove slowly
by his side, and found he was quite childish. I said to
him, "Father B., what is the matter with you?" and
held up my horse to hear his complaint. The good
man exclaimed, "O, I am killed! I am killed! my
feelings are killed!" I said, "Where are you going?"
He replied, "Home."—"Well, now, I will assist you
into my buggy, take you up to my house, and, if I do
not get a chance to send you home, will send one of
my own boys to take you." After he was seated in
the buggy, I said to him, "What hurt your feelings
so?" He replied, weeping, that the Roman Catholic
Bishop had been in Jefferson, and his pastor "had
given him his pulpit for to go through his fooleries,"
and his pastor sat and heard him, and he could not
bear it. He said, "How can I live when I see the
sanctuary of God profaned?" I endeavored to divert
the old gentleman's mind from his troubles, by talking

about his nearness to the land of rest—the upper sanctuary, where nothing that maketh a lie shall enter in.

OBTAIN AN OLD SCHOOL-HOUSE TO SPEAK IN.

After pondering the thing in my own mind, and mature deliberation and prayer, I concluded to try, if it was among the possibilities, to obtain a place and deliver a course of lectures on Romanism. But I would not fight the enemy on his own ground. I went down to the village one day, saw Senator George Guinnip, and asked him if he thought it was possible to obtain the school-house for me to deliver a course of lectures on Romanism? He thought it would. He was an unconverted man, but said he would see Esq. Peck ; he thought there would be no difficulty in obtaining the house for that purpose. I told him, if he could, I would deliver a lecture, every Sabbath afternoon, at half-past two o'clock. The house was obtained, the appointment given out, and I was notified that all would be in readiness.

I went at the appointed time, and found more people there than could well get into the old school-house. I remarked to them, "I am glad to see so many friends present, to-day, but am afraid that you are going to be disappointed. I shall not lecture to-day *directly* on Romanism, but will give you a talk upon the Divinity of God's Word—because, if you do not believe the Bible to be divinely inspired, I shall in a measure be deprived of a great deal of testimony that will be very much needed through my course of lectures. Now, I wish to say to you, if I come here, it will be a great satisfaction for me to know that I am not speaking to Infidels. There will be three sources from which I shall draw my proofs. First, the Bible. Second, the history which I shall read to you from my books.

23

Third, my experience, and the observations that I have had where Catholicism predominates. And now, if I proceed, I want to tell you at the starting point, that I make no compromise with the old mother of harlots, the abomination of the earth. She has a great many connections, who may be traced down to the thirty-second cousin. You must not expect that I shall show her any mercy. When I strike her in the face and eyes, and you see the moral blood begin to run, and I hear you whining and saying that you are too hard upon the old lady—that she's done a great many bad things, but nevertheless she's done some good ones—now, so sure as 1 hear anything like this, I shall be certain that some of her relations are present." I de-delivered my lecture, for it was thought not best to call it " preach."

OPPOSITION OVERCOME.

I had not progressed far in my course, before I caught the tidings, from almost the wings of the wind, that "Eld. Sheardown is a vulgar man, and makes use of very low language." I did not calculate to review the Bishop only, but at the same time to pay some atten-tion to his sympathizers. The next Sabbath, I re-marked, before the congregation, (which was always very large,) " Now, some of you have been hurt. You think the blows have been too severe ; consequently, I find a report going around here that I have made use of improper language. Now, I do not want you should lay this to my parents, for I was well brought up ; neither to my education, for, as far as that went, I was correctly instructed ; and, as it regards my knowledge of the world, of men, and things, I can say without boasting, that I have forgotten more than many of you ever knew. But I can tell you this, that the language

I have made use of, is not yet, according to your standard, half as severe as what you will find in God's Word." Every few Sabbaths, there would be some fault-finding to review as I passed along.

UNPLEASANT CONTROVERSY.

At length one person said to me, "There is a strange report about you, sir, in the village." I replied, "Well, that is nothing new; but what is in the wind, now?" —"Why, sir, it is reported that you have lied."—"Ah! indeed."—"And others say that either you or Mr. —— has lied."—"In what does the lie consist?"—"You have said, sir, that you were invited by Mr. —— to come to this village and lecture on Romanism, which you never were."—"Very well, I am not troubled about that. I have said so, and I say so now." I named these things in my afternoon labors, for I meant that everything that was said about me or done to me should come square out before the public. I said, "Next Sabbath, if God will, I shall look at this thing in the face, and meet it in a way that I think every individual will be satisfied who has lied. If it is susceptible of proof that I have, I will get down upon my knees before this community and confess my wrong, until this village shall be shaken as with a moral earthquake."

CALUMNY REFUTED.

This brought the mass of the people together the next Sabbath. After services, I stated the report, and hoped that there might be some mistake, some where, because, for a minister of the Gospel to be charged with lying, is a great thing; but to be proved a liar, is awful. I stated to the congregation the conversation that took place, (while sitting in the buggy,) before referred to. After I was through, the P. clergyman arose (for he was present,) and said, he had no recollection of ever having said anything of the kind; that something might have been said, so remotely that the speaker might have considered it an invitation, but he did not think what he had said was even an apology for an invitation. I then repeated over verbatim, the conversation that had taken place on the highway. I then turned to the brother who was with us on that occasion, and said, "Now, Bro. D., did not your pastor make those statements and requests?" He answered, firmly, with an unfaltering voice, "He did, sir." That appeared to be the end of all strife in the mind of the public. Not very long after this, the clergyman closed his labors, and I do not know that I have ever seen him since.

SERMONS ON THE MOSAIC LAWS.

After laboring on Romanism for six or seven months, every Sabbath afternoon, I came to a close on that subject, and promised, if they would give me a hearing, I would deliver a course of sermons on the Mosaic Laws—the rules and regulations of the Jewish hierarchy. I did this in order to try my strength relative to holding a congregation. I soon found, that, in a good measure, I had secured the attention and good feeling of the people in general.

REMOVAL TO JEFFERSON.

In 1848, I resigned my charge in Reading, and moved to Jefferson. In a financial point of view, this was one of the greatest mistakes of my life. I had bought me a very pleasant little home, thirty acres of land, with house, barn, and fruit of every kind almost, and in a fair way to finish up the last payments of my contract, when I was advised, by brethren who I thought were good financiers, to sell that precious little home, and purchase a house and lot in the village where I was to perform my labor of building up a church. I did so, and now this house and lot are all my earthly possessions. Had it been in the former homestead, it would have made a desirable place for the evening of life.

But the work was fairly before me. The field to be occupied was somewhat difficult. Still, there was every inducement to labor on, hoping that, by and by, we should be numbered among the churches of the earth. We retained the old school-house in peace as a place of worship, but always by far too small for us.

COMMENCE TO BUILD.

It had pleased God in His providence to send among us, Bro. Alfred Bellamy and wife. He was a business man, ardently pious and benevolent—in fact, my right hand man. We saw that we could not do anything unless we built a church edifice. Means, we had but very little. However, we had some prospect that the earth would help the woman, and we commenced getting our timber and other materials together, in the winter of 1849.

When the summer of that year arrived, it brought with it that dire malady, the Cholera, which overset all our plans. Some of our subscribers were dead, some moved away, and others were either not able or not willing to do what they had promised or previously said they would. The day looked to us very dark. However, we took courage, got up a new subscription, and concluded to build the house. After looking over what we really wanted to meet the emergency of the case and the expectations of the community, we saw that it would cost us from twenty-five hundred to three thousand dollars. Contract let, and lesser expenses calculated, we found we could not foot up with less than throe thousand. There was a great deal of turning pale and trembling in view of the consequences. Our subscriptions would in no wise begin to reach the expense.

While in this dilemma, Bro. Bellamy was in the city buying goods. I was on my bed, sick. The friends in the village had built a very nice Union school-house, and it looked as though the old building was left for us until we could erect a house for God. While in this condition, my son came into my room and said, "Father, the Trustees are going to sell the old school-house." I asked him when? He said, "To-night." Then I felt heart-sick: nothing but the good providence of God could save us from being cast out upon the common. I told him to attend the sale, ascertain what it was sold for, and who bought it. When he returned, he informed me that the notice of sale was illegal, and that the sale was put off, I think for two weeks, in order to give correct notice.

Before the time had arrived, I was off my sick bed, and my brother had returned from the city. I said to him, "Now, I want you to buy that house." His remark was, "Why, it is literally worth nothing." I replied, "It is worth everything to us: it is our rallying point." After pressing him, he finally remarked, "I will buy it if you will stand in the gap for one-half the purchase money." I told him to go ahead. He sent a person on the night of the sale, and bought it, I think, for a hundred or a hundred and ten dollars. Its real value was very trifling, only it made us a shelter from the storm and from heat.

TROUBLES ABOUT OUR OLD PREACHING ROOM.

But we had not got out of our troubles. Very soon, we had notice served upon us to remove it from the corporation grounds. Then one great thing was, How can it be moved? but the greatest was, Where shall we put it? While walking through the village, looking for some vacant place where we could put our tent, I met a gentleman whose name I did not know. He said, "Well, Elder, I understand that you are ordered to remove your church."—"We are," was the answer, "but that is not the worst, sir; I can not find a place to set it."—"Well," said he, "I have got two vacant lots on that street. I am going West, to be gone a year or more, I do not know how long. You may remove it on to the east lot, with pleasure, only, when I tell you it must be moved or sold, I shall expect you will do it." I thanked him very kindly and told him that any time when he wished us to take it down or take it out of the way, we would certainly do it. I immediately started for the boat-yard, to try to get the loan of a capstan, cable ropes, and chains, necessary for the removal; raised a dust; and mustered help enough, from the brethren and friends, to take it to its new location. There was a great deal of wracking and cracking about the old shell, yet it held together, and the next Sabbath we were happily located in the old house on a new site.

That village had some peculiar advantages—such as its canal, and its steam-boat navigation on the lake—which made it a rallying point for boats lying in the large basin over the Sabbath. Here was a field of labor that met my heart's desire—for I always loved to preach to seamen and boatmen—and I thought to become a kind of Bethel chaplain. I told my congregation I wanted to preach on the lake shore, or else go down to the long pier and preach to the boatmen. I also asked for something that would designate the place where I should hold forth; and then described the ensign jack—a good size, with cords to it, so that I could easily bend it to one of the long poles which the boatmen always had upon their boats. I soon received a beautiful flag, with "Bethel Church" painted upon it, and, a short time after, another, what the sailor calls a swallow tail-jack.

PREACHING TO BOATMEN.

Now, I was equipped, outwardly, to my content. The villagers would turn out together, down to the boats, making me often a very large congregation. A friend, the pastor of one of the other churches, was desirous to share with me the happiness of preaching to the boatmen. I cordially took him in as a partner, but still found I had to do the greater part of the preaching. He was confined to his manuscript, and could not extemporize; consequently, if it proved to be a windy day, his craft would not hold up to the breeze, and his manuscript would be on a lee-shore. But I always felt ready and willing to aid the dear brother when those winds of affliction beat upon him, and we had good times.

Our meeting house progressing, we were moving on, hoping against hope that one day it would be better with us than now. But at last we appeared to come to a stand. Brethren and friends would say, "Now, Elder, we must stop this work. It will be a disgrace to us to get into debt more than we can pay." I replied, "I do not want that we should get in debt, but I want that we should redeem all our contracts, and let the work progress. Now, brethren, if you are willing to dispense with preaching once in a while on a Sabbath, I can gather up, pretty soon, five or six hundred dollars." They thought it was doubtful, but were willing it should be tried. I knew the churches all through the country, and had no fears but what I should get. aid. I started for my old ground between the Lakes. Tried Trumansburg, Covert, Farmerville, &c. All responded cordially, cheering my heart in the work. While I was laboring in this way, the trustees were paying out money as fast as I could obtain it.

One Saturday evening, about nine or ten o'clock, my wife came to my room and told me that Mr. —— wished to see me. My heart fluttered as soon as I heard his name. He was one of our workmen, and our trustees were pledged to see every mechanic paid when he needed it. I said to the gentleman, " Well, sir, what do you want?" He appeared to pause, as though he did not like to do his errand. I said, " Speak on. You want some money, do you?" He said, " Yes, sir." —"Very well, how much do you want?"—"I should like," he said, "to be paid up."—"How much are we owing you?"—"About sixteen dollars." I replied, " Well we can cut this work short. I have not got any money of any account. Mr. Bellamy is from home; but here, sir, I married a couple an hour or two ago, and there are two dollars that I got for it; take that, sir; it will last you over the Sabbath." He said, " When can I have the balance?"—"You shall have it on Monday forenoon." I had it not—could have borrowed it of any of my friends on the street, but that I dared not do. He went off, apparently well satisfied, (and so was I to think that I had the two dollars for him.)

A BENEVOLENT MORAVIAN.

The Sabbath came. I went to my appointment, in the morning. In the congregation was a very good hearted man, (then irreligious,) who, as I was passing through the streets to my afternoon appointment, came up to me, somewhat excited, and said, "Elder, make haste and get to the school-house. I dined," he said, "at the Washington house, to-day, and there were a gentleman and lady from New York; they told me where they had been to meeting in the forenoon, and inquired if there was any meeting in the village in the afternoon? I said, there, is a man who preaches this afternoon, but it is in a miserable old school-house, scarcely fit for decent people to go into. Now, make haste," he said, "make haste, they are passing up the other side. I want you to get there first and give them the best seat we have." I could not help smiling at his earnestness, and the thought of giving the gentleman and lady the best seat we had, for their was very little superiority, as it regarded seats, in our school-house church. They were old benches, broken down and patched up, which the loitering school boys had well nigh destroyed with their jack knives. However, I had been in but a few moments before the strangers made their appearance. "There they are! there they are!" exclaimed my friend, "look out for them! give them a good place!" (This man had been through the Mexican war, and learned to obey orders; and he spoke as though it was my duty to obey everything he commanded.) Our congregation came together as usual. I tried to preach as best I could, from a passage in Romans. It was a doctrinal subject. I saw, by their countenances, that the strangers fellowshiped the truth. When I had got through my sermon, I told my congregation, that the next Sabbath I must spend in the city of Rochester, for we must have some more funds. My own heart was very tender, and for a few moments the dear brethren and sisters appeared to be in the valley of Bochim. I dismissed my meeting, after which I introduced myself to the strangers. They apppeared to be courteous, kind, Christian people.

In the morning, I thought I would go down to the port, or what is more familiarly termed "the steam-boat landing," thinking perhaps I might get my eye on those friends, and shake hands with them again, as I had learned they were going down the Lake. While standing, looking at the bustle on the wharf as the boat was taking in some freight, "spat" came a man's hand on my shoulder, and behold it was the soldier again ! He said, in great haste, " Elder, the gentleman. and lady who were at meeting yesterday, are at the Washington house, and wish to see you before they go away. Run," he said, "with all speed, sir, for they will be going down to the boat very soon." I went to the house, inquired for their room, knocked, and re. ceived admission. The gentlemen said, "Sir, I could not leave this place without I saw you again. I was deeply interested in the precious truth you preached to us yesterday afternoon. When we were preparing to retire last evening, as is our custom, at home or abroad, to kneel down and pray, it appeared to me I could not pray. The thoughts that occupied my mind, sir, were these: Now, here is one of God's ministers, with a few poor brethren and sisters around him, who are struggling to build a house of worship; and what is my duty, in view of their circumstances? I did not think, when I left home, that any benevolent object might present itself; consequently, I am unprepared. I do not belong to your denomination. I trust we belong to Christ's Kingdom, however. I am one of the United Brethren, commonly called Moravians. I should like to spend some time with you, but we must go down on the boat. Now, sir, there are twenty dollars. Please accept, and may it encourage your heart to labor on." So that, on Monday forenoon, I was able to redeem my pledge to the mechanic, pay him up, and have money on hand.

COMPLETE OUR HOUSE.

. We struggled on and completed our church edifice, which cost something over three thousand dollars. It is a beautiful little house, well adapted to a rising village. We began to come to a conclusion of the whole matter. I saw that we were coming out in debt about a thousand dollars. This I had anticipated, all the way through. And in talking with Bro. Belamy, we came to the conclusion that the money should be borrowed, so that every man, employed on the work, should be paid up, before we entered it for worship; (and I do not recollect that there was a man who could righteously say, You owe me one cent.) The next thing was to find the man who had the money. I knew him, and thought we could get a loan, by giving security on the property. The gentleman was willing to do the business, but, before we come in possession of the money, he did not like the security. The house might burn down, and the lot would not be worth a thousand dollars. Some of my brethren come to me with the trouble. I remarked to them; "If that is all the difficulty, we can turn him out the insurance as collateral security: then he will be perfectly safe." He accepted the proposition. All our debts for materials and work, were thus paid off. We entered that edifice perhaps with as much gratitude as ever any poor little church did.

ORGANIZATION—INDEPENDENCE.

In raising the interest at Jefferson, some sticklers for the square rule may think us a little loose in our management. When we were very small, we organized ourselves into a church, and attended all the ordinances of God's house as regularly as though we had been recognized for twenty years. We called no council for fellowship, for reasons that were best known to ourselves. However, some of the pastors and deacons, in the churches between the Lakes, approved our course. We reported to the Seneca Association our numbers, increase, and diminution, as regularly as though we had been one of their body, (though this was not entered on their Minutes.) We looked up to the Association as a child would look up to his father. When the time came, we called a council for fellowship, and received the hearty recognition of a large class of our brethren.

BETHEL SERVICES—INCIDENTS.

I have referred, to labor performed in the open air on board of boats in the harbor, and some very interesting scenes we had. They were generally as orderly a congregation as we find in our churches. Once in a while we found a man, intoxicated, who would act under that influence. I remember, one Sabbath, having thrown our banner to the breeze, we opened services by singing, (and the friends did sing, and many of the boatmen assisted them, with a will that would almost make a Christian believe that they were on board Old Ship Zion, just entering the port.) But as I arose to pray, the intemperate man was a little noisy. I spoke very calmly to him, "Now, sir, be still—we are going to pray." He stammered out, (for his tongue was very thick,) "Lord, I was just agoing to pray myself." Some kind friends took hold of him, peacefully led him away, and he troubled us no more.

On another occasion, we went down to the boats to hear a stranger preach.. He had not proceeded far before it appeared evident that his knowledge of
24

human nature was not very extensive. He endeavored to open the pit of eternal darkness, and to show
the boatmen that that was their doom, and I thought
he told them a great many things that they were truly
guilty of, and perhaps many things that they were not:
in fact, when he was through, it appeared as though
he had made them out to be the most desperately
wicked of all men. Indignation seemed to flash from
many eyes during the sermon. It was evident that all
the bad feeling that they possessed was aroused from
the very bottom.

After his labors were over, I remarked to them,
" Next Sabbath, many of you will be here again. You
will have made your trip, so far. Some will be waiting
for the tow-boat to go down the lake, and others perhaps will be for working their way up to Corning.
Now, I wish to say to you, if God will, I shall be here
with an invitation for some of you to furnish us with a
setting-pole on which to hoist our colors." Then I
added, with some degree of sternness, " I shall preach
to you, and tell you what I think of boatmen."

I redeemed my pledge. But, as I passed along the
boats, there appeared to be an unusual coldness and
indifference manifested. Instead of the usual kind invitation, " Come on board my boat! Come on board
my boat!" I had to ask the privilege of some three or
four boats, before I could get consent to establish our
quarters. I endeavored to preach to them as much of
Jesus as I could possibly crowd into the time allotted.
But it was very evident, from their countenances
generally, that they were very desirous to know what
the speaker thought of them.

THE PENNSYLVANIA PACKET BOAT CAPTAIN.

At the close of the sermon, I remarked, " Now I

have my pledge to redeem. I have not yet told you what I think of boatmen. Boatmen are exposed to many temptations. There are many sinful ways into which they are often drawn by their avocation, and I am sorry that it is so, but I tell you that I believe that boatmen have some warm places in their hearts if we can only get down to them. But this does not satisfy you. You want to know something more relative to my thoughts. Well, now, in order to do this, and give you clearer perceptions of what I think of you, I will relate an anecdote that I read in a paper some time ago. The circumstances were in substance as follows :

"In an adjoining State, the Railway cars came to their terminus at a given place on one of the Canals of that State. The passengers there changed from the cars to the packet. But, on board the cars, there was a poor invalid, a young man who had been living West. He had the consumption, and was very near to his end; his great anxiety was to live to reach home, that he might die in the arms of his dear mother. The passengers in the car did not like his company, and they proposed to inform the captain of the packet, that, if he took that sick man along, they would not go with him; and they appointed one of their number to carry the message to the captain of the boat. After he had heard what they had to say on the subject, he inquired, "Gentlemen, is there no one to speak for the young man? Where is he?"—"He is in the car, but we shall not go with you if you take him."—"Very well," replied the captain, "We will see about it. I want to see the young man for myself." He went into the car, and the next thing they saw was the captain, with the young man in his arms. The captain carried the sick boy to his boat, gave him the best berth he had, and told his cook to attend to him and give him any nourishment that he could take. The travelers were very indignant at the conduct of the captain, and still declared that they would not go on board of the boat with that man. The captain looked at his watch, and said it was so many minutes before he should start. The passengers waited to see the result, whether he would leave them or not. By and by, the word was given, "Cast off the lines, boys!" There was a general rush to the packet. After they were on board, calm reflection appeared to take her seat upon her throne, and one and another began to relent that they had been so forward in endeavoring to deprive the young man of his passage. It resulted," according to the account that I saw in the paper— not because the young man was really needy, but as a token of respect, or in other words to palliate their former conduct—"they made him up a very handsome purse, and thanked the captain for his perseverance and manhood. Now, that was none other than Capt. Samuel D. Kerns, well known to many Pennsylvania boatmen!

"I have related this anecdote to show to you what I think of boatmen. They have got hearts, they have got souls. With all their faults, I love them still." There were perhaps but few boatmen present, but what were in tears; their hearts had been reached, at least sympathetically.

One word more in relation to the church in Jefferson. They did not financier, perhaps, as well as they ought to have done; their debt, for money borrowed to pay for building, was heavy upon them; but, after hard struggling, and with the assistance of the Seneca Association, they finally lifted the debt. The little church is living along, and I believe will maintain its visibility.

They still remain a member of that Association which has been to them a foster-mother.

CHEMUNG RIVER ASSOCIATION—ITS CHURCHES.

In 1842, it was talked up amongst the brethren about forming a new Association, to be called the Chemung River Baptist Association. It held its first anniversary with the Campbell and Irwin church, Steuben county. This association 'was made up of some of the old churches, such as Big Flats, Catlin and Dix, Caton, Factoryville, Smithport and Elmira, (now called the First Church of Elmira, for they have become two bands,) and eight other churches which had been organized about 1840 and 1842, making in the whole fifteen churches, with twelve ordained ministers, four licentiates, and a membership of 1,282. Some of the churches have changed their names since their original organization.

Elmira and Fairport was originally Elmira, being named after the town, (not after the city,) and is now called Horse Heads, (sometimes, "Fairport.") There are some interesting things in relation to this church. It was gathered by the Rev. P. D. Gillette, in part an offshoot from the Big Flats church. I thought, in its early years, it was composed of as good elements as any church in my acquaintance. They had a meeting house, known by the name of the "Marsh Church." It was a singular name, but true to the letter, for it stood in what might be termed a peninsula, or rather an island, in a marsh. I asked Bro. Gillette why build a house in such a place? He said it was "the geographical center, and you know some people are more tenacious about the exact center than they are to have a good location a short distance from that center." I always thought that the Horse Heads, in nature, was the very

place for a house of God. I was present at the time of
the organization of this church, when it took its present location. Elder Jackson had the pastoral care of
the original church, and was anxious for it to remove
its stand-point to the place just named. But brethren
and sisters, whose hearts were bound up in the old
hive where they had seen so much of the grace of God,
were unwilling to break up, and instead, perhaps, of
endeavoring to conciliate, too harsh measures. were
pursued in order to accomplish the desired end. I remember Bro. Jackson informing me of the course that
had been taken. It appeared that he and a number of
brethren and sisters had consulted in relation to the
change, and they were willing to be led by him. He
then gave me the text from which he preached, and a
synopsis.of his sermon, from Amos, 6th chapter and
12th verse: "Shall horses run upon the rock? will one
plow there with oxen? for ye have turned judgment
into gall, and the fruit of righteousness into hemlock."
He had with him nineteen or twenty, I think, who
took letters at that time to lay the foundation of this
new organization, and some very good brethren and
sisters they were, and some equally good were left behind, much grieved in spirit. A council was called for
their fellowship; much was said in relation to the
capability of the little church to sustain the Gospel
amongst them. I remarked that I would be decided
in reference to their organization, and the fellowship-
ing by the council, providing Eld. Jackson, having cast
in his lot with them, designed to stand by them as their
pastor, until there should be a mutual agreement between pastor and people that it would be best to dis-
solve the connection. The reply was, "I have made
up my mind, as long as the church is suited, to stand
by them. I have no intention of anything else." I

think, in two or three weeks, I heard that Bro. Jackson had gone to Orleans county, some supposed in view of settling, and the first thing that I knew was that he had moved his tent. Notwithstanding, the church survived; God has given them good pastors, (none better than the present incumbent, Rev. Philetus Olney." They are a strong, working, useful church. Several of their members I have been personally acquainted with, thirty-five years at least.

The First Church, Elmira, I have been intimately acquainted with ever since its organization. Some of the original members still live, while others long ago have gone to their rest. I might refer to names that still survive amongst them—none more dear to me than one of their present deacons, Bro. Joseph Grover. I shall have occasion again to refer to this church.

The church at Campbell and Irwin did not exist when I first traveled through that region. The Hornby church had a common center on the upland, some miles off, called Robbins' Hill. In passing to and fro over the country where this church is now located, I used to preach in a place called Cobbs' barn. They were mostly Presbyterian people who cared for me— warm hearted, not troubled with a great deal of sectarianism—but in those days, and I believe it is so yet, any individual who brought to them the bread of life was cordially received. I was invited, when I passed through that way, to make it my home at a Mr. Pierce's. And a home indeed it was for the traveling pilgrim. It pleased God to convert his wife, and I baptized her. This was hard work for her dear husband. He thought all his earthly comfort was gone. But, some months after, he was convinced, that, instead of having lost his earthly comfort, it had become dearer to him than ever before, for he was made the happy recipient of divine grace, and enjoyed in a great measure the comforts of God's salvation. In conversing with him one day, he said, "Elder, do you wish to walk out?" I replied "Yes, no objection." We walked down the road, some thirty rods perhaps: he led me into the bushes, and came to a certain place, where we stopped. "There," he said, "is the spot that I have picked out, in my own mind, as a place to build a meeting house." It was a beautiful site, being an eminence overlooking the beautiful land known as Cooper's plains. (In fact, all that part of the valley of the Conhocton is delightful.) The time appeared to have arrived when Robbins' Hill, the favorite center of the old church, was no longer adapted to meet the necessities of the people. Many precious souls had been converted within a reasonable distance of this point, which had impressed the mind of my dear Bro. Pierce as the proper rallying place for those who had been hopefully converted to God, and for others for whom we prayed that they might follow in the same precious way.

In the arrangement that was to be made in reference to houses of worship, it was agreed to change the locality of the old church to a place called Hornby Forks. This would make it convenient for quite a number of the brethren and sisters on Nash's Hill, who had been considered a part of the mother church—the old church in Catlin. The Campbell and Irvin meeting house was built upon the site my brother had selected. The Hornby Church built their house at the forks, just referred to. Now, the brethren and sisters in the valley of Mead's creek can go to their place of worship without climbing the hill. The other brethren, living on the upland, can be very comfortably accommodated at their common center. Though many of the dear brethren and sisters who I baptized through that region of country sleep the sleep that knows no waking until the resurrection of the just, I hope to hail them in the first resurrection. Among the departed are Dea. J. Underwood, sister St. John, and others whom I might name. Dea. St. John, I understand, is yet living, but his toils are almost ended.

The Caton church, which I have referred to before, was organized in 1832. It was always very gratifying to me to meet these churches by their delegates in association.

CHAPTER VIII.—1852 TO 1865.

NEW ENTERPRISES.

In 1852, by advice of brethren of the Seneca Association, I went to try to raise a church in some of the new villages, west of Elmira, on the New York and Erie Railroad. I tarried at Addison, over one Sabbath, but, on looking over that field, did not see anything calculated to induce me to hope that a Baptist interest could speedily be raised in that place, and so I continued on up to

HORNELLSVILLE.

This appeared to be one of the most thriving villages on that part of the line, being the terminus of the western section, and the point of junction with the railway to Buffalo. There was a large, floating population. I found people dwelling in partly finished habitations, in shanties, and, in some instances, large barns had been partitioned off for the accommodation of families. Everything looked like thrift and activity. I found in the village a brother and sister Owen, with whom I had been acquainted when they were young people. He was converted in Elmira. His wife I had baptized into the fellowship of the church in Reading, in her early years. They were well posted in relation to the field for labor. There was no Baptist church in the place, and not to exceed half a dozen Baptists.

HORNELLSVILLE CHURCH FORMED.

We engaged a hall on Main street for a place of worship. It was well located, but in some respects was not a desirable place—for, like all public halls, in such villages, it was used through the week for all kinds of performances. Sometimes, when I went to attend worship on Sabbath morning, I would find theatrical apparatus, curtains, and paintings, as they had been left on Saturday night. But we kept on laboring, and things began to look favorable. The Hornellsville church was organized, October 15, 1852, with fourteen members, and attended all the ordinances of God's house as best they could.

LOOK OUT FOR A PLACE TO BUILD.

I had been in the village but a short time before I began to look about for some vacant lots suitable for a meeting house. There was a corner, at Church and Canisteo streets, which appeared to me the most desirable location, for the purpose, in all the place. If my memory serves me, the lot is about eight rods on one street, and twelve on the other. Upon inquiry, I could not at first find any one who knew who owned it. One day, I stopped a gentleman on the street to chat a moment or two with him, and said, "Sir, can you tell me who owns this corner?" He said he thought the lots were not owned by any person in the village. They had been held by some gentlemen who had been speculating in land and building houses for sale, but they had closed their business, and where they had gone he did not know—"but if any one can give you the-information, probably Esquire L. can."

I waited upon Esquire L., who informed me that the owners resided in New Hampshire. After gaining what information I could, I asked him if he would do me a kindness. He was not, strictly speaking, a religious man, and (I was told) held views, on the subject of future punishment, directly opposite my own. But that made no difference to me as far as my business with him was concerned. I remarked, "Now, sir, I expect you will stand fire—that is, I want to talk with you, confidentially—do not want my conversation to come out upon the street. I desire you to write to these gentlemen—inasmuch as you have business transactions with them—and please to inqure if these lots are for sale, and, if so, what will be the price of them?" One of the owners wrote that the lots were for sale, but he had not power to sell them, as his partner was at the West, transacting business—he thought the price would probably be six hundred dollars. He gave us his partner's address, for any further information. I requested Esquire L. to write to the gentleman, West. We received no answer—waited some time— wrote again to New Hampshire—learned that the Western partner had changed his location, and then addressed him at his new residence. He promptly replied that the lots were for sale, but should not name the price, as he expected to be in Hornellsville, soon, and would dispose of them in person.

The thing we most feared, now threatened us—if he should offer them for sale, there were certain land speculators who in all probability would give more than we could be able to offer. A few days after this information, another letter was received, saying he had declined coming east, and the lots could be had for six

25

hundred. I immediately said to my legal friend, "Now, sir, will you please write again to the gentleman in New Hampshire, giving him what information you have had from his partner, or enclose his letter that he may see for himself—asking him to appoint you his agent to manage this business? The lot I want to build a church upon, and that is the reason why I did not wish this correspondence to be made public." He replied, "I should have no objection to do this, providing you were calculating to purchase the property for yourself; but your church, sir, is too small, and too poor either to buy lots or build a house." I replied to him, "The few Baptists in this village, with all the reproach that is heaped upon them, are not the representatives of the Baptist denomination in the State of New York. If we have not the money, there are those who have." The reply was, "They may have the money, but can you obtain it?" I said to him, "Sir, how long will you give us to settle this point relative to the means?" He replied, "If I have got anything more to do about this, I should like to do the business up pretty soon." "Well, sir, in twenty-four hours, I will set your mind at rest."

I knew who had the money. I consequently got into the cars, came down to Elmira, called upon the pastor of the Baptist church, and made known my errand. I told him we wanted six hundred dollars, and that six hundred dollars we must have. The property was well worth the money for any individual to take, even on speculation. He said, "Where is your mind made up to make a call?" I told him, in the first place, we would call on Brother Riggs Watrous. He was a business man, and I endeavored to present the thing to him in a business point of view. He said at once, "I will take an equal share of the six hundred dollars, in one hundred dollar shares, providing Deacon Howell, Brother Grover, Brother Canfield," and one other whose name has escaped my mind, "will do the same." I obtained the four for one hundred dollars each, and Brother Watrous, if my memory serves me, was to advance two hundred dollars to make the thing complete. Brother W. inquired, "Now, when do you want this money?" "Not until Mr. L. gets the deed." "It will have to be acknowledged in New Hampshire and in Wisconsin, which will take some time to get around. If my figures tell truly, it will be along about the first week in January." I said to Bro. Watrous, "Now, we want something to show that this is a bona fide contract—that you are holden for six hundred dollars when the papers shall be presented." He remarked, "I will straighten up all that. I will give you a line to Mr. ——, one of the most wealthy merchants in your village, who is doing a large business with me, and he will satisfy Mr. L. that all is right in this thing." I arranged the business, and my friend L. appeared to be very happy that we had got things in such a safe train. He said, "I have been to see Mr. ——, and he informs me that the paper is just as good as any Bank in the State."

We called a council, to see if they would fellowship the little church, early in January. They arrived overnight, and among them were some of those dear friends who had agreed to advance the funds. Brother Watrous had put the money in his pocket, when he started for the council, and, I think, in the morning's mail, the papers arrived. The next day the money was paid over, and all was right. Next, we wished those brethren to give the little church, through their trustees, an article to run five years. So far, we had secured some foothold in that village. If we had no credit there, it was a clear case that brethren abroad had confidence in us.

COMPELLED TO LEAVE HORNELLSVILLE.

My health failed me after I had been there about fifteen months, and I was under the necessity of retiring from the field, thinking my earthly work was done. There was but one sermon more that I thonght I should ever preach, and perhaps not that. I was under pledge to preach a dedication sermon, for what was called a Mission church, between five and six miles south from Elmira, to be known as the Pine Woods Church, but which eventually took the name of SOUTHPORT.

THE HOUSE COMPLETED.

The church in Hornellsville felt very severely the necessity which rested upon their first pastor to resign his charge. But his successor went on to build the house. It is a beautiful, brick structure, an honor to the village, to the pastor, and to the people who accomplished the work. I believe it cost something over four thousand dollars. Embarrassed with their land debt, and something for building, it kept them (as it is often termed) "under the harrow." But the ladies were most indomitable in perseverance, and have done their part, and sometimes I thought more than their part, towards liquidating their debts and making the internal part of the house desirable. The Chemung River Association, as they have always done, were ever ready to aid in whatever way they could. The church had unnecessary trouble, and caused their friends much anxiety, in consequence of their own somewhat divided state, when Satan got the advantage of them. But I believe they are now clear of debt, (much of it having been paid by the Elmira brethren)

—are in comfortable union—and happy under the labors of Brother Seely. Although they have had many trials, they have also much to encourage them—a young minister strong to labor, a fine field, and as I was informed last evening, their village contains four thousand inhabitants. There is, I believe, no Baptist church within five or more miles: consequently, they have a large margin on the outside of their border. My heart would rejoice could I see them again in the flesh, all walking together in the bonds of unity and peace.

DECEASE OF ELDER BAINBRIDGE—ELMIRA.

I feel sad to-day, just having received the tidings that Rev. S. M. Bainbridge, pastor of the Central church in Elmira, has suddenly paid the debt of nature, and gone to his rest. I had known him from his College days, and was acquainted with his family and with his wife's family before they were married. It has brought my mind back to the changes which have taken place in the Baptist interest in that young city. The First Baptist church was organized in 1829. The place was originally called "New Town," and I had heard much of it under that old name. When I first saw it, I found that, as is often the case, we judge of the magnitude of a thing by the accounts we hear of it, but are disappointed when it is presented to our vision. More than forty years ago, when first visiting the place, I was like the boy who was looking all around for the Fourth of July, when in reality he was in the midst of it! My thoughts revert to the days of Bro. Philander D. Gillette, whose remains, with those of his brother, Daniel H., have for years been slumbering in the ground. We often conversed in relation to the Baptist interest in Elmira, and often knelt together and prayed that God might bless and prosper that little, infant band. I had often said to brethren in the First church, "Now is your time to colonize; the little one has in a measure become a thousand; you have wealth enough, numbers enough that you might spare, and territory on which they might pitch their tent—and in a few years, under God, they might stand up by your side like an only son, full of life and vigor, by the side of his father, while his father's locks began to tinge with gray, his countenance furrowed with the cares of human life." I feared, if they did not make the sacrifice, and do what appeared to be God's will and their duty, the day might come when some unexpected whirlwind might pass over them and leave them in a very unhappy condition. I am sorry that my fears have been too much realized. There are few if any among the churches more endeared to me than the First Baptist church in Elmira. There are also dear brethren and sisters, in the Central church, whom I love in the Lord. I hope the time is not far distant when these two churches may enjoy all the good feeling, love, and harmony that it is their privilege to enjoy as the redeemed people of the Prince of Peace.

I have said that I felt sad, to-day. And something more. I feel like a reed shaken with the wind. With me, "the grasshopper is a burden, and desire fails." I am realizing very sensibly, my mortality. Had it not been for the love and deference I owe to my brethren of the Chemung River Association, I could never have made up my mind to comply with their request to give them these few dottings of my checkered life. I feel at times as if haunted by a specter, that, after having done and said all I have to do and say on this subject, my friends will feel towards it as a certain old man said relative to himself. After hardly ever seeing a school for sixty years, he supposed, while almost in his second childhood, that he was well qualified to teach. I saw him pass my door in the morning, and said to him, "Where now?"—"Going," he replied, "before the school inspectors to be examined." On his return, I inquired, "Well, how have you come out?"—"I have been run through the mill," he replied, "and have come out—all bran!" In the judgment of charity, I think the brethren may say of me, as the old man said of himself. My nervous system is taxed to its utmost capacity while this work is progressing, and I sometimes feel afraid that it will fall into perfect wreck and ruin before I shall get to the close—the end—which is near at hand.

NEW PINE WOODS CHURCH IN SOUTHPORT.

Having resigned my charge, through indisposition, at Hornellsville, in the spring of 1854, I sought again to enjoy the sweets of HOME, and rest in the bosom of my family. I had left my companion in Havana, (three miles south from Jefferson,) with my second son, Dr. S. B. Sheardown. She had become infirm, and afflicted with paralysis—and my son felt desirous of having her continually under his own eye.

When called to leave Hornellsville and the dear brethren I loved so much, and where I had anticipated bringing them through the building of their house, I had about made up my mind to spend the remnant of my days, as much as possible, free from the labors and cares through which I had so long toiled and traveled. But God thought otherwise. I received notice from Bro. Chandler, then pastor of the First church in Elmira, that the house of worship for their Mission church was about finished, the day set for the dedication service, and they still depended upon me to preach the sermon.

THEIR MEETING HOUSE.

The building of that house was a good work. It is a neat superstructure, situated in a pleasant place. The whole cost I do not now recollect, but .it certainly could not have been less than twenty-five hundred dollars, calculating the grubbing, for it was built in the woods. The grading and fencing, together with the edifice, must have amounted to the sum specified, beside the building of a row of sheds for the accommodation of horses and carriages. Three of the brethren of the First church, living in that region, lifted very heavy. I think I never saw men of their means do better than they. They must have paid, at the least calculation, twelve hundred dollars towards making that place of worship what it now is. Deacons HOWELL, GROVER, and BROWN were the three strong men to whom I now refer.

BLESSING ADDED.-

The time having arrived for the services, I tried to preach the dedication sermon. The Lord was pleased to give the dear brethren evidences of his approbation, and sanction the good work that they had done, by convicting sinners under the very first exercises of the meeting. It was thought best to continue our meetings a few days, and see what the result would be. The pastor, and some of the brethren and sisters, from Elmira, came up, and aided in the good work. God gave me strength to preach once or twice every day for six or eight weeks. It was a soul-refreshing season. Bro. Chandler baptized the converts, as pastor of the church in Elmira, for as yet no church was organized in connection with the house just dedicated. The church, I believe, was organized in May, and received recognition in July.

After having labored through the protracted effort, Dea. Howell remarked to me that they were anxious I should take the pastorate. I had been acquainted with him for thirty years at least. He acknowledged that there were some drawbacks. The *first*-was, aside from those, who had lifted so hard to build the house, the generality of the brotherhood were in rather limited circumstances. I conversed freely upon the subject, and yet see, in my mind's eye, his tears, when he said, " I wish, Elder, we could give you what you ought to have, but I know we can not." I remarked to him, I never had had many trials or much trouble about salary business.

COMPENSATION—TEMPTATIONS ABOUT THE MINISTRY.

Satan had sometimes tempted, to allure me from my chosen field of labor, and so had men, both orthodox heterodox, and also men professing no religion at all.

I. TO QUIT THE MINISTRY.

One wealthy, enterprising man, said on one occasion, " Now, Eld. Sheardown, sell your horse, or give it away, and quit your preaching. You know as much about business as one-half of the merchants I am acquainted with. If you will, I will purchase you a stock of goods, and find you a place where you cannot help but get rich." I replied, " I had rather have nothing with a clear conscience, than be rich with a guilty conscience, having forsaken God, and the blessed vocation of preaching His Word for the sake of filthy lucre." I have wept and prayed a great many times with that man, since the time referred to, around his own family altar. He sometimes would say, " Elder, don't you remember when we talked about selling the old horse ? I never should have made that statement, if I had known in my own heart the blessedness of the Gospel at that time."

II.   TO GAIN A LARGER SALARY.

On another occasion, I received a letter from a friend in one of the cities, saying that their people were going to be destitute of a pastor, and were quite desirous of obtaining my labors. " Now, if you answer this by saying you will come, you may expect a call, very soon."   I pondered this in my mind, looked over the · loñg, hard years of labor and toil, on the mountains, through the valleys, and across the rivers, and it appeared to be time that I should look for a more easy field of labor.   Riding alone one day, 1 almost decided that, all things considered, it was my duty to accept the call, if given.   But I had no sooner come to the conclusion, than a voice came as from the Throne of God, " *With whom hast thou left these few sheep in the wilderness ?*"   I had then on my hands two or three little churches, that were unprovided for.   " With whom hast thou left these few sheep in the wilderness?"   I replied to myself (and perhaps audibly,) " Lord! I would not leave them in their present condition, for all the wealth they have in their city ; nor has all their influence power to draw me there."

III.   TO TURN UNIVERSALIST.

There was another individual, with whom I was intimately acquainted—an excellent neighbor, kind in every sense of the word; I have baptized many in a beautiful little stream near his house, when his doors were always open to accommodate the candidates returning from the water; I have preached many sermons in his barn ; he was always cheerful, and ready to accommodate,—but, in his religious views, a Universalist.   One day, in conversation with him, he referred to my straitened circumstances, and how difficult it must be for me to get along with my large family. "Now," said he, "I love to hear you preach, with some small exceptions. If you would only make a little change in your doctrine, come out on a full, free, and universal salvation, I can put you right into a good living, of at least six or eight hundred dollars a year." I replied, "God said, Buy the truth and sell it not."

After having stated these facts to the deacon, he said, "Well, do you think you can live on four hundred dollars a year?" I answered, "Yes"—I had never had so large a salary, with the same hope of obtaining it, in my life; and that fact he knew almost as well as I did.

The *next* obstacle that appeared to be in the way, was the difficulty in obtaining a house. "There is a little house," he said, "adjoining my farm, owned by Bro. Striker," but he would be ashamed for any stranger to come and visit his minister living in such an inconvenient place. I remarked to him, "It makes but very little difference to me what kind of a place I live in—I had just as soon live in a shanty by the way-side, as anywhere—if I could only say to my friends, I am only stopping here until such times as the church can build a parsonage." "That," he replied, "is what every church ought to have, and I think we must try and do it." I then answered, "If you will make the effort to build a parsonage, we will be contented to move into the house you speak off." He replied, "It would be very difficult to obtain a site, for people do not like to sell off a small patch of their farms to put a house upon, because there would·be always more or less uneasiness growing out of fowls trespassing, and other little things, for 'tis the little things that make the great troubles. If you come with us, you must make up your mind to be on the lookout. There may be some little place for sale. And now, if you can be obtained under these circumstances, I will guarantee that every contract on the part of the church shall be fulfilled, to the very letter of it."

BECOME A SETTLED PASTOR.

I entered into an engagement with that new interest, to take the pastoral charge, and removed my wife and youngest son from Havanna. I never saw her more happy in a removal than she was when settled on the plank-road, in the very bosom of friends who had known us so many years. And_I must say it was equally satisfactory to me, after having been tossed about for so many years, to find that we were safely moored in such a quiet harbor. We looked forward for years of comfort, as well as toil, and, though an infirmity had got its hand upon us both, yet our motto remained the same, to die with our harness on. Neither of us thought, that, in two short months, we should be severed from each other by the scythe of death, and become separated for all time.

DEATH OF MRS. ESTHER G. SHEARDOWN.

Mrs. Sheardown sickened about the last of June, and died on the 20th of July. (See Appendix.) I felt, when I kneeled by her bed and prayed after she had breathed her last, as though I was cut loose from all my moorings. Our life had been a checkered one; but, however dark and gloomy everything around might be, we always had sunshine in our domestic circle. I have said but very little in relation to my wife. One reason has been, it is painful to me to review the past, because in that I view my severe loss. Not that I am not blessed in my present relations, nor that my second companion is not everything to me, now so late in the afternoon of life.

We laid our beloved one away in the place of her choice, (Havanna,) near by the field where she had spent so many years of toil and labor in her domestic circle, in the church, and out of the church, around the sick bed, and every place, by day and by night, where her help, or any comfort, physical or spiritual, could be rendered. The burying ground in which she was laid, was disposed of by corporation order, and her remains, with the greater part of the others there interred, have been removed to a cemetery of some thirty-five acres, overlooking a beautiful landscape, where the Seneca lake can be seen, like a broad, silver belt, for near one-half of its length.

In my lonely condition, some of my children or grand-children were almost continually with me. One of my daughters let me have her own hired help to keep house for me, and myself and our youngest son were wrapped in the habiliments of mourning. After something like a year had passed away, I took my present companion, Mrs. Lorrin Alexander, widow of Amos R. Soper, of Pennsylvania.

DEACONS HOWELL AND BROWN BUILD A PARSONAGE.

After this digression we will return to the parsonage. I met on the road, one day, a gentleman, who said to me, "Elder, did you know that Mr. Cook wished to sell his place?" I said, "No, sir." He replied, "I understand he does." I inquired if he knew what he would ask for it? He did not know, positively, but thought he would take six hundred dollars. It was one of the most beautiful building spots on all that plank road. I communicated the information to my good Deacon Howell. He remarked he would see, and ask John what he thought about it. This John was the junior deacon, the present Dea. Brown. He was not wealthy,

26

but one of those whole-souled business men whose heart is like a globe, and as full of benevolence as the sun is full of light. They talked this matter up between themselves, and agreed to buy the place. The first thought was to repair the house that was upon it, or build an addition, but when they came to examine the house, after having made the purchase, they found that it had been built in those days when timber grew very large. It was put up in bents, with posts and girders large enough for a barn a hundred feet long. It was thought best to abandon the old house entirely, and take it out of the way, dig a cellar, and put up a new house on the old site. Those two men prosecuted the work, paid all the contracts and bills, and when the last draw of the painter's brush passed up the edifice, all was square, ready for the pastor to take possession of. For this house, with its two acres of ground, orchard and garden, I allowed them one hundred dollars a year rent. I labored untiringly to improve the ground, lay out the garden anew, fix up the door yard for a flower garden and shrubbery, (for I always loved flowers,) and endeavored to make everything as desirable as possible. There was a very nice, comfortable barn built upon the premises, so that there was little or nothing lacking to make it a beautiful home.

Those deacons held the property in their own hands. This sometimes was a trouble to me, because I knew they designed to deed it to the church, through its trustees. It was very evident that Dea. Howell, though not very aged, was failing. His dear companion—a woman in Israel, indeed, who yet survives—said to him, "David, you are very sick: had you not better make arrangements about that parsonage?" He replied, in his weakness, "O, yes—I wish John was here." Just about that time, Dea. Brown walked in, when the dying man said, "John, I am very sick. Ought we not to do something about that house and lot?" The young deacon said, "Yes, what do you wish to do, uncle David?"—" Why, you know I want to give my part to the church. Will you give yours?" —"To be sure," replied the junior. A professional brother from the First church in Elmira was at once obtained, and the business was finished. Those two men gave to the church a property which cost them from sixteen to seventeen hundred dollars.

LOSS OF DAVID HOWELL—A GOOD MAN INDEED.

Bro. Howell was momentarily nearing the eternal world. At times, his pains were excruciating, but we knew that the blessings of God were buoying him up under all his affliction. After his death, his companion, for the benefit of science, gave her consent for a post mortem examination. I was present, and the fact was demonstrated that he died with cancer in the stomach.

So passed away from life's stage, one of the most upright, devoted, Christian men. As an officer in the church, he was always in his place, unless sickness or absence from home prevented. He was indeed the minister's friend—the pastor's companion. Very seldom did a week pass, but he visited the pastor's house, inquiring if the family were well—if they needed any supplies—to talk about the interests of Zion, the great, important truths of the Gospel—then pray, and depart on other errands of good, or return to his avocation in life, or to his house to enjoy the comforts that could always be found around his happy board. Few infant churches have been blessed with such a worthy man, and fewer perhaps have been so suddenly deprived of his labors and influences.

When the church was organized, it was expected

that Dea. Grover also would cast in his lot with us, as we thought he could be more useful in this new location. To our great regret, he concluded to retain his standing with the old church in Elmira. He had contributed heavily towards the erection of our house, and lived convenient to it. His decision taught us that we must not put our trust in man.

DEACON JOHN BROWN'S BURDEN.

Dea. Brown had always leaned upon Dea. Howell's wisdom and judgment in managing the affairs of Zion. But when the chief duties devolved upon him—often with fear and trembling, and with very diminutive views of himself—Dea. Brown bowed his neck to the yoke, and gave his shoulder to the burden, with a willing heart and ready hand. I recollect hearing a minister, while preaching before the Seneca Association, say that he had once in a while seen a minister indeed, but he had never seen a deacon. But I think I have seen as many deacons fill their office with credit to themselves and honor to the church, as I have of ministers. Things went on very pleasantly. We had an excellent Sabbath-school, through the summer season, of which Deacon Brown was superintendent. I have known few men better calculated to superintend a school than he is. And I have known him from his early years, for some of his family were converted under my administration, and joined the church in Caton.

With that young church on the Plank Road, I spent many happy days, as well as days of grief. I used to go up into what was called "the Woods," to Deacon Brown's saw-mill, and I don't know but I preached as good sermons in that mill as I ever preached. We had an out-station at a school-house, pretty much surrounded by the native forest, where everything looked familiar and desirable. Another station was six miles down the river, about two and a half miles north of Wellsburg. God was pleased to give us, from time to time, evidences that we had not labored in vain nor spent our strength for naught.

A CHANGE DESIRABLE.

The query, perhaps, may arise in the minds of some, Why leave such a pleasant location? And here let me say, that I did not leave for want of a place in the affections of my people, neither because I had lost my attachment to them. In the first place, the field itself was contracted. Within the distance of six miles on that plank road, there were five meeting-houses, which spoke well for the people, at least in appearance. Yet, after all, considering the extent of the field, some of the ground was very sterile. But this was not the chief reason why I thought it duty to resign my charge. The church appeared to be bearing a burden, financially, that was too heavy for them. It wore upon my mind when I saw the desperate effort that they were willing to make to sustain their pastor, and especially the portion of it assumed by my beloved deacon. He was raising a family, his wife was in feeble health, his doctor bills and other expenses were high, and I noticed that if anything was done in a money point of view, the first inquiry was, "What has Dea. Brown done?" He must do the first, and that was not all; he must do the last also, for it appeared that he was "ordained to make up all deficiencies." I looked over some other little churches, which might be considered within reach of the pastor of that church, providing he was in the vigor of life, where the labor might be divided so as to have two charges, and he might be able, under God, to keep up both interests; and thus,

two churches might comfortably sustain a pastor.
This determined my mind relative to making a change.
I never assigned the dear brethren all my reasons for
declining to serve them longer, because I feared lest,
peradventure, Dea. Brown might feel himself aggrieved,
and, rather than I should resign, he would not only do
what he had done, but perhaps more than his means
would justify—for, if he had but one dollar, and he
thought his pastor needed that—he would give it as
freely as he ever breathed the air of heaven.

EXCHANGE FIELDS WITH ELDER THOMAS MITCHELL.

I had learned that Bro. Mitchell, of Troy, Bradford
county, Pennsylvania, was about to resign his charge,
and desired to preach half his time in Columbia and
Wells, and the other half with some other church that
he could conveniently reach. I talked the thing up
with my brethren, advised them to look at it and enter
into an arrangement, (if it should appear to suit all
around,) with Bro. Mitchell. I was considerably acquainted with him, and from the first esteemed him
very much as a minister of Jesus Christ and a brother
beloved in the Lord. They entered into negotiations
with him, which resulted in his engaging to labor with
them one-half of the time. This was a great relief to
my mind. I feared their being left entirely destitute, lest they should become discouraged and should
lose the vivacity and willingness to labor for God that
they had manifested from their earliest existence as a
church. Their ranks were liable to be thinned by
removal and death, and they needed a pastor with a
sympathizing heart, who could cheer and encourage
them in the divine life. Bro. Mitchell removed into
their parsonage, and commenced his labors. They
were much united in him. Perhaps, I was acquainted

with their views as much or more than any other individual. And all whom I ever heard speak on the subject, felt as though God in his providence had sent But he undertook to serve a *third* church, also, which them the one best adapted to their circumstances. proved too much for his strength, and he felt compelled to vacate that field. He now labors with the. church in Springfield, Bradford county.

MY REMOVAL TO TROY.

The church in Troy were thus destitute of a pastor. I had made some acquaintance with them, while aiding Bro. Mitchell, two short terms, in extra religious efforts. I received a call to take the charge of that church. I accepted their invitation, and it was literally a *change* of pulpits and people between Bro. Mitchell and myself. I thought I knew something of the wants of the church, and inasmuch as it was getting late in life with me, I might there spend (God willing) a few more years in endeavoring to build up the waste places of Zion.

In October, 1860, the dear brethren sent over their teams, and moved us to this place, where we now are. Our advent into Troy was marked by one peculiarity, which was calculated to try our faith. We were successful in obtaining the house we now live in, (the property of Judge Wilber,) with the pledge that, if it suited us, we could have it as long as we wanted it. Though too far a distance from our house of worship to be really convenient, yet it has answered a very good purpose. One of my brethren's house was next door to my own, on the bank of a branch of Sugar Creek. I had anticipated taking much comfort, for I thought I could run in at any time, ask counsel, exchange thoughts, lay plans for future usefulness, &c.

DISASTROUS OVERFLOW OF SUGAR CREEK.

But God's ways were not our ways. We had been about a week in our new domicil, and just got the things stowed away, our winter's supply of vegetables in the cellar, and it began to look very much like "living." The brother and myself went down to East Troy, something over three miles. The day was remarkably rainy. On our return, in the edge of the evening, I asked the brother (Andrus Case) if he thought that the water would not be too high for us to pass through the Pond Road? He smiled and said, "O no, sir." Still, my mind was pretty well impressed that the creek must be very high, for I had considerable experience among the mountain streams of Pennsylvania, in Potter and Tioga counties. However, there was nothing to obstruct our way, and we arrived safe at home. Seeing the creek was rising fearfully fast, I went in and told Bro. Case it was getting rather wild. He replied, "There is no danger—the water wont hurt anything," and (if I am correct) he was so composed that he retired to bed pretty early in the evening. I did not feel like sleeping, but, watching the stream, found it was breaking over the bank by the corner of my barn, and assuming a very threatening aspect. The wrecks of bridges, buildings, and so on, began to come down, quite rapidly—the night, impervious darkness—my garden, under water some two feet—my cellar, full. Very soon, the kitchen part of Bro. Case's house went down stream. That began to stir my feelings. Next, his dining room sailed away, (Those two parts appear to have been added after the main body of the house was built.) People were out with their lanterns, wading in the water in every direction except near the stream. They all felt confident that the water had done its last work as it regarded Bro. Case, and that the main body of the house was so permanently fixed that it could not go off. However, such was the amount of drift-wood lodging against the dam, that at length, as with one fell swoop, the flood broke through, carried away the bulk-head on our side of the stream, swept his beautiful dwelling, with all its contents, into the surging mass, and—as though it was decreed to make a finishing blow at all he had on the banks of the creek—his barn, well stored with winter supplies on a lot he owned on the other side of the stream, a little below, was taken bodily with all its contents, and much of the lot itself was washed away. So the Lord in his providence took from our beloved brother, as with a stroke, the greater part of his hard earnings. It was a heavy blow. We felt intensely for him. But God has been pleased to abundantly bless him, and we think he may say with Job, that he has now more after the affliction, than he had at the beginning.

OUR VILLAGE—STIRRING BUSINESS QUALITIES.

Having survived the flood, I was next ready to look out upon the land that I was designing to labor in. And first I would say, in relation to Troy itself, that I was as much disappointed, in its business capacity, as I was in the appearance of New Town, to which I have referred. In all the villages in which I have been, I think I never saw one, of the same population, carrying on the same amount of business that is done in Troy. There is nothing between Elmira on the North and Williamsport on the South, and I knew of nothing East or West within at least twenty miles, that can be called a business town like it. It is to me always cheering to see active men, with their hands full of employment.

I recollect passing through here, thirty-five or more years since, in company with P. D. Gillette. We had a short preach, in a little school-house, to a small congregation, but—so great are the changes and improvements—I see no landmark by which I can determine where it was that I first labored, in this region. We passed on to the ever-hospitable abode of that large-hearted, beloved brother, the late Dea. Jesse Edsall, of Columbia, (Columbia and Wells church.)

DIGRESSION—THE MILLPORT, AND THE LINDLEY AND LAWRENCEVILLE CHURCHES.

Before commencing my experience with the Troy church, I am wondering what has become of the church in Millport, and also that at Lindley and Lawrenceville! They used to have their place with the churches composing the Chemung River Association, but of late years we do not see them. Both have been subject to fainting away, every once in a while, but I have never heard that either of them had entirely given up the ghost.

For some time, I have doubted the ability of the brethren in Millport, to retain their visibility. Their location is not the best. Yet I have hoped that the interest in that place might live, providing the strong and wealthy church at the Horse-Heads would throw their arm around it, so that they might remain as a branch church if no more.

But I see no reason why the Lindley and Lawrenceville church should be in its present condition. Its location is good, with a community from which should be gathered a Baptist church of some strength. It was organized in 1841. I well remember its recognition, when our venerable father, Alfred Bennett, preached from that memorable text, "The Church of the living God, the pillar and ground of the truth."

They appeared to commence under favorable auspices
—have had several pastors—and for some years kept
up their meetings regularly. In relation to them, (as
also to several other small churches on the southern
tier of towns in New York, and the northern tier in
Pennsylvania,) I have thought that the great failing
has been the want of adaptation in their pastors to the
work on which they have entered. They may all have
been good men. But it demands peculiar talents for
gathering churches. And to build up under such circumstances, requires missionary habits of life, unshaken
confidence in God, indomitable perseverance, and good
common sense.

LABOR ON, AND CONFIDE IN THE GREAT JEHOVAH.

Moreover, I have often feared that many pastors
cripple their own energy by doubting and fearing lest
peradventure they may not be sustained. I know no
other way but for a preacher to do his full duty and
trust in God. I may be permitted to testify on this
subject, because, in all the ministerial labor that I have
done, and the churches which under God I have been
enabled to build up, I never had anything from a convention or missionary fund, save in Jefferson and Hornellsville. And we can erect our Ebenezer to-day and
say, Hitherto hath the Lord helped us!

And now a few words in relation to the church
over which God has permitted me to preside for four
years past. First I would say, I have not accomplished
all that I hoped to do, but I can truly add that I have
done what I could. I have not kept back anything
that I thought was for the glory of God and the best
interests of Zion. I have tried to give my hearers the
cream of my long experience and observation. I have
thought as intensely, perhaps, as I have ever done, to

bring forth things both new and old. In sickness and in health, I have received from them nothing but kindness and attention. I have some as choice brethren and sisters as can be found anywhere. They have my affections—they live in my heart and in my prayers.

THE GREAT DEFICIENCY AMONG US, AS WELL AS AMONG OTHERS.

But, as a church, we are not what we wish we were. Perhaps the principal lack is that of MORE ARDENT PIETY—more love and affection for each other—more the appearance of a unity of brotherhood, as one common family. Not that I am disappointed in coming here. Many years ago, I learned that the great want of the church generally, in these latter days, is a strict discipline, and more thorough teaching in the doctrines of the Gospel of Christ. We need to master the great fundamental truths of religion—vivid perceptions of the deep things of God, as revealed unto us in the New Testament—to see more clearly the necessity of divine sovereignty and human agency going hand in hand— with a good understanding of our peculiar views as Baptists—carrying out in our lives the Gospel we profess—and walking up to our covenant obligations with God and one another. No doubt we are often weak when we might be strong, were we better acquainted with God's claims upon us. And we can only attain to this by a growing knowledge of the will of God concerning us, as revealed in the. volume of divine inspiration.

LOCAL HISTORY.

For the early annals of the Troy Baptist church, I am indebted to its late pastor, and am grateful for the privilege of embodying it in this work—[see Appendix.]

THE BIBLE TOO MUCH OVERLOOKED.

It appears to me that there is among the body of Christians a fearful lack in this one thing—*we know by far too little of the Bible* One great cause of this, is because we read almost everything but that "BOOK OF BOOKS." We hear in every church, in prayer circles, in conference meetings, in religious conversations, but very few quotations from the sacred Word—and many professed quotations from the Bible are made up from some other book, or something we have heard or formed in our own minds, and taken it for granted that the Bible says so!

A PREACHER SADLY AT FAULT.

When I hear such mis-quotations, it reminds me of a certain Baptist minister, who, when he arrived at the place of his appointment, (which was in a school-house) found that he had left his pocket Bible at home, and there was no Bible present. He said, very confidentially, "It makes no difference, friends: I shan't take a text that you won't find between the lids of the Bible. It is certainly there, though I can not give you the chapter and verse. Now my text is, 'Stripped for the race and harnessed for the battle.'" After the services were over, a Presbyterian deacon said to him, "Elder D., your sermon did very well. I have no fault to find with it. But your text is not in the Bible." The minister replied, rather short, "Yes, sir, it is in the Bible."—"Well, my brother," replied the deacon, "if you will find it, come to me, put your finger upon it, and let me read it, I will give you my horse and buggy for the information." The minister searched diligently, by the help of his Concordance, but could find no "Stripped for the race and harnessed for the Battle."

The deacon saw him some time after, and said, "Why

27

didn't you come for my horse and buggy?"—"Why," he confessed, "I could not find the text."—"Do you know the reason, sir?"—"I suppose," replied the minister, "it is not there." There was a preacher who was too little acquainted with his Bible, and here was a deacon, trembling upon the borders of the grave, with his mind so stored with God's Word that he knew assuredly the words the preacher used for his text were not in that sacred volume.

And here is the great difficulty with us at the present day. We do not read and treasure up in our hearts and in our memories, as our fathers did, the blessed promises of God's Word, the glorious truths of divine revelation. O, that we would make a simultaneous start as Christians, and in this respect return to the good old paths of those who have gone before us!

GRATEFUL TO CHRISTIAN FRIENDS AND NEIGHBORS.

I feel happy in my relation with my brethren here. I have always been conscious that the churches here had to bear more with me, than I had to bear with them; and the only difference is, that the members have to bear with the failings of *one*, while the pastor has to bear with the failings of *many*.

And I am very much indebted to this community. I have never found more friends, outside of my church, than I have found in Troy. As far as I am concerned, I do not think their equals can be found—unconverted people, and people of other denominations, give decided evidence that their friendship is of a genuine cast.

You have stood by me, Christian friends and fellow-citizens! in sickness in my family, and in death also. When my dear son died among you, so soon after his return from the army—on the 12th of January, 1864, (his 25th birthday,)—you had tears to mingle with my own ; you were ready with every act of kindness that human sympathy could prompt. And when—in the June following—my own breath was quivering upon my lips, and pulsation had so far ceased that it went abroad, (even to the Association, and to the public press,) that I was really dead, brethren, sisters, friends and neighbors never ceased in their kind administrations, by day or by night.

APPENDIX.

ANSWERS TO INQUIRIES.

The foregoing is the continuous narrative of Bro. Sheardown, taken as described on page 12. In answer to points suggested, he has made the following additional statements :

How many believers have you baptized ?—"Something over 1,400." It will be remembered that for eight years in England, and some time in America, he preached without ordination ; and in protracted meetings, and on some missionary fields, the pastors generally attended to that ordinance.

How many sermons have you preached?—" I think, 12,000 sermons delivered by me during my ministry, would be quite a low estimate, and should not be surprised, if the exact number could be ascertained, if there were some thousands more. Between 1830 and 1836, while missionating, my sermons averaged nine a week—468 a year. In protracted meetings, I often preached three times a day for weeks in succession. In Penn Yan, during one meeting, I preached 79 sermons, (from two to three per day,) there being but one sermon, by another brother, while I was preaching those 79—then, becoming somewhat exhausted, others preached alternately with me." As his public efforts cover half a century of time, and thirty years were most fruitful in varied labors, we should presume he may have made 20,000 religious addresses.

How many different meeting-houses, taverns, school and private houses, mills, &c., have you preached in?—"I could not undertake to say."

How many churches have you been pastor of?—"I was active in originating seven churches, and in resuscitating several others, of most of which I was regarded as pastor, for a longer or shorter period. But, excepting Troy, (and perhaps Southport,) I never settled as pastor over a church formed by others."

DATA IN THE LIFE.

1791—Born, near Great Grimsby, Lincolnshire, Eng-
    land.
1805—Entered upon mercantile apprenticeship, aged 14.
1809—Removed to London, aged 17.
1812—Baptized in Hull, (Yorkshire,) aged 21.
1813—Commenced public religious efforts.
1814—Married Miss Esther Grassam.
1815—Received formal liberty to Itinerate.
1818—Removed to Pontefract—Distress in England.
1820—Spring.   Visited France and Holland.
    "   Fall.   Settled in America, at Covert, Seneca
    county, N. Y.
1821—May.   My family reached me.
1822—Attended the first Seneca Association.
1824—United with the Covert Baptist Church.
1826—Settled in the woods of Catlin, Chemung county.
1827—Gathered a Baptist Conference.
1828—Organized Catlin Baptist Church—was Licensed.
1829—Ordained to the work of the Gospel ministry.
1830—Commenced Mission work in Pennsylvania.
1832—Caton Church formed (in " No. One.")
1834—Re-organized the present church in Reading.
1844—Removed to Reading as the pastor.
1848—Engaged in new interest at Jefferson (Watkins.)
1852—Engaged in new interest at Hornellsville.
1854—May.   Removed to the Plank Road in Southport.
    "   July.   Death of Mrs. Esther G. Sheardown.
1855—Married Mrs. Lorrin A. Soper.
1860—Pastor at Troy, Bradford county, Pa.

ORDINATION SERVICES.

[From page 17 of the Catlin (now Catlin & Dix) Church Book—then kept by A. C. Mallory, Clerk—we extract the following account of the proceedings of a Council held on the 11th of February, 1829.]

PASTOR ORDAINED.

By request of the Baptist church in Catlin, a council convened in the log-house of Anthony Pierce, consisting of the following delegates from sister churches:

First Ithaca—Eld. John Sears, Bro. H. Wilson.

First Covert—Dea. Lewis Porter, D. Wite.

First Hector—Eld. J. Reynolds, S. Dolph.

First Lodi—Eld. J. Fisk.

First Elmira—S. Moore, Dea. J. Carpenter.

The council organized by appointing Elder John Sears, Moderator, and J. Fisk, Clerk. After which the church presented Bro. Thomas S. Sheardown, for examination, relative to ordination. The council, after mature deliberation, unanimously

Resolved, That we are satisfied with the Christian experience of the candidate, his call to the ministry, and view of Christian doctrine and practice.

Resolved, That we proceed to the ordination of Bro. Thomas S. Sheardown.

Resolved, That Eld. Sears preach on the occasion.

Resolved, That Eld. Reynolds make the ordaining prayer, and lay on hands with Elders Sears and Fisk.

Resolved, That Eld. Reynolds give the charge.

Resolved, That Eld. Fisk give the right hand of fellowship.

Resolved, That Eld. Sears address the church and society.

The Benediction by the candidate.

TRIBUTE TO MRS. ESTHER G. SHEARDOWN.

BY A LADY WHO KNEW HER INTIMATELY.

I rejoice to learn that God has spared the life of our revered father Sheardown, until he has completed the history of those labors which were so eminently successful in the extension of the Redeemer's kingdom. I hail its publication as a coveted heritage, which we shall delight to transmit to our children.

But I remember, while I think of those untiring labors and sacrifices, of ONE who shared them all for many long years—not, indeed, before the public gaze, but, in the seclusion of her own quiet home, enduring hardships and bearing burdens, which must otherwise have rested upon him, thereby preventing him from engaging in those labors. I feel that, as David of old required the spoil of battle to be divided with those who stayed by the stuff,·making it a statute and an ordinance for Israel unto this day, so some honor is due to her memory for those unostentatious labors.

It is impossible for us, at this day, to have an adequate conception of the privations endured by the early settlers of our country, even when most favorably situated. But when we think of her living in a log house in the wilderness, often with none but her little children around her—feeding the cattle with her own hands, because no child was old enough to do it—in case of sickness, doctoring and nursing and watching the children—yea, and in one instance, when sudden illness came upon one of them, and she expected it must die before the morning, not daring to leave it, and, none of the others being old enough to go far for assistance in the darkness, preparing to lay out that little one with its own mother's fingers—then we have a faint conception of some of the trials, which she cheerfully endured, that her companion might break the bread of life to the famishing.

One point deserves particular notice. Let her sorrows and privations in his absence be what they might, they were kept from him as much as possible, so that his mind should not be over-burdened with care. His return was always hailed with joy, by the whole family. But, much as she enjoyed his society, and necessary as might be his presence and aid to her comfort, she ever bade him go when those earnest Macedonian calls came —as they so often did—and followed him with incessant prayers for the blessing of God upon his labors.

For many years, his salary or compensation for preaching, was very small, rendering it necessary for her to use all the economy and ingenuity which she possessed to meet the wants of an increasing family. She could remember when it was different with her: and doubtless there sometimes arose before her vision the scene of that bridal morning, when her husband conducted her to her new home, furnished, from garret to cellar, with everything essential to comfort, and where the wedding breakfast awaited her, prepared by her own servants. She could recall, too, succeeding days of prosperity. But, if the recollection of those by-gone days gave a keener edge to the privations she was enduring for Christ's sake, it was borne without repining. I do not believe a member of the church ever heard her boast of what she once possessed, or murmur on account of present privations. Patiently, she strove to discharge every duty. Her family were always comfortably clad, appearing in the house of God neat and tidy in their apparel.

While there were none of the family old enough to

take charge of the rest, she was prevented from sharing her husband's labors abroad. But the church at home always enjoyed her presence and her counsels, in all its meetings, when it was possible for her to be there; and although we were sad because our loved pastor was absent, yet we were cheered by her exhortations and faithfulness in the service of Christ. The younger members of the church where she so long lived, looked up to her as to a mother in Israel, and many are the tender recollections of her loving kindness and anxious solicitude for their spiritual welfare, which some of them still cherish. She also strove to lead her own family in the narrow way, gathering them around the family altar in his absence, and commending them to a covenant-keeping God. As they grew in years, they showed their affection for her by relieving her, as much as possible, from the burdens she must otherwise have borne—at times, taking the whole charge of the family, that she might accompany him in his labors of love, (a privilege which she much enjoyed, and well improved.) In the later years of her life, she had less of earthly care, and her religious privileges were greater, until finally she sunk to rest, beloved by all who knew her. Truly it may be said of her, "The memory of the just is blessed."

J. E. H.

FROM REV. BENJ. R. SWICK.

Adams' Basin, N. Y., June 19, 1865.

Rev. Th. S. Sheardown, Troy, Pa.

My Dear Brother—I have been thinking of you this morning, and concluded to write to you of the days that are past.

On the 2d of January, 1831, I was buried in baptism, and, as I trust, came forth from that grave to walk in newness of life. From the first, I was impressed with the duty of preaching the Gospel, but was anxiously inquiring how one so unlearned, and so poor in the things of this world, as I was, could ever be put into the ministry, to proclaim the unsearchable riches of Christ. In the providence of God, you came to Wayne, Steuben county, and preached, in a school-house near the outlet of the Little Lake. You employed as a text, the words of our Redeemer, as recorded in Isaiah, 50th Chapter 4th Verse: "The Lord God hath given me the tongue of the learned, that I should know how to speak a word in season to him that is weary." The *earnestness* of your manner in pointing out the wants of "the weary," and the *knowledge* of him to whom "the tongue of the learned" had been given, made an impression upon my mind that has never wholly passed away. Then and there was firmly fixed in my heart the necessity of presenting important truths with holy zeal. From that time until I began, in much feebleness, to preach the Gospel, there was an almost hourly recurrence of my mind to the doctrine deduced from that beautiful verse, and to the manner of its enforcement. Although I have never used that particular text for sermonizing, yet, for more than thirty years, I have "kept in memory what you preached to me," and, as I hope, "believe not in vain."

If time and space would allow, I should take pleasure in referring to your first field of labor, in Catlin. I once tried to preach to your people, when we, accompanied by a number of brethren, retired to a log house, in that then new country. We spent the first hours of the night in telling what the Lord had done for our souls, and then laid our weary bodies down upon the floor, to rest for a few hours, preparatory to another day of toil and night of preaching—for it was a time of the outpouring of the Spirit in that place. I should like to refer at length to the time when " Old Schoolism" had well nigh swallowed up the church of which I was pastor, in Hector. God sent you to my aid, and made you his instrument as a deliverer.

As you are nearer your home to-day, and as I hope to meet you again when we both have passed our Jordan, may I not ask you to pray for me that my faith fail not? And may the God of all grace strengthen your heart, and, after you have suffered all his will, perfect and settle you in his heavenly kingdom! Love to all.

Truly yours,

B. R. Swick.

SKETCHES OF SERMONS.

The following outlines of discourses were taken down, nearly thirty years ago, by a brother, who says in relation to them, " These sketches may convey some idea of Eld. Sheardown's mode of treating a text, but I never knew him to take any written plan into the pulpit, or use one on any occasion. I do not believe he ever wrote one. He was among the most difficult of men to follow after, to make a report. I have many times taken pencil and paper, at the commencement of his sermon, and, after getting down perhaps two or three ideas, would become perfectly oblivious to all thoughts of writing, and find myself, at or near the close of the service, with mouth half open, and tears and sweat running profusely.

Text—Isaiah 50, 11 : " Behold, all ye that kindle a fire, that compass yourselves about with sparks: walk in the light of your fire, and in the sparks that ye have kindled. This shall ye have of mine hand, ye shall lie down in sorrow."

Introduction.—The Christian has the promise of heaven and happiness—but these are not for the sinner.

The word of God is compared to fire, and its effects to a furnace. Those characters kindle a fire of their own—one which God has not kindled. But their fire has neither *light* nor *heat.* It is counterfeit, and counterfeiters grow more skilful. Hence, ungodly men all have some creed. There are about seventeen hundred different systems of religious belief. We notice,

I. *Some of the fires which men kindle.*

1st. To blunt conscience, some kindle the fire of Atheism. 2d. Others, for the same purpose, deny

such parts of the Bible as they cannot comprehend—
yet they cannot tell which part is revealed, and which
is not. 3d. Others deny the immortality of the soul.
4th. Some embrace Universalism. 5th. Some trust in
their morality. 6th. Others expect to reach heaven
because their pious parents had them sprinkled in infancy. 7th. Some trust in church membership, like
Nicodemus, the High Churchman. But Jesus said,
"Ye must be born again." Members of other churches
satisfy themselves with the mere forms of religion.
They enlist, but do not fight. 8th. Some try to live
religion alone—make no profession, &c.

II. *The consequences of so doing.*

"Ye shall lie down in sorrow." This term, "lie
down," has reference to the end of a journey. O, the
sorrow of that soul that has expected heaven, and lies
down in hell! "They shall have it at God's hand"—
no escape. Be not deceived!!

Text—Zechariah 3, 9: "Upon one stone shall be
seven eyes: behold, I will engrave the graving thereof,
saith the Lord of hosts, and I will remove the iniquity
of that land in one day."

Introduction.—Jesus Christ is often spoken of under
the figure of a stone. "Behold I lay in Zion for a foundation, a stone, a tried stone, a precious corner stone."
Notice, that the eyes are not in the stone, but looking
"upon" it.

1st. The eye of God was upon Christ, for the fulfil-
ment of the covenent between them. 2d. The eye of
divine Justice. 3d. Angels were looking ministers, &c.
4th. The eyes of wicked men—they recoiled, mocked,
whipped, &c. 5th. Devils looked. 6th. Saints looked.
7th. The eye of Mercy was upon him.

"I will engrave," &c. Anciently, the corner stone

had the initials of the architect engraved upon it. So Christ—and he showed the engraving when he said to Thomas, " Reach hither thy finger," &c. " He hath upon his vesture and upon his thigh a name written."

" Remove the iniquity," &c. " Christ has become the end of the law for righteousness to every one that believeth." " By his stripes we are healed." " Now no condemnation," &c. Christ has " spoiled death," &c.— He has dragged death and hell at his chariot wheels— when he rose, a mighty Conquerer, &c.

His *manner* during pulpit ministrations was peculiar to himself, and no attempt at imitation could be made without spoiling the picture. Before service, he would walk the aisles, singing, and shaking hands with each one who came in. In prayer, he left the impression upon his hearers that he walked and talked with God. In reading hymns, and preaching, he gestured much. After reading his text, he usually laid the Bible upon the seat behind him, and, as he warmed in the work, would sometimes, lay off his coat, then his cravat and collar, and, for about an hour, would pour forth, in a manner indescribably attractive and impressive, thoughts that were a " wonder to many."

A. C. M.

A FUGITIVE EPISTLE.

[At the time of Bro. Sheardown's removal to Southport, his goods were sent to him from Havanna, but—
very unfortunately—one box, containing his choicest
private papers, &c., became mislaid, and he has since
had no tidings from it. The loss to him, in preparing
the sketch of his long and checkered life, was great,
but has been very well supplied by his most remarkable
memory of minute particulars as well as prominent
events. There happens, however, to have been pre-
served in the family, *one letter,* to the wife of his youth,
which we venture here to insert, as a *specimen* of his
yearnings for the endearments of home, even while his
whole heart was engaged in carrying out the spirit of
Paul's exhortation to Timothy: "Watch then in all
things; endure afflictions; do the work of an evangelist; make full proof of thy ministry."]

WALWORTH, January 10, 1843.

MY DEAR ESTHER,—Having a few moments to spare,
I have commenced another epistle to you, hoping you
received my last in season. When we cannot see each
other, it is good to converse in black and white, for
thoughts on paper are better than none at all. Through
the mercy of God, my health is good as usual. "The
Lord is my portion, I shall not want." The field is a
hard one, but God has done a good work here, and I
hope will do more. I shall not finish this, until I sum
up in this place. May the Lord bless you, my sister—
good night!

Wednesday Evening.—Another day is past, and I am
seated in my room, thinking about you and the dear
children. When I think of home, in a moment I seem
to be there. But, alas! I will say no more about it, or
you will think I am *homesick.* You have always in-
dulged me in my childish notions, and if I live to get
home I expect you will still have to bear with me.
Through mercy, my health is very good. Had a visit,

to-day, from Bro. Griswold, the pastor with whom I hold my next meeting. He is a good soul, and has a precious wife. I think I shall have a good home, and this I know will be pleasing to you. I am as happy as circumstances will permit. My love to the children. Yours, my dear sister, in a precious Saviour—good night!

Thursday Evening.—We have had a good meeting. I have labored hard, but my health holds out well. I have got two fine new flannel shirts, which you know I stood in want of, and how many more clothes I shall have to get before I come home I cannot tell, but you can trust me not to get anything but what I really want. What adds to the pleasure of the evening, is your letter, which came safe to hand just as the meeting was out. The consolation it afforded, almost over-powered me, for I had been thinking, last night, whether you would answer my letter or not. Nothing could have been more seasonable to me. Do not neglect sending to the office, as I may write often. I would say something more, but I remember you showed my letter to the girls, so you must guess for yourself. Now, my dear sister, you know I love you. Good night, &c.

Friday Evening.—The day and the night are both alike unto the Lord. My health is yet good, but I find my sheet is filling up, and I have said nothing about Bro. French and wife, who made their appearance in our meeting. The snow was going so fast they had to go home, but I visited with them about all night, and a good visit it was.

I have found a better pen, so I thought I would write a little more this evening, for to-morrow night I expect to be very tired. Covenant meeting at one o'clock. It will be hard work to get the converts out, for there are few members in the church that have any musing qualifications. Tell John, if he is a faithful boy, he will have a suit of clothes for his name. I may go and spend a week with Bro. French before I come home. That, you will perhaps think, is too bad—to visit any one before I visit you. But I think you made me pr mise to do so: if not, I know you will forgive me, for you are aware that I never lay out many nights on my way home.

I am thinking about old John Bunyan's "Grace Abounding to the Chief of Sinners." That is the foundation of my hope.

Now, my dear sister, what other pledge can I give you of my heart being yours, than you have had for nearly thirty years? My love to the dear children and converts—good night!

Saturday Evening.—Have had a good day—the Lord be praised—four were received by letter, and twenty-one by experience, and I expect a few more in the morning. I hope the Lord will be in our midst. I hope you will have a good day in Catlin. I know not what to say about the business that is to take place on the 25th inst., only that I cannot be there. I feel for you, my dear Esther, but that will not relieve you. May the Lord support you! I hope nothing will take place to injure the cause of Christ. You must give my love to the children: keep them as comfortable as you can, and dispose of everything to the best advantage. Let the girls manage, and you keep as still as you can. Don't let me come home and find you, as I did the last time, all worn out: if I do, it will almost kill me. Good night, my dear sister—may the Lord bless you!

Sunday Evening.—This must finish. Have had a good day—twenty-three strong candidates were baptized, most of whom came out of the water rejoicing in the Lord. Bro. Bennett did up the business about right. I open to-morrow evening, if God will, at Marion. Expect to have a visit from Eld. Church, of Rochester, next Thursday. Tell Samuel to take good care of the stock. If you get tired of paying postage, you must say so. My love to the converts, and brethren and sisters. I am, dear Esther,

Your affectionate husband,

T. S. SHEARDOWN.

TO HIS CHILDREN.

[One of the daughters of Bro. Sheardown, has furnished a few letters from the father, while evangelizing, from which we make characteristic extracts:]

January 31st.—Perhaps this is the most wicked place I ever saw. It contains about 2,000 inhabitants. The church was very low, and everything seemed against us, yet the blessed Lord has, in great kindness, come down to His people. Seven were baptized yesterday, and three have told their experience to-day. Our house was flooded to overflowing. May the Lord pour down His Spirit upon this community, and save, from the wrath to come, a multitude of souls! How much we need faith and unshaken confidence in God! I expect to see a great display of redeeming grace in this benighted region, and the Lord of hosts in his war chariot of salvation riding through in great power and majesty, destroying the works of Satan.—February 1st. "The Lord (said David) is on my right hand: I shall not be greatly·moved." My health is as usual—my lungs somewhat torpid. The pastor and his wife are Holy Ghost Christians—first-best workers—may the Lord make them a great blessing to this place! Everybody comes to meeting. We are every day putting on more team: the Gospel plow is in to the beam, and if under God we can put on strength to take her through, shall cut a large and deep furrow. Holy Spirit, come! You must excuse a short letter, as I am in great haste. I shall write to mother this week. My love to all the dear friends. Tell —— I am yet praying for her—she must see well to her soul. I am, dear children,

Your affectionate father,

Thos. S. Sheardown.

APRIL 14th.—According to promise, I drop you a line to say that I arrived safe in this place, up to the eyes in mud. But the situation of the roads was nothing compared with the situation of the church, which is split up and divided, so that, out of one hundred members, often, not more than five brethren attend the meetings. There are large congregations of sinners in the evenings, and some are under conviction, but there is little strength in Zion. There are more unconverted people in the place than I ever saw for the number of inhabitants, and if we can get the church in its place, I shall expect a mighty revival, but at this time all is dark.—APRIL 16th. Yesterday was something of a good day. Eight or ten members were out; the rest were strangers, and people of other denominations. Evening, a large congregation; one soul converted, and some deeply convicted. "Lord, send prosperity." If there is a breach made in the walls of infidelity, I shall expect to see a mighty breaking down. Visited a Deist yesterday, and asked the privilege to pray. He said he would not say that I should not pray in his house: I might pray for myself, but not for him. So I bowed down and prayed for myself and just such a man as he is. I think he must have thought, if it did not mean him, it must have meant his brother. He and his wife attend meeting, and I have a great anxiety for their conversion.—*Sabbath afternoon.* A full house, this morning. Preached from Numbers 35: 12. Had a conference with the brethren in the vestry, and they gave their pledge to attend this week more than they have done. Four souls are rejoicing in God, and I hope for many more. The ague is beginning to show itself here. My health is not very good, to-day. I have a very good home—accommodations just what I wanted—two good rooms, and a good bed with clean and warm flannel sheets. Pray for me. "All is well."

January 4th.—"Through the mercy of God, I continue to this day." There is nothing I have ever known on earth that will compare with the season we have had here. It required special meetings, and help from sister churches, to remove the rubbish out of the way. Some members were excluded, and some restored. For an old place, I have never seen so much ignorance [in spiritual things.] One young man, a member of the church, when asked by the pastor, in a special meeting, if he meant to try to live religion, said he did not know—he had not made up his mind yet! I thought, "what will come next?" At length, the Lord appeared for us. Last night, there were about sixty on the anxious seat—backsliders, and convicted sinners—and ten we hope have been converted. To-day we had a season of fasting and prayer. It is the middle of the third week, and we are only beginning to work. With a few exceptions, I have been preaching all the time to the church. Some new cases came forward to-night. May the Spirit of the Highest come down! I have been loading and firing all the time, and am almost tired out. Lord, give me strength.—January 6th. Things are a little better—anxious increasing—some more conversions—but a great want of deep travail in the church. They want me at Palmyra, Webster, &c., &c.—January 9th. In the multitude of business, I have delayed my letter until now. We have over twenty converts, and I expect to hear of more in the morning. Some went home much pressed down in spirits : may they find the Fountain of Life to-night! The snow is all gone, and we are in the mud as flat as a griddle, but I hope for more snow if it is the Lord's will. I am beginning to sound the converts about going into the water on Sunday next. If I do not get home until spring, perhaps may send for mother to visit with me when I get through.

JANUARY 24th.—God is doing a great work here—between sixty and seventy converts—about 150 anxious —and this only the second week.—The situation of things in Reading is all new to me, and I am perfectly unprepared to say anything upon the subject. If I had any inclination to go there, I should be the last man to manifest it until the ground were clear. I have always loved the brethren and sisters in Reading, but that is not to say that I should preach for them. I have no time to reflect upon such important engagements as long as I am in a protracted meeting. I expect to return home in March, if God will, and then will pay the subject the attention its importance demands. My health is better than I could expect—for which I would be very thankful. Yours, &c.

FEBRUARY 18th.—I embrace a few moments, stolen from the time afforded me for rest and reflection, to inform you that I am in rather better health than when I left you. My labor is of the hardest kind, but God is here. He has converted a goodly number of the youth, and is just beginning to pull down the tall oaks of Bashan. There is trouble in the camp of the enemy. The Prince of Darkness is full of wrath. He cannot break his chain, but 'tis frightful to see him gnaw his tongue for pain as we expose his hidden iniquities. We hope, by the grace of God, to strip the veil from his dark abode. We are at work against some of his strongholds, such as bar-rooms, gambling shops, houses of ill-fame, &c., and he begins to think it is hard times. His kingdom in this ungodly village must take a severe shaking. The pastor is a man after my own heart, and I have everything as it should be at my stopping-place. Thanks to my heavenly Father, "the lines have fallen to me in a pleasant place." You must be satisfied with a short letter—so many are dinging at me, some to hold a meeting, and others offering a large salary to become their pastor, &c. I seldom retire before 12 or 1 o'clock, and arise by candle-light in the morning. My heart and hands are full, but God is with me. Love to all the dear friends. Yours, &c.

FEBRUARY 22d.—Yours came to hand this morning, for which I was very thankful. Many things in it gave me much pleasure. That your family visit was harmonious and pleasant, was gratifying news. I should have been happy to have been at home, but I am about my Master's business. We are holding upon the Arm of strength. The Lord is on our side, we will not fear what man can do. Souls are coming into the kingdom—some thirty-five converts, and a number of anxious. We had one baulky horse in the team, who threw himself and fell directly in the gateway, and we thought we should have to try to get him up or skin him on the ground—but, finally, put a rope to his leg. There are more churches than ministers. If it is my duty to come to Reading, the door will be opened by the brethren in season. My health has been very poor, but I feel smart again, and better than I have done for some months. Yours, &c.

FOR A DAUGHTER'S ALBUM.

Youth has fled, and manhood's failing,
　Silvered locks, and furrowed brow,
Trembling limbs and painful feelings—
　Think, O think upon me now!

Soon I'll pay the debt of Nature,
　Soon shall part with those I love ;
Jesus smiles—O, blessed feature !
　All in all in Heaven above.

Dear Eliza! you shall meet me
　Far in yonder world of light ;
In Heaven above, I hope to greet thee
　Filled with rapture and delight.

Jefferson, April 12th, 1850.　　　　THOMAS S. SHEARDOWN.

Mrs. ESTHER G. SHEARDOWN.

[From the correspondence of Prof. ALEXANDER TEN BROOK, in the "New York Baptist Register," of Utica, we extract the following tribute to the memory of the model wife of a pastor:]

JULY 24, 1854.

Having spent a day in visiting friends at Factory-ville, in company with my classmate, Rev. J. T. Seeley, now of Dundee, on the Seneca lake, I am again at El-mira. The principal object for which we came hither at this time, was to be present at the recognition of a church at Pine Woods. I alluded to it, once before, as made up of original members of the Elmira church, whose help at the village is no longer needed, and pro-mises to be very efficient in this new interest. The recognition was to have been on the 19th inst., but an afflictive providence defeated it.

Mrs. Esther Sheardown, the wife of the chosen pastor, having been for some time very ill, and her death daily expected, died on the 20th, at the age of sixty-one years. She was born in the city of Hull, England, and there baptized, forty-six years ago; and, forty years ago, married, in the same place, Rev. T. S. Sheardown. It is enough to say of her that she was the worthy wife of one, who, although he may not be reckoned among the great men of the world, (as he himself would doubtless object to this,) was neverthe-less the man whom, for the past twenty-five years, God has chosen to bless in the conversion of men, and the building up of the churches, beyond any man that has ever labored in this section of the State. Those churches, in Chemung, Steuben, Allegany, Yates, Seneca, and Monroe counties—for he has been greatly blessed in preaching several times of late in the city of

Rochester—little know how much they are indebted to
his wife for the labor which he has performed. She
made it her greatest care to so attend to the family,
and even in some respects to the church, in his absence, as to make it possible for him to be almost constantly engaged in those evangelical labors, at home
and abroad, by which thousands have been made to
rejoice. The same desire was shown on her death-bed,
by inquiring, on the morning of her last Sabbath on
earth, in the near prospect of death, about his readiness
to go to his public duties. She expected to die, and
had nothing to do but make arrangements for it. She
called Rev. C. N. Chandler, pastor of the church in Elmira, and mentioned to him the text from which she
wished him to preach, to the people, a sermon on the
occasion of her funeral; and on Thursday she expired,
in the ever-brightening hope of a blessed immortality.
She was buried, the following day, at Havanna, where
one of her sons is settled. The sermon on the occasion
was from Rev. 14, 13: "Blessed are the dead," &c., the
passage which the deceased had selected.

FROM EBEN B. CAMPBELL, Esq.

Phelps' Mills, Clinton Co., Pa., Feb. 27, 1865.

Rev. Thomas Mitchell:

DEAR SIR—I am glad indeed that the auto-biography of my dear friend, Rev. Thomas S Sheardown, is about being published, and would wish to have at least ten copies.

About the year 1841, I became acquainted with Bro. Sheardown, through my first wife; and the late Bro. Elijah De Pui, of Tioga, where I resided, always spoke of him in the most kind and feeling manner. After moving to this place, about 1847, my wife urgently pressed me, time and again, to ask "father Sheardown" to come here and preach the Gospel. But it seems as if it had been ordered that my dear wife was no more to hear that voice call sinners to repent, and, ere he could arrange to come, she was called to her home on high.

In the winter of 1860, father Sheardown came, and preached nine evenings at the Mills—aiding our pastor, Bro. J. Anderson Kelly, (now Agent of the University at Lewisburg.) In a short time, many of the workmen, their wives and children, became alarmed at their situation, and the result of the meeting was the conversion of some thirty precious souls. It was a remarkable work of grace, and we feel among us, to-day, the effects of that blessed season. Some of the converts have already gone to their rest, and I am truly happy to say that, out of all those spared, not one has turned again unto the world.

One interesting conversion, which occurred about the time of that revival, I will give at some length. Three young men were about starting to school. One of them became deeply concerned for his soul's salvation. The time arrived for the school to open, and his

companions urged him to leave with them. He replied,
"No—I will find Christ, first." He did find Him,
united with the Jersey Shore church, and then went
on to his studies. In April, 1861, he was among the
first of those of our noblest and best youth, who volunteered for the preservation of the flag of our country.
He wrote home, often—and although, in his letters to
his pastor, he said the camp was a hard place in which
to lead a Christian life, yet he seemed thoroughly devoted to his Saviour. In June, he was accidentally shot,
by one of his comrades. He told them not to feel bad
—it was all right—God was about to call him home—
exhorted them to be prepared for death : and, in four
hours after receiving his wound, he fell asleep in Jesus.
The church brought his body. home, and have erected a
suitable monument in memory of ALBERT KISSELL.

Time presses me. I could give pages of interesting
matter from scenes arising through those blessed
meetings.

Remember us kindly to Bro. Sheardown and wife.
Our earnest prayer is that God will lead him very
gently down the declivity of life, and give-him an inheritance, incorruptible and undefiled, in Heaven,
there to meet those redeemed souls whom he has
been an instrument in bringing to the cross.

I am yours very truly,   E. B. CAMPBELL.

TESTIMONIAL OF CHEMUNG RIVER ASSOCIATION.

[In the Minutes of the eighteenth session of this body, held with the church in Hornby, September, 1860, we find the following proceedings:]

In place of the closing sermon, Father SHEARDOWN gave some very touching and pleasant reminiscences of the Association, saying, he had been with it, from its birth, until now; had seen the churches planted and grow up, under the toil and watch-care of himself and his brethren; and referred to the history of particular churches, and to the struggles and self-denial of individual members, in such a manner as to melt every heart, and bring tears from every eye. All felt that it was good to be there, as they sat at the feet of the father and received his benediction.

The following preamble and resolutions were then unanimously adopted :

"As our venerable father in the ministry, Rev. Thomas S. Sheardown, who has been for so many years a member of this body, and whose faithful and efficient labors have done so much in enlarging and building up the churches, is about to remove to another State, therefore

"*Resolved*, That we look upon his removal from this body with deep regret, and that we will ever remember him, in his relations to us, with feelings of pleasure and gratitude, especially as a safe counsellor, a valuable friend, a defender of the truth, sound in the faith, and abundant in good works.

"*Resolved*, That we cordially recommend him to the confidence and fellowship of all of God's people, everywhere, and especially of the church and community to which he is soon to remove."

FROM A RETURNED MISSIONARY.

Covington, Pa., July 17, 1865.

Brethren Worden and Case:

I have been so anxious to learn the principal facts in the history of Eld. Sheardown, that I had resolved to make several journies, of twenty miles or more, to learn from his own lips some of the incidents of his remarkable life. I am thankful that the dealings of God with him are now recorded, and that a book is to be published which will permanently embalm what would otherwise perish with his mortal life.

Since my return from Burmah, I have not only admired him as a preacher, but loved him as a father. I shall never forget the prayer he offered after my first attempt to preach before the Tioga Association. His warm sympathy deeply affected me. And the prayer (as on other occasions) was so marked by directness, unction, fervency, and choice words, that almost the whole audience was bathed in tears.

Since then, I have often heard him preach. His familiarity with the Bible, his profound knowledge of human nature, reasoning powers, glowing imagination, good voice, ease, and grace of expression, coupled with strong faith, devotion to his Master, and a yearning love for souls, render him a prince of preachers.

His memory is a treasury of illustrations. On one occasion, wishing to show that plainness in preaching, though apparent severity, was real kindness, he spoke of an English ship, that was almost wrecked, a short distance from a certain fort. As the ship's crew were about to give up in despair, the guns of the fort opened upon them. "Alas!" cried those on board, "the howling storm and hungry waves have almost destroyed us, and now our friends on the shore are about to complete

our misery and destruction by firing upon us." . But
those were friendly shots—for, as they flew harmlessly
over the ship, they conveyed to it the rope, by which
the sailors were all brought safely to the shore. The
ministers of Christ are like those friendly guns—start-
ling and terrifying in their denunciations of sin, but
aiming at the highest welfare of hearers in their eternal salvation.

On another occasion, at a covenant meeting, a number of candidates were received for baptism. A note
of discord was sounded, which threatened to mar the
harmony, and destroy in a measure the good effect of
the meeting, if it did not lead to subsequent bitterness.
"Stop, brethren," said Eld. Sheardown,—"we must be
careful what we do and say in the presence of these
converts. Two old sheep were quarreling—and, as
they rushed to butt their foolish heads, a lamb in its
innocent gamboling ran between them, and was instantly killed." The influence of this little story was
most happy—the objectionable matter was dropped,
and harmony was restored to us.

Yours, affectionately,

G. P. WATROUS

INCIDENTS.

The writer, conversing with Eld. Sheardown upon his pioneer experience, heard him state that coming home one night, late and weary, he found at his barn eight strange horses, to be fed and cared for. They belonged to persons coming to settle in Catlin, or who had gone that way to spend the night in social intercourse. He went at the work cheerfully, accomplished it thoroughly, and only alluded to it to show the influx of population, and the peculiar demand for patience and large room often required by new settlers.

When young in the ministry in America, and still wearing that serviceable English drab coat, he was invited to preach to a large congregation where he was not generally known. An aged sister asked who that man was who had just entered the pulpit? She was informed that it was "the new minister, from Catlin." She sighed as she remarked, "Well, we sha'n't have much from him—I don't know what he looks like." While the stranger, however, made strong and rapid progress in his sermon, the late hopeless objector kept jogging the elbow of the sister next to her with the information, "He's a perfect sing'd cat—a sing'd cat!"

As an illustration of the arduous character and wide scope of country covered by his labors, this anecdote may suffice: A preacher (then lately ordained) undertook to carry out Elder Sheardown's engagements, during one missionary voyage of something like a fortnight's duration. On his return, the substitute confessed: "I did the best I could to keep up with the Elder's appointments, but came out three days behind, although I wore the skin from the back of my horse, and my shirt was not dry for two weeks."

Several persons were endeavoring to drive an undesirable mastiff out of a preaching place, when he ran to the desk where the Elder was standing. The latter coolly remarked, " *Without* are dogs," and gave an "effectual" kick which sent the interloper out of doors.

On one occasion, the Universalists had made extraordinary efforts to keep people away from a revival meeting—but in vain. The house was crowded, pulpit and all. While waiting for the moment to open services, Eld. Sheardown asked a convert, standing upon the pulpit stairs, to say a few words to the people, expressive of his feelings. He had been rather a prominent man among the unbelievers, one of whom, standing under the pulpit, looked up, and exclaimed audibly—probably, however, not intending to be uncivil, but astonished beyond measure—"It beats the Devil! they've got Mr. ——!" (calling the convert by name.) The Elder brought his hands together pretty loudly as he rejoined, " I always thought the Universalists believed there was a Devil!"

Speaking of the late " beloved disciple," John Peck, of New Woodstock, N. Y., and of his two sons, Philetus and Linus, as all excellent men and superior preachers, Eld. Sheardown added, "Indeed, I never knew an Elder Peck who was not a full half bushel." A lady who was present, observed, "That is rather complimentary—my mother was a Peck."—"Very well," was the response, " then you are just half a Peck."

One soweth and another reapeth.—In one case, Elder Sheardown felt almost cast down in view of the fact that he had seen but little fruit from a most earnest consecration of himself and Christian friends to the good of souls in a public effort. Not long after, while he was laboring quite a distance away, a precious revival was enjoyed on his late field, and many of the converts "dated back" their awakening or their converting exercises to the comparatively forgotten time of Eld. Sheardown's preaching. This fact, related to us by the "reaper" who gleaned the sheaves of the "sower" who had not that opportunity, should be an additional incentive for laborers to "sow beside all waters," and to trust in God that the fruit of sincere efforts for human good and divine glory will appear in due season.

Good singing always had an inspiring effect with Eld. Sheardown, and his large fund of "psalms and hymns and spiritual songs," enabled him to strike the right key-note at any stage of protracted or other religious exercises. One of the most affecting and melting prayers we ever heard offered, was in 1864, before the Baptist State Convention at Williamsport, Pennsylvania, on behalf of a little company of superior singers, over whom his compassionate soul yearned, for the reason that some among them had never learned to sing, in spirit, the song of redemption. An incorrect or feeble performance of that part in worship, was sometimes a drag upon his mental activity. It is related that in an instance of comparative failure, he observed —with the slight English accent which sometimes marks his speech—" You must sing that *hover*."

In his forgiving disposition, he has overlooked one personal misfortune. While preaching in Troy, one evening in the winter of 1862, he. put his favorite young bay mare under the meeting house sheds, from which she was taken away, with the harness, cutter, two robes, driving gloves, and whip. He has never since heard from the animal, nor from the graceless thief in that character. We do the latter (we hope) justice in venturing the opinion, that he could not have known Eld. Sheardown, and did not even guess that the finest establisment there, by him selected, belonged to a poor old Baptist minister!

HISTORY OF THE TROY CHURCH.

This body, situated in Bradford county, Pennsylvania, was originally known as the *Burlington Baptized church.* That part of Burlington township in which were most of its members, and where its house of worship was located, having been erected into a new township, called Troy, the church after a time changed its name, and, since 1822, has been known as the "Troy Baptist church." About 1799, a church of the same order was founded on the Towanda creek, and another also on Sugar creek. The latter was of short duration, and the former changed its name and location so often as to have almost lost identity. The same may be said of the Alba-Canton interest. So that the TROY church may perhaps be regarded as the oldest, and SMITHFIELD, (organized two years after Burlington,) as the second oldest, *continuous* Baptist organization in the county.

In the Book of Records of the Troy church, are found these prefatory remarks:

"In the year of our Lord 1808, a number of brethren and sisters came to this place, from Vermont State—among which, were Eld. Elisha Rich, and his son, a preacher—and dwelt in this wilderness a few months, feeling themselves as scattered lambs among wolves, and also feeling themselves weak and feeble. Finding a goodly number of professors in no Gospel travail, things were trying to their souls. They often desired a visit from the Holy Spirit of God, to gather them together. Eld. Rich and his son preached in the place—but nothing especial occurred, until about the first of November, 1808, when Jesse Hartwell,* a missionary from the Massachusetts Baptized Society, visited us; whose labors seemed to us like cool water to thirsty souls."

An extract from Eld. Hartwell's Journal, as found in

---

*Born in Rowe, Mass., February 27, 1771—died in Lake county, Ohio, November 21st, 1860, in his 89th year. His son, Jesse Hartwell, D. D., born in Buckland, Mass., in 1795, died in 1859, while President of the University at Mount Lebanon, Louisiana. Both were able and laborious ministers of the New Testament.

the *Massachusetts Baptist Missionary Magazine*,* will
be of interest to the reader, as it contains a brief account of travels in this region of country, and of the
consummation of labors in connection with the organization of the Troy (then Burlington) church :

"Monday, Nov. 1, [1808.]—Rode from Tioga Point [Athens]
up the Chemung river twelve miles to Eld. Goff's.   Tuesday,
Nov. 2, rode with Bro. Goff and others to a place called Sing
Sing, fifteen miles further up the river.   Nov. 3, preached before the Chemung Association.

"This is a very needy country, and calls most loudly for
missionary labor of any I know of in all the western part of our
land.

"Friday, 5th, rode up the Chemung river twelve miles to
Post Town [Painted Post]—preached five times.   Nov. 8, rode
back to Sing Sing, and preached at 10 o'clock.   Then rode
eighteen miles to Eld. Goff's, and preached in the evening.
Rode this day thirty miles, and preached twice.

"Tuesday, Nov. 9, rode seventeen miles, through dismal
woods, with scarcely any road, to Sugar creek, expecting a
meeting at 2 o'clock : but my appointment had not been received.   I was fatigued, weary, and almost sick, and very glad
to rest ; but I am not willing to live for nothing.

"After preaching a number of times on Sugar creek, I
crossed the Highlands to Towanda creek, and, following that
down to the Susquehanna river, I went on preaching once,
twice, and three times a day, until Tuesday, 15th, when I returned to Sugar creek.

"On Wednesday, Nov. 16, after I had preached from Psalm
27th, 4, a number of brethren and sisters, lately moved into that
wilderness, and some who had been long mourning in a lonely
state, came forward with letters of their standing, made a relation of their Christian experience, and adopted the Sandisfield
Articles of Faith.   By the advice of Eld. Rich and a number of
brethren from a distance, I gave them the right hand of fellowship as a church of Christ, commending them to God and the
word of his grace, which is able to build them up in the most

---

*This was probably the second—if not the first— distinctly Baptist periodical
in America, the first number appearing in September, 1803, in book form.
Originally, it comprised only two numbers, of 32 pages each, per year.   The
issues were subsequently increased to three, four, and finally twelve, per
year.   It is still published, in Boston, as the *American Baptist Missionary
Magazine*, devoted to the foreign mission work.   The early numbers embalm
many memorials of the self-denying ministers, sent forth to plant the standard of the cross on our frontiers.   It also narrates the conversion to Baptist
views of Messrs. Judson and Rice—the growth of the mission spirit among
our people—and the workings of the General Convention (and Union) to this
time.

holy faith, though in this wilderness. On this occasion, our hearts were enlarged, and our souls filled with brotherly love. It seemed somewhat, I imagine, like Paul's bidding his brethern farewell—we talked and prayed till midnight, and almost break of day. This was a season of comfort to many souls. I tarried the next day, and preached, and baptized an old man who was added to the church. * * * * * * * *

"I have been gone, on this journey, eighty-four days—have ridden ten hundred and seventy-six miles, preached one hundred and three sermons, and heard five—attended five church meetings—and seen much of the goodness of the Lord."

In its constituent membership, the church was very small, (not exceeding Noah's family in the Ark.) It consisted of *eight* individuals, namely: Eld. Elisha Rich, Elisha Rich, Jr., Russel Rose, Moses Calkins, James Mattson, Phœbe Rich, Pegga Rich, and Lydia Rose.

The spring after their organization, they resolved to select a burying ground, and erect upon it a house for the worship of Almighty God. On the 12th page of the old church book, we find this record:

"Church met, March 25th, 1809.—After the usual devotional exercises, and the reception of two persons as candidates for baptism, voted to choose a committee to search for a place for a grave-yard, and a suitable site for building a meeting house. Aaron Case, Elisha Rich, Jr., John Barber, and Eli Parsons, were chosen as that committee."

We turn over a leaf of this same book, and find the following suggestive item:

"May 6th, 1809.—Church met in the meeting-house—opened by singing and prayer."

It will be observed this last record was made just *one month and thirteen days* after the appointment of the building committee. The house was built of hewed logs, with galleries on three sides, and is said to have been a neat, commodious and substantial structure for those times.

The site of this original rallying place for the church, was within the limits of the old Cemetery, one mile east of the present village of Troy. The building has wholly disappeared, and with it all the constituent members of the church, as well as the greater part of those who in early times worshipped within its consecrated walls. In those grounds they repose, awaiting the coming of their Lord; there are the treasured jewels of very many of the villagers, and of the inhabitants of the country around; and to that spot look many of the living as the place of their final rest.

The present, larger house of worship, in the southern part of the village, was constructed about 1832.

The church has had mingled seasons of prosperity and adversity. Peace, and consequent advancement, crowned the first two years of its existence. During that period, its membership was increased from eight to ninety—*sixty* of whom were baptized into its fellowship—an increase not surpassed in the history of our denomination in this country, considering the sparseness of the population.* Since that time, the church has enjoyed other revivals, and many precious souls have been gathered into the kingdom through its influence. Including the present incumbent, it has had twenty-two pastors. May its coming years be more glorious than its former !　　　　　　　T. M.

---

*In 1819, Smithfield reported 86 baptisms. The same year, Columbia reported 59 baptisms, and 28 the year following—87 in two years. These were indeed refreshing seasons in the respective churches.

THE CHEMUNG ASSOCIATION,

Constituted in November of 1796, was the earliest, and for a time the only Baptist corresponding body, in a wide extent of thinly-settled country now comprising many large bodies of the same faith and order. Its constituents were FIVE small churches—*Chemung*, (near Wellsburg, in New York and Pennsylvania,) recognized in 1791; *Fredericktown*, (which had a meeting-house in the town of Wayne, east of Crooked Lake, N. Y.) founded in 1794; *Romulus*, (Seneca county, N. Y.) founded in 1795; *New Bedford*, (now Owego, N. Y.) organized in Feb. 1796; and *Braintrim*, (in Wyoming county, Pa.) organized in 17—.

Some information respecting this body is derived from a manuscript of the late Eld. Smiley, in the hands of his son, Dr. T. T. Smiley, of Germantown, Pa., and from a pamphlet of the late Eld. Joel Rogers, in possession of H. G. Jones, Esq., 133 South Fifth street, Philadelphia. From 1805 to 1830, (excepting for 1818,) are printed Minutes. The earliest pastors named are Roswell Goff, Peter Bainbridge, Ephraim Sanford, David Jayne, Amos Eaglestone, Samuel Sturdevant, Thomas Smiley, Jehiel Wisner. The sessions generally continued two days—sometimes, three. The progress of the Association may be mostly traced in the following table:

Times of Annual Meeting.	Where held.	Reception, Dismission, and other changes among the Churches.	Churches.	Baptized.	Whole No. of Members.
1st—1797—At Chemung			5	*	108
2d—1798	do.	—Received *Bath*, N. Y.	6	90	211
3d—1799	do.	—Rec *Tawanda* and *Sugar Creek*, both in Pa.	8	12	275
4th—1800	do.	—Rec. *Chenango* † Braintrim reported "dissolved," (mostly joined "Eld. Jacob Drake's Connexion," in Luzerne county, Pa.)	8	*	329
5th—1801—Chemung.		—Sugar Creek extinct	7	*	264
6th—1802—Romulus.		—Chenango extinct	6	*	280
7th—1803	do.	—No changes	6	27	313

Times of Annual Meeting.	Where held.	Reception, Dismission. and other changes among the Churches.	Churches.	Baptized	Whole No. of Members.
8th—1804—New Bedford, (Owego.)—Dismissed Romulus and Fredericktown to the Cyuga Association............			6	*	272
9th—Oct. 30, 1805—Tawanda.—Only two churches represented.......			4	1	73
10th—Oct. 29, 1806—Chemung —No changes...........................			4	18	143
11th—Nov. 4, 1807.—Owego.—Rec. *New Town.* (afterward Almyra, or Elmira,) and *Owego Creek*, both in N. Y........			6	2	173
12th—Nov. 3, 1808—New Town (Almyra.)—No changes................			6	10	185
13th—Nov. 1, 1809—Chemung.—Rec. *White Deer* and *Burlington.* both in Pa..................			8	13	286
14th—Nov. 7, 1810—Burlington.—Rec. *Alba.* Pa., and *Spencer* and *Hector*, both in N. Y................			11	56	382
15th—Nov. 6, 1811—Elmyra.—Rec. *Smithfield*, Pa.................			12	16	427
16th—Oct. 7, 1812 do. —No changes................			12	43	457
17th—Oct. 6, 1813—Chemung & Elmyra.—Romulus restored. Chemung took the name *Chemung & Elmyra*...			13	20	569
18th—Oct. 5, 1814—Burlington.—Rec. *Columbia* and *Tioga*, both in Pa. Owego took the name *Tioga, N. Y*......			15	59	661
19th—Oct. 4, 1815—Elmyra —Alba reported disbanded................			14	62	697
20th—Oct. 2, 1816—Tawanda.—No changes................			14	41	719
21st—Oct. 1, 1817—Burlington.—Rec. *Little Muncy*, (afterward *Madison*,) Pa................			15	36	753
22d—Oct. 7, 1818.—Spencer.—Rec. *Canton*, (near Alba,) Pa			16	*	833
23d —Oct. 6, 1819—Smithfield.—Rec. *Caroline*. N. Y.—Dis. Bath to the Steuben Association................			17	199	1066
24th—Oct. 4, 1820—Tioga, N. Y.—Rec. *Berkshire*, N. Y., and *Delmar*, and *Orwell & Ulster*, both in Pa.—Dis. White Deer and Little Muncy to the new Northumberland Association.—Again dis Romulus.—Towanda took the name *Towanda & Franklin*, (and, afterward, *Franklin*)			19	71	1081
25th—Oct. 3, 1821—Chemung & Elmyra.—Rec. *Springfield, Columbia & Wells*, and *Warren*, all in Pa....			19	113	1021
26th—Oct. 2, 1822—Canton.—Rec. *Asylum*, Pa.—Burlington became *Troy*, Pa. Tioga, Pa., became *Sullivan*, Pa., and the present *Tioga, Pa.*, was rec'd...			21	95	1116
27th—Oct. 1, 1823—Big Flat.—Rec. *Norwich Settlement*.† Elmyra became *Big Flat*. Orwell & Ulster became *Orwell & Sheshequin*, sometimes "Orwell & Wysox," (and now, *Rome*.) Dis. Spencer, Tioga, N.Y., Caroline, Berkshire, and Owego Creek, to the new Berkshire (now Broome & Tioga) Asso'n................			22	59	1080
28th—Oct. 6, 1824—Smithfield.—Dis. Hector................			17	15	721
29th—Oct. 5, 1825—Tioga, Pa.—Rec. *Athens & Ulster*. Dis. Norwich settlement................			18	21	781
30th—Oct. 4, 1826—Troy.—Dis. Shippen, (Shipping, or Delmar) to Allegany Asso'n................			16	8	756
31st—Oct. 3, 1827—Canton.—No changes................			15	114	831
32d —Oct. 1, 1828—Big Flat.— do.			15	102	901
33d —Oct. 7, 1829—Chemung & Southport.—Rec. *Windham*, Pa. Dis. Big Flat to Seneca Asso'n................			15	19	763
34th—Nov. 6, 1830—Athens & Ulster.—No changes			15	16	652

*No. of baptisms in these years, not known.

†In which State, not indicated. "Chenango" is supposed to have been near Binghamton, New York, and " Norwich Settlement" west of Tioga county, Pa.

Our file ends with 1830. In the twelve years preceding, *thirteen* of the *thirty-two* churches which had belonged to the Chemung, had been dismissed to other Associations on the borders of the original body. Campbellism and Antinomianism, at that day, were rending the churches. From time to time, the members seem to have concluded to *disband the old organization* and unite with such others as would best promote their peace and the prosperity of the Redeemer's kingdom. In 1834, was formed the *Canisteo River* Association, and, in 1835, the *Bradford*—the latter embracing *five* churches of the county in its origin, (the same number as constituted the original Chemung Association,) and soon absorbing nearly if not quite all of the regular Baptists in Bradford and Tioga counties, Pennsylvania.

In the same year, (1835) a so-called "Chemung Association," claiming to represent eight of the thirty-two churches which had owned that name, convened with a "Sullivan church," in Charleston, Tioga county, Pennsylvania. Of these *eight* churches, *three* were unrepresented, and *one* withdrew, leaving only *four* remnants of churches, with 246 members, as the real strength of the body. Representatives of those 246 persons, however, proceeded to formally *disfellowship* "*what are falsely called benevolent societies, founded upon a moneyed base.*" and by name *exscinded from their* "*correspondence*, the Philadelphia, Abington, Bridgewater, Franklin, Madison, Steuben, and all other Associations," guilty of aiding such organizations! The promulgation of that Bull seems to have been "the fore-ordained means" of arresting the growth of an erroneous claimant to the name of an old and honored but virtually disbanded body. The writer, at least, has not heard of any advancement by it for some

years—while those Associations, which it excommu-
nicated, have been signally strengthened and blessed
by the great Head of the church.

That the original Chemung Baptist Association was
an earnest and efficient Christian body, its enlargement,
and the precious revivals it enjoyed in its earlier and
better days, abundantly demonstrate. A few references
to some of its Minutes, clearly show that its *principles*
and *practices* were directly contrary to the do-nothing
policy of the " falsely called" Old School order.

The burden of the preaching of the Chemung's wilderness pioneers, was the same as that of the first
Baptist, who missionated over eighteen hundred years
ago: " REPENT—BELIEVE—BE BAPTIZED." We have
the figures for twenty-eight sessions, which report
1338 baptisms—an average of nearly fifty, added to the
churches, yearly, of such as it was hoped should be
saved. Modern Old Schoolmen do not thus urge repentance and belief upon sinners, and baptisms as a
result of religious reformations are lamentably uncommon among them.

In 1807, Eld Roswell Goff—the highly esteemed
Patriarch of the Association—preached from the text,
" We, then, as workers together with Him, beseech
you also that you receive not the grace of God in vain"
—a text most decidedly of the Fullerite type.

In 1808, Eld. Hartwell, from the Massachusetts Baptist Missionary Society, preached, and the Association
sent by him a letter to said Society, " requesting mis-
sionaries to come to this land, and meet with us at our
associations."

1810, the Circular letter was a strong Scriptural
argument for the temporal support of ministers of the
Gospel by the church members. One of the Articles of
Faith, (1822) reads: " We believe that they that preach

the Gospel shall live of the Gospel, and that it is the church's duty to communicate to their ministers, and all other church charges, by *equality.*"

In 1812, in reply to a query respecting a minister who had been "repeatedly intoxicated, repeatedly admonished by the church, yet still continues it, What shall they do, suppposing he would still wish to confess it?" The Association promptly condemned trifling in such a serious matter, by saying, "We, advise you to put him from among you. See 1 Cor. v: 11."

In 1813, "Bro. Smiley read a letter from Bro. Mathias to this Association, containing pleasing accounts from India, and also of singular outpourings of the Spirit of God in some parts of both our Eastern and Southern States. We rejoice in the reviving news.

"Under a feeling sense of the ill success of the Gospel in many parts of our land, and of our being involved in War, we recommend to all our churches to set apart the fourth Wednesday of November next as a day of fasting and prayer."

In 1815, "a letter was read from Bro. Luther Rice, agent of the Baptist Board of Foreign Missions, accompanied with sixteen copies of their Report. We wish the work to prosper; and have appointed Bro. Smiley a standing secretary to report for us to the Board, and to receive what intelligence it has to send us." This endorsement of missions among the heathen, is often repeated.

In 1816, $41 were raised for Associational Missions, and Brethren Goff and Ripley were engaged to labor as itinerants for one month each. In 1817, Bro. Smiley was recommended for compensation for similar services.

In 1820, "a sermon was delivered by Eld. D.

Dimock, and a missionary sermon by Eld. E. Comstock, and a collection taken."

In 1821, was formed the "Chemung Baptist Missionary Society." The members and objects of the Society are defined in two sections : "2. This Society shall be composed of such persons as shall subscribe to this Constitution and pay into its funds at least one dollar annually." (A "moneyed base," surely.) "3. The object of this Society is to furnish the means of preaching the Gospel among the destitute within or near the the boundaries" of the Association.

The Minutes for 1826 contain the financial report of the Society, which we copy to show that prominent supporters and *recipients* of "benevolent societies founded upon a moneyed base" were among those who afterwards condemned the same and would like to be accounted "Old School Baptists:" [See the next page.]

The assistant treasurers were—John Knapp, Franklin; Dea. A. Hibbard, Troy; Eld. Jos. Beeman, Columbia & Wells; James Gerould, Smithfield; Wm. Evans, Esq., Springfield; Dea. I. Baker, Columbia; Dea. J. Luman, Roulet; Eld. H. West, Orwell.

Annual Report of the Treasurer of the Chemung Baptist Missionary Society.

C. B. M. SOCIETY, DR.

1825. Oct. 7.	To paying Eld. James Clark in part for services to the N. Y. State Convention (as appointed) in property	$26.61
	To same, cash and order, 4.83, and 8.56	13.39
Oct. 15.	To paying Eld. H. West for services	50
Nov. 2.	do. do. do.	3.00
Dec. 9.	do. do. do.	4.00
do.	do. do. his expenses	37
1826. July 1.	do. do. for services	1.50
Aug. 16.	do. do. do.	10.11
do.	do. do. his expenses	56
1825. Oct. 15.	To Dea. Roswell R. Rogers for services	2.31
1826. Aug. 30.	do. do do.	23.61
Feb. 1.	To paying Eld. L. Baldwin do.	1.42
Feb. 2.	do. Eld. J. Beeman do.	50
do.	do. B. G. Avery do.	3.50
Aug. 16.	do. do. do.	2.25
do.	do. Eld. Jas. Parsons do.	1.94
	To. disc. on rye, 6 b. at 37½ cts. per b.	2.25
Aug. 30.	To balance to new account	17.32
	Total	$115.08

SAME, CR.

1825. Sep. 1.	By balance on hand	$15.34
Oct. 4.	By donation by Mrs. Ruby Mitchell	1.95
	pair socks by Mrs Katherine Drake	45
	cash per Miss Nancy Otterson	25
	do. Eld. Baldwin	11
	F. M. S. in Charleston, tow cloth, 11¼ yds.	2.81
Oct. 6.	By contribution at the close of the Association, $9.65, which by request was divided, viz: to Eld. J. Sawyer $4.82, leaving to the Society's use	4.83
Oct. 15.	By Orwell & Wysox F. M. S., by Eld. West	2.76
Nov. 2.	By Franklin do. by Dea. A. Knapp	3.37
do.	By Col. & Wells do. by Eld. J. Beeman	1.50
Feb. 1.	By do.	3.25
	By Canton do. by Eld. Baldwin	1.00
1826. Feb. 3.	By Jackson F. Aux. Soc., by Eld. West	1.75
Aug. 16.	By Asylum F. M. S., do.	2.48
	By collection on the missionary tour	1.50
	do. by Eld. Baldwin	42
	do. by Eld. West	8.87
Aug. 30.	By members on subscription	33.25
	By do. whose accts. are yet in Assis. Treas. hands	28.70
		$115.08

WILLIAM J. GREENLEAF, *Treasurer C. M. S.*

In 1830, (our last Minutes) it was "Voted to take up a contribution for the New York Baptist State Convention," and that "we approve of the labors of Bro. James Clark (appointed by said Convention) among us." They also recommend that every church contribute at least one shilling per member to support ministers from abroad.

[Correspondence of the (Utica) " New York Baptist Register."]

COLUMBIA, Bradford county, Pa., August 18, 1832.

DEAR BROTHER—The Baptist church in this place has been blessed with a shower of divine grace. Immediately after the Association, in October last, it pleased the Father of mercies to pour out his Spirit, in awakening professors from a state of lethargy, and sinners to a sense of their danger. Twenty-three have been added by baptism, and a number by letter. In May last, I visited the church in Roulett, in Potter county, and found them in a low state. They had not met for one year. There was a meeting appointed, and the presence of the Lord seemed to be manifest. From that time the work increased, and seemed to inspire professors with new life, while the cry with the sinner was, " What shall I do to be saved ?" In July, I visited them again, and found many rejoicing in the love of a Saviour. The second and third Lord's day, I had the satisfaction of burying eleven in the waters of the Allegany, and Bro. Avery, three. May the great Shepherd of the church continue his blessings, until this wilderness shall bud and blossom as the rose: and unto His name be all the glory !   JOSEPH BEAMAN.

The foregoing references are sufficient to prove, that —in sentiment and in action—the real Chemung Association harmonized with the first associated Baptists on this continent,* and with evangelical disciples everywhere. Earnest Christians have ever combined "faith and works." The scriptural records of primi-

---

*See the reprint of the first one hundred years' records of the PHILADELPHIA (the oldest Baptist Association in America,) for sale at 530 Arch St., Phila.

tive churches show that the entire membership were expected to aid, by their time and by their means, in efforts for the world's regeneration. The Apostle Paul would compel no one, and would burden no one—"for God loveth a cheerful giver"—yet among his teachings of a practical nature we find these are most explicit: "If we have sown unto you spiritual things, is it a great thing if we shall reap unto you carnal things ?"— "EVEN SO HATH THE LORD ORDAINED, that they which preach the Gospel, should live of the Gospel."

In the light of the facts, therefore—and with the figures before us—it seems clear that the so-called "Old School" is but a *newly-formed "ism."* It doubtless embraces some sincere Christian friends: but does it not become all such seriously to inquire if they have not been misled from the good old paths? They may occupy ground.and claim names, hallowed by precious associations, and yet may have lost their first love, as truly as have those organizations on the sites of the seven churches of Asia. Let them return to the counsels and the walks of our heroic, faithful ancestors, who believed in the awfully solemn import of the last command and promise of our Divine Redeemer—"Go ye into all the world, and preach the Gospel to every creature. He that believeth, and is baptized, shall be saved; but he that believeth not, shall be damned."— "And, lo, I am with you always, even unto the end of the world."

BAPTIST ASSOCIATIONS.

ON AND NEAR THE GROUND OF THE OLD CHEMUNG.

FORMED.	STATES LOCATED IN.	CHURCHES.	MEMBERS.
1796—Chemung, in N. Y. and Pa —absorbed.		—	——
1801—Cayuga, in N. Y.		18	1793
1803—Drake's Yearly Meeting, Pa.—absorbed, 1818.		—	——
1807—Abington, Pa.		33	2384
1814—Ontario, N. Y.		15	1294
1817—Steuben, N. Y.		19	1887
1818—Susquehanna, Pa —dissolved, 1826.		—	——
1821—Northumberland, Pa.		31	2232
1822—Seneca, N. Y.		15	2032
1824—Berkshire—now Broome & Tioga, N. Y.		26	2463
1826—Bridgewater, Pa.		14	1107
Allegany, (probably Old School) location, &c., we know not.		—	——
1827—Cortland, N. Y.		21	2121
1827—Monroe, N. Y.		26	3063
1834—Canisteo River, N. Y. and Pa.		12	542
1835—Bradford, Pa.		16	802
1842—Chemung River, N. Y. and Pa.		19	1910
1842—Tioga, Pa.		15	776
1843—Wyoming, Pa.		17	1095
1843—Yates, N. Y.		11	798
		308	26.249

In 1791, appeared CHEMUNG, the first Baptist church in that region—and, the same year, Eld. SHEARDOWN was born, in far-distant England. · In 1796, convened CHEMUNG, the first Baptist Association in the Central portion of Northern Pennsylvania and Southern New York. There are also, mingled with the above, several Welch, German and unassociated churches, as also Freewill and other orders of Baptists. It is a pleasant thought, that within the probable out-stations of those five feeble, scattered, pioneer bands, there are now over 300 churches, with 30.000 members, and 150.000 adherents of Baptist congregations, gathered within the life-time of the subject of this work, whose labors have been more of less felt throughout much of the field.

CORRECTIONS.

As the Editing Publisher was not able to read the proofs, some errors have occurred in printing the foregoing sheets. Those merely typographical it is hoped will be readily overlooked. The following are deemed worthy of notice:

Page 54, line 17, "villages" should be *villagers*.
 57, 1, "ever" should be *even*.
 58, 9, omit the word "in."
 62, 31, "keel" should be *heel*.
 63, 10, "could" should be *would*.
 83, 11, "Printed" should be *Painted Post.*
 104, 25, "stores" should be *stones*.
 106, 27, "bad" should be *hard*.
 " 33, "28" should be 38.
 114, 10, "to necessity" should be *the* necessity.
 133, 30, "country" should be *county*.
 137, 31, "may" should be *my*.
 141, 15, "am" should be *was*.
 170, 20, "boys laying" should be *logs lying*.
 191, 2, "appears" should be *appeared*.
 195, 32, "of" should be *or*.
 213, 17, "process" should be *progress*.
 217, 29, "pin-head" should be *pier-head*.
 252, 26, "corner room" should be *lower rooms.*
 257, 29, omit "the" before "Siloam."
 281, 10, "Smithport" should be *Southport*.
 300, 15, omit "an" before "infirmity."
 307 transpose 4th and 5th lines.
 313, 18, "confidentially" should be *confidently*
 325, 16, "our" should be *over*.
 327, 31, "recoiled" should be *reviled*.
 329, 15, "then" should be *thou*.
 330, 22, insert *other* before "letter."
 " 36, "musing" should be *nursing*.
 332, 4, insert *some* before "characteristic."

INDEX.

NEW YORK STATE REFERENCES—PERSONS.

PENNSYLVANIA REFERENCES—PLACES.

PENNSYLVANIA REFERENCES—PERSONS.

REFERENCES TO VARIOUS PERSUASIONS.

GENERAL TOPICS REFERRED TO.

TEXTS REFERRED TO.

☞ The delay in the issue of this work has added to it several pages of matter. Had it been printed on the larger size of type as at first intended, it would have considerably exceeded 400 pages.

———

Should any reader desire to propose any addition, correction, or advice—for the benefit of a revised edition if called for—please communicate freely to Eld. S., at Troy, Pa., or to O. N. Worden, Lewisburg, Pa.

———

E. B. Case, of Troy, Pa., will personally attend to the sale of this work in certain regions where Eld. S. is best known, and will DELIVER it at Two Dollars.

Those desiring it by *mail or express*, will please address O. N. Worden, Lewisburg, Union county, Pa., giving very plainly their Post Office (or Station,) County, and State. Receipts will be taken from Postmaster and Expressmen, for books sent by them at the risk of the purchaser.

Sent by mail, pre-paid, for	$2.25	per Volume.
By Express not pre-paid,	2.00	" "
do. do.	21.00	" 11 Copies
do. do.	40.00	" 21 "

———

None but National money received. For sums over $10, it is safer to send Post Office money-orders, or checks on the Lewisburg National Bank—payable to the order of O. N. Worden.

SECOND THOUSAND.

The *first thousand* copies of "Life and Times of Sheardown" being mostly sold, the SECOND THOUSAND is placed in the Binder's hands.

The following leading papers of TEN religious denominations, and of various political parties, have furnished most commendatory notices of this work:

National Baptist, Public Ledger, German Reformed Messenger, a Lutheran paper, American Presbyterian & Genesee Evangelist, Philadelphia; Chronicle, and Journal, Lewisburg; Church Advocate, Lancaster; Lycoming Gazette, and Bulletin, Williamsport; Tioga County Agitator, Wellsborough; Potter Journal, Coudersport, Penn'a—Christian Advocate, Examiner & Chronicle, The Independent, Evangelist, and Observer, New York city; Northern Advocate, Auburn; Courier, Seneca Falls; The Advocate, Buffalo, N. Y.—Christian Era, Boston—Zion's Advocate & Eastern Watchman, Portland—Christian Secretary, Hartford—Journal & Messenger, Cincinnati; Religious Telescope, Dayton; Evangelical Messenger, Cleveland; Christian Herald, Kalamazoo, Mich; Christian Times & Witness, Chicago.

Others have referred to it in similar terms, but their notices are not at hand.

Among many influential and intelligent gentlemen, of different churches, who have voluntarily expressed in writing their gratification with, and their approbation of, "Sheardown," are the following:

Justin R. Loomis, LL. D., President of the University at Lewisburg; Henry Harbaugh, D.D., of the College at Mercersburg; Rev. A. K. Bell, D D., Allegheny City; Hon. Eli Slifer, Secretary of the Commonwealth, and Hon. Charles R. Coburn, Superintendent of Common Schools, Harrisburg; Rev. E. D. Fendall, and Hon. Henry C. Hickok, Philadelphia; Rev. P. S. Worden, late Principal of M. E. Seminary, Binghamton; Smith Sheldon, Esq., New York.

Price reduced !

The abolition by the late Congress of various Book taxes, with the sales of the *first* thousand, have enabled the Publisher to reduce the price of the *second* thousand. I will hereafter sell as follows:

Single Copy, by Mail or delivered at my expense	$1.50
" " without any expense to me	1.35
Ten or more copies at cost of purchaser (each)	1.10

A Lithograph has been thought preferable to a Photograph for this issue.

Sincere thanks are due to editors and others who have manifested an interest in the sale of this work. In the multiplicity of books, a special good word, repeated, by those who may regard this as worthy of a large circulation, will be of material value.

Some kind criticisms and suggestions have been gratefully received—and any others will be welcome—inasmuch as a revised and enlarged edition is not improbable, (provided costs of paper and printing come down.)

All orders &c to be addressed to

O. N. WORDEN, Lewisburg, Union Co., Pa.